UNTAMED DESIRE

Desire, Oklahoma:
The Founding Fathers 1

Leah Brooke
writing as
Lana Dare

MENAGE EVERLASTING

Siren Publishing, Inc.
www.SirenPublishing.com

A SIREN PUBLISHING BOOK
IMPRINT: Ménage Everlasting

UNTAMED DESIRE
Copyright © 2011 by Lana Dare

ISBN-10: 1-61034-227-5
ISBN-13: 978-1-61034-227-8

First Printing: January 2011

Cover design by *Les Byerley*
All art and logo copyright © 2011 by Siren Publishing, Inc.

Printed in the U.S.A.

PUBLISHER
Siren Publishing, Inc.
www.SirenPublishing.com

DEDICATION

To all the wonderful Facebook ladies who make me laugh every day. Thank you for your comments and questions and for taking the time to visit me.

But most of all, thank you for your support.

UNTAMED DESIRE

Desire, Oklahoma:
The Founding Fathers 1

LANA DARE
Copyright © 2011

Chapter One

Margaret Simms used the back of her hand to wipe away yet another tear that leaked from the corner of her eye. She watched in a kind of stupor as several of the men from the Shenandoah helped lower the pine box into the damp earth, having a hard time believing the scene playing out before her was real. She'd expected it for some time, had thought herself prepared for it.

She wasn't. How did someone ever prepare for something like this?

Her only real family was dead.

To make it even worse, her father's death made the always lingering ache for Eb and Jeremiah Tyler almost unbearable. She wanted them here. She wanted them to take her in their arms and tell her that everything would be all right.

They'd always made everything all right for her.

Anger crept in, slicing through the numbness. She didn't need them and never would again.

Swallowing another sob, she stiffened when an arm came around her shoulders, only to slump again when a voice sounded low in her ear.

"Your father was a good foreman—and a good friend. He'll be missed, Maggie. I know you must be afraid, but you're not alone, honey."

Maggie looked up over her shoulder into the eyes of her father's dearest friend, a man who'd always been like a second father to her, Ace Tyler. She couldn't help but worry that the lines on his face appeared much more pronounced today, and his own eyes were wet with unshed tears. Forcing a faint smile, she leaned into him. "How do you always know what I'm thinking?"

Ace Tyler had been her father's friend since before she was born. Her parents had lived in town when her father first started working at the Shenandoah, but her father had come to live at the ranch when her mother died, shortly after her birth. Since then, the housekeeper, Esmeralda, had pretty much taken over raising her.

Mr. Tyler squeezed her shoulder again. "I've known you since you were a baby. We all had a hand in raising you. Eb and Jeremiah always knew what you were thinking, too. Remember?"

"They're gone." She couldn't talk about them today. It hurt too much. She needed them there beside her as much as she needed her next breath.

But they were gone, and had been for a long time.

Pushing back the anger that rose again, she forced a smile, not wanting to upset the older man.

"And now Daddy's gone. Thank God I still have you and Esmeralda."

"There are other people that love you, and you know it."

Maggie shrugged, her gaze sliding involuntarily to one of the ranch hands who stood beside the grave, holding a shovel and staring at her hungrily. "Fred doesn't love me."

Mr. Tyler's gaze followed hers. "No, he doesn't, and I'm glad you're smart enough to know that. I don't like that look in his eye. He wants you, and he's not doing anything to hide it anymore. He tells everyone on the place he loves you, but I don't think Fred loves anything but himself. Seems the young man has plans to marry you. He'll soon find out just how wrong he is about that."

Irritated, she turned away. "He already has. I've already told him that we can be nothing more than friends."

In fact, Fred's advances had started making her feel uncomfortable, so she'd already told him to stay the hell away from her.

Twice.

But Mr. Tyler didn't need to know that. She didn't want Fred to lose his job because of her, and she was confident she could handle him.

"Your daddy threatened to shoot him if he came near you again. Your daddy's not even in the ground and Fred's sniffin' around you. I won't have it, Maggie."

Maggie sighed, knowing that only his boss's presence kept Fred from approaching her. "He just came over to tell me he was sorry about Daddy."

Ace nodded. "I'm sure that's what he said, but he's lookin' for more." Pushing her hair back from her face, he smiled gently. "Honey, your daddy's been sick quite awhile now, and you've been a godsend to him. But now it's time for you to live your life. Time for you to get married and have babies you can teach to do all the things that, according to the Reverend Perry, you're not supposed to do."

Maggie smiled as she knew Mr. Tyler meant her to and looked again toward her father's grave, the lump in her throat growing.

The ache for Eb and Jeremiah grew, when she'd been sure it couldn't possibly get any bigger.

Smiling through her tears, she looked up at the older man, desperate to change the subject. "I tried to get Daddy to marry again, but he always said you were two peas in a pod. You both lost your wives young, and yet neither one of you ever remarried."

Mr. Tyler's hold tightened briefly on her shoulder as he turned her and started toward the buckboard. He walked stiffly, as he usually did when his old bones protested the cold and the damp. "We both knew that there'd be only one love in our lives. Anyone else woulda just been second best. That's no way to treat a lady."

Leading her back to where the others had gathered, he didn't say anything, just held her arm to steady her over the rough ground of the cemetery. He helped her into the buckboard, placing a blanket over her skirts before starting the ride back to his ranch.

Other than the men who'd taken Esmeralda back already, the ranch hands who'd come to the funeral rode on either side of them, their boots polished and most of the dust beaten from their cowboy hats.

A few had been left behind to bury her father once she was out of sight, and Fred didn't look happy to be one of them. There was no doubt in her mind that Mr. Tyler had done it on purpose.

She looked around again in vain for her best friend, Savannah Perry. The only thing that would have kept Savannah away today was Reverend Perry's refusal to let her come.

Stan Perry was the minister in Kansas City and didn't care for his niece's friendship with Maggie. He had a hair-trigger temper that went off with very little provocation, something he kept carefully hidden.

But Maggie knew.

And worried.

He hated Maggie and everyone who worked at the Tyler ranch. A greedy man, his jealousy ate at him until nothing remained but bitterness. He'd hidden his hatred from Eb and Jeremiah, but once they left, he hadn't bothered to hide it from her, warning Savannah to avoid Maggie right in front of her.

"You stay away from that heathen, Savannah. You hear me? The Tylers own her as much as they own all those cows and horses. She runs wild over there with all those men. She even rides and hunts like a man. It ain't seemly, I tell you. It just ain't seemly."

He turned to Maggie, lifting his chin and looking down at her, not bothering to hide his distaste. "Stay away from her, Margaret. I don't want her turning out like you or her mother."

Savannah's mother had moved in with her brother when the father of her unborn child was killed in a gunfight in Savannah, Georgia, before they'd had the chance to get married. Maggie had long ago lost count of how many men she'd been through since then. Two years ago, while riding in a carriage with one of her beaus, the carriage tipped, killing her.

Savannah had lived alone with her uncle ever since.

Mr. Tyler, in his usual headstrong way, had arranged for another minister from the next town to handle her father's service. It would give Mr. Perry another reason to hate her, but she no longer cared what he thought.

Her only concern was Savannah.

Mr. Tyler snapped the reins and glanced over at her, his jaw tight. "Your friend would have come if she could. Her uncle's not right in the head, and he's getting worse. Now that your daddy's gone, I'm responsible for you, which'll make him hate you even more. I don't want you around the Reverend Perry unless others are around. I don't trust him."

Staring straight ahead, she nodded, firming her lips. "Savannah usually meets me in town anyway. I'm worried about her." The secret she'd unwillingly kept could no longer be contained. Looking around to make sure the others weren't close enough to hear, she kept her voice low. "I'm afraid he hits her, but she won't admit it."

Mr. Tyler's face hardened. "Suspected as much. He's been warned already, but I'll keep a closer watch."

Maggie breathed a sigh of relief, trusting that Mr. Tyler would indeed watch out for her friend. "Last week I saw bruises on her arm. She moved slow, like she hurt, but I can't get her to talk about it."

He nodded once. "I'll take care of it. You just stay away from him."

They rode in silence for about a mile, both obviously lost in their own thoughts. The ranch hands didn't speak much at all, although several looked her way with sympathetic smiles. She'd known most of them her entire life and smiled back, grateful for their presence.

When the wind kicked up, Maggie tugged her shawl more closely around her. She wore the warmest one she owned, but still it didn't hold off the damp chill in the air, a chill that seemed to go all the way to her bones.

She'd been cold ever since she'd seen her father lying on the stable floor holding his chest. Now, nothing she did seemed to warm her up.

If only Eb and Jeremiah were here, they would make her warm and get rid of this lonely emptiness inside her.

"I sent for Eb and Jeremiah."

Maggie sucked in a breath and froze, her heart stopping as her stomach dropped to her toes. The air seemed to shimmer around her as her world tilted and a warm glow ignited inside her.

A glow she hadn't felt in years.

Thank God!

Please God, no!

Both thoughts went through her mind repeatedly, one after the other.

A chance to see them again.

To watch them leave again.

She'd never survive it a second time.

Her heart beat furiously now, and she closed her eyes as memories she'd pushed back for years rushed to the surface, forcing her to relive the pain of their desertion all over again.

She must have misunderstood. Longing for them so desperately, she'd heard what her heart wanted to hear. She had to swallow heavily before she could speak, the disappointment like a blow to her chest. "Wh—what did you say?"

Mr. Tyler's face softened, amusement and understanding shining in his eyes. "You heard me, Maggie. I sent a telegram right after Buck died and paid to have it delivered as soon as possible. We're gonna stop in town on the way back to the ranch and see if they answered."

Maggie fought for air as a wave of dizziness washed over her.

Her fondest dream.

Her worst nightmare.

Her head spun, filling her with a sense of unreality. She couldn't face them again.

She just couldn't.

They left, and after days, then months of crying for them, of lying in her bed at night wishing she could talk to them one more time, she'd finally come to terms with the fact that she'd never see either one of them again.

To have them come and go again now...

Fighting the anger building inside her, she turned to Mr. Tyler, fisting her hands so he wouldn't see how badly she shook. "Why would you do that? Why would you send for them? The funeral's over, and there's nothing they can do. Send them another telegram, and tell them it isn't necessary. I'm sure they're far too busy to come anyway."

Please let them stay away.

He scowled down at her. "Funny, I never remember you being so addle-minded before. You know damned well that both of my sons would do anything for you. Of course they'll come. They love you. And you love them."

She looked away, her face burning and the knots in her stomach getting tighter and tighter.

They'd loved her like a little sister, while in the years since they left, they were all she ever dreamed about. No other man could ever hold a candle to either one of them. It was too cruel to expect her to go through the agony of losing them again.

Frantic now, she grabbed Mr. Tyler's sleeve. "Please send another telegram. I don't want to see them."

He shook his head, his stern look cutting her off in mid-sentence. "Don't you dare say something you're gonna regret. I won't cotton to your lies any more now than I ever have. You miss them, and you've been thinking about them nonstop since Buck died. You need them, and they'll be here for you. You'll see."

Shaken, she took a deep breath and looked away from the hopeful look in his eyes, wondering if she'd ever feel normal again. She had to get him to see that it would be better to leave everything the way it was.

If Eb and Jeremiah came back now, someone was bound to get hurt. Her.

Forcing a small smile, she did her best to appear composed while the knots in her stomach grew and rose in her throat, threatening to choke her. "I don't know where you got the idea that...anyway, I think it's just wishful thinking on your part to get Eb and Jeremiah back here. You've been like another father to me my whole life, and I don't want to see you getting hurt. Please don't put things like that in your head. It's only going to hurt both of us."

Hating that he must be missing his sons dreadfully to even attempt to get them to come home, Maggie touched his arm, smiling in sympathy.

"I know you miss them, but you still have me. I loved growing up with two fathers."

Mr. Tyler met her smile with his own. "Don't be afraid. Everything is gonna work out just fine. If my sons have their way, your children will have two fathers, too. Just you wait and see." He grinned at her stunned expression and called out to several of the ranch hands to go ahead of them to the ranch, rattling off a list of chores he wanted done. No matter what happened, there was always work to be done. Others would stay in town with him to load up the buckboard with supplies.

A trip to town was never wasted.

Before she had a chance to say anything else, he jumped down from his seat to hurry into the telegraph office, showing more energy than he had just moments ago. His words kept racing through her mind, filling her with a sense of foreboding and an undeniable yearning.

Your children will have two fathers, too.

How could he know how much she needed both of them? Why didn't he lecture her about the futility of wishing for something that could never be?

Heat and chills washed through her, one right after the other, as she waited for Mr. Tyler to reappear. She couldn't keep her hands still, but she couldn't make anything else move. Dizzy now, she held on to her seat for balance, blind to the activity in the street and the people all around her, her thoughts consumed with only one thing.

Eb and Jeremiah Tyler.

They'd both been the biggest part of her world, her entire life. She'd spent every spare minute with them from the time she'd learned to walk. They'd taught her to ride, to fish, and tried to teach her to hunt.

They'd teased her for being too soft-hearted when she didn't like it. A reluctant smile played at her lips when she thought about how many rabbits they'd let get away after she begged them not to shoot them.

They loved their father and Esmeralda and respected Maggie's father, but everyone knew that their biggest soft spot was for her.

At least, that's what she thought.

Right before they left, there'd been a huge fight in the big house between the men and Mr. Tyler and her father but no one would ever say what the fight was about.

The next day they'd mounted two of their father's horses and left the ranch and hadn't been back since.

That was five years ago.

A mental picture of Eb and Jeremiah Tyler rose in her mind with alarming ease. She could still picture the dark brown hair that neither one of them liked to take the time to get cut whipping below their hats the way it did when they rode.

She clearly remembered Jeremiah's golden brown eyes and the dimples that had the women in town vying for his attention and throwing themselves at him every chance they got. His eyes had always been full of laughter and mischief, a man who would race to hell and back just for the fun of pulling the devil's tail.

Eb's eyes, on the other hand, always looked far too serious for someone so young. His sharp hazel gaze always seemed to be watching—assessing everything around him.

But they'd warmed when he looked at her, the green twinkle in them when he smiled her way never failing to steal her breath.

She'd grown up with them, and they'd always treated her more like a sister than their friend and made it plain to everyone that they considered themselves her protectors.

Everyone knew that if Maggie wasn't happy, neither was Eb or Jeremiah, and no one wanted to be on the receiving end of their tempers, the tempers Maggie faced head-on, much to the amusement of the other ranch hands.

When Maggie was only five, the Perrys came to Kansas City. Eb and Jeremiah, had taken her to town to visit Savannah, who'd been six and the only other girl her age around. As the girls became best friends, they'd quickly taken Savannah under their protective wings and indulged both girls endlessly.

Eb and Jeremiah bought Maggie hair ribbons and peppermint sticks, and she'd always been able to go to them to talk or to ask questions. It had never mattered to her that they were the boss's sons.

They were just hers.

They'd become so important to her that she couldn't imagine life without them.

But something had changed right before they left, something that put a distance between them she didn't understand, and one they wouldn't discuss with her.

And it hurt.

Memories raced through her mind, one after the other, until the final memory she had of them forced itself to the forefront, the one that remained forever burned into her mind no matter how hard she tried to forget.

The day they'd left the Shenandoah.

She could still remember the sounds, the smells of that day as though it had happened only yesterday. It had been springtime, the smell of sweet hay and wildflowers in bloom a cruel mockery of the sadness in her heart.

Eb had been twenty-six, Jeremiah, twenty-four, several years older than her own sixteen, when they'd packed their belongings and come to say goodbye.

Heartbroken, she stared after them until she could no longer see their dust, her world crumbling as they rode away from her.

She often wondered just how long she would have stood there with tears running down her face if her father hadn't come to get her.

She hadn't received a letter from Eb and Jeremiah for almost a year.

The brief letter expressed their hope that she was doing well and a reminder to stay out of trouble now that they couldn't be around to get her out of it.

She'd cried for days.

Since then, they'd written a letter or two a year, telling her about the land in Oklahoma that they'd won in a card game. Over the next few months, they'd won enough money playing poker to buy acres and acres more of it, so much of it, they'd said, that they owned everything as far as the eye could see.

They'd hired a dozen men and started raising cattle. While digging wells, they'd struck oil and had to hire dozens more.

It seemed they'd had nothing but good luck since they left.

They no longer had any reason to come home.

They wrote of desperados, the obstacles they faced living in Indian Territory, and hardships from the weather. Every letter, though, had been full of enthusiasm, as though they loved the life they lived now and relished each and every challenge.

For men like them, who lived for challenges and danger, nothing could be more exciting—or rewarding.

They were rich men, richer than even their father, and had a big ranch that they'd devoted their entire lives to. The last letter she'd received from them, months earlier, mentioned the house they'd begun building and the difficulties in getting supplies.

She'd never really understood why she'd cried when she read it. After all, she'd known they would never come home again, but just reading about them building a house she would never see hurt unbearably.

It made their desertion so final—so permanent.

They'd never mentioned missing her, and after her first tear-stained letter to them, she hadn't said it either. Except for the infrequent letters, it appeared they'd forgotten her altogether.

In her letters, she'd never spoken of how lonely the ranch seemed without them. There hadn't seemed to be any point. She'd only written about the ranch and the men they knew and told them very little about herself. Each letter she'd written had gotten shorter and shorter as she'd found it increasingly difficult to write to two men she no longer even knew.

Men who would soon be looking for wives and starting families of their own, if they hadn't already.

The thought of it cut like a knife.

At the sound of whistling, she looked up, swiping away a tear as Mr. Tyler came out of the telegraph office with a lightness to his step that hadn't been there before. The huge grin splitting his face made her stomach clench in both fear and excitement.

Would she get to see them one last time?

He hurried over to her, his twinkling eyes a painful reminder of Eb's. "They're already on their way. They'll be here day after tomorrow. I know you're worried now that Buck passed, honey, but everything'll be all right now." He waved his hand against the dust in front of his face when several horses and another buckboard passed. "My sons were right in gettin' outta here. Kansas City's gettin' too damn crowded."

Maggie couldn't draw enough air into her lungs, the dizziness getting even worse. "They're really coming?" She pressed her lips closed to stop the flow of questions she didn't dare voice.

Mr. Tyler, in the process of supervising the loading of the buckboard, turned his head to meet her eyes. "Of course. I told you they would. They know you need them now."

With those words, the pressure building inside her chest broke free. Sobbing, she buried her face in her hands and slid to her knees on the buckboard.

They were coming home.

For her!

Oh, God, it was a dream come true.

Mr. Tyler helped her back into her seat, catching her when she stumbled. "Easy, little girl. Don't you worry about a thing. Eb and Jeremiah'll be here soon."

Hardly able to believe it, Maggie couldn't stop crying as they rode back to the ranch, earning indulgent looks from the ranch hands that rode along either side of them.

Eb and Jeremiah were coming back to the Shenandoah!

Could she dare hope that one of them would marry her? If so, everything would be the way it should be, and she'd finally have the man she wanted. She'd long ago come to terms with the fact that it didn't matter which one. She loved them both so much it terrified her.

It was a secret she would have to keep the rest of her life.

Especially from them.

* * * *

On the way to the train station, Maggie couldn't sit still, literally shaking with excitement and bouncing on the hard seat.

Mr. Tyler chuckled as they arrived, and he brought the horses to a stop. "Calm down, girl. You're as wound up as a cat in a roomful of rockers."

In her haste, she jumped down and snagged her dress on a rough piece of wood. She impatiently yanked it, wincing at the sound of material ripping. Holding on to her hat, she ran to Mr. Tyler and hurried with him up the steps to the platform.

"Do you think the train's on time? What if they changed their minds? Are you sure they're coming?"

Chuckling again, he gave her his arm to cross the platform. "No, honey, they didn't change their minds. They're coming. Hear that? They're here."

The sound of the train whistle made her heart trip. She shaded her eyes and turned to watch its approach, the loud noise making conversation impossible.

It didn't matter. She had nothing else to say, all her thoughts centered on seeing Eb and Jeremiah again.

Bouncing from one foot to the other, she gripped Mr. Tyler's arm as she watched the train approach. She couldn't wait to laugh and talk with them like before. They'd be able to ride and tease each other and take trips to town together.

Dinner would be a joyous event once again, and after dinner, she'd go walking with one of them, the one who would marry her, and he'd kiss her under the moonlight.

She'd be touched like she never had before and give herself over to a man for the first time in her life.

Just thinking about those big, strong hands moving over her naked form sent a wave of longing through her that weakened her knees.

Lost in her thoughts, she nearly stumbled when Mr. Tyler pulled her out of the way of the passengers getting off of the train and those who came rushing to meet them. She blinked, startled to realize that the train had already come to a stop. Her heart raced and her breath came out in short bursts, the anticipation of seeing Eb and Jeremiah again hitting her hard. Wiping her damp palms on her dress, she scoured the crowd for them, her gaze flying over and dismissing each passenger who disembarked.

The last time she'd seen Eb or Jeremiah she'd been little more than a girl. She'd changed quite a bit since they left. She'd become a woman and, for the first time in her life, felt self-conscious about her curves.

What would they think about the way she looked now?

Pulling the shawl more securely around her, she stilled as a strange sensation washed over her, a deep awareness that brought everything around her into sharp focus. Gradually, the sounds disappeared until the only thing she heard was the sound of her own heartbeat.

She slowly raised her head, alarmed at the tingling that went up her spine and settled at the back of her neck. Taking a deep breath, she swallowed heavily, turning her head, her eyes inexplicably drawn to the passenger car on the right.

Two men emerged and stepped off the train, each with an arm raised as they donned their hats, effectively preventing her from seeing their faces. Both men towered over the people around them and moved with a confident stride in her direction, their heads lowered in conversation as they approached, the brim of their hats keeping her from seeing the upper half of their faces.

Their dark suits did nothing to camouflage the primitive, almost savage power radiating from them. Something about the way their suits hugged their massive frames and the way they moved hinted at a wildness that had others giving them a wide berth. The holsters they wore low on their hips almost appeared to be a part of them, and although they each carried bags, both men kept their right hand free as though out of habit.

People stared, the easy grace in which they moved and their obvious strength mesmerizing as they cut through the crowd.

Tightening her hand on her shawl, Maggie stared, just as transfixed as everyone else. Instead of staring at them, she knew she should be looking for Eb and Jeremiah, but she just couldn't tear her gaze away from their compelling presence.

She was still staring when, as one, they lifted their heads, their eyes unerringly targeting hers, the blast of heat from them scorching her, even from twenty feet away.

Gasping sharply, Margaret stepped back, straight into Mr. Tyler, who reached out to catch her shoulders.

Shaking her head, she tried to take another step back. "No. No. No."

Except for their eyes, she barely recognized the Eb and Jeremiah that kept moving closer as the men who'd left five years earlier.

Hard. Cold. Undeniably breathtaking—the strength and purpose in their strides impossible to ignore.

Her mind screamed at her to run, but she remained rooted to the spot, unable to get her feet to listen to her brain.

As though they'd heard her breathless denial, both men's eyes sharpened, their already granite-like expressions hardening even more.

This was not the Eb and Jeremiah she knew. Not the Eb and Jeremiah she'd dreamed of all these years. The barely restrained power in their movements hovered so close to the surface she would swear she could see it.

Her heart beat frantically against the hand she tightened on her shawl. She couldn't look away as they stepped closer.

Eb never took his eyes from hers as he closed the distance between them, the green sparks in them creating a strange warmth throughout her body that made it difficult to breathe.

"Hi, little girl. Damn, you've turned into a real beauty."

His skin had darkened, making his eyes appear even more brilliant, the lines in his face more pronounced than she remembered. The deep cadence of his voice seemed to strum over her skin, causing little shivers everywhere. To her horror, her nipples pebbled and poked at the front of her dress, becoming so sensitive she couldn't stand the fabric of her dress against them. Frozen in place, she couldn't react in time to avoid the arm Eb whipped out and wrapped around her.

He yanked her against him, lifting her to her toes to bury his face in her throat. "And you filled out just fine. All woman now, aren't you, Maggie?"

Her hands went to his shoulders, not even trying to catch her hat as it flew off, the combination of his warm breath on her neck and the incredibly hard body he held her against totally overloading her senses. A whimper escaped before she even knew it was there, tears pricking her eyes that appeared out of nowhere.

Had he always been this big? This hard? This...overwhelming?

This wasn't her Eb!

Taking a deep breath, she closed her eyes as his scent wrapped around her, a scent she thought she'd forgotten but that affected her in a way it never had before. It called to everything feminine inside her, making her feel weak and yet strong at the same time. It filled her with a hunger she didn't quite understand but that made her crave feeling him naked against her.

His hair, even longer than it had been in the past, brushed her cheek, and she turned her face into it without thinking, reveling in the feel of the silky strands against her skin. It made her ache to feel it elsewhere, to feel it in places no one else had ever touched before.

His voice, his hard looks, the way he held her—no, this man didn't seem anything like the Eb she'd known.

A total stranger.

And it broke her heart—at the same time making her want him in a way she'd never even dreamed she could want.

Confused, she clung to his solid strength, her body seeming to mold itself against his. The feeling of safety that she'd never even realized had been missing warmed her from the inside out and brought more tears to her eyes.

Mr. Tyler chuckled from somewhere behind her. "I knew it."

What was she doing?

Pushing against Eb's shoulder, she fought her way out of his hold, alarmed at the hard muscle that shifted beneath her hand. Her chest heaved, and she stumbled back against Mr. Tyler, avoiding Eb's hands when he tried to steady her. Panicked, she slapped at him. "No. Don't. Please. Don't touch me." The words came out in a frantic rush, breathless and shaky.

Her neck still tingled where Eb's lips had touched it, the same tingling that had made itself known in her nipples where they'd brushed across his chest. The ensuing heat travelled with alarming speed from her nipples to her clit, and she pressed her thighs together against the juices that now coated them, shifting restlessly as the tingling made its way to her pussy.

Shaking with fear of not only the loss of control of her own body, but also the changes in them, she turned to look away, only to find Jeremiah standing on her other side, holding her hat out to her and looking at her as though he'd never seen her before. Mortified that he'd witnessed her reaction to Eb, she tremulously reached out for her hat, only to have her hand snatched in his. Before she could even try to pull away, she found herself yanked against his chest.

As Eb had done, Jeremiah wrapped his arms around her to pull her close and buried his face in her throat, his low groan vibrating over her neck and sending a shiver down her back. "Damned if you ain't a beauty. I'm sorry about your daddy, honey. Everything'll be all right now. We'll take care of you."

Maggie closed her eyes, her fingers digging into Jeremiah's wide shoulders as she fought the wave of longing that raced through her, longing so strong her knees gave out. His own silky hair blew against her face, the clean scent of it increasing the wild hunger inside her. The heat intensified until her pussy burned, the sensation so intoxicating she had to bite her lip to keep from crying out against it.

Jeremiah ran a hand over her hair, pulling her even closer to absorb her involuntary shudder. "Everything will be all right, honey. I promise."

Eb moved in from her other side, both men effectively surrounding her with their big bodies. "I'm sorry about your daddy, Maggie. I wish we could have been here with you for his funeral. We got here as fast as we could." Each took an arm, keeping her between them as they greeted their father, and made their way along the platform and down the stairs.

Thankful for their support and dismayed that she needed it, she allowed them to guide her away from the train station and to the waiting horses. She trembled so badly she would have stumbled if they hadn't steadied her. Grateful that they'd traveled to town with two extra horses for Eb and Jeremiah to ride back, she moved to the buckboard, anxious to put some distance between them.

She jumped, unprepared for Jeremiah's hands circling her waist and lifting her with remarkable ease onto her seat. Turning her head, she expected to see Mr. Tyler, only to find Eb on the seat beside her instead.

Whipping her head around, she saw Mr. Tyler mount one of the free horses. Amid greetings and laughter, the other men waved and started toward the ranch. Shaking hard now, she reached for the blanket she didn't need and watched with a sinking heart as the others rode away. "I thought you and Jeremiah would be riding the horses."

Eb's eyes narrowed beneath the brim of his hat. "Dad can ride. I want to talk to you a bit, see how you're doing. I'm real sorry about your daddy, honey. He was a good man and loved you very much.

But I don't want you to worry about anything. We'll take good care of you, and I know you'll like Oklahoma." He expertly flicked the reins, his strong hands easily controlling the horses as they started out.

Stunned, Maggie whipped around. "What are you talking about? I thought you were moving back here. I'm not going to Oklahoma."

Eb nodded calmly. "Yeah. You are." He turned his head, his eyes raking over her face, his matter-of-fact tone scaring her more than if he'd yelled. "Everything's ready for you."

They hadn't come back to her after all.

Blinking back tears, Maggie snorted inelegantly, not about to let them see her heartbreaking disappointment. "If that's your way of asking me to visit, I'll pass."

The thought of watching them walk away again nearly doubled her over in pain. Her fingers refused to be still, tangling in the ribbons of the hat she held on her lap as she avoided looking directly at either one of them.

Keeping her chin up, she vowed to keep her heartache to herself, which would mean avoiding them as much as possible. Sensing Eb's stare, she involuntarily turned toward him, folding her arms across her chest in what she hoped looked like defiance instead of a way to hide her trembling.

His eyes narrowed, barely visible beneath the brim of his hat. "I think your tongue got even sharper while we've been gone. We'll talk about this later."

"I'm not leaving Kansas City."

"Hmm."

Aware of the curious looks Mr. Tyler and Jeremiah sent her way, Maggie pressed her lips together in an effort to hold back her tears. Angry with herself for getting her hopes up, for actually believing she could have the life she wanted, she remained silent and stared straight ahead, absently listening to the three men's conversation.

Her thoughts turned to her future and what she would do when they left again.

They rode to where a small grove of trees stood at the turnoff to the ranch, and Eb pulled the reins to bring the horses to a stop. "Dad, why don't you go on ahead? We'll meet you at the ranch in a bit."

"No!" Alarmed, Maggie shook her head, not wanting to be alone with either one of them.

Ignoring her, Mr. Tyler nodded once in Eb's direction and shot a glance at Jeremiah, a knowing gleam in his eyes. "Take your time." With a wave, he took off, kicking up a cloud of dust.

Jeremiah stopped close to her other side, crossing his wrists over the saddle horn, his eyes unreadable beneath the brim of his hat. As soon as his father was out of range, he leaned forward and shot a glance at Eb. "Problem?"

Eb shifted in his seat beside her. "Appears so. What's wrong with you, Maggie? I thought you'd be happy to go with us."

Aware of their burning stares, she kept her eyes forward, watching Mr. Tyler fade into the distance. Once he disappeared from view, she glanced at Jeremiah before turning in her seat toward Eb, inadvertently hitting his leg with her own. Scooting away, she placed a few more inches of space between them, rubbing her knee where it tingled.

Tongue-tied, she cleared her throat. "If that's why you came back, you wasted a trip. I have no intention of leaving the Shenandoah."

Jeremiah used a knuckle to push the brim of his hat back, allowing her to better see his eyes. His teeth flashed white against his tanned skin, the twinkling in his eyes making the gold in them even more pronounced. "Oh, you're coming with us. I've seen your stubbornness before, but it usually wasn't directed at us. I know you're mad because we left, but it was for your own good. You'll come back home with us for the same reason."

Maggie wondered what she'd ever done in her life to deserve the cruel joke fate had decided to play on her. To have Eb and Jeremiah appear and know she had to watch them leave again hurt almost too much to bear.

She took a deep breath and let it out slowly. "I understand now why your father sent for you. Now that Daddy's gone, he wants you to take responsibility for me." She thought she couldn't hurt any worse.

She was wrong.

Eb reached out and lifted her chin, holding it and forcing her to meet his eyes. "Is that all he told you? Didn't he tell you why we left in the first place?"

Maggie shook her head. "Daddy said you left because Kansas City was too crowded for you." Looking up from beneath her lashes, she eyed them both. "I always thought it had something to do with the fight the four of you had the night before you went away."

Eb's lips thinned. "You always were smart. We fought with Dad and Buck about you." At her look of surprise, he nodded. "We knew you were too young, but we wanted our intentions clear from the start. We told your daddy we were willing to wait for you, but he didn't want to hear it. He was right, but things are different now. He's gone, Maggie, and we've made a home for you in Oklahoma."

"What do you mean? You told Daddy you wanted to take me to live in Oklahoma?"

Eb's eyes narrowed, a small smile playing at his lips. "No, Maggie. We told your daddy our intention to marry you."

Maggie's breath caught as she looked from one to the other. Could it be true? Her heart sped up, making it difficult to breathe. "Which one of you wants to marry me?"

Eb's expression never changed. "Both of us, Maggie. You're going to marry both of us."

She couldn't believe they would be so cruel. "That's not very funny." The sooner they left again, the better.

She looked at Jeremiah, expecting him to laugh at his brother's cruel joke, but he just kept staring at her.

Both of them kept looking at her as though *she* were the stranger, their eyes raking over her body in ways they never had before. It felt as though she'd been sleeping all the years since they left, numb and unfeeling. Suddenly, all of her senses became heightened, almost to the point of pain.

Jeremiah tilted his head, his eyes narrowing. "He's serious, Maggie."

Shaking her head, Maggie twisted her hands together. "That's not possible, and you know it. A woman can't marry more than one man. Are you having trouble deciding which one of you is going to have to marry me? Why would you even say such a thing?"

She started to turn away, yelping when Eb grabbed her arm and whipped her back around again.

Cupping her jaw, he forced her head up, his eyes sharp. "Because it's true. You're going back to Oklahoma with us. That's the end of it, Maggie. It's for your own good, and you'll do as you're damned well told."

Jeremiah moved closer from the other side, shooting a warning glance at Eb. "Your daddy wouldn't believe we could make it work here, and after the fight you referred to, we had to admit he was right. So we left to find a place where we could both have you. And we have. We can live with you the way we want to and nobody will say a word against us. One word, one wrong look from any of the hands and they're gone." He reached out to brush a hand down her hair. "And they already know it. We've got a good life there, Maggie, one that you'll be a part of."

His eyes went down her body from her head to her toes, lingering on her breasts and making her burn everywhere. "And with you looking like that, being married to you is looking better and better."

Angry now at his disregard for just how much pain they'd caused and their arrogance at assuming she'd be ready to fall in their arms, she snapped at them. "Are you crazy? You've been gone for five years, walked away without a backward glance, and you come back here and try to tell me you want to marry me? You want me to be a wife to *both* of you? You expect me to leave the only home I've ever known and move to Oklahoma?" Shaking her head, she stared straight ahead. "No. Leave me alone and go back to your precious ranch."

The fact that she was actually considering their offer infuriated her.

Jeremiah's jaw clenched. "No, Maggie. When we leave, you're coming with us."

She spun to glare at Eb, fighting the panic that started to set in. "We're not friends anymore. Just leave me alone and go back to your damned *good life* in Oklahoma."

Eb's eyes flashed. "When did you start cussing? I'll hear no more of that from your lips, is that clear?"

Maggie sneered at him. "Go to hell. In case you haven't noticed, I've grown up, and what I do is none of your business. You left, remember? Without telling me anything. I don't owe you anything anymore, not even friendship. And I *don't* have to listen to you anymore."

Jeremiah's eyes narrowed and darkened. "Oh, we've noticed that you've grown up, honey. And you *will* do what we say."

Eb flicked his wrists, his eyes softening as he put the buckboard in motion. "We *are* here to help you. We didn't talk to you about all this years ago because you were still too young. We've waited long enough for you, Maggie, and there's no reason to wait any longer. We're getting married tomorrow. While we're here, everyone will have to think it's just you and I, but at the end of the week, you're coming home with us to our ranch where you'll be wife to both of us. Openly. That's that, Maggie."

The way he spoke, the authority she'd never heard from him before, scared her more than she cared to admit. He'd always been bossy and self-assured, but this was beyond that. He spoke as if he'd become used to his word being law and that he neither expected nor would tolerate any arguments.

Maggie smiled serenely while her insides fluttered. "No."

Jeremiah kept pace alongside them. Shooting another warning glance at Eb, he grinned, showing off his dimples and making her breath catch. "It *will* be a good life for all of us, Maggie. Everything we've done, we did so we could have you with us."

"Without even asking me what I wanted. No, you didn't do it for me." The sharp edge of betrayal cut deep. Blinking back tears, she looked down the road to the Tyler spread, her hands tightening on her hat. These weren't the young men who'd gotten her whatever she wanted, the ones she'd always counted on to make everything all right.

These men were arrogant and bossy. Hell, they'd just arrived and already started issuing orders.

Feeling more alone than ever, she straightened in her seat and swallowed the lump in her throat.

"It's obvious neither one of you cares enough about me to get married. You say *marry*, but neither one of you would be a real husband. What you're really doing is taking care of me because your father expects it. I appreciate the offer, but I'd rather have a man who wants a real wife."

Eb tugged the reins, bringing the horses to a sharp halt, sending her flying out of her seat with a cry. He caught her easily with one arm before she could fall and pulled her onto his lap. "Oh, you're going to be a real wife, Maggie. Make no mistake about that."

Settling her struggling form across his thighs, he lowered his head, his eyes holding hers. The muscles beneath her bottom shifted as his strong arms wrapped around her, pulling her against an equally hard chest.

At the age of twenty-one, she'd been held before, even been kissed a few times but nothing in her meager experience could compete with the feeling she got from being in Eb's arms.

So strange and yet so heartachingly familiar.

He brushed his lips over hers, the gentle caress surprising her with its power. Like a jolt of lightning had struck her system, everything came alive, as though her senses had been lying dormant, waiting for him to awaken them.

Alarmed at the softening of her own body against his, she pushed at him in a panicked effort to get away, only to grip him tightly instead.

The strong contrast between the tenderness of his kiss and the strength of his arms made her dizzy. Panicked, she struggled to get away, frightened that she'd surrendered so easily

The soft brushes of his lips on hers never faltered as he tightened his arms around her, holding her until her struggles ceased. Only then did he relax his hold and deepen his kiss.

Maggie's eyes fluttered closed on a moan as he used his tongue to tease the seam of her lips, not faltering until she allowed him inside. Her hand went to the nape of his neck, her fingers threading through the cool strands of his hair as though she'd done it a hundred times.

Following her automatic retreat, his tongue slid over hers, tangling with it until she surrendered and touched her tongue to his.

The fire Eb and Jeremiah had already ignited inside her flared to life 'and began burning out of control. Rubbing herself against Eb in a frantic attempt to ease the tingling heat in her nipples, she was alarmed that she only managed to make it worse.

Jeremiah touched her leg. "That's it, Maggie. Let go. You're ours."

The brim of Eb's hat shaded her face and created an intimacy that only Jeremiah's presence seemed to penetrate. The awareness that he watched Eb kiss her heightened her senses and almost made her feel as though he were a part of it. The sensation increased when she felt his hand slide under the hem of her skirt to caress her ankle.

Eb explored her mouth with a thoroughness that left her breathless, the barely leashed hunger in his kiss both alarming and irresistible.

One of his strong hands supported her neck while the other settled at her waist, squeezing lightly and making her squirm against him, silently urging him to touch her where she needed it most. He obliged her, his hand sliding up so slowly it made her breath hitch until he touched the underside of her breast. She gasped as it slid higher and closed over it, her heart beating frantically as he held it there, not moving at all while she writhed restlessly to get even closer.

He swallowed her moan, his hand tightening briefly when she pushed her breast more firmly into it, and with a groan, he sank into her, deepening his kiss until she saw stars and gripped him in a frantic attempt to keep from flying away. His hand shifted, his fingers gentle as he pressed his palm against her nipple, his low groan sending another wave of electricity through her.

Flames licked at her everywhere as his touch grew bolder, the raw possessiveness in his kiss adding to the feeling of being totally taken over as his fingers plucked at her nipple through her dress. Shaking uncontrollably, she rocked on his lap, whimpering as the burning between her thighs became unbearable.

When he lifted his head, she opened her eyes to find him staring down at her with an intensity that shocked her.

With a small, indulgent smile, he flicked his thumb back and forth over her nipple. "You'll be a *real* wife to both of us. You'll live on our ranch and bear our children. Now stop fighting us. We'll leave for Oklahoma at the end of the week."

Still wrapped in a cocoon of warmth and pleasure, she stared at him blankly before glancing sideways to see Jeremiah watching them with the strangest look on his face. Snapping out of her stupor, she fought her way out of Eb's arms, putting as much distance as the seat allowed between them. "No. It was just a kiss. I…You surprised me. That's all." Unsteady, she held on to the side of her seat, trembling and so weak she was afraid she would fall off. What the hell had he done to her?

Mad at herself and them, and hurt that they thoughtlessly ignored her objections, she looked straight ahead and wrapped her shawl around herself again, fighting for some semblance of control. Now that Eb no longer held her, the cold crept back in, making her ache all the way to her bones. Lifting her chin, she did her best to keep her voice steady, not daring to let them see how easily they'd won so much of her surrender. "Please take me home."

Eb snapped the reins, his face once again like stone. "Your home, Maggie, is a ranch in Oklahoma. Get everything packed that you want to take with you. We leave at the end of the week."

Chapter Two

Barely holding on by a thread, she knew she'd fall apart if she didn't get a few minutes alone to get herself back under control. Leaving Eb and Jeremiah at the stable talking to Jasper, Maggie turned away, looking over her shoulder and mumbling an excuse that she wanted to change out of her good dress.

Both Eb and Jeremiah whipped their heads around, spearing her with their sharp gazes before nodding, wordlessly giving their consent.

Hiding her anger and the uncomfortable suspicion that they would try to rule her if she allowed it, she started out, involuntarily pausing when Jeremiah called her name.

"We're not finished talking with you yet, Maggie. We still have a few things to discuss."

Maggie nodded, her knees shaking as she started walking again. She had no intention of finishing *that* conversation, her body still humming from the one they'd had several minutes ago. She knew they expected her to return after changing, the warning in their eyes making it blatantly clear.

They'd just have to be disappointed.

It would be a small but satisfying victory to disobey them, but she couldn't face them again right now, even if she'd wanted to.

She hurried back to the house she'd shared with her father and ran straight into the bedroom. Stripping out of her dress, she started to toss it aside but held it to her breast instead, staring at herself in the mirror.

Her eyes looked too bright and too big for her face, her skin pale. Her lips looked swollen and dark, almost bruised, and when she licked them, she could still taste Eb.

Tracing her fingers over the bodice where Eb's hand had been, she closed her eyes, no longer seeing herself but the image of his face as he stared down at her, his eyes hooded and shot with green.

The arrogance and possession she understood and expected, but the surprised wonder was something she didn't think she'd ever forget.

Shaking off the image, she tossed the dress aside to don a pair of the pants she usually wore and a shirt that had seen better days.

This clothing suited her, the familiarity comforting her, something she desperately needed right now.

Almost as much as she needed to talk to Savannah.

Her friend's failure to meet her yesterday morning at the general store worried her, especially after Savannah's absence after the funeral, and Maggie wouldn't feel better until she checked on her.

She usually snuck out to the Perrys' house at the outskirts of town whenever she knew Savannah's uncle wouldn't be there and met her friend every week at the general store to talk.

Maggie went early, desperate to see if Savannah was all right and to tell her about Eb and Jeremiah coming back to town.

When Savannah didn't show up at the general store Maggie knew something had to be wrong.

She'd gone out to their house last night and snuck around back, looking in the window to see Savannah reading from the Bible to Reverend Perry. Frustrated that she wouldn't have a chance to talk to her friend, she'd reluctantly left. With all the rush and excitement of getting to the train station and Eb and Jeremiah's arrival, thoughts of Savannah that had been pushed back came back now with an urgency that couldn't be denied.

Maggie took the shortcut through the woods, both to get there faster and to keep anyone from town from seeing her and reporting it to Eb and Jeremiah if they came looking for her.

The fading daylight made Maggie a little nervous, so she rode as quickly as she could through the dense cluster of trees, dodging branches and careful to keep her horse from tripping.

Approaching the small barn behind the Perry home, she slowed and slid from the saddle, careful to keep out of sight. Darkness had fallen, but with the lanterns lighting the way to the barn, enough light shone that she could be seen if anyone looked her way.

She left her horse where he would be hidden by trees and carefully made her way through the trees and bushes and over the uneven ground to the edge of the woods where the trees met the Perrys' yard.

The light coming from the dilapidated structure told her that the barn was in use. As she got closer, she heard the Reverend's voice, condescending and raised in anger as he delivered his usual dire threats of hell for those who didn't follow his teachings to the letter.

Ramblings was more like it. That man could go on and on about nothing longer than anyone Maggie had ever met.

For once she could be thankful for it, hoping it would give her some time to talk to Savannah.

She knew she'd find her friend in the kitchen, where she'd be busy preparing refreshments for the Reverend's flock. The Reverend worked Savannah incessantly telling her repeatedly that he did it to keep her out of trouble.

Maggie figured it was because the good Reverend wanted a slave to see to his every need and Savannah never complained.

She had a feeling her best friend was up to something, but she couldn't get Savannah to tell her anything. She'd been too quiet lately, something that worried Maggie a lot.

She'd known her friend a long time, and one thing she knew for sure.

A quiet Savannah was a dangerous Savannah.

Savannah cooked and cleaned and had to help write her uncle's sermons for him. She mended his clothes and cleaned the barn for him after his meetings while the reverend went to bed. She prepared cakes and fresh lemonade for his meetings and had to deliver the cakes and pies that she slaved over to those he saw as beneficiaries to his cause. He volunteered her services to see to the sick and read to them because he was too afraid of catching something to go himself.

In addition, she had to read to him from the Bible every night, and he kept her up until all hours, interpreting it to suit his own needs.

Savannah never complained, but Maggie couldn't help but notice how distracted her friend seemed lately. She'd commented on it several times but could never get Savannah to confide in her.

She'd go crazy if she didn't find out what her friend was up to.

No amount of begging or threatening could get Savannah to talk.

Something had to be done, though, and soon. Maggie didn't trust the gleam in the reverend's eyes one bit and feared for Savannah's safety.

Maybe she should talk to Eb and Jeremiah.

Picturing *that* confrontation made her smile.

If the reverend had been scared of the old Eb and Jeremiah, she imagined he'd soil himself if he saw them now.

On that cheery thought, Maggie started up the steps to the back door.

"I'll kill him."

Startled by the deep, masculine voice coming from Savannah's kitchen, and intrigued by the frustration and affection in the tone, Maggie paused on the second step, glancing over her shoulder toward the barn to make sure no one could see her.

"Mr. Matlock, you shouldn't be here. Please go before my uncle finds you here."

"When I kissed you, you called me Wyatt."

Maggie's mouth dropped open. What? Savannah kissed him? This was definitely a conversation she'd love to eavesdrop on, but she couldn't stand outside for long or someone might arrive late at the meeting and see her.

"Please go!"

The panic in Savannah's voice spurred Maggie into action. Glancing over her shoulder toward the barn, she raced up the rest of the stairs and hurried inside, careful not to slam the door behind her.

Shocked to see that instead of one man, *two* men stood in the kitchen, one on either side of Savannah, Maggie stopped short just inside the door.

Both men spun at her entrance, their hands going to their guns, stopping just short of drawing them. Eyeing Maggie warily, they took a protective stance in front of Savannah, appearing irritated at the interruption.

Maggie didn't flinch, concern for her friend overriding everything else.

"Who are you, and what are you doing here?"

Taking a few steps closer, Maggie's alarm grew when she recognized them.

They'd arrived in town several weeks ago, and when Maggie first saw them, she'd assumed they were outlaws.

Their loose-limbed strides had folks giving them a wide berth as they walked through town, their dark eyes razor-sharp and constantly moving. Their lean muscular builds drew plenty of attention from both nervous men and fascinated women, but neither man seemed particularly interested in either one.

They had the kind of presence seldom seen in Kansas City.

A picture of the way Eb and Jeremiah looked as they came toward her in the train station rose in her mind, a sharp reminder of the only other men she'd ever seen who had that ruthless look about them.

They didn't look so ruthless right now. In fact, both looked more than a little frustrated.

Cursing the fact that she'd forgotten her own guns in her rush to get away from the ranch, she considered screaming.

The one on the right shifted his weight as though in anticipation to move after her if she tried to escape. When he stepped closer to the lantern, she found herself fascinated by the red glints in his otherwise dark hair. "Don't scream. We won't hurt either one of you. We're friends of Savannah's."

Eyeing her red-faced friend, he sighed, the exasperation on his face easing some of Maggie's fears. "Even if she doesn't want us to be."

"Savannah, are you all right? Who are these men?"

To her surprise, Savannah laid a hand on each of their sinewy forearms, sharing a look with them, the intimacy in their eyes making Maggie feel like an intruder and wiping away the last of her uneasiness.

Things just kept getting more and more interesting.

The men's expressions softened, the change in them remarkable as they stepped aside to make room for Savannah to pass. Their eyes never left her as she approached Maggie, the affection and annoyance in them unmistakable.

When Savannah turned her head, the light caught an ugly mark high on her cheek.

Outraged, Maggie gasped, grabbing Savannah's shoulders to turn her more fully toward the light. "Savannah! Damn it, Savannah, when did this happen? Where else are you hurt? Why didn't you come to me?" Furious when her friend flinched, she released her immediately.

Savannah pushed the loose tendrils of hair from her face with the back of her hand, wincing when her hand brushed the bruise. "Shh, he'll hear you. Please, Maggie, just go. I'm fine, I promise. Everything will be all right, but he can't find you here."

Outraged, Maggie spared a glance at the barn. "Savannah, he hit you! You can't keep quiet about this anymore. Eb and Jeremiah came to visit. I'll tell them."

"No."

The other man came forward, the shadows in the room making his dark looks appear even more threatening, but at least he smiled. "I appreciate that you want to help your friend, but we'll take care of this. You should go."

Shaking her head, Savannah stepped away from them. "I can take care of this all by myself. I want all of you to go. I promise you, I have this under control."

Maggie eyed both men and put her arm around Savannah. "I can't just sit around and do nothing. What kind of friend would I be if I just left her to two strangers?"

The unsmiling one inclined his head. "Fair enough. We're lawmen and can be trusted to not hurt your friend. My name is Hayes Hawkins, and this is Wyatt Matlock."

Maggie hugged Savannah, running her hands over her to see if she flinched again. She paused, shooting a grin at her friend. "The one who she kissed?"

Savannah gasped and pulled away from her, her face a bright red. "Maggie! How did you know—I mean—"

Maggie crossed her arms over her chest, hurt that her friend hadn't confided in her, but thrilled that she apparently had a beau.

If Maggie had to leave Kansas City, nothing would please her more than to know that Savannah had someone to look after her. Eyeing the man on her left with new respect, she couldn't help but smile at the way he stared at Savannah.

Wyatt Matlock eyed her friend as if he wanted to eat her alive, while the other man stood stone-faced, dividing his attention between her and the window.

Maggie winked at her. "I heard you talking when I was walking up the back steps. I'm glad, Savannah. He'll stand up to your uncle. That's something I'd love to see."

The other man's face hardened into a look that frightened Maggie just a little and reminded her of Eb in a rage. "Her uncle will be dealt with. You'd better leave before he finds you here."

Shaking her head, Maggie wrapped an arm around Savannah. "No. You're the ones who'd better go. Reverend Perry would have a conniption if he found you two here."

Wyatt reached for Savannah. "I'm not worried about the reverend."

Savannah stepped back out of his reach and glared at him. "I want all of you to leave. Your butting in is only going to make it worse. If you—" She turned to encompass the two men watching her attentively. "If any of you care about me at all, you'll leave now before my uncle finds you here."

When all three began to speak, she lifted a hand. "I mean it. Now just go. Please."

Her voice broke on the last word, making both men shift uncomfortably and tying the knots in Maggie's stomach tighter. Knowing that the reverend would be calling for refreshments soon, Maggie reluctantly nodded.

"If you agree to meet me tomorrow at noon behind the general store, I'll leave. If not, I'm staying."

"Savannah! It's hot in here. Where's that lemonade?"

Savannah blanched at her uncle's demand and kept her voice at a furious whisper. "Fine. I'll meet you there. Now just go. If I don't get out there, he'll be coming in here looking for me. Get out of here. All of you. Hurry!"

Maggie stood firm. "First I want to know if you're hurt anywhere else."

Shaking her head, Savannah pushed Maggie toward the front room. "No. This was an accident. I'll see you tomorrow. Don't you dare tell anyone."

Savannah glanced nervously at the two men who'd followed them. "Please go before my uncle comes in here. And don't come near me again."

"Savannah!"

Maggie cringed at the impatience in Reverend Perry's voice and shot a glance at the other men, a little surprised at the raw fury on Hayes' face. "We'd better go before he gets really mad and takes it out on Savannah."

She touched Savannah's arm. "I'll see you tomorrow. If you don't meet me, I'm coming back with Eb and Jeremiah."

"Damn it, Maggie."

"I mean it, Savannah."

"All right! Just go."

Maggie left the kitchen and went out the front door, swearing under her breath when Savannah called out to her uncle. She paced back and forth right outside the door, pacing as she waited for the men to join her. As soon as they did, she confronted Wyatt.

"How long have you known Savannah?"

He took her arm and led her around to the side of the house, looking back over his shoulder toward the house. "Since a few days after we came to town. We've seen you with her. You're her friend, Margaret, aren't you?"

"I am." She kept her voice low and watched as Hayes came out, barely glancing at her as he went ahead of them to look around the corner. "You'd better not cause any trouble for her."

Spinning, Hayes speared her with his gaze. "The last thing we want is to make trouble for Savannah. We'll be there tomorrow when you meet her, though. We want to talk to her, too."

Tugging her arm out of Wyatt's grasp, Maggie took several steps back. "That won't be necessary. Besides, I want to talk to her alone."

Wyatt crossed his arms over his chest, all arrogant male, something she'd had enough of today. "So do we. I'll make a deal with you. We'll give you some time alone with her if you'll afford us the same privilege."

Maggie lifted her chin. "That's up to Savannah."

Hayes came back to stand on the other side of her. "Then no deal."

He cursed, whipping an arm out to pull her behind him. "Two riders are coming. I think it's the Tylers. I heard about them earlier. Who are they? Your guardians?"

Maggie panicked at the thought of Eb and Jeremiah finding her and starting a ruckus when it just might get Savannah in trouble.. "No, but I have to leave before they get here. You'd better get out of here, too."

Wyatt glanced over his shoulder in the direction Eb and Jeremiah approached. "We'll wait until you're gone." At her wary look, he smiled. "We'll leave, I promise. We've got some things to do before we see Savannah tomorrow."

Maggie paused and turned, asking the question that had bothered her ever since she saw the way Hayes looked at her friend. "Why do I get the feeling more than one of you is interested in Savannah?"

Wyatt shared a look with his friend, staring after him when Hayes bit off a curse and walked away. Turning back, he sighed impatiently. "It's a little hard to explain. Let's just say that we both care about what happens to her and leave it at that."

He turned away abruptly and took several steps before coming to a halt. With his hands on his hips, he turned slowly, glancing again in the direction Eb and Jeremiah approached before turning to her, his expression softening. "I heard from the shopkeeper in town that Eb and Jeremiah Tyler want to take you with them when they leave Kansas City. Don't worry about your friend. We'll take care of her."

Before she could reply, Hayes came back and grabbed her arm, pulling her with him to the corner of the house. "Savannah just went into the barn. Go."

Maggie stopped, digging her heels in when he tried to push her toward the trees. "We're not done talking about this. If I find out you've hurt Savannah, I'll let Eb and Jeremiah loose on you."

Hayes went still, menace in every line of his body. "The last thing we want to do is hurt Savannah. Now, go before someone sees you."

"What about you?"

His cold smile sent a chill up her spine. "I'm going to have a little talk with the reverend first. Now, get out of here before you're spotted."

His slow wink relieved her, assuring her that they'd take care of Savannah. Maggie cursed the fact that she wouldn't be there to witness their little talk with Reverend Perry. Reluctantly turning away, she crouched low and headed for her horse, cringing when she heard the icy snap of Eb's voice from behind her.

"Who are you, and what the fuck are you doing with Maggie?"

Knowing Eb's temper, Maggie cursed and quickly mounted to race toward the side of the house where he and Jeremiah surrounded the other two men. She looked over her shoulder toward the barn, hoping no one heard them and barely managing not to yelp when Jeremiah whipped an arm out and yanked her from her horse to his.

"You're not going anywhere until we find out what the hell's going on." His threatening tone startled her, sending a fissure of fear down her spine and sounding nothing like the playful Jeremiah from her past.

She automatically grabbed at him, afraid of falling, but it immediately became apparent she shouldn't have worried. The muscles in his arm bunched and shifted under her hand as he settled her in front of him.

"Please. We have to go."

She turned to Eb and, to her horror, saw he had his gun aimed at Hayes and Wyatt with practiced ease. "No!" Remembering the need for silence, she glanced toward the barn again and whispered furiously. "They're friends of Savannah's. We've been worried about her."

Hayes stepped forward, inclining his head toward the gun, but not looking the least bit intimidated. "I appreciate your concern, but we have no designs on your woman."

Wyatt looked around the corner of the house just as Savannah came out of the barn with two empty pitchers and hurried toward the house. Frustration poured off of him. "Maybe now's not the best time for introductions. Get her out of here. We've got some business to attend to with the good reverend before we go."

Jeremiah tightened his arm around Maggie when she shivered. "Maggie, these men haven't touched you?"

Shaking her head, Maggie eyed Eb nervously. "No. I swear. Please. I'll explain it all later. We have to get out of here before Reverend Perry sees us. Wait!"

Crossing her arms over her chest, Maggie smiled coldly. "I don't care if he sees you. Savannah's in trouble. Her uncle hit her. She has a black eye."

Eb's eyes widened, and then narrowed. "What? That son of a bitch! Wait here."

Hayes stepped forward, holding up a hand. "No. I appreciate your concern, but Wyatt and I, we'll take care of it."

Eb didn't even spare him a look and started past him.

"Take Maggie home, Jeremiah. I'll take care of this."

Hayes blocked his way, placing a hand on the horse's neck. "No." He waited until Eb met his gaze and inclined his head toward Maggie. "If this was her, wouldn't you want to take care of it yourself?"

After a brief silence, Eb smiled coldly, glancing at Maggie and nodding once. "Absolutely."

Wyatt came forward, crossing his arms over his chest and raising a brow. "Then you'll let us take care of what's ours."

Maggie cringed at his arrogant tone and could hear her own heartbeat as the tense silence dragged out, knowing from experience how dangerous a situation like this could become.

Finally Eb nodded and stuck his gun back in his holster, his expression grim. "I expect to hear the whole story."

Wyatt inclined his head, saying nothing.

Breathing a sigh of relief, Maggie slumped against Jeremiah, turning her head to catch his words.

"No one here wants trouble, Maggie. Just calm down. Are you sure you're all right?"

Maggie nodded, her head brushing against his jaw. "I'm fine." She covered the hand he placed over her stomach, keeping her voice at a whisper. "Eb wouldn't really have shot him, would he?"

"Of course. Just be still."

To her surprise, he reholstered his own gun, one she hadn't even been aware he'd drawn, and placed his hand over her thigh.

"Savannah! Hurry up with those cakes."

Hayes' eyes iced over. "First things first." He disappeared around the side of the house with Wyatt right behind him.

Maggie pushed against Jeremiah's hold. "Let go of me so we can get out of here."

Jeremiah adjusted his hold, pulling her more firmly against him, settling her so that his cock pressed against her bottom. "I like you where you are just fine."

Gathering the reins of her horse, Eb moved closer, reaching out to touch her thigh, his caress sending a blazing trail to her folds, where it spread to her pussy and clit. "We're going to talk about this, honey. You're gonna learn real quick to do what you're told."

Unsettled when her pussy clenched, leaking moisture, Maggie looked away, trying to keep her breathing steady. She wrapped her arms around herself against the chills that went through her, despite the warmth of Jeremiah's body along her back. As they started back through the woods, Maggie fought for the bravado they'd cut through with alarming ease, assuring herself she'd done what she had to do.

She didn't care whether Eb and Jeremiah approved or not.

They weren't the only ones who'd changed in the last five years.

* * * *

Eb shot a look of impatience at his brother and turned his horse toward the woods, intending to have it out with Maggie as soon as they got back to the Shenandoah.

He'd only been around her a day and already she seemed hell-bent on driving him crazy. The spirited young girl they'd left behind had become too independent and headstrong in their absence, something he and Jeremiah would have to take care of right away.

Distracted by her incredible beauty, a body that would rival any of Trixie's girls, and beautiful eyes that breathed fire one minute and darkened with passion the next, he could tell already that he would have a hell of a time keeping her in line.

He'd spent hours riding with his father and brother as his father showed them the changes he'd made to the ranch, but his mind had been on Maggie the entire time.

Everything about her fascinated him, and every moment he spent with her just made him want her more. She held his attention like no other women ever had, even with their experienced ways and erotic tricks, which he enjoyed but that left him cold.

The warm, sweet scent of Maggie's impossibly soft skin nearly brought him to his knees.

He'd expected her to be grown up. He just hadn't expected the grown up version of her to affect him so strongly. The scent of her, those full, voluptuous curves, that pink mouth and the fullest, softest lips he'd ever kissed had sent his senses spiraling, and he hadn't been able to get them under control since.

For a man who prided himself on his control, it was a hard blow to take.

It angered him that she could shake him so easily, and with no apparent effort. The desire to shake her just as badly raged inside him along with the hunger for her that seemed to grow each time he saw her.

He wanted to yank those pants down to her knees and fuck her long and hard from behind and teach her who was in charge, while giving her more pleasure than she could imagine. He wanted to hear her scream his name and beg for more and come hard, gripping him with her pussy and coating his cock with her juices.

Damn it, he wanted her to want him as much as he wanted her. He'd never have the upper hand with her as long as she had this hold over him.

Hell, he'd only been back a few hours and he could already feel his control slipping.

The thought of fucking her with his brother, the two of them taking her ass and pussy at the same time and filling her completely had his cock throbbing painfully.

Maggie wouldn't stand a chance of denying them. Once they'd taken her and she knew the full pleasure to be found in their arms, she'd be much easier to control. They could provide or deny pleasure as they needed to keep her in line, and maybe then he could rein in this wild hunger for her.

This kind of desire weakened a man and would keep him from doing what he had to do.

Once he had her and he and Jeremiah had the upper hand, everything would be as it should be.

Tonight would be the perfect opportunity to give her a taste of desire and to give her a taste of what would be in store for her when she defied them.

And she would.

It would also fulfill his need to have the power over Maggie every man should have over his woman.

Her silence now bothered him. Of course he preferred that she remain silent as they rode through dark woods, but in the past, she'd usually chatted like a magpie. He and Jeremiah would have spent the entire trip back impatiently telling her to be quiet until they got out of the woods and listening for any sign of trouble.

It troubled him that he couldn't read her moods as easily as he had before, something that unsettled him more than he wanted to admit. He studied her expression but couldn't figure out if her silence came from anger or fear.

Hell, for all he knew, she could be planning something.

They came out of the woods on the western edge of the Tyler land, several hundred yards from the main house. Once they emerged from the trees, Eb rode beside his brother, taking in Maggie's stony expression. The light from the moon allowed them to see her better, but she just stared straight ahead, not looking at either one of them.

Where was the girl who used to follow them everywhere and hang on their every word?

The rebellious nature she appeared to have developed toward them set his teeth on edge. When she was younger, he'd usually been amused at her antics and quick-fire temper, even when it had been directed at him. But in the past, she'd always deferred to him and teased Jeremiah, saving her stubbornness and defiance for others.

To have them directed at him now put distance between them he didn't care for a bit.

She'd been spoiled over the years, something he admitted he'd contributed to, but he couldn't allow that any longer. She'd be living in a cruel land, where wild animals and wilder outlaws roamed free, and she wouldn't be allowed to have the freedom she had here, and she'd damned well just have to get used to it.

If anything happened to her because he'd failed to protect her, he'd never forgive himself. Although Maggie was well suited to ranch living, he could see that in order to keep her safe, he'd have to keep a tight rein on her.

He hadn't counted on how much freedom she'd be allowed as she got older, freedom he would have to take from her.

Starting now.

Both he and Jeremiah stopped their horses when they were still too far for anyone at the ranch to see or hear them.

The bright moon allowed him to see Jeremiah's expression, frustration, anger, and hunger warring for supremacy.

Eb understood his brother's emotions well and knew Jeremiah would be just as relieved when they got Maggie settled down.

He moved his horse to stand in front of her and sat unmoving, grinding his back teeth together when she wouldn't look at him. Waiting her out tried his patience, and by the time she finally looked up, his impatience had turned to anger and added a bite to his tone.

"I don't know if the rules you've been living by have changed or not, but you'll live by our rules now. You won't go to town again without our permission, and you won't go anywhere alone." Smiling coldly when she glared at him, he folded his arms across his chest, a warm satisfaction welling inside him at her display of emotion.

At least he knew he had her attention now.

Lifting her chin, she glared at both of them. "You can't just show up here after five years and try to tell me what to do."

Eb pushed back the urge to shake her and exchanged a cool smile with Jeremiah while moving in closer. "You're wrong about that. We're marrying you and taking you home with us. Your life is with us now, and you'll do as you're damned well told."

Damn it, he itched to spoil her again, but he couldn't take the chance of doing it now. The sooner he forced her to become malleable, the sooner he could do all the little things that earned him one of her sweet smiles.

Jeremiah gripped her chin, forcing her to face him, his hand sliding up to rest beneath the swell of her high breasts. "It's for your own good. You'll only get yourself in trouble if you don't obey the rules we give you."

Maggie stunned Eb by pulling out of Jeremiah's grip and crossing her arms over her chest, in an apparent attempt to mimic his pose. She only managed to push her breasts higher, giving him a tantalizing glimpse of the upper curve of their round fullness. She gave him her most haughty look, but he heard the catch in her breath.

"Then I guess I'd better stay here where I'm safe. Besides, I like being here in the city. Why would I want to live out in the middle of nowhere? Now, if you'll excuse me, I'm tired. It's been an eventful day."

Eb gritted his teeth, fighting the urge to yank her against him and kiss her until she surrendered. He met her smug smile with a cold one, not about to let her rile him into anger. "It's about to get even more eventful, sweetheart, and no matter what you say, you're coming to the Triple T with us."

She lifted her chin, making him hungry for the taste of those full lips. "I'm staying here."

Jeremiah lifted her by the waist, turned her, and settled her across his lap, grinning when she struggled. "No. You're coming with us. We've made a home, Maggie, one that you'll like. Life's much different there than it is here, and it's dangerous. Yeah, it's in the middle of nowhere, but that's so we can live the way we want to with you. The only way we can keep you safe, though, is if you do what we tell you."

Maggie cocked her head in that way she had when she was at her most impudent. "If you're so damned ashamed of me that you only want to live with me in the middle of *nowhere*, why the hell would you come back for me?"

Eb gritted his teeth, wondering why her smart mouth, which he used to find so adorable, now gave him the urge to turn her over his knee and paddle her ass. "We're not ashamed of you, damn it. But the three of us can't live together—"

Her sassy smile made his hand itch to connect with her curvy behind. "That's what I've been saying."

"Damn it, Maggie." Stopping short, he clenched his jaw and took a deep breath to calm himself, not about to give her the satisfaction of making him lose his temper. "You can't have two husbands in a town like Kansas City. Be careful, little girl. I'm running out of patience with you."

Maggie's chin went up, sparks flying from her beautiful eyes and making his cock impossibly harder. "I'm a grown woman, not a little girl, and I know that having two husbands is against the law."

Taking another calming breath, Eb had to make a conscious effort to relax his jaw before he could speak. "I know that. You won't legally have two husbands—"

"Then what's all this about? You said you both want to marry me. I think living in Oklahoma has affected your brains. I will have two husbands. I won't have two husbands. Nothing more reassuring to a woman than a man who knows what he wants."

Jeremiah ran a hand up her thigh. "We know what we want, Maggie. We've known it for a long time. You damned well will have two husbands. Not legally, but every other way. Let me show you." He sunk into her.

Watching them, Eb could find no better way to describe it.

His brother wrapped his arms around Maggie and pulled her to him while bending over her, his hair falling to cover both of their faces.

Eb's cock came straight to attention as he watched Jeremiah's hand slide over Maggie's full breast, his lust even stronger when he imagined his brother watching him touch Maggie the same way.

Maggie pushed against his shoulder at first, but within seconds grabbed on to them, her little hand fisting in Jeremiah's jacket.

Clenching his jaw against yet another surge of need, he couldn't help wondering what that little hand would feel like stroking his cock.

He couldn't wait to find out.

* * * *

Maggie automatically grabbed Jeremiah's shoulders to steady herself, even though it immediately became obvious that his strength made it unnecessary.

Still, she held on, loving the feel of the muscles shifting beneath his jacket, and she couldn't quite hide a gasp when her nipples brushed against his chest.

Hard arms wrapped around her and pulled her against a chest much wider than it had been five years earlier. Cupping her jaw, he lifted her head, his eyes intense as they searched hers. "Husbands in every way, Maggie."

She held her breath as he bent his head and caught her lips with his own.

With a hand cupping the back of her head and the other at her waist, Jeremiah surrounded her with his heat and strength, warming her inside and out.

Maggie shivered as his tongue slid over hers, gasping when his silky hair brushed over her cheek. She hadn't even felt the cold until his warmth began to seep in, warmth that grew with every sweep of his tongue.

When his hand slid to her breast, she went limp in his arms, amazed at the hunger that took hold almost immediately and soon raged inside her. Every slide of his hand over her nipples sent an answering pull to her slit. Each clench of her pussy released more of her juices, her clit tingling more with each slide of Jeremiah's tongue over hers.

Her clit burned, swollen and with an ache that no amount of squirming could relieve. Her breasts warmed and swelled, and Jeremiah's attention to her nipple only made it worse.

He pinched lightly, forcing a cry from her which he met with an answering groan.

Desperate for attention to her other nipple, she rubbed against him, thrilling at the warm hard feel of him.

No matter how tightly he held her, she couldn't seem to get close enough.

When he lifted his head and pinched her nipple harder, the cry she released startled even her. The sharp jolt of pleasure to her pussy and clit had her writhing in his hold, gulping in as much air as she could in an effort to fight off the dizziness.

She could feel Eb's gaze on her and knew he watched her surrender in Jeremiah's arms, something that should have embarrassed her but instead sent her lust soaring.

Breathing heavily, she stared up at Jeremiah, trying to read his expression, but the brim of his hat blocked the moonlight from his features.

His hand gently massaged her breast, the possessiveness in his touch just as potent to her senses as the pleasure it gave her.

"You'll be my wife, too, Maggie. Make no mistake about that."

His soft tone held both tenderness and a hint of danger, a combination that proved lethal to her resistance.

"Impossible." But some little part inside her knew that she could never give herself to anyone else.

The years that she'd missed them and their possessive gentleness wiped away all her defenses, sweeping her along until Eb and Jeremiah were the only solid things in her world.

Jeremiah's hand slid under her shirt and closed over a breast. "Mine." The rough texture of his palm against her nipple sent an answering wave of hot sizzles through her, making her clit pulse.

Crying out as the sensation grew, she kicked her legs as her abdomen tightened and more of her juices flowed. Twisting restlessly, she whimpered in her throat, beating against Jeremiah's shoulder in frustration, and then held on for dear life as another wave shot through her.

"Give her to me." Eb's raw, gravelly tone sounded as though he'd just swallowed splintered glass.

Jeremiah's hand moved from her breast down to her hip and under her bottom. "No. I've got her."

Lifting her high against his chest, he swung one leg over his horse's back and slid from the saddle, his secure hold never faltering.

Eb came forward, running a hand up and down her leg as Jeremiah strode several feet away and lowered her to the blanket Eb had obviously spread.

Jeremiah settled himself on one side of her while Eb did the same on the other, neither man relinquishing his hold on her.

Maggie couldn't breathe in enough air, couldn't get close enough.

Completely surrounded, she'd never felt so small, so powerless and yet safer than she could ever remember feeling. Being this way with them released a bubble of happiness inside her, an effervescence that made her light-headed and increased her desire for both of them even more.

Her breath came out in frantic gulps as she writhed on the blanket, fighting her growing need, unsure if she could take any more.

This had to be some kind of dream. The men who'd always been larger than life to her wanted her and seemed enthralled with every inch of her. When both men reached for her, she sucked in a sharp breath and forgot how to breathe altogether.

Their warm, firm hands touched her everywhere at once, from her arms and shoulders to her breasts, from her hips and thighs to her abdomen and stomach, making everything in their path come alive with awareness.

Eb's fingers, both firm and caressing, stroked her jaw, turning her toward him. "You grew into a beautiful woman, Maggie, one who's smart and daring." He tapped her chin. "Maybe a little too daring. It was adorable when you were younger but won't be tolerated in Oklahoma. There's too much danger. You're going to have to get used to doing what we tell you so we can protect you. Our wife." His mouth covered hers before she could respond, his hand warm on her breast.

Or is it Jeremiah's?

When a firm hand covered her other breast, the knowledge that both of them touched her nearly sent her over the edge. With a whimpered moan, she held on to them as the last of her control over her body slipped effortlessly into their hands.

Eb's hand went into her hair, keeping her head turned toward him as he deepened his kiss, moving his lips over hers and sliding his tongue inside.

Restless and edgy, Maggie couldn't stop writhing as their hands moved over her. The cool air on her bare breasts was like nothing she'd ever felt before, the decadent sensation sending her senses soaring.

Her nipples pebbled even more, the cool caress of air contrasting sharply with the heat of their hands. Eb teased a nipple, running his work-roughened palm over it in slow circles, lifting his head to stare down at her as though mesmerized by her reaction.

At the same time, Jeremiah traced his fingers over her other breast, and to her frustration, he avoided her nipple completely.

The contrast of hot friction on one and cold need on the other made her more aware of both. She couldn't lie still, twisting from one side to the other in an effort to satisfy the craving building inside her.

Lying between them, she neither knew nor cared which one of them caressed her. It didn't matter as one touch blended into another.

Eb's voice sounded even deeper than before. "Look how she's trying to get you to touch her nipple."

Jeremiah groaned. "God, she's going wild."

Stunned that they talked about her as though she wasn't even there and the tension in their deep voices as they did, Maggie shivered.

An awareness began to grow inside her, an awareness of the touch of her lovers' hands that gradually made it possible to tell one from the other.

Jeremiah's teasing hands moved over her lightly, his fingers strumming over her flesh from one place to another and making her tingle everywhere. She couldn't anticipate where he'd touch her next, but he seemed to be determined to touch her everywhere.

His fleeting touch slowed occasionally to give her extra attention here and there, but she never knew when or where it would be or how long he would remain in one spot before his devious fingers made their way to another.

It drove her wild.

Eb, on the other hand, savored. He explored each inch of her body with a thoroughness that left her reeling. He touched, he pinched, he tasted, and the different textures of his fingers, lips, and tongue against her sensitive flesh brought every nerve ending alive and teased them mercilessly before moving on to another.

It stole her sanity.

The knowledge added an intimacy that had been lacking

She wondered briefly if they felt the same but couldn't dwell on it as the combination of their caresses impossible to resist and robbing her of all reason.

She just knew she wanted more.

She held on to Eb with a hand in his hair, knocking his hat off and fisting her fingers in the silky strands. The entire area between her legs tingled hotly, growing hotter as their hands roamed over her, Jeremiah's light caresses keeping her guessing while Eb's firmer touch explored each place on her body with a possessiveness that made her melt..

With the other hand, she held on to Jeremiah, digging her heels into the blanket to arch toward him in an attempt to get him to touch her other nipple.

The ache had become unbearable, her nipple pebbling tighter as the cool night air caressed it. His warm fingers, only inches away, made the cold feel even colder, making her crave the heat of his touch even more.

Eb continued to manipulate her breast, running a rough palm repeatedly over her nipple so lightly she wanted to scream, as though fascinated by it.

Jeremiah teased her, running his fingers from her breast to the waistband of her pants, and back up again, doing it over and over. Her stomach muscles quivered under his hand, her abdomen becoming so tight it hurt.

Eb bent to kiss her again. "So sweet. I think this marriage is going to work out just fine."

Turning her face toward him, Jeremiah brushed her lips with his. "Damned fine."

Maggie licked her lips, savoring the combined taste of both of them as much as she loved their combined caresses. "I can't believe you're both touching me. It feels so good." Oh, God, nothing had ever felt better. The closeness she'd missed with them came back with a suddenness that had tears stinging her eyes.

Different now than when she'd been younger, the intimacy between them was that of a man and a woman needing to be as close as possible to each other. More fulfilling, it made her want even more.

Jeremiah pinched her nipple, nuzzling her neck. "It'll feel even better in a little while."

Eb's hand went to the fastening of her pants. "Much better. Let me show you."

Maggie shook her head from side to side in denial of her loss of control, but couldn't get the words out before Jeremiah covered her mouth with his, swallowing her cries when Eb's lips began a slow journey down her body. Her cries became distressed whimpers when Eb began to lower her pants, allowing the cool air to touch parts of her that had never been exposed outdoor.

Already learning how thoroughly he explored every part he touched, she wondered if she'd ever survive that kind of attention on her clit and pussy, which already had become so sensitive she feared even one of Jeremiah's fleeting caresses would be too much.

Eb used his weight to hold her legs down, hooking his arms over them, effectively stilling her squirming. He slid his hands up her thighs, lingering about halfway up and massaging gently before continuing higher and using his thumbs to part her folds.

The cold breeze caressed her exposed slit, the juices wetting her folds and clit, making the feeling even more intense. Crying out, she fought their hold, unable to remain still at such a decadent sensation.

Jeremiah's long, drugging kisses made her dizzy, and she arched her back, lifting her breasts in invitation. With a groan, he finally gave her what she needed.

He ran the palm of his hand over a nipple before pinching it lightly between his thumb and forefinger, gradually increasing the pressure and tugging it upward, the sharp pleasure making her clit swell and tingle even more.

Eb kept her clit exposed, making her writhe in frustration, but his hold on her hips kept her from getting away from him.

Caught up in the passion in Jeremiah's kiss, the ribbons of pleasure from the sharp tugs on her nipples, and the raw sexuality of having her clit so exposed, she wasn't prepared for the touch of Eb's tongue.

The soft warmth brushing her clit hit her like a bolt of lightning, and she screamed into Jeremiah's mouth as her entire body jerked in his arms. Unable to believe her body was capable of such an erotic sensation, she bucked her hips against it, but couldn't budge Eb at all.

After a few strokes of his talented tongue, strokes that robbed her of reason, she no longer wanted to.

She lifted now, not to push him away, but to get more, her cries becoming frantic when his tongue slid over her clit, circling it and then stroking it with fast little flicks.

Eb lifted his head, allowing the cool night air to caress her clit again, drawing a tortured moan from her. "Jeremiah, I want to hear her."

Jeremiah lifted his head, no longer muffling her cries and whimpers, only to lower it over her other nipple. He swirled his hot tongue all around it before catching it with his teeth to tug on it.

Maggie couldn't hold back her cries against such incredible pleasure. The animalistic sounds splitting the night air alarmed her, especially when she realized they came from her. "Please! It's too much. Oh, God. What are you doing to me?"

Eb's hands tightened on her thighs, his tongue delving within her folds, unerringly finding just the right place to keep the pressure inside her growing.

She couldn't take much more. She never wanted him to stop.

How could she have lived her entire life without ever knowing that this kind of pleasure existed?

Jeremiah's mouth felt too hot on her nipples, as he used his lips and tongue on one and then the other. The cool breeze blowing across the wetness he left behind sent even more sizzles to her clit, made hotter by the strokes of Eb's tongue.

The swell inside her kept growing, the bubbles racing through her veins adding to the pressure.

Suddenly, it burst free.

Frightened at the intensity, she cried out as it showered her with sparks that raced over every inch of her body. They kept falling over her, the pinpricks of heat going on and on and rendering her senseless. The sheer ecstasy of it blinded and deafened her to everything else.

Her body tightened and bowed of its own volition, once again taken over by Eb and Jeremiah.

Jeremiah's soft murmur went unheard, his words drowned out by her own cries. Eb slowed the strokes on her clit, each flick of his tongue now like a jolt to her system, making her jerk in Jeremiah's hold.

Wrapping his arms completely around her, Jeremiah pulled her close, running his hands up and down her back. "Hell, honey. If I'd known you'd be like this, we would have come to get you a year ago."

Eb came up on her other side, burying his face in her neck and caressing a bare thigh, sliding a warm hand around to cup her bottom. He slid his hand between her thighs from behind and pushed a finger into her. "If you didn't seem so surprised by the pleasure, I'd think you'd done this before."

Trembling and holding on to Jeremiah's shirt, it took several moments before Eb's words penetrated. The finger poised just inside her pussy felt strange and very intimate, but she couldn't keep from tightening on it. Too embarrassed to face him, she buried her face deeper into Jeremiah's shirt, breathing in his masculine scent. "Are you asking me if I'm free with my affections?"

How could they expect her to talk to them now? Lethargic and shaky, she wanted nothing more than to hide someplace warm until she could rebuild her defenses.

Eb pressed his thick finger a little deeper. "I'm asking if you're still a virgin. Have you let anyone fuck you, Maggie? Don't lie to me because I'm about to find out the truth."

Moaning, Maggie buried her face deeper. "Leave me alone."

Jeremiah cupped her jaw, his thumb and fingers firm but gentle on her cheeks as he held her face turned, backing away and staring down at her. "Never. We want to know if anyone's taken what belongs to us."

Eb had already started to press his finger deeper, not stopping until he pressed against her barrier firmly enough to draw a whimper from her. "She's intact." He removed his finger and patted her thigh as though she were a horse that pleased him.

Mortified, Maggie pushed out of Jeremiah's hold and struggled to her feet, losing her balance when her pants tangled around her ankles. "How dare you! Neither one of you is ever touching me again!"

It infuriated her even more when both men started laughing. Still trembling from her first orgasm, she felt far too vulnerable to face their callousness now.

Eb somehow managed to slide a hand over her naked bottom as he helped her up. "Calm down, honey. You have to admit it's a little funny to tell the men you're going to marry that they're never going to touch you again. Come here. Let me hold you. You're still shaking."

Embarrassed at the level of intimacy they forced on her and furious that he and Jeremiah appeared to know of her feeling of helplessness, she pushed at him, inwardly cursing her weakness. "No. I don't want you to hold me. I want you to go back to Oklahoma, to the ranch you love so damned much, and leave me the hell alone." Trying to pull away from him, she fell again.

She wanted to cry at their coldness but held her tears at bay, not wanting them to see any further signs of weakness.

Not willing to risk falling on either one of them again, this time Maggie decided to take the time to fasten her pants before she tried to get up.

But it appeared Eb and Jeremiah weren't through.

Eb toppled her onto her back and leaned over her.

"We're never leaving you alone, Maggie. You're ours, and you're coming with us."

She had a hard time keeping her mind on fastening her pants with Eb nuzzling her jaw and Jeremiah raining kisses over her naked breasts. Without meaning to, she arched, offering her breasts and tilting her head to give Eb better access. "Damn it. Stop!"

She pushed away from them and finally managed to get to her feet, her chest heaving.

Eb stood when she did. "You sure do smell good, Maggie. We'll have to buy a barrel of whatever's making you smell like that and take it with us."

Her hands shook so badly she couldn't fasten her shirt. "I already told you I'm not going with you." Frustrated, she tied the ends of the shirt together and started for her horse.

Jeremiah stood and came after her. "We'll talk about it over dinner. I'm sure Esmeralda kept it hot for us."

"No."

Eb folded the blanket and stowed it, his movements practiced. "Why weren't you there for dinner?"

Maggie mounted her horse, anxious to get away from them as soon as possible. She still felt shaky and vulnerable, as though she'd lost something to them and didn't know how to get it back.

It appeared to have had no effect on them at all.

Sucking in a breath, she turned her horse, not wanting them to see the unshed tears in her eyes.

"I ate dinner at the big house because my father was foreman. He and Mr. Tyler used to talk about the ranch while they ate. My father's gone now. I figured the new foreman would be there."

Eb stilled. "My father hasn't appointed a new foreman yet, and even if he had, you know better than that. We're getting married tomorrow, and you'll be moving into the big house until we leave. You'll eat at the house from now on."

Jeremiah came to stand beside her horse, laying a hand on her thigh. "You know damned well we all expected you to be there. You only did it to piss us off. You succeeded. Now come up to the house and eat your supper."

The heat from Jeremiah's hand spread, sending a shock of renewed awareness to her clit, making it tingle with renewed vigor. Unsettled that she'd almost leaned into him, she bit back a groan and straightened.

"I'm not hungry. I'm tired, and I just want to go to bed."

She started off, but Jeremiah grabbed the reins, effectively stopping her. "We don't want you going to town tomorrow without us. We're going to do some things around here in the morning with Dad. That'll give you time to put on a pretty dress."

She remained silent, not agreeing to anything, knowing they were both so arrogant they'd see her silence as acquiescence.

They apparently did.

Eb had already mounted his horse and rode close to her other side. "Dad and Buck spoiled you rotten. Don't fight us on this, Maggie. We haven't even discussed the fact that you disobeyed Dad and went to the Perrys' home—something we're going to deal with."

Maggie struggled to appear unaffected by their authoritative tone, which in the past had always been reassuring to her because it had always been directed at others. Directed at her, it sent a chill down her spine and made her uneasy, and it took a tremendous amount of effort to keep her voice steady.

"I didn't disobey Mr. Tyler. He told me to stay away from Reverend Perry, and I did. He never even knew I was there."

Eb and Jeremiah rode silently beside her, their stares burning into her as they edged her toward her house instead of the stable.

Jeremiah gestured toward her front door. "Just go in, Maggie. We'll take care of your horse."

Desperate to be alone, she picked up the pace, glad they didn't insist that she move into the big house tonight. She slid from the horse, not even glancing at Eb or Jeremiah, her emotions too raw to face either one of them.

She started for her front porch, pausing as Eb called out to her.

"Stay here until we come get you tomorrow, Maggie. Do you hear me?"

Maggie nodded once. "I hear you." She hurried inside before either one of them could say anything else. Once there, she locked her door, something she'd never done before, and sank to the floor, leaning back against the door as tears welled in her eyes, blurring her vision.

The moonlight from the small window provided the only light, but she didn't even bother getting up for a lantern. Sitting there on the floor of her kitchen in the semi-darkness, she pulled her knees close to her chest and wrapped her arms around them, waiting for her trembling to stop.

How could they make her so weak, and with so little effort?

When Eb and Jeremiah left five years ago, she'd been little more than a girl. The feeling of friendship she'd always felt toward them had just begun to ripen into something more when they disappeared from her life.

She'd never dreamed she could have these sexual yearnings for both of them and didn't know what to do about it. Although their solution sounded perfect on the surface, she couldn't see how she could live the rest of her life with two men as her husbands.

It simply wasn't done.

Was it?

Could *she* do it?

Rubbing her arms, she pushed herself to her feet and looked out the window in time to see Eb and Jeremiah leave the stable and make their way to their father's house.

From this distance, she couldn't see their faces, but she'd know their smooth, arrogant strides anywhere.

A surge of pride welled within her as she watched them. Eb and Jeremiah had made something of themselves, fighting the odds to build something bigger than she could imagine. It didn't surprise her.

She'd always known them to go for what they wanted and get it.

But this time, she couldn't let them win. The tenderness for them growing inside her frightened her on so many levels. If she gave in to them, they'd run roughshod over her. They knew she'd grown up physically, but other than when they touched her, they treated her as the child they'd left behind.

She knew men and women got married all the time with much less than friendship between them, but with the way she felt about them, marriage to both of them would bring her a life full of heartache.

But how would that be different from what she had now?

If she stayed here, she might actually one day love a man who could love her in return. She could forget about Eb and Jeremiah and have a happy life.

Who was she trying to fool?

Eb and Jeremiah had been out of her life for the past five years, and not a day had gone by that she didn't miss them.

She would marry them, of course.

She'd never be able to survive watching them ride away again.

As much as she'd like to dig her heels in until she knew if they'd ever see her as a woman, she couldn't resist being with them. It was as if she'd been asleep all these years, just waiting for them to return to come alive again.

She turned away from the window and wiped her eyes, vowing to herself that somehow she'd get Eb and Jeremiah to one day look at her the way Hayes and Wyatt looked at Savannah.

Chapter Three

Sitting in his father's study, Eb stared out the window that faced the small house where Maggie slept, fighting the urge to go over there and crawl into bed with her. It filled him with a deep satisfaction to know that by this time next week she'd be settling into the house they'd built for her, sleeping in the bed he and Jeremiah had built for her.

She might complain now, but he knew he and Jeremiah could make her happy, provide for her, and satisfy her sexually. Confident that he and his brother could make everything right just as soon as they got her to Oklahoma, Eb sighed and sat back, wishing they were already back home.

But he knew she needed a little time to get used to it, pack her things, and say her good-byes to the people she loved.

She needed some time alone to think about her future, which was the only thing that kept him from crossing the yard right then.

Her reluctance to go with them didn't anger him as much as his own failure to anticipate it. Their little Maggie had grown up, and although her stubbornness and defiance had gotten worse, she displayed a vulnerability he hadn't ever seen in her before.

Perhaps if he and Jeremiah talked to her a little more about the Circle T, she would feel more comfortable in going with them.

It would also give him something to think about besides the way her ass twitched when she walked in those pants she insisted on wearing. He didn't mind them and had already decided to let her keep them, both because he considered them more practical for living on the Circle T and because he thought that indulging her might soften her up enough to stop arguing with him so much.

Every time she opened that sassy mouth, he could think of nothing but shoving his cock inside.

He tossed back two fingers of whiskey, hoping the burn would relieve the ache in his groin. He loved sex in its many varieties, and it had been too long since the whore wagon had stopped at the Circle T.

Hell, who was he trying to fool?

He'd gone months at a time without a woman, but having Maggie in his arms had turned him inside out. Knowing that she was a virgin and belonged to him had his lust for her still raging even an hour after he walked away from her.

She was too innocent to fake such passion the way the whores could when it suited them. Her virginity excited him in a way he'd never imagined before. Everything they did to her was new, and the knowledge that she'd never before been touched by another man filled him with a possessive hunger that wouldn't be denied.

The knowledge that every reaction was genuine and surprising to her just made him want to give her more. The fire inside her increased his own need and he couldn't help fanning the flames, amazed that his own passion for her burned even hotter.

Her moans and whimpers would no longer be enough. He wouldn't be satisfied until she screamed.

Fuck. Thinking about Maggie screaming as he fucked her only made his cock harder.

He got up to pour himself another drink, hoping his father's strong whiskey would enable him to calm down enough to sleep. After taking another sip, he sat back down and stared at Maggie's dark house, unable to stop thinking about the way she felt writhing in his arms.

Hell, he could still taste her, and the taste of her fired his loins like nothing ever had. His cock pressed painfully against his rough pants, throbbing and even leaking moisture.

If he'd only fucked her, he could have gotten this hunger out of his system and would already be asleep.

Once he married her, he'd fuck her long and hard as often as possible and gradually build the intimacy that women always craved. When they gained her trust and got rid of some of her nervousness and the sexual tension she didn't yet know how to handle, she'd become comfortable in her role as their wife. Things would settle down then and he and Jeremiah would have a woman who would warm their bed, satisfy their lust, and make their house a home. He wanted a good, solid woman who knew ranch life and understood the hardships—someone   who'd   give   him   children. Someone...comfortable.

He shifted again, grimacing as his cock protested. He sure as hell wasn't comfortable right now.

Changing his position yet again, he thought back to the day all those years ago that he'd decided that she would belong to him. At the time, he'd been seeing a woman in town and had just about decided to marry her. When he'd accidentally overheard her talking about how rich she would be once she married him and that she'd be even richer when his father died, he'd gotten rid of her in a hurry and turned a deaf ear to her pleading for another chance.

He came home with a sourness in his stomach, only to find Maggie waiting for him with news that one of the newborn kittens had died.

All thoughts of the other woman fled.

A fourteen year old Maggie had tears swimming in her eyes as she held the kitten for him to see, but shrugged matter-of-factly when he tried to console her.

"These things happen, Eb. You know that as well as I do." Despite her words, her voice broke, and she hurriedly looked away.

Staring down at her, Eb watched her cradle the lifeless kitten in her arms, her eyes huge in her face when she looked up at Jeremiah's approach.

Jeremiah met his gaze over Maggie's head as he bent to kiss her hair. "Come on, honey. We'll go help you bury him."

Eb walked with them to the edge of the woods that bordered the property, standing aside with Jeremiah as Maggie picked the perfect spot. He stood next to her, his arm around her shoulder for support as Jeremiah made short work of digging a hole. Afterward, she nodded and thanked them and went back to work as though nothing had happened.

It broke his heart.

Death was a common occurrence on a ranch the size of their father's, but the death of Maggie's kitten had everyone walking around on eggshells and doing their best to cheer her up.

She tried to play it off as though it didn't bother her, but several of the men caught her wiping her eyes throughout the day.

Over supper that night, he looked into her sad eyes and knew she would one day be his wife.

It happened just that fast, a decision that he knew in his heart was right as soon as he made it.

She understood ranch life and was strong enough to work through bad days and sweet and innocent enough to cry over a kitten—nothing like the cold woman he'd left in town only hours earlier.

The problems arose when he told Jeremiah, only to learn his brother felt the same way. Jeremiah adored Maggie and always had, and Eb knew he should have stepped aside and let his brother have her.

But he couldn't.

Something inside him demanded that she belong to him, and he'd told his brother so.

When they'd heard from several new hands his father had hired that some men who lived out west shared their women, the idea had taken root that they could have Maggie in the same way. Nothing in the years since then had ever changed their minds. In fact, the more he and Jeremiah had talked about it, the more it had made perfect sense.

They'd both known her since she was an infant and had helped take care of her since she'd gotten big enough to follow them around. She'd been a huge part of their lives, and leaving her had been one of the hardest things they'd ever done.

Her safety and security was at stake, and he knew he and Jeremiah could take care of her better than anyone.

They'd carved out a world where they could live with her the way they wanted to—in a way they no longer even questioned.

He'd missed her more than he would ever have imagined. He and Jeremiah had found themselves talking about her at odd moments, imagining what the ranch would be like once she came to live there.

She'd been little more than a child when they left Kansas City, but even then he could tell she would be a beauty. She'd drawn people to her like a moth to a flame, something that had always been a source of pride to them, especially since they'd both had a hand in helping to raise her.

When he received the telegram from his father, he'd been anxious to get to her, worried that she'd be scared and unsure of her future. The picture of the way she'd looked with the dead kitten in her arms had him racing to get to her. He'd arrived, anxious to see her again, and assumed she'd be anxious for their comfort and grateful to have her future assured.

Instead, she'd stared at him as though he were a stranger.

Hurt and angry, he'd yanked her against him, both to punish, but also because he'd been unable to resist it.

He knew he'd have a difficult time explaining the life he and Jeremiah wanted to have with her, but he hadn't expected to have her thwart his plans to marry and move to Oklahoma. It pricked his pride that she hadn't asked one question about her new home. He and Jeremiah had worked their asses off to build a place they could live with her, and it infuriated him that she'd showed no interest at all in it.

He closed his eyes, remembering her soft little cries of pleasure. Smiling reluctantly, he shook his head. Beautiful, soft, and curvy in a way that felt perfect against him, she had to be the most responsive woman he'd ever touched.

But she was also as hard-headed as a mule.

He was just contrary enough that the combination excited the hell out of him.

At the flare of a match, he turned his head to see Jeremiah lighting the lamp on the table closest to him. Taking another sip of whiskey, Eb leaned back, propping his feet on a footstool, wincing when his cock protested the movement.

"Where's Dad?"

"He went to talk to Larry, the new foreman. He'll be here in a few minutes." Jeremiah blew out the match and took a seat in the chair next to Eb, a chair which also afforded a view of the small house across the yard. Taking a deep breath, he bent forward, staring out the window. "She's always been stubborn, but not so hard-headed that she wouldn't listen to us, especially after what just happened out there. After she came I thought she'd be more agreeable. Hell, she just got more prickly."

The cold fist around Eb's heart tightened as he stared down into his glass. "We shouldn't have stayed away so long. I swear, I thought I knew Maggie inside and out, but she's not the same, and it pisses me off. Did you see the way she looked at us at the train station?"

Jeremiah nodded. "It's like we missed something. We weren't around when she became a woman. She's so familiar and so different at the same time. I want our Maggie back."

Eb kept his voice low so as not to be overheard in case his father came back. "She's skittish—understandable after us leaving for so long and her father's death. She'll eventually see that what we're doing is best for her and calm down. Tomorrow we'll take her to town with us when we go to the general store. Afterward, we'll stop at the preacher's and get him to marry us and check on Savannah at the same time. That'll cheer her up."

Still staring out the window, Jeremiah nodded. "I want to know who those two men were." Turning his head, he met Eb's gaze. "Did you happen to notice how both of them seemed to be interested in Savannah? You don't suppose they want to marry her the way we want to marry Maggie, do you?"

Leaning forward, Eb cradled the glass he held, staring into it. "They'll never be able to live that way with her here, and they both appear to be smart enough to know it. One of them is gonna get hurt."

Jeremiah grunted and looked away, staring toward Maggie's dark house again.

Even in the low light, Eb could see the muscle working in his brother's jaw.

"What the hell's wrong with you?"

Jeremiah shifted in his seat. "All your plans for tomorrow. Seems you've got it all worked out when it comes to Maggie."

Something in his tone had Eb sitting up. "You weren't jealous tonight, were you? How the hell do you plan to share her without seeing me touch her?"

Shooting to his feet, Jeremiah moved to the window, pushing the curtain aside. "I didn't expect it. I didn't expect...her." Dropping the curtain, he turned away. "Fuck it. Just leave it alone, Eb. You're the one who's marrying her anyway."

Eb's stomach knotted. None of this was working out the way he'd planned. They'd expected to come home, have Maggie fall into their arms with gratitude for taking her away from here, and each show her the affection they'd always felt for her. They'd have children with her, heirs who would one day take over the ranch.

A comfortable life with a woman they'd practically raised and who knew all about the hardships of living on a ranch.

They'd be content, which was all he ever wanted.

He had it all worked out, damn it! It was supposed to have been so easy.

He sure as hell hadn't expected to have his legs knocked out from under him by a woman he thought he knew, or to argue with his brother over a woman they'd decided years ago to take care of together.

Surging to his feet, he joined his brother at the window, his gut burning. He and Jeremiah would have to settle things between them before they could ever hope to become a united front for Maggie, both to lean on and to look to for guidance. Staring out, he took a deep breath and blew it out slowly, considering his words before speaking.

"When we were at the train station and I held her—hell."

He scrubbed a hand over his face in frustration. He'd never even considered having this kind of conversation with his brother. The whores they'd shared required no conversation on his part, other than what they did in bed.

He hadn't foreseen any of this at all. How could he have been so stupid?

Staring at her dark house, he tried not to think about his cock that even now demanded attention. "My cock was hard as a rock and stayed that way on the ride here." Allowing a small smile, he glanced at Jeremiah. "Damned uncomfortable. When I kissed her, I didn't expect the damned punch to the gut. It was the same tonight. I sure as hell didn't expect to go so far with her, but the way she responded— hell. She was drenched and tasted delicious."

With a look of disgust, Jeremiah started to turn away. "Go to hell, Eb."

Eb grabbed his brother's arm to stop him. "Don't go off half-cocked. I'm not trying to make you jealous."

Jeremiah jerked his arm away. "Then what the hell *are* you trying to do?"

With a sigh, Eb shook his head. "I'm trying to tell you she's got me turned inside out, too. When we decided to marry Maggie together, we agreed to share everything, remember? Yeah, so I've already had a taste of her, and I damned well can't wait for another. If you don't like it, that's too bad. I'm not walking away, so you're gonna have to get over it."

Disgusted with himself and his brother, he turned away. "We've stuck together on just about everything since we left here. It's the only way we managed to get where we are. This is Maggie, Jeremiah. Marrying her and taking her back to Oklahoma is too important for us to fight about. How the hell are we going to give her the security she needs if we're always fighting? She's got to be able to count on both of us. She's got to know we're united on everything that has to do with her."

Jeremiah sighed, bracing his fists on either side of the window. "I know that, Eb. Even when we disagree about her, we can't let her see it. She needs to know she can count on both of us to be strong for her. We can't do it by squabbling. I know it, but when she called out your name when she came...Hell, I don't know. Of course I can't expect her to yell both names. But I was watching her face and—damn it!"

Rubbing his stomach where a knot tightened, Eb sighed. "Yeah, I guess I would have been jealous, too." He paused, throwing back the rest of his whiskey. "It *is* a little different with Maggie, isn't it?"

Jeremiah shrugged. "Yeah. Fuck this. I'm going to bed."

Eb watched him leave, suddenly realizing that sharing a woman, even one they both knew as well as they knew Maggie, wouldn't be as easy as they'd first thought. Standing, he moved to pour himself another whiskey, but changed his mind and set the glass on the table.

Whiskey wasn't the answer. He needed a clear head to think this through.

He was still staring out the window when his father walked in about an hour later.

"Son, what are you doing in here? I thought you'd gone to bed."

Eb looked over his shoulder. "I had some thinking to do, Pa."

"I wondered when you'd get to it."

Surprised, he turned to face his father fully. "Excuse me?"

His father smiled, apparently not the least bit intimidated by his tone, a tone that back home would have had outlaws scurrying. "Thinking about how you and Jeremiah are gonna share a wife. Did you disagree on something?"

"Not exactly."

"You will. Better figure out how you're gonna handle it."

"Already have."

Eb stood and headed for the door. "We can't let our jealousies affect Maggie. She needs to feel safe, no matter what. It looks like we're going to have to talk about some rules."

* * * *

Jeremiah came downstairs before dawn the next morning after a nearly sleepless night, only to find Eb already sitting at the breakfast table drinking coffee. "You're up early."

"Never went to bed."

Pouring himself a cup of the dark brew, Jeremiah looked over his shoulder at his brother, something in Eb's tone troubling him. "Oh?"

Eb sighed. "Sit down. We need to talk."

An hour later, both men sat laughing, looking up as Esmeralda hurried into the kitchen, tying her apron around her.

Smiling, she went to the back porch and came back with a basket of eggs. "You two seem to be in a good mood. It's nice being back home again, isn't it?"

Thinking of the sounds Maggie made as she fell apart in his arms and the conversation he'd just had with his brother, Jeremiah sat back, happier than he'd ever been in his life. "Yeah, it's good to see the ranch again, but I can't wait to get home."

Eb held up his cup when Esmeralda brought the pot over to refill it. "I love that place. Hope Maggie likes it."

Their father walked into the kitchen, greeting everyone, and took a seat, smiling his thanks to Esmeralda when she filled his cup. "I'm sure she'll love it. Have you talked to the preacher yet?"

Jeremiah stood and went to the window, trying to peer around far enough to see Maggie's house. "We're going to town right after breakfast. We've got to load up on all the supplies we can, and then we'll stop at the preacher's. Where's Maggie?"

Their father looked up from his coffee, raising a brow, a faint smile playing at his lips. "She's your responsibility now. Did you make sure she had supper last night? After you two tore outta here, Esmeralda and I ended up eating alone."

Jeremiah gritted his teeth, not liking the reminder. "She said she ate already and the only reason she ate here was because Buck was foreman. Said she figured the new foreman would be joining you, and she didn't want to be in the way." He looked toward the door again, wondering where the hell she could be.

Their father set down his cup so hard it should have broken. "And you let her get away with that? Maggie knows better and so should you."

Esmeralda smiled at their father, patting his shoulder. "She's just trying to avoid them, and she keeps moving to avoid Fred."

"Who the hell's Fred?" Eb and Jeremiah both barked simultaneously.

His father took another sip of coffee, looking entirely too amused. "One of the hands. You really don't know what's going on with Maggie at all, do you? Buck told him to stay away from Maggie, but ever since he died, young Fred's been pantin' after her."

Jeremiah could actually feel his temper soar. "It sounds like we have a lot to talk to Maggie about."

Eb's eyes narrowed as his eyes shifted from the door to his father. "Maggie tell you that?"

Their father took a sip from his cup. "No, but I know everything that happens on the Shenandoah, and Esmeralda keeps a sharp eye on Maggie. Always has. Did you forget that, too?"

Grimacing, Eb didn't meet his father's eyes, instead looking back at the door to the kitchen, making Jeremiah wonder if he was thinking the same thing he was.

Did they know what he and Eb did to Maggie last night?

Why did he care? She belonged to them, damn it, and they could do whatever the hell they wanted to with her, and it was nobody's fucking business. His gaze shifted to the door again.

He respected his father and Esmeralda, but needed to make that clear. "I appreciate what you've done for Maggie, and I know how much you both love her, but, like you said, she's our responsibility now. We'll handle her."

Esmeralda plopped the basket of biscuits on the table with more force than necessary. "I thought when you came it would help her deal with her father's death. But now she seems even worse. You've got to get her mind off of it and get her excited about moving to your ranch."

Eb reached for a biscuit. "Once she's there, she'll be fine. She's been worried about Savannah, but that's being taken care of."

Jeremiah helped himself to one of Esmeralda's biscuits, hoping the biscuits Maggie made tasted just as good. "You've all spoiled her. She doesn't like to be told what to do and goes out of her way to defy us. That could be dangerous on the Circle T, and we won't allow it."

It had been a long time since he'd found the need to explain himself to anyone, and it didn't sit well.

Eb came to his feet, looking anything but happy. "She should have been here by now."

Jeremiah joined him, eager to see what the hell was keeping Maggie, and tossed over his shoulder. "Dad, you and Esmeralda meet us at the church."

"Reverend Perry ain't gonna like it."

"I don't give a damn what Reverend Perry likes or not. Meet us in town in a couple of hours."

Ten minutes later, he fought to rein in his temper.

Eb's expression appeared to be carved from stone as they faced the ranch hand who worked in the stable. "How long ago did she leave, Jasper?"

* * * *

Still fuming, Jeremiah saddled his own horse, cursing under his breath the entire time. "She's spoiled rotten, damn it. I'll bet she thinks if she makes us mad enough, we'll leave her here. What the hell's gotten into her? Why isn't she happy to be going with us? She's always been crazy about both of us."

Eb finished with his own saddle. "I don't know what the hell's going on with her, but I'm going to find out."

Jeremiah hadn't slept worth a damn all night, unable to get the passionate sounds she made or the feel of her soft skin out of his mind. His cock had stayed hard enough to drive nails for hours after he went to bed, and he'd finally had to take himself in hand to get some relief.

It hadn't helped.

"Where the hell do you think she is?"

Eb led his horse out of the stable, anger making his movements stiffer than normal. "If I know our Maggie, she went exactly where we told her not to go. She's in town."

Jeremiah grimaced. "She doesn't listen worth a damn."

Smiling coldly, Eb mounted. "Then I guess it's up to us to teach our little bride to behave herself."

Jeremiah's cock stirred with anticipation. The only spankings he'd ever given in his life had been the playful ones to the whores that frequented the ranch. It didn't take long for him to discover how arousing it could be to have a firm ass to enjoy at his leisure, especially when a spanking done properly could make a woman wet and needy. He didn't know how he'd be able to administer one to Maggie as punishment without thinking about how the smooth cheeks of her bottom would look beneath her pants.

But then again, he didn't have to.

Eb started out, looking over at Jeremiah. "Let's find her and give her the paddlin' she deserves."

Jeremiah chuckled and looked around to make sure no one would overhear him. "It's a shame we can't give her the kind of spanking Trixie and Lacy like. One of those bare ass spankings with wandering fingers."

Eb shot him a look, his eyes alight with devilish anticipation. "Why do you say that? She's ours, and we can spank her any damned way we want to."

Lust and a sense of power and possessiveness swelled inside Jeremiah, making his heart beat faster and his cock ache all over again. "Ours. Hell, that's going to take some time to get used to. All ours. Let's go get her. I'm dying to know how Maggie'll react to a spanking like that."

They rode toward town in silence for several minutes, giving Jeremiah a chance to think. Having Maggie in his arms last night had been nothing like fucking the whores he was used to. "Do you think we'll ever be able to take Maggie together, the way we used to with Lacy and Trixie?"

Nodding once, Eb adjusted his pants over his cock. "We'll teach her. You heard her last night. She came, didn't she? Maggie's gonna love sex. We're just gonna have to go slow."

Jeremiah didn't want to mention the fact that Eb had been mostly responsible for Maggie's orgasm. He wanted to be the one to give her the next one. He wanted, *needed*, to hear his name on her lips when she screamed her release.

Although he'd known her as long as his brother had, he knew she looked to Eb first and considered Eb's word law, sometimes even taking it over her daddy's.

The jealousy he'd experienced rose up again and knotted his stomach. He vowed to himself that he would do whatever he could to get her to see him in the same way and realize he could take care of her just as well as his brother.

He'd changed quite a bit in the years they'd been away, and it was high time to show her that.

Years ago, he'd been a man who couldn't commit to one woman and spent as much time as he could fucking as many as he could. He liked his fun, and he sure as hell liked to gamble.

That's how he'd won the damned land they lived on.

Hell, it had been a long time since he had the kind of fun he looked forward to right now.

They'd show Maggie a different side of them, one that he hoped like hell would throw her off balance enough for them to get the upper hand, and give her the kind of pleasure that would make her putty in their hands.

* * * *

Irritated to find no one home at the Perry spread, Jeremiah rode beside his brother to town, his anger and impatience growing. He didn't know what the hell had put a burr under Maggie's saddle, but he couldn't deny that the way she kept trying to avoid them hurt.

A lot.

The noise and the dust in the street from passing carriages annoyed the hell out of him, making him even more impatient. Looking up and down every street they passed, Jeremiah grimaced, wondering if he'd ever find Maggie in this crowd. "Were there this many people here when we left?"

Eb scowled, his expression growing darker by the minute.

"Didn't seem like it."

"It's too damned noisy."

Eb turned to him, his eyes narrowed. "You used to love to come to town. Couldn't wait to get your chores done so you could play poker with one of Starr's girls on your lap. As I remember, Candy was your favorite."

Shaking his head, Jeremiah's eyes went to the saloon across the street. "It seems like a long time ago. Hell, I can't even remember any of the other girls' names."

"There she is."

Jeremiah turned to follow Eb's gaze, searching the area beside the general store. "Where?" He turned his horse to follow his brother, deftly cutting through the crowd.

Eb nodded. "She ducked behind the general store. I'd know that walk anywhere. She's wearing pants again."

"She's never been allowed to wear pants to town. Seems she's doing everything she can to defy us." Jeremiah hated the fact that he didn't know what was going on in Maggie's hard head. The feeling that he'd missed a part of Maggie's growing up saddened him more than he'd like to admit.

Eb tethered his horse and started for the small alleyway beside the general store, anticipation lighting his eyes. "She's testing us. She's about to see what happens when she crosses the line." He turned the corner and came to a dead stop.

Jeremiah stopped short of running into him, his hand already on his gun. He'd only heard that growl once before from his brother— when another man had drawn a gun on him during a poker game.

That hadn't ended well for the other man, and he wondered if this would have the same outcome.

Maggie stood talking to Savannah under the watchful eyes of the two men they'd seen the night before. She turned slightly at their approach, frowned, and turned her back to them.

A red haze blurred Jeremiah's vision.

Eb glared at the two men, his fists clenching at his sides. "This is the second time finding you with our woman."

Hayes had a scar down his cheek Jeremiah hadn't noticed before, a scar that made him look even more sinister as he nodded grimly. "Can't say I blame you for being fired up. I'm Hayes Hawkins. My interest isn't in your woman, but mine."

Jeremiah didn't make a habit of butting into another man's affairs, but this was Maggie's friend. "It appears to me you both have more than a passing interest in Savannah Perry."

The other man stepped forward. "Wyatt Matlock. I know what you're thinking, but for Savannah's sake, I'd appreciate it if you could keep this to yourself."

Hayes seemed to have a hard time keeping his eyes from Maggie's dark-haired friend, who'd also grown up to be a beauty in their absence. "Don't take offense, but from what I hear in town, the two of you both want Savannah's friend."

Jeremiah narrowed his eyes. "It's none of your business."

Eb folded his arms across his chest. "I got the feeling last night that both of you have an interest in Savannah, and you've just confirmed it. Although I'm glad she'll have someone to look after her, you'll never be able to live that way with her here. She's been Maggie's friend for a long time. I won't have her hurt."

Wyatt stared over to where Savannah and Maggie stood talking, his expression grim. "We have no intention of hurting her."

Inclining his head, Eb kept his voice low. "See that you don't. Tell Savannah that her uncle's marrying us today. I'm sure she'll want to be there for Maggie."

"Your Maggie probably already told her."

Eb chuckled, his expression softening for the first time. "Maggie doesn't know."

Wyatt and Hayes both turned. Wyatt shared a look with his friend before turning back to Eb. "Oh?"

Jeremiah glanced at them, but his focus stayed on Maggie. She usually braided her hair but apparently hadn't taken the time this morning, so her long blond hair hung in a disarray of tangled curls down her back.

Shrugging, he reluctantly dragged his gaze from her to the other men. "Maggie's having a hard time accepting that both of us want to marry her. Except for when she greeted us at the train station, she's done nothing but argue and defy us since we got here."

Eb narrowed his eyes in Maggie's direction. "She was told she could no longer come to town without permission but sank spurs first thing this morning and came anyway."

Maggie hugged Savannah and started over to where the four of them stood. Lifting her chin, she narrowed her tear-filled eyes at both of them. "You promised you would take care of her. I'm trusting you to be men of your word."

Wyatt smiled tenderly. "Yes, ma'am. We'll take good care of her. I promise."

With a glare, she started past Jeremiah, who whipped out an arm to stop her.

Despite her struggles, Jeremiah pulled her back to stand in front of him, taking in her stony expression. "You're in a heap of trouble, little girl."

Hayes and Wyatt didn't spare them another glance, instead rushing over to stop Savannah when she tried to sneak away around the other side of the building.

When Maggie tried to pull away from him, Jeremiah tightened his hold and started back toward their horses.

"Where's your horse?"

* * * *

Maggie tugged again, alarmed when she couldn't shake his hold. She hadn't expected them to find her as quickly as they had. "Hell and damnation. Let go of me."

Eb grabbed her other arm. "I already told you I don't like you swearing. Now where's your horse?"

Embarrassed at the looks she was getting, Maggie stopped struggling. Even those who didn't know Eb and Jeremiah stepped aside. After a glance at their angry faces, she couldn't blame them. "In front of the saloon. I figured you wouldn't look for me there. Hey, did you see Hayes' scar? I didn't see it last night. I told him it makes him look like a pirate."

Jeremiah's eyes narrowed, his lips thinning. "How the hell would you know what a pirate looks like? Have you been flirting with other men?"

Maggie shrugged, enjoying his show of jealousy and flare of temper. "I read about one in a book and it all sounded so romantic. Savannah's a lucky woman. Hey! Stop pulling me."

Neither one of them loosened his hold as they led her to their horses. Once in the saddle, Eb reached down, plucking her from Jeremiah's grip and setting her in front of him.

Aware of the curious stares, she forced herself to sit still, not wanting to make any more of a scene than they already had. Every wiggle moved her against the hard bulge pressing against her bottom and sent her senses reeling. At Eb's answering groan, she did it again.

Memories of the previous night wouldn't be kept at bay, no matter how hard she tried to ignore them. Her breasts felt hot and swollen where they rested on his forearm, her nipples tingling with remembered pleasure at his and Jeremiah's ministrations.

Trying not to think about the answering pull to her clit, she turned her head, keeping her voice low.

"You're acting like a brute and I don't like it."

Eb tightened his arm, sliding it back and forth under her breasts in a way that no longer left her in any doubt that he did it on purpose. "I've got news for you, sweetheart. I'm not acting."

Shivering at his tone, she wiggled against his cock again in retaliation. She smiled up at him over her shoulder, knowing it would infuriate him. "You can't come back after all these years and tell me what to do. Go back to that ranch of yours and just leave me alone."

Eb's jaw clenched, making him look even more menacing. "We already told you many times, when we go back to the Circle T, you're coming with us."

Jeremiah leaned closer, his expression one of impatience. "If you hadn't run off the ranch at the crack of dawn, you'd know we're getting married today and could have worn a dress."

Maggie looked away, the pain of having her dream of a life with them so different than she'd planned it.

"You could have told me last night. Maybe I don't want to get married today." She just wished she had a little more time to get to know them again before standing in front of a preacher.

It probably wouldn't matter anyway. She knew she would be miserable without them.

Eb's hand flexed on her stomach. "You've been defying us ever since we got home. It's time we took care of that."

At his matter-of-fact tone, a cold chill went up her spine, turning to sizzling flames when his lips brushed against her ear. Eb's voice always went quiet when he was at his most threatening, something she'd learned long ago.

But his tone now held an erotic intimacy to it that made the threat dangerous in a far different way.

Something inside her thrilled at it, something feminine and vulnerable that ached to give in to his dark masculinity but feared that if she let him see how easily he could get to her, he would never think of her as anything more than an easy conquest.

She wanted to challenge him—*them*. She wanted to make them conscious of her in a different way, and she had to admit a part of her wanted to make them pay for leaving her five years ago.

Let them stay awake at night thinking of her the way she'd stayed up most of last night thinking of them. Let them wonder what she was thinking or feeling.

Let them need her to want only them as much as she needed them to want only her.

They'd barely touched her and already her body needed more.

Her nipples pebbled and became so sensitive that even the brush of her shirt over them became unbearable. The rub of Eb's hand over her belly pulled the material of her pants tighter against her so that the movement of the horse rubbed them against her clit.

When they stopped at the saloon, several people surrounded them, tossing questions at Eb and Jeremiah, mostly about how long they would be staying.

Eb kissed Maggie's shoulder. "We just came back to get Maggie. We're on our way to the preacher's to marry her right now. You're all welcome to join us."

Keeping her smile in place had to be one of the hardest things she'd ever done. She looked over her shoulder at him. "I already told you—"

He bent his head until the brims of their hats touched, his faint smile and the intent look in his eyes making her forget what she'd been saying.

"I want you wearing my name as soon as possible. I won't leave here without you, Maggie. Dad and Esmeralda are both worried about you. Can't you ease their worries a little?"

Feeling a tug of remorse, Maggie squirmed, her breath catching at the hardness beneath her bottom.

"Damn it, Eb. That's not fair. You know I'd never do anything to hurt Esmeralda or your father, but can't you see that it's too soon?"

Eb's eyes sharpened. "Nothing's better for you than being with us. It's already been far too long."

Angry once again at his arrogance and the fact that he and Jeremiah could come and go as it suited them, Maggie set her jaw. "Then why did you stay away?"

Lifting his head, Eb turned his horse to follow Jeremiah.

"Because that was the best thing for you then."

Maggie turned away to stare in front of her, blinking back tears. "You don't even want to marry me. It's just a way of having control over me."

Eb chuckled, the deep sound ominous. "Honey, you have no idea how much control I'm going to have over you. You're marrying me if I have to paddle your ass and carry you into the church over my shoulder. Or, you can behave and walk in like a good little girl and marry me without raising a fuss. Your choice, Maggie, but either way, you'll marry me today."

The image of being over his lap for a spanking leapt into her mind, making her clit swell, demanding attention. Making her tone as firm as possible, she glared over her shoulder at him, doing her best to hide her reaction. "Ebenezer Tyler, you'd better not even think about spanking me."

Her words ended on a gasp as he pressed his cock against her bottom.

He nipped her earlobe, his hands tightening on her waist. "You've already got one coming for disobeying us and coming to town without permission. I'll take care of that as soon as we get back to the ranch."

Gulping in air, Maggie involuntarily tilted her neck when his lips moved lower. God, it felt so good when he touched her this way. Hell, it felt good when he touched her *any* way. "You expect me to marry you after you threaten to spank me?"

Eb chuckled at her question, which came out in a breathless whisper. "Something wrong with your hearing, honey? I didn't threaten anything. I told you that you've already got one paddling coming, and if you give me any trouble about getting married, you're gonna get another."

It took tremendous effort to remain stiff in his arms when she wanted nothing more than to slump against him. "You can't just issue orders and expect me to fall in line. I'm not one of your damned ranch hands."

Eb scraped his teeth down her throat, the underlying threat in his deep voice sending a wave of longing through her. "There's something you'd better get through that hard head of yours, Margaret Mary. You belong to me and Jeremiah. I can do whatever I want with you." He stopped his horse in front of the church and gestured toward the doorway where Mr. Tyler and Esmeralda stood, both wearing their Sunday best and grinning from ear to ear.

"You gonna do this the easy way or the hard way, Maggie? It doesn't matter to me. It'll all come out the same in the end."

Forcing a smile for Mr. Tyler and Esmeralda, she spoke softly through gritted teeth.

"You're a heck of a lot meaner than you used to be."

Inclining his head, Eb slapped her thigh. "Have to be. I've never been mean to you, so you have nothing to worry about."

"You said you're going to spank me. That's mean."

Eb gripped her chin and forced her to meet his eyes. "A spanking is my way of getting you to obey me. Your life could depend on doing what you're told. It's for your own good."

His lips brushed her ear, his tone both amused and decadent. "Besides, honey. Your spanking is gonna make you so wet you'll be begging to come."

Jeremiah dismounted and came to stand beside them, holding out his arms for her. "You ready?"

Maggie jerked out of Eb's hold and glared at him. "You could just talk to me instead of threatening me all the time. And no one would ever like to be spanked."

Raising a brow, Eb slid his hand over her stomach, sending a wave of heat to wash over her. "You're going to eat those words, Maggie, and I tried to talk to you and you don't want to listen. Won't always have time to explain things to you, and I shouldn't need to. When we tell you to do something—or *not* to do something, you need to listen. If I have to beat your ass to get you to behave, I will."

His hands tightened on her hips. "Now be a good girl and go with Jeremiah, or I'll paddle your ass right here in front of everyone."

Jeremiah circled her waist and pulled her from the horse, holding her against his body a good foot off the ground. His hooded eyes held a promise of retribution and, by the twinkle in them, one he would enjoy immensely.

"I don't know what's put a burr under your saddle, but you're going with us. In the meantime, you'll convince Dad and Esmeralda that you're happy and looking forward to your new home."

Lifting her chin, Maggie held on to his wide shoulders, barely resisting the urge to pull herself even closer and rub against him. "And if I don't?"

Jeremiah slid her down his body with deliberate precision, his eyes full of the knowledge of what it did to her. "Once you get the spanking you have coming to you, you'll have your answer. Now let's go get married—and remember that you're marrying me, too. I'll be just as much a husband to you as Eb. Now put a smile on that pretty face, and let's go make you a married woman."

* * * *

Standing in front of Savannah's scowling uncle, a sense of inevitability and destiny calmed Maggie at a time when she should have been really nervous. It was as though everything in her life led to this moment, and even with the distance Eb and Jeremiah kept between them, she knew marrying them was the right decision, the *only* decision she could have made.

Confident that over time she could make them see her in a different light, she hid a smile at the look of confusion on the reverend's face when Jeremiah came to stand next to her instead of standing next to his brother.

Reverend Perry's usual sour expression was noticeably absent, amusing her further. He'd always been scared to death of Eb and Jeremiah, but now he looked downright terrified.

What a wonderful wedding present.

Eb and Jeremiah each stood holding an arm as though afraid she would flee. Turning her head, she saw the happiness on Mr. Tyler and Esmeralda's faces and smiled back at them reassuringly.

With her father's death, she felt more out of place on the Shenandoah than she'd expected, still uneasy about living in a home that no longer felt like it belonged to her. Although she appreciated Mr. Tyler and Esmeralda being there for her, she needed to start a new life.

She knew it would take time for Eb and Jeremiah to see her as a woman and not the young girl they'd left behind. Once she explained to them that only concern for her friend had led her to defy them, they'd realize she hadn't done it out of immaturity and perhaps they'd have a chance to talk.

She was dying to know everything she could about her new home and longed for the easy camaraderie she'd so desperately missed.

To Maggie's surprise, Savannah walked out from behind a curtain that led to the back and came forward, avoiding her uncle's glare. She came to stand behind Maggie and leaned close. "Don't worry about me anymore, Maggie. I'll be leaving here tonight. No, don't turn around, and don't say anything, and for God's sake, don't worry. I've saved up enough money to get away."

Maggie bit her lip, scared for her friend and lifted her gaze, meeting Reverend Perry's assessing one. When Eb and Jeremiah each reached for a hand and squeezed, Maggie wanted to cry. Their support reminded her too much of the Eb and Jeremiah she'd grown up with and crumbled the last of her defenses.

Thrilled that Savannah would soon be able to escape her uncle and relieved that she had men like Hayes and Wyatt to look after her, Maggie couldn't hold back a smirk.

Reverend Perry's expression turned even colder, his face becoming an angry red.

Until he turned his harsh gaze to Eb.

Eb stepped forward, his eyes narrowed into slits. "You ever look at Maggie that way again, Reverend, and I'll forget you're supposed to be a man of God. Hurry up and marry us before I shoot you."

Alarmed at his ice-cold tone, Maggie stared at Savannah's uncle, shocked when the older man swallowed heavily, all color draining from his face. Turning, she looked up into Eb's face and froze as what felt like an icy finger traced her spine.

His eyes glittered and became impossibly darker, making him look positively lethal. It told her without a doubt that he'd changed even more than she'd suspected.

He wouldn't really shoot him, would he?

She tried to pull her hand out of Eb's, but he squeezed threateningly, never taking his eyes from Reverend Perry.

If possible, Savannah's uncle paled even more. Averting his gaze, he turned to Jeremiah and cleared his throat, his fingers clumsy as he flipped through the pages of the Bible he held. "Uh, which one of you gentlemen will be marrying Miss Simms?"

Eb inclined his head. "I am. Get to it."

From the bench behind them, Mr. Tyler chuckled. "Boys, I think you're scaring the preacher. He ain't one of them gunslingers or cattle rustlers you're used to shootin'." He paused and she heard the bench creak as though he'd moved. "Although you might want to ask him about those bruises on Savannah's arm."

To Maggie's astonishment, Hayes and Wyatt came from behind the same curtain Savannah had come through.

Wyatt glared at the reverend, who hurriedly looked away. "That's already been taken care of."

Maggie turned to look over her shoulder at Savannah, unsurprised to see that her best friend's face had turned bright red. "Anything you want to tell me?"

Savannah's eyes slid to where Hayes and Wyatt stood with their arms crossed, their expressions fierce. "No. Let's get on with the wedding. And don't you dare tell anyone what I'm planning! I don't want anyone trying to follow me."

Facing the reverend, Maggie stood between Eb and Jeremiah, her head spinning as she took her vows. It hit her all at once that this was really happening, that her life would be forever changed after speaking a few words. Shocked that both Eb and Jeremiah slid a silver band onto her finger at the appropriate time, Maggie stood in a daze as the brief ceremony ended.

"I now pronounce you man and wife. You may kiss the bride."

Maggie's heart nearly pounded out of her chest as Eb turned her toward him, his eyes dark and possessive as he lowered his head.

"Hello, Mrs. Tyler."

Automatically grabbing his shoulders for support, she pursed her lips for a perfunctory kiss, but it seemed Eb had other ideas.

Whipping an arm around her, he pulled her close and covered her mouth with his, immediately applying enough pressure to force her lips open. In spite of the fact that they had an audience, he kissed her deeply, sweeping her mouth with his tongue in a kiss that made her tingle all the way to her toes. As always, he took his time, kissing her leisurely as though he planned to stand there all day and do nothing but kiss her.

Her nipples pebbled almost immediately and she rubbed them against his chest, moaning at the contact. Only then did he lift his head, a smug smile teasing his lips as his eyes raked over her face before turning her toward his brother.

When Jeremiah tangled his fingers in her hair and lowered his head, Maggie froze at Savannah and the reverend's gasps and tried to push away from him, but Jeremiah would have none of it. Marking her as his, he ate at her mouth hungrily, not satisfied until he overcame her struggles and she fisted her hands in his shirt to pull him closer.

With one hand in her hair and the other at the small of her back, he deepened the kiss, swallowing her moans and lifting her to her toes. He lifted his head slightly, studying her face as though looking for something. Apparently satisfied with what he saw, he smiled down at her, running his hand down her hair as he released her.

"Maggie Tyler. I like the sound of that."

Eb thanked the reverend coldly and turned away, smiling at Savannah. "Savannah Perry, you're even more beautiful than your momma was."

Savannah blushed and looked at her hands. "Thank you, Mr. Tyler. Congratulations. To all of you. I really have to be going."

Maggie reached out a hand to stop her, but Savannah had already started for the back, with Hayes and Wyatt following closely behind. The reverend took a step toward his niece, stopping abruptly when Hayes whipped his head around and shot him a razor sharp look.

White-faced, and obviously shaken, Savannah's uncle turned away.

Jeremiah eyed him coldly over his shoulder and took her arm, leading her toward his father. "Leave it to the men, Maggie."

Taken aback at his cold tone, Maggie looked over her shoulder as he dragged her along, alarmed to see Eb talking to Reverend Perry.

He kept his voice low, but his cold tone carried, the fury on his face unmistakable.

She tried unsuccessfully to pull out of Jeremiah's grasp. "What's he doing? Let go of me. I want to hear what he's saying."

Jeremiah yanked her back and handed her off to his father, who waited to congratulate her. "Brat. You always did love seeing Eb and me give someone hell."

Absently accepting a hug and a kiss on the forehead from Mr. Tyler, Maggie tried to look around Jeremiah's huge frame, but he wouldn't let her. "You're both so good at it, and I've never seen you yell at someone who didn't deserve it. I want to know what he's saying to him. Let me go talk to Savannah."

"No. Let's go eat. Hayes and Wyatt are taking care of Savannah. Don't interfere."

"But I want to see Savannah!"

Mr. Tyler took her other arm. "Instead of eating in town, let's go back to the ranch. Esmeralda prepared a meal, and we wouldn't want to hurt her feelings."

Eb came up behind her and placed a warm hand on her back. "No, we wouldn't. Let's get out of here."

Maggie grabbed the front of Eb's shirt before she thought about it, reacting the way she would have in the past. "What did you say to him? Did he get mad? He looked pretty scared to me. Please tell me you threatened to shoot him again. Would you really shoot him?"

The flash of heat in his eyes and the way his big body stilled as he looked down to where she touched him reminded her that things between them had changed dramatically.

Touching him sent a thrill through her like it never had in the past. The muscles under her hand tightened, and his eyes became hooded and sharp, settling on her lips, the hunger in them making her lips tingle.

Darting her tongue out to ease it, she shivered at the low groan that vibrated under her hand as his eyes narrowed on her lips in a look that she felt as clearly as a caress.

Unable to stop herself, she leaned forward, closing the few inches between them to touch her breasts to his chest. She bit her lip to keep from crying out at the sharp jolt that went to her pussy, fisting her hand in his shirt as her knees threatened to collapse.

Her clit throbbed, and she couldn't help but stare at his mouth, remembering how good it felt on her swollen nub. Her breath caught when his tongue touched his bottom lip as though remembering the taste of her.

Jeremiah came up behind her, rubbing her shoulders, and pressed his own hardness against the small of her back.

Her head dropped back against his chest in an automatic attempt to get closer to him.

Jeremiah's hands went to her waist. "Did you forget about me already?"

Sensing an urgency in his tone, Maggie groaned and turned her face to look up at him. "How could I ever forget you? God, I love when you touch me. Are you really my husband, too?"

Jeremiah ran a finger over the hand she flattened on Eb's chest, tapping her rings. "That's my ring there, too. I'm your husband just as much as Eb is."

She looked up into Eb's face, a little concerned by the impatience she found there and gasping as Jeremiah's arm came around her waist, his hand settling on her abdomen.

Pressing, he ran his lips over her hair. "And I'll never let you forget it."

Leaning against Jeremiah while touching Eb filled her with a hunger so strong, she would have gladly let them undress her right there. When Jeremiah bent to kiss her neck, she automatically reached for Eb. "It feels different when you touch me together."

Jeremiah ran his busy hands up her sides as he continued to nuzzle her neck. "Different how?"

Maggie locked her knees to keep from falling as her hands slid from Eb's shoulders. "It's more. When you both touch me it makes me tingle all over." She probably shouldn't have admitted it to them, but her thoughts tumbled out before she could stop them.

"Come on, honey. Let's get back to the ranch so we can both touch you in private." He pressed his cock against her ass, his hand coming around to settle on her stomach. "I'm looking forward to spanking this sweet bottom."

Fascinated by the low growl that rumbled through Eb's chest and the overwhelming feel of having both of them touching her, it took a minute for Jeremiah's words to penetrate. When they did, she pushed out of their hold, putting some distance between them before whirling to face them. With her hands on her hips, she shot daggers at both of them.

"That's not fair. I don't deserve to be spanked. I was worried about Savannah and had to come see her. You should understand that and stop threatening me."

Jeremiah shrugged. "We do, but that's not the issue. You didn't tell us any of this and just went out on your own to handle something that we should have known about. We told you flat out that you're supposed to ask for permission to come to town, and you didn't. We would have come with you."

"I wanted to talk to her alone."

Jeremiah stepped closer, stalking her as Eb circled from behind. "But you weren't alone, were you? How can we keep you safe if we don't even know where the hell you are or who's going to be with you? I'm your husband, Maggie, whether you want to believe it or not, and I take my responsibilities seriously."

Eb bent from behind, startling her, his voice a warm whisper across her cheek. "The right kind of spanking will get that point across. You'll remember it every time you're about to do something you're not supposed to do and hopefully think twice before disobeying us again."

The silky cadence of his deep voice reminded her too much of the way it had sounded right before he slid down her body to bury his face between her thighs, something she sure as hell didn't need to be reminded of right now.

She had the uncomfortable feeling she'd greatly underestimated the lengths they would go to in order to get her to obey their every word. She also had a sneaky suspicion that both Eb and Jeremiah had a few tricks up their sexual sleeves that she knew nothing about.

She readily admitted to herself that she was excited to learn more, hoping the feeling of closeness she got when they touched her intimately would increase over time.

Besides, she wanted more of that wonderful feeling. Nervously licking her lips, she looked up at Jeremiah through her lashes. "I don't like to be threatened."

Eb moved to her side, his eyes flaring with green heat as he followed the movement of her tongue. Running a finger down her neck, he bent until their noses practically touched. "There are two kinds of spankings, and you'll quickly learn the difference. One you'll beg for. The other, the kind you've got coming, will have you regretting whatever you did to deserve it."

* * * *

Since Mr. Tyler and Esmeralda decided to ride the horses back to the ranch, Maggie found herself scrunched between Eb and Jeremiah on the seat of the buckboard. Shifting restlessly as they rode out of town, Maggie stared down at the two thin bands on her finger. Looking toward the people who waved at them, she kept her voice low enough not to be overheard. "I wonder what these people would think if they knew that I was married to both of you."

She glanced over at Jeremiah, surprised to find him watching her. "What if you meet another woman and want to get married? You're not really married to me, after all."

Jeremiah's expression hardened. "I thought we just covered this. I damned well am married to you, and after tonight, there'll be no doubt in your mind that I'm your husband."

Transferring the reins to one hand, Eb used the other to lift hers until the sun glinted off her new rings. "We know what folks around here would think. That's why we left. At home, this'll be accepted. We just have to keep it quiet until we leave so there's no trouble with Dad. As soon as we get on that train, the fact that you belong to both of us is gonna be out in the open."

Avoiding Eb's intent stare, she glanced at Jeremiah. "Are there lots of other women there?"

Just thinking about the other women they'd been with tied knots in her stomach,

When the wind picked up, Eb shifted his body to block it, a gesture that appeared automatic, and one she'd never seen from anyone before. "Not a one. You'll be the only woman on the place. None of the hands are married. We're gonna have to do something about that."

Incredulous, Maggie turned. "Why would any woman go to a place like that? She'd be absolutely alone and defenseless against dozens of men. If the men are anything like you, a woman wouldn't stand a chance of defending herself."

Jeremiah turned to look at her thoughtfully before glancing at his brother. "She's got a point. The only way any women would come would be if we promised them safety."

Eb patted her thigh, not appearing to notice the effect it had on her. "We can put an advertisement in the paper and post some signs. Tell women who want to come that they'll have a place to live and be looked after until someone claims them."

"What if they don't want to be claimed?"

Jeremiah turned to grin at her, his smile all arrogance. He ran a hand up her thigh, seemingly unable to stop touching her. "All women wanna be claimed, darlin'."

Maggie snorted and turned toward him, a little taken aback at the flash in his eyes when she'd automatically moved her leg closer to his. "Men."

As they cleared the outskirts of town, Eb handed the reins over to Jeremiah, sharing a look with him as he pulled Maggie onto his lap. "If they don't, they'll still be looked after by everyone, but I've got to tell you, we really don't want any women coming that aren't looking to be claimed. That's the whole point of having them come. I've got a lot of single men living there, and I sure as hell don't want you being the only woman for miles around. Women who come are going to have to listen to the men to be safe until they have a man of their own."

"So if women come there, they'll have to agree to be claimed or else be bossed around by every man there?" When she tried to move away, he tightened his arms around her and smiled.

"You stay right where you are. Yes, they will. Just like you'll have to listen to the other men when we're not around."

Maggie eyed them both suspiciously, crossing her arms across her chest and pulling her coat closer. "Would a woman be able to say no to a man who wanted to claim her?"

Jeremiah reached out to run a finger over her knuckles. "You're thinking about a woman like Savannah. Yes, she would be able to say no, but if she's claimed and she doesn't deny the claim, she'd become that man's responsibility, and he would have to provide for her and protect her."

Thinking of her own situation and fearing what the other men would be like in Oklahoma, Maggie grimaced. "What would happen if a woman married someone and he mistreated her?"

Eb frowned down at her, tapping the underside of her chin. "You're just full of good cheer today, aren't you?"

Jeremiah sighed. "We'd take care of it. I know you're thinking about Savannah and hoping you can talk her into leaving—yeah, I saw your face when you wanted to go after her. I know you better than you think, Margaret Mary. If Savannah or any other woman came to the Circle T, we'd watch out for her and have our men do the same. Satisfied?"

"The Circle T? Where did that name come from?"

Eb reached for her hand, touching the rings he and Jeremiah had placed there. "Our brand is three T's in a circle with the tops touching. You've got the same mark on your rings."

Shocked, Maggie lifted her hand to take a good look at the rings she wore. Sure enough, each band was plain except for the mark he spoke of. "You put your brand into my ring? And why three T's instead of two?"

Jeremiah grinned. "One's for you."

Eb took her hand in his again. "Now you're branded with our mark, too."

"Branded?" Maggie tried to pull at her rings. "I'm not cattle."

Eb grabbed her hand, his eyes narrowed. "You pull those rings off your finger and you'll regret it."

Unsure of what he would do, Maggie stopped tugging at the rings, alarmed when Jeremiah pulled on the reins to bring the horses to a stop under a tree on Shenandoah land. "What are you doing?"

Grabbing her chin, Eb forced her to look at him. "Those rings are a brand anyway, and you'll leave them where we put them."

Tugging her hand away from his, she tried to get off his lap, but he wouldn't let her. "I'm not your property."

"I don't want any man you come across to have any doubt about who you belong to. You belong to us, and you'll wear the brand to prove it."

Jeremiah turned in his seat, shooting a glance at his brother, a slow smile spreading across his face as he reached for her. "I guess our wedding day is as good a time as any to prove that to you."

Alarmed at the look on his face, Maggie jumped up, surprised that Eb let her. Her relief was short lived when Eb held her arms behind her back while Jeremiah deftly undid her shirt, baring her breasts to the cool breeze.

Pulling her back down to sit on his lap, Eb kept her arms clasped in his behind her back, which thrust her full breasts out, her nipples pebbled with a combination of need and the cool air.

"How dare you! Let go of—Oh!"

Eb nipped her earlobe just as Jeremiah tapped a nipple with his callused finger.

Jeremiah's eyes flashed at her gasp, his smile softening. "All ours."

Adjusting his hold, Eb gripped both of her wrists in one hand, sliding the other over her stomach. He bent, startling her by running his lips over a bare shoulder. "So soft."

The hand on her stomach slid higher to cup a breast, his thumb flicking back and forth over an aching nipple, making her gasp again. "Hard little nipples and the softest skin."

Maggie arched, her breath coming out in pants as fire shot through her from her breasts to her pussy, the raw sensation making her toes curl Her clit felt so swollen and hot that she couldn't sit still and moved restlessly on Eb's lap.

Thinking her hands were free, Maggie tried to grab Eb's shoulders, only to find that he'd used the ends of her shirt to tie her wrists together.

Jeremiah circled her other nipple with the tip of his finger, not staying in any one place and leaving a trail of sizzles in its wake. "You've got a spanking coming, sugar. One that you won't soon forget."

Shaking her head, she closed her eyes on a moan, crying out when he tapped the nipple he'd teased so mercilessly. "No, I don't want a spanking. Please, it's too much. Don't tease me like this anymore. Give me what you did last night."

Even though they'd been outside when they'd bared her last night, the darkness had allowed her to hide in a way she couldn't now. Eb didn't even allow her to hide her face against his neck the way she had with Jeremiah the night before.

Instead, he nuzzled her jaw, fisting his hand in her hair as he covered her breast with his other hand. The friction from his work-roughened palm sliding so gently over her nipple had her shifting restlessly and crying out at the sharp explosions of pleasure at her slit.

When Eb leaned her back over his arm and brushed his lips with hers, she tried to arch into him, desperate for his kiss. He kept her in place with a hand in her hair, using his other to pinch her nipple just hard enough to send another flash of heat to her clit.

She kicked her legs as her pussy clenched, sucking in a sharp breath when she felt Jeremiah's hands at the fastening of her pants.

His low, amused drawl nearly made her come right then. "It looks like she's ready."

Maggie moaned, trying unsuccessfully to hold still while he unfastened her pants. She couldn't wait to have him touch her clit and give her that wonderful feeling again.

Jeremiah's deft hands yanked her pants to her knees, exposing her to their gazes. He slid his hands up her thighs to her slit and used his thumbs to part her folds, allowing the cool air to blow over her clit the way Eb had the night before.

Unable to lie still, Maggie bucked in Eb's arms. That gathering feeling kept getting stronger, and she wanted the release she knew they could give her. "Yes. Give it to me. Please make this ache go away."

Eb nipped her bottom lip. "I'm afraid we can't do that. It's time for your spanking."

Before Maggie could react to his shocking statement, Eb had her flipped to her belly over his lap. She could feel the rough fabric of Jeremiah's pants on her inner thighs as he wedged a knee between them, effectively pinning her pants to the seat of the buckboard.

Kicking her legs, she screamed at them and tried to get up, but with her hands secured behind her back, she had no leverage at all. She stilled as a rough hand slid slowly over her exposed bottom and had to strain to hear Eb's low, gravelly voice.

"All ours."

A hard slap landed, startling a yelp from her, and then another, heating what the cool air had already chilled. The heat on her bottom felt like nothing she'd ever experienced before, more overwhelming than painful. In no time at all, the warmth crept between her thighs, sending another, even stronger surge of awareness there.

Alarmed, she fought their hold, not even able to budge when Eb laid an arm over her back.

"Fighting it will get you nowhere. Soon you'll have no fight left in you."

"Let me go."

To her surprise, Eb bent to kiss where he'd slapped her. "Never."

"Someone will see."

Jeremiah slid his hands from the backs of her knees to her thighs. "No one's here but us, Maggie. If someone was coming, we'd hear 'em. We wouldn't let anyone else see you this way."

To Maggie's amazement, the warmth and the vulnerable feeling she got from being exposed and over Eb's lap had more moisture leaking from her pussy and made it impossible for her to stay still. Not wanting them to see her damp thighs, she tried to squeeze her legs together, kicking at Jeremiah to get free. "Let me up, damn you!"

When the wind kicked up again, the air caressing the heated area between her spread thighs startled her so much she stilled.

Jeremiah's thumbs went to her center and teased her pussy entrance. "She's soakin' wet, Eb. Looks like she likes her spanking."

"No, I don't!" Mortified, Maggie squirmed again to no avail, sucking in a breath when Jeremiah parted her folds with his thumbs and started to stroke her. She lifted into his touch before she could prevent it, embarrassing herself further.

"Look at her lifting up and shaking her ass at us. Hell, Eb, it looks like we married ourselves a wildcat."

Eb's hand smoothed over her bottom, a gesture that was somehow both affectionate and threatening. "This wildcat's gotta learn that when we say something, we mean it."

Surprised and more than a little frightened by her body's betrayal, Maggie shivered again at the carnal need that grew inside her.

How could a spanking frighten her and arouse her at the same time? Her face burning, she rubbed her cheek against Eb's leg, thankful that neither man could see her embarrassment.

Jeremiah's thumbs slid through her folds, keeping them parted and sending her senses reeling. "Let's explore our new bride."

Her entire slit, from her clit to her bottom, burned, completely exposed to their gazes. She'd heard about sex before, but never anything like this.

"Men aren't supposed—oh, God—to see women this way. You can't—oh, please!"

Eb lightly slapped her bottom again, chuckling when she cried out and shifted restlessly. "The difference is that you're *our* woman and we can see you any way we want to. Jeremiah, it seems our little Maggie's shy about us seeing her this way. She'll soon get used to us touching and licking everything, won't you, honey?"

They couldn't be serious! How could anyone get used to this?

Jeremiah slid a fingertip inside her, drawing even more of her juices from her, and ran his finger over her folds, coating them with her moisture. "Nice and wet." He tapped her clit, making her jolt and whimper, the tingling there growing stronger by the second. "Her clit's swollen and too sensitive to touch. I can't give her any attention there until I take care of her ass."

"Get to it, then. She's got a few more slaps coming." Eb slapped her bottom again, this time keeping his hand over the heat he'd ignited and holding it in.

Not trusting the sound of that, Maggie fought to close her thighs and rub them together. The pressure inside her kept building, even stronger than before, and she wanted the release she knew would end the torment. "What did Jeremiah mean by that? What are you going to do to me? You don't have to spank me anymore. I won't go to town again without telling you. I promise. I want to come."

Jeremiah chuckled, moving his leg out of the way when she tried to rub against it. "But, honey, you seem to like being spanked this way. Why would we stop?" He stroked her pussy one last time before withdrawing and, to her mortification, leaned down to kiss one of the cheeks of her bottom.

"I don't want to be spanked like a naughty little girl. I'm a woman, damn it. Let me up." The pool of lust that settled low in her abdomen made her pussy clench in spasms she couldn't prevent. She couldn't stop wiggling, so close to that delicious release she could almost taste it. "Please do something."

"I'm about to—and we're certainly not spanking you like a little girl. Believe me, darlin', we know you're all woman." Jeremiah's hand covered the lower part of her bottom as he slid a thumb through her juices. "Let's see how well you like having something in your ass."

Maggie froze as he parted the cheeks of her bottom, exposing her bottom hole to the cool breeze and their hot gazes. "What are you doing? Oh, God!"

She panted, chills racing up and down her spine as Jeremiah's slick thumb touched her most forbidden opening. "Don't touch me there."

Oh, God! They couldn't. They wouldn't.

A slap landed on her bottom again, right above Jeremiah's hand, this one sharper than any of the others. "We're going to do more than touch your ass, Maggie. We're going to fuck you there. How else did you think you would take us together? Your ass belongs to us just as much as the rest of you."

Maggie opened her mouth to protest but squealed instead when Jeremiah applied pressure, the pinch of her bottom hole stealing her breath as the ring of muscle gave way. "Oh, my God. It's inside me."

Jeremiah pushed a little deeper. "Just a little, honey. You're going to fuck yourself on my thumb while Eb's beating that beautiful ass of yours. You're going to take all of it, Maggie."

She fought their hold, but every time she moved, it shifted the tip of Jeremiah's thumb inside her, the stark intimacy of the feeling making her shiver all over and her words come out on panting breaths. "No. I won't. It pinches. Take it out. Just spank me and be done with it."

Another slap landed at the same time Eb reached under her to pinch a nipple. "Don't make the mistake of trying to tell us how to punish you, Maggie. You're ours, and we'll punish you as we see fit. You knew you'd be spanked for leaving the ranch, but you chose to do it anyway. We want to make sure you understand what you've got coming to you if you ever disobey us again."

Tapping her nipple, he bent low. "If you misbehave in the future, it'll tell us you need this kind of attention."

Jeremiah slid his finger through her slick folds and touched it to her clit. "You're not only going to accept it, you're going to participate in your own punishment."

Maggie tried again to kick her legs, but Jeremiah had them pinned. "No, I won't. I'll hate you for this."

Jeremiah's finger on her clit teased her mercilessly, but she couldn't move against it to get the friction she needed.

Eb slapped her ass again, which moved her on Jeremiah's finger, but also forced a little more of his thumb into her bottom, drawing her attention there. "You won't hate us. You'll be begging us to fuck you."

Maggie groaned hoarsely, too conscious of the thumb invading her ass to think about much else. "It burns."

Rubbing the heat into her bottom, Eb pinched her nipple again. "Honey, it's just Jeremiah's thumb. It's gonna burn even more when one of us works a cock into you."

Maggie couldn't be still, needing Jeremiah's touch on her clit more than she'd ever needed anything in her life. As soon as she focused on her ass, Eb pinched her nipple, focusing her attention there. Concentrating on her nipple and moving on Jeremiah's finger, she inadvertently took more of his thick thumb in her bottom.

Just when she thought she'd go over, another slap on her ass pulled her back, tormenting her, the pleasure so strong it threatened her sanity.

She tried in vain to rub against Jeremiah's finger, knowing it would be enough to send her over.

With a soft chuckle, Jeremiah slid his finger away, using it to tease her folds and pussy opening.

Furious now, she kicked her feet, stilling when his thumb went deeper. "You moved, damn you. Put it back!"

She bucked in Eb's arms, inadvertently working herself on Jeremiah's thumb. It burned, but the burn only seemed to heighten the pleasure, driving her into a frenzy of need. Trying to kick at Jeremiah, she clawed at Eb's leg, screaming her frustration at both of them.

"You bastards! I hate you."

The slaps continued, lighter and more infrequent now as Eb and Jeremiah spoke in low tones, but her own cries kept her from hearing what they said. She struggled to get the attention to her clit she needed, coming up more fully on her knees in order to reach his finger.

It pushed Jeremiah's thumb deeper, and her inner muscles tightened on it of their own volition, making the burn even hotter.

"That's it, honey." Jeremiah released her legs, finally allowing her to move.

Rocking now, she shuddered, finally able to rub against Jeremiah's finger just as his thumb thrust deep. "Yes. Oh, God. Yes!"

The tingles that radiated from her slit warned her that she was about to go over, to experience that wonderful bliss of the night before.

Without any warning, Jeremiah's finger moved away.

Furious and desperate to come, Maggie flailed on Eb's lap. "No. No! Put it back. Give it to me."

Another sharp slap on her bottom didn't dissuade her as she bucked, frantic for release.

"No, Maggie. That's it for you." Eb ran a hand over her bottom, holding her down on his lap until she stilled.

Maggie couldn't stop tightening on the thumb in her ass. "No. Please, do something."

They wouldn't really leave her like this, would they? Waiting breathlessly for the touch that would put her over, she froze, squeezing her eyes closed on a moan as the cheeks of her bottom were parted wider.

Jeremiah slid his thumb almost all the way out of her, paused, and slowly pressed it back in again. "No coming, Maggie. That's your punishment. If you behave, we'll do this anytime you want and make you come over and over. Now, be still so I can stretch you a little."

Blinking back tears of frustration, Maggie gulped in air as she struggled to adapt to the deliberate strokes. Lying there over Eb's lap with her ass in the air and her thighs parted wide, she whimpered in distress against Eb's leg.

His hands stayed on her back, holding her down, but caressing her at the same time. "You like having your ass fucked, don't you, Maggie? Wait until we get you stretched a little more, and we'll fill it with cock. That's enough for now, Jeremiah. Her ass is gonna feel that for quite a while."

He ran his hand over her bottom one last time as Jeremiah slowly slid his thumb from her, teasing her by circling around her tingling opening as he withdrew. After untying her hands, Eb helped her to her feet, holding on to her when she swayed. "Now we're gonna sit at the table with Dad and Esmeralda and eat the fine wedding dinner she prepared."

Out of her mind with need, Maggie reached down to touch her clit herself, growling at Jeremiah when he caught her hand.

"No, Maggie. No coming for you." He slid her pants up her thighs and fastened them, ignoring her struggles.

At the same time, Eb leaned in to take a nipple into his mouth, sucking gently.

With her hands now free, she grabbed his shoulders, crying out when her knees buckled.

Releasing her nipple with a pop, Eb caught her, his hands firm on her upper arms, tightening when she cried out in rage and tried to swing at him. "Don't leave me like this. Stop playing with me. Are you men or not? You said you're my husbands. You're supposed to finish it."

He shook her once, his voice snapping like a whip. "Stop it right now! I know you're all riled up, but behave yourself. You're gonna learn we mean business, Maggie, one way or another. It's hard work running a ranch, and I don't have the time or the patience to be getting you out of trouble because you didn't mind me. I don't want to be distracted worrying about you." His unrelenting tone and the determined look on his face told her that he'd have no tolerance for any infractions.

Humiliated, horrified, and angrier than she'd ever been in her life, Maggie swiped the hair out of her face and glared at both of them. "We're not in Oklahoma, and I'm not in any danger. There was no reason to…"

"Spank your beautiful ass?" Jeremiah added helpfully.

"Ooh!" She stomped her foot and then regretted it when Eb's eyes went to her jiggling breasts. Reaching for the ends of her shirt, she covered them, her breath catching at the feel of the material sliding over her nipples.

Jeremiah slapped away her trembling fingers to fasten her shirt himself. "Let me do that, or we'll be all day here waiting for you."

Maggie clung to him as he righted her clothing, moaning at the feel of the rough fabric sliding over her sensitive skin. Unable to believe they would actually leave her this way, she shifted restlessly, trying to rub against Jeremiah. "You're mean and hateful to do this to me."

Overwhelmed by the tingling of her skin, she couldn't inject the heat in her tone she strove for.

Eb slid a hand inside her shirt and tweaked a nipple. "I don't want to hear anymore. My cock is hard enough to pound nails after that, and I'm in no better mood than you are." Grabbing her chin, he got right in her face. "And I'm stronger and meaner than you could ever be, so don't push it. Sit down and behave. We'll both fuck you good after supper, but you're gonna stew in your own juices awhile."

Jeremiah picked up the reins again and started down the road to the ranch. "You're not mad because Eb spanked you, honey. You're mad because you liked it, *and* you also liked having my thumb up your tight ass."

Her face flamed, her cheeks growing so hot she would have fanned herself if they hadn't been looking. "I'll never forgive either one of you for that."

Eb slid a finger between her thighs, unerringly stroking her clit. "Sure you will. Now put on a happy face for Esmeralda and the others." At her scowl, he raised a brow and stroked her once again before removing his hand. "If you don't, I'll haul your ass upstairs and spank you again—this time, where everyone can hear your cries."

Chapter Four

Maggie didn't remember much about dinner.

Seated between Eb and Jeremiah with her body still humming and her bottom still warm, she found it difficult to sit still and impossible to concentrate on the conversation going on around her. She couldn't even remember what she ate, some of whatever Eb and Jeremiah stuck on her plate because they kept lifting a fork to her mouth every time she stopped eating.

Torn between wanting to hurry up and finish so she could go home and nervous about being alone with them again, she did her best to smile at Mr. Tyler and Esmeralda's teasing, but for the life of her couldn't even remember what they'd said.

She'd never known an arousal could be so intense or that it could last so long. It bordered on pain, and she wondered if she'd be able to slip across the yard to her house, lock herself in the bedroom, and try to relieve it.

Jeremiah leaned close, his voice a low whisper in her ear. "Stop fidgeting. Your bottom isn't that hot. Accept your punishment like a good girl. Now smile and finish your supper. You're not eating anything, Maggie. Come on, honey, have another bite."

Mr. Tyler and Esmeralda both beamed, obviously thinking Jeremiah had whispered sweet nothings in her ear.

Smiling obediently, Maggie promised herself that one day they'd pay for doing this to her.

They had the upper hand now, mainly because they'd changed so much she didn't know what to expect from either of them, but she'd always been able to find a way to get back at them for something in the past. As soon as she got her bearings again, she'd make them pay.

On that happy thought, she took another bite from the fork Eb held to her lips, stilling when he leaned close from her other side.

"The way you reached for yourself out there convinced me that we're gonna have to get something for you, something that'll keep you from rubbing that clit when we're not around."

Maggie froze, almost choking on her food and looking up at him through her lashes. Her face burned as she tried to imagine what he could be talking about, but the devious look in his eyes had already given her a clue.

She looked away, embarrassed that she'd even attempted to touch herself in front of them. She still couldn't believe she'd done it.

"I can't believe you would remind me of that. You're no gentleman."

"Isn't that the truth? Get that frown off your face. Smile for Dad and Esmeralda. Yes, I think something in leather should do the trick. I'll order it tomorrow—one with a nice little metal knob that'll fit in your ass."

Maggie blinked, not quite sure she knew what he meant, but she would bet it didn't bode well for her.

When the meal finally ended, Maggie stood to help Esmeralda clear the dishes.

The older woman waved her hand, shooing her away. "No, you are not washing dishes on your wedding night. Go on with Eb and Jeremiah, and I'll see you in the morning." Smiling, she slid a glance at the men. "Oh wait! Maggie, can I see you in my room for a minute?"

Maggie nodded and stood to follow Esmeralda, her lips firming when the men also stood and Eb caught her arm, his gaze boring into hers as a half-smile played on his lips. "You can go."

Not giving him the satisfaction of seeing her anger at his calm display of authority, she smiled sweetly and fluttered her lashes. "I don't need your permission."

He grabbed her arm when she would have stormed past him, bending close and keeping his voice low. "You're gonna learn just how wrong you are about that. Go with Esmeralda. We'll wait for you outside."

Glaring at him over her shoulder, Maggie started past him, stopping abruptly when she ran into Jeremiah, who gripped her shoulders and leaned close to whisper in her ear while running his hand over her hair in an apparent gesture of affection.

"Behave yourself. Don't go upsetting Esmeralda. Damn, you smell good. I'll bet you taste just as good."

He released her to approach Esmeralda, grabbing her the way he used to and dipping her while raining playful kisses over her cheeks.

The older woman giggled, the sound making everyone else smile and reminding Maggie of happier days.

Jeremiah had always been a flirt and teased Esmeralda mercilessly, grabbing her often to dip her as he did now, or sometimes lead her into a dance.

As she had in the past, Esmeralda giggled and tried to shoo him away, her face bright red when he finally stood her upright again.

Jeremiah grinned and tugged her braid where it had come loose from the coil she always wrapped it in. "You still smell like cinnamon and biscuits. Maybe we should leave Maggie here and take you to the ranch instead."

Mr. Tyler looked up from his coffee. "Over my dead body."

Esmeralda finally evaded him, shooing him away and still, smiling as she put an arm around Maggie's shoulders and led her to her bedroom. Once inside, she closed the door behind her, shaking her head. "That boy will never change."

Still chuckling, she leaned back against it, her eyes brimming with unshed tears. "You're a married woman now. I'm sure your daddy would be happy to know you're being taken care of. What fine men they've become, huh? They're more than capable of looking after you, and I know how much you've missed them."

Maggie couldn't help but smile at Esmeralda's enthusiasm. The housekeeper had always had a soft spot for Eb and especially Jeremiah. "I miss Daddy so much. It happened so fast it doesn't even seem real. I keep expecting to turn a corner and find him there."

Patting her shoulder, Esmeralda tugged Maggie's arm, leading her to the bed. Sitting next to her, Esmeralda hugged her, wiping away a tear and sniffing delicately. "I know this all happened so fast. I've always thought of you as a daughter, and I'm so relieved to know that Eb and Jeremiah are going to take good care of you. Is there anything you want to ask me about tonight?"

Maggie's face burned, for the first time realizing that everyone would know what Eb and Jeremiah did to her tonight. "Will it hurt?"

Patting her shoulder, Esmeralda smiled, wiping away another tear. "It hurts just a little, but it doesn't last. I'm sure Eb and Jeremiah will make it easy for you. After the first time, it won't ever hurt again."

Maggie didn't believe that, especially after the spanking she'd just received. Eb and Jeremiah seemed to care a great deal about being physical. She didn't know how to ask Esmeralda about the other, not sure how to put into words her anxiety about having a cock pushed into her bottom.

She didn't even know if it was possible, or if they'd just said it to scare her. It sounded pretty real to her.

Patting her hand, Esmeralda jumped up. "I have a present for you. I made it for you and have kept it put away to give to you on your wedding day." Esmeralda went to the chest at the foot of her bed and came back with the most beautiful shawl Maggie had ever seen.

Accepting it, her eyes pricked with tears. "Oh, Esmeralda! It's so beautiful. You do the most intricate work."

Maggie held the shawl up, taking in the detailed stitches, surprised at the soft texture. Hugging the older woman, Maggie squeezed her eyes closed against the tears blurring her vision. "Thank you so much. I'll think of you every time I wear it."

Esmeralda smiled through her own tears. "It's a little something to keep you warm and give you a hug when I can't. I'm going to miss you so much."

"Oh, Esmeralda, I'm going to miss you, too. Do you think I'm doing the right thing?"

Esmeralda's smile widened. "Of course you are. You're a married woman now, Maggie. Your place is with your husbands."

Maggie smiled reassuringly, not wanting to alarm the older woman. "I know. It's just that I'm a little scared of leaving. I'm sure everything'll be fine once I get settled in my new home."

"That's my girl. Now go on." She gestured toward the window. "Eb and Jeremiah look a little impatient."

Maggie followed her gaze to look out the window to where Eb and Jeremiah both stood, talking to their father. The sun had started to set, and she knew it would be pitch dark very soon and that both men were anxious to be alone with her before then. Hugging her shawl to her breasts, Maggie nodded. "Good night, Esmeralda. Thank you."

Maggie walked slowly through the kitchen and out the back door. The need had dulled to a persistent ache but hadn't gone completely away. Clutching her shawl tighter, she took a deep breath and walked around the corner, pausing when Eb and Jeremiah both turned to her.

Jeremiah wordlessly held out his hand, a brow going up when she hesitated. His eyes sharpened as he wagged his fingers. "Come on, Maggie. It's time to go."

* * * *

With his cock harder than he could ever remember it being in his life, Jeremiah walked beside Maggie across the yard, fighting the nerves that knotted his stomach.

He wanted to make tonight good for Maggie, but after what happened on the way here, he didn't know if he could hold out long enough to give her what she needed. He'd played with many women before, some alone, some with Eb, but never in his life had he been primed like tonight.

He had to keep reminding himself that she was still a virgin, despite what they'd done to her. Her uninhibited response made it harder to remember that.

Smiling to himself, he had to admit that marrying her had to be one of the smartest things they'd ever done.

A woman who could work on a ranch, who was more beautiful than any woman he'd ever seen, and who turned to fire when they touched her would have been hard enough to find. The fact that the woman they'd already decided on, who was also a friend, made it that much sweeter.

He couldn't believe the woman with a body made for sin and mouth made for sass was their little Maggie.

Damn, she was irresistible.

Building a new life somewhere else hadn't been easy, but they'd done it for Maggie. Thinking of her cute smile, her sweet, playful disposition, and her eyes so blue it almost hurt to look at them got them through the roughest times.

He paused, his eyes narrowing when he saw a young man about Maggie's age sitting on the bench right outside her door. "Who the hell's that?"

He started forward, not waiting for an answer, his hands already tightened into fists. "Who the hell are you, and what are you doing here?"

Maggie started forward, gasping when the younger man jumped to his feet and reached for his gun. "Fred, no!"

Jeremiah drew his in a move so automatic he never even thought about it anymore, clearing leather before Fred even closed his hand over the butt of his gun.

Out of the corner of his eye, he could see Eb jerk Maggie behind him with one hand, holding a gun pointed at the younger man with the other.

Maggie tried to pull away from him, but Eb held firm, putting his body between her and the other man.

"Get behind me and stay there, Maggie. I mean it."

The younger man puffed out his chest and straightened in an apparent effort to make himself look taller. "I'm Fred Johnson, Maggie's beau. I work here on the Shenandoah. You two better get off Mr. Tyler's spread before he catches you. He don't cotton to strangers, especially around Miss Maggie."

Keeping Maggie out of the man's reach, Eb smiled coldly. "Well, Fred, I'm Eb Tyler, Maggie's *husband*, and this is my brother Jeremiah. Maggie's our responsibility now, and I don't want to find you around her again. Get out of here, and if you value your life, you'll stay the hell away from her."

Satisfied at the way the younger man paled and then reddened, Jeremiah caught Maggie's fist when, out of the corner of his eye, he saw it flying at him. "Settle down, Maggie, before you hurt yourself."

This young man was apparently the one his father had talked about. Just the thought of someone sniffing around Maggie pissed him off.

She tried to pull out of Eb's hold, her long hair flying. "Damn it, you've got no right to pull a gun on Fred. This is none of your business."

The fact that she defended him pissed him off even more.

Eb holstered his gun before grabbing her shoulders. "He tried to draw on us, Maggie. A man doesn't draw a gun unless he's planning to use it. And in case you've forgotten, *wife*, you *are* my business."

Maggie tried to push Eb out of the way, struggling to look around him, her eyes darting to Jeremiah and the gun he still held trained on Fred.

"You wouldn't really shoot Fred, would you?"

Jeremiah smiled coldly, not taking his eyes from Fred. "Just waiting for him to go for that pistol."

He barely restrained his laughter at the look on Fred's face. He stood almost a foot taller than the younger man and outweighed him by about a hundred pounds, but the other man kept glancing at Maggie and then back at the gun pointed at him as though weighing his chances.

"Maggie, you got hitched?" Fred's face hardened, his hands fisting at his sides. "I guess I wasn't good enough for you. You had to marry the boss's son."

Jeremiah saw red at the insult to Maggie, his fingers tightening on the trigger. "I'd be careful if I was you, boy. Now you can walk away quietly and keep your job, or I can kick your ass all the way to the ranch border." He smiled again, keeping his voice low. "Or you can reach for that pistol and end the whole thing. Your choice."

Smiling, he gestured toward Fred's holstered gun. "I'm hoping you'll go for that pistol."

Eb went to the door, opened it, and pushed a struggling Maggie inside. "Make up your mind quick. It's our wedding night, and we're anxious to get to our bride."

"We?" Fred looked from one man to the other.

Jeremiah raised a brow, cocking his pistol. "You got a problem with that?"

Maggie fought to come outside again but couldn't get past Eb. "Damn it, Jeremiah, leave Fred alone. I can take care of myself."

"No. Get in the house, Maggie. Now."

Muttering something under her breath that Jeremiah couldn't quite hear, she stormed inside.

Jeremiah took a step closer to the younger man, hiding a smile that Fred's bravado appeared to have fled now that Maggie was gone.

Fred backed away, nearly tripping over his own feet. "I don't want to lose my job. Tell Maggie I'll see her around."

Eb's eyes narrowed. "No, you won't, and if I catch you anywhere near her, I'll make sure you regret it. Get lost." He turned his back on the other man and went inside, leaving Jeremiah alone with Fred.

Holstering his gun, Jeremiah never took his eyes from Fred as he scurried across the yard toward the stables. With his hands on his hips, he took several deep breaths, trying to get his unwarranted fury under control.

He didn't really blame Fred for going for his gun. The younger man hadn't worked here when they left five years ago and didn't know them. He admired his fierce defense of Maggie.

His anger came from Maggie's defense of Fred. He was jealous, plain and simple.

Irritated at himself, he went into the house, closing and locking the door behind him, anxious to get to Maggie. He expected to find her and his brother already wrapped around each other, and it irritated him that he was jealous of that as well. Hearing her voice raised in anger, he stopped in the middle of the kitchen.

"Damn it, Eb. I could have handled him. You and Jeremiah can't tell me who I can talk to and who I can't!"

"You're wrong about that, darlin'."

Jeremiah's lips twitched at Maggie's growl of outrage. Continuing into the front room, he paused, leaning against the doorway and watching in fascination as she paced angrily back and forth across the room, stopping only to rail at Eb.

"I'm not a child anymore, and you've got to stop treating me like one. There was no need to threaten him that way."

"When a man goes for his gun, he should know the consequences."

Maggie stamped her foot. "Oh! You make me so mad. He's just a boy. There was no need for you and Jeremiah to pull your guns on him." She looked up and, spotting Jeremiah, included him in her outrage. "No need at all. You're nothing but animals. You act like cavemen, the way you treat women! You should both be ashamed of yourselves."

Jeremiah didn't allow his amusement to show. Damn, he'd forgotten just how exciting Maggie could be in a temper. It made him itch to tame her and had his cock hard in an instant.

"It's a different world where we live now, Maggie. As tough as you think you are, you'd be defenseless there. Rules keep it peaceful in an uncivilized land. Having a woman there is just going to stir some of the men up, especially until we get some of those catalogue brides to come. You said yourself they've got to be protected."

"But we're not in Oklahoma, and I wasn't talking about me!"

Eb raised his arms over his head and stretched. "That's how we are now, Maggie, and you're just going to have to learn to live with it. Seems you've got a lot of mad to get rid of. Maybe it has to do with being aroused still from your spanking."

"I hate you. Both of you."

Grinning, Eb removed his boots and crossed one foot over the other. "If you hate us for arousing you, you're really gonna despise us by morning." He leaned back and raised a brow expectantly at Jeremiah.

Amused at his brother's willingness to let him take the lead, he turned to face Maggie. Nerves and lust fought for supremacy, and not wanting either Eb or Maggie to see the nerves, he led with the lust.

He went for her shirt, ignoring that she batted his hands and tried to pull away. Grabbing her wrists in one of his hands, he raised them above her head and pulled her shirt over to cover her face so she couldn't see them.

With her hands out of the way and her face covered with the shirt, Jeremiah paused, smiling as she continued to rail at both of them, and decided to have a little fun with her. As she struggled, cursing both of them, her full breasts jiggled, their pointed tips making his mouth water. Turning, he smiled wordlessly to his brother.

Eb needed no second invitation.

Without his boots on, Eb moved quietly across the room, and to Jeremiah's surprise, reached out to pinch both nipples.

Maggie froze, her gasp making his cock twitch.

Jeremiah grinned. "Seems like only one way to get your attention, Maggie. I guess we know how to handle you when you start your nagging."

"Nagging? Nagging! I'll show you nagging, you…you animal."

Eb pinched her nipples again before releasing them, earning another gasp from her. "Being needy put you in a real sour mood. It puts me in a damned foul one. You might want to remember that."

Jeremiah slid his hand down her soft belly and undid her pants, letting them fall to the floor. "Spanking you excites us and puts us in a real nasty mood when you're being punished and can't take you. You might want to think about that the next time you decide to disobey either one of us."

Eb squatted and held her legs still so he could work her boots and pants off, leaving her naked except for the shirt covering her face and upraised arms.

Jeremiah waited until Eb stood before yanking her shirt off, leaving her standing completely naked between them.

God, she was even more beautiful with her face flushed and her hair flying like silk around her as she fought to break his hold. His cock pressed painfully against his pants, made worse when he wrapped his arms around her to hold her still. "That's enough, Maggie. Settle down. You're just gonna hurt yourself."

Her soft curves moved against him, making him want to taste and explore every delicious inch of her. Having her warm and naked in his arms, he groaned, needing her more than he'd ever needed anything in his life.

His brother's wife. No, his wife, too, damn it, and despite what the law said in his eyes, she belonged to both of them.

He shot a glance at Eb, tensing at this critical moment. All the years of talking and planning came down to this. As her legal husband, Eb had every right to take her and toss Jeremiah out the back door.

And he wouldn't be able to do a damned thing about it.

Eb's face appeared as if it had been carved of stone. He met Jeremiah's gaze and nodded once. "She's both of ours, remember?" Reaching around, he slid a hand over the cheeks of Maggie's luscious bottom. "But when the time comes, I'll be the first to take her ass."

Relief made Jeremiah's knees weak. Keeping his voice at a whisper, he raised a brow. "You know once I take her, there's every chance she'll be carrying my child. She'll be mine, too. No turning back."

Eb looked down at her, running his finger over her clit. "There's no turning back for either of us. There never was."

Maggie's gasp was like a stroke to his cock, making him want to plunge it into her warm body and hear that gasp again and again. He lifted her slight weight to carry her to the small sofa, groaning at the soft, smooth skin under his hands.

Shaking her head, Maggie eyed Eb. "You can't take my bottom."

Eb touched her bottom hole with a finger and pressed until she cried out. "Oh, yes, honey, I can. I will."

Jeremiah touched her silky curls before parting her folds and teasing the entrance to her pussy. "This belongs to us now, too." Bending, he licked a nipple, drawing another of those exciting gasps from her. "All of you belongs to us now."

The blue in her eyes fascinated him, more brilliant now as her eyes went wide with shock and a slight trace of fear even as they darkened in arousal.

Sliding his hand to her waist to keep her still, he nibbled at her bottom lip. "We won't hurt you, honey."

He didn't give her a chance to respond, desperate to know if she'd go up in flames the way she had with Eb. Taking her mouth with his, he slid a hand beneath her hair to gather her even closer. Her nipples poked at his chest, stroking his need to even greater heights.

When she tried to turn her head away, he tightened his fingers on the back of her neck to keep her in place, applying pressure with his lips until she opened for him. He immediately swept her mouth with his tongue, starving for the taste of her surrender.

When her tongue hesitantly touched his, he felt it all the way to his cock.

Drunk on the combination of relief and lust, he lost himself in the feel of her soft curves.

He pressed his cock against her soft belly, swallowing her whimper and groaning when she wiggled against him. The fire in her delighted him, and he swept his thumb over her pebbled nipple, greedy for more of it.

She's a virgin.

Groaning, he reluctantly broke off his kiss, lifting his head to stare down at her, a wave of possessiveness washing over him at the glazed look in her eyes. He took several deep breaths, knowing he had to calm down before he took her.

Eb groaned from beside him. "Damn, darlin'. You've got the prettiest little pussy I ever saw. I've gotta have another taste." He nudged Jeremiah to the side, spreading her legs wide to make room for himself between them.

Jeremiah watched in fascination as his brother parted Maggie's folds with his thumbs. "Hell, if that ain't a sight."

Her pink folds glistened with her moisture, making his own mouth water. Maggie gasped and tried to sit up, but Eb chose that moment to push back the hood hiding her clit and stroked the tender pink nub he exposed. She jolted, crying out, the sound sending a burst of fire to Jeremiah's cock.

Fuck. Playing with a woman had never gotten Jeremiah this close to spending before.

He couldn't tear his eyes away from the sight of Eb holding Maggie's legs high and wide as he lowered his head, his brother's face a mask of dark passion as his tongue traced her folds. Unable to stand the confinement, Jeremiah pulled off his boots and freed his cock, cursing at his clumsiness.

The look of passion and pleasure on her face made her beautiful features even more stunning.

This was Maggie, his Maggie, *their* Maggie.

Reaching out, he traced a finger over one of her little pink nipples, a little concerned that his hands were too rough to touch something so delicate. Frowning to himself, he gently traced over one, and then the other, worried that their play earlier had hurt her.

When she cried out, he almost pulled back, but paused when she arched, pushing her breast more fully against his hand. The sounds coming from her had him fighting back his own fierce arousal, those little catches in her breath threatening to do him in.

Damn it. If he was going to spill his seed, it would be inside her, not on the fucking floor.

"Eb, oh, God! It feels so good."

The need to hear *his* name on her lips snapped his control. Taking her hand in his, he wrapped it around his cock and held it there when she tried to pull it away, keeping his hand on hers until she opened her eyes and looked into his.

"Touch me, Maggie. Say my name." Reaching out, he took a nipple between his thumb and forefinger, his cock jumping in her hand at her whimper.

"Jeremiah." It came out on a breath, her eyes unfocused on his.

Clenching his teeth, he groaned and took several deep breaths in an effort to hold back his orgasm. "Bad idea. Hell. Let go, honey, before I spill."

He reluctantly pulled her hand away from his cock, which already leaked moisture. He ran his hand over her as she twisted and cried out, having never felt so protective or so much a man than at that moment.

His gaze swung back and forth from her face to where Eb ate at her, his own mouth watering for a taste of her sweet juices. His brother avoided her clit but kept her writhing against him. Wishing he had more light so he could see her better, Jeremiah ran his hands over Maggie's body, over her breasts and stomach and back to her breasts again, already addicted to the texture of her soft skin, and found he couldn't stop touching her.

He took great delight in the way her taut womanly curves trembled under his palm. He pinched one nipple and bent to take the other into his mouth, closing his eyes in bliss at the feel of the tight little berry against his tongue.

When she cried out sharply and grabbed his head, tangling her hands in his hair, he sucked her nipple harder and applied more pressure to the other, groaning his relief and supreme satisfaction when she moaned his name.

If he'd ever been this aroused before, he didn't remember it. His cock jumped, leaking more moisture, his balls drawn up so tight it bordered on pain.

Eb straightened, chuckling softly when Maggie thrashed and kicked at him. "No, honey. You can't come yet." He got up to light several lanterns and brought them over as Jeremiah gathered her warm softness against him.

Maggie beat at Jeremiah's shoulders. "Please make it stop. Give me more. Please don't leave me like this again."

Jeremiah ran soft kisses over her collar bone, his entire body primed to take her. "Eb, I'm gonna finish her off. Look at her. The poor thing's in agony." Hell, so was he. Seeing her writhing in pleasure, hearing the primitive sounds coming from that sweet mouth made him wild to have her.

Shaking his head, Eb moved in at her side, rubbing a hand over her mound. "It'll be better for her when you take her virginity."

Jeremiah's cock throbbed with the need to plunge into her. Nodding, he adjusted her on the sofa, turning her so her bottom hung over the edge. The sight of her glistening pussy had to be the most beautiful thing he'd ever seen in his life. "The damned sofa's too small. Let's get her to bed." He slid his hands under her to lift her, pausing when she fought him.

Maggie arched her body. "No! Here. Now. Hurry."

Eb threw off his own clothes and leaned over her. "We'll take care of you, darlin'. Jeremiah's going to take you first. We'll give you everything you need."

"First?" She moaned again, twisting restlessly. "Oh, God. You meant it. You're both going to take me."

Poising the head of his cock at her opening, Jeremiah sucked in a breath at the feel of her warm juices coating the head of his cock. Placing his hand flat on her abdomen, he teased her clit with his thumb and slowly began to push into her. "Of course we meant it, honey. Easy now. Just let us take care of everything." Careful to use the same gentle tone he used when dealing with skittish horses, he crooned to her, having no idea what the hell he said.

His brother seemed to understand his predicament and bent to rain kisses over her jaw and shoulders while running his hands over her breasts. "Look at me. I want to watch your eyes when Jeremiah takes your virginity. You belong to both of us, Maggie."

With one quick thrust, Jeremiah broke through her barrier, wincing at her shocked cry as he sank into heaven. His entire body shuddered with the need to move, but he fought it, giving her time to become accustomed to being filled. He'd never been more grateful for his brother's presence than when Maggie cried out in pain and fought to push him off.

Eb's hands tightened on her shoulders, his smile out of place in his granite-like expression. "Don't fight him. It's all right, darlin'. It won't hurt anymore, I promise. Be still. Shh, don't cry. We'll give you what you need. Just let that soft pussy settle a bit."

Hearing Eb's gentleness and control made Jeremiah feel like a heel. He shot a look of gratitude at his brother before bending over her and gathering her close as he fought for the words to reassure a virgin. "I'm sorry, honey. Shh, it won't hurt anymore, I swear. God, you feel so good. I promise I won't move until you're ready."

He stayed as still as he could, letting her adjust to being taken for the first time in her life.

The thought had him struggling desperately for control, fisting his hands on the sofa on either side of her. "Fuck. Hellfire and damnation! So fucking tight. So hot."

When Maggie moaned and started to move, he thought the top of his head would fly off.

Gritting his teeth, he withdrew slightly and sank deep again as he pressed his thumb to her clit. "Yeah, that's it." He loved to talk dirty while fucking a woman, but this was Maggie, and for the first time in his life, he found himself at a loss for words. He wanted to ease her fears and let her know that he considered her special, but he couldn't think of anything except how good her tight pussy felt rippling all over his cock. "Your pussy's so damned tight, honey. Can you feel the way you're squeezin' me?"

Maggie's face turned bright red as she tightened her legs around his waist and looked away. "You're both watching me. Don't look at me." She moaned again, closing her eyes when Eb's hands moved over her breasts and began to play with her nipples.

Eb took Maggie's bottom lip between his teeth, tugging and then releasing it. When her eyes popped open, he grinned, holding her gaze. "Of course we're gonna look at you. I'm gonna stroke your clit while Jeremiah's fucking you."

If possible, her face got even redder. "I can't believe I'm letting— Oh!" She kicked her feet as Eb's middle finger touched her clit, her knuckles white where she held on to him.

Jeremiah groaned and began to move, having to consciously loosen his hold so he didn't bruise her hips.

She seemed so damned small and delicate in his arms, something her passion sometimes made him forget. Her inner muscles gripped his cock with every thrust, so tight and hot his cock ached as tingles settled at his spine.

Meeting his brother's eyes, he groaned. "I can't last. Too fucking tight. Too good."

Eb nodded, clenching his jaw. "Go ahead. I'll finish her off."

"Like hell. We both will." Jeremiah knocked his brother's hand away from her clit and began to thrust forcefully. He was too lost in her, too far gone to do anything else, and vowed to himself that he would make it up to her. With his fingers digging into her firm bottom, he held her against him and surged deep, groaning loudly as his seed exploded from him.

The force of it was like nothing he'd ever felt before and left him shaking. Motionless, he held her as still as he could until his cock finally stopped pulsing, leaving him drained.

Hell, he'd died and gone to heaven.

"Move."

Eb's tortured command spurred him to action.

Still shaking, he managed to withdraw from her and move aside to slump heavily against the sofa. He caressed her, his hands clumsy, and with a groan he bent to tug a nipple with his teeth while reaching down to stroke her clit.

Eb thrust into her with a low groan. "Jesus, she's tight. Come on, darlin'. Come for me. Let me feel this tight little pussy clamp down on me."

Jeremiah drew back when his fingers inadvertently brushed Eb's cock.

"It's happened before, Jeremiah. Don't you fucking stop touching her."

Each word dripped with sex, his brother's dark tone even getting through to Maggie.

Her eyes popped open in shock, closing again on a groan when Jeremiah slid his fingers over her slick clit and began to stroke in earnest. A few strokes later, her eyes shot open again and she grabbed for him.

"Oh! Oh, my God. It's happening."

Jeremiah sucked in a breath at the surge of possessiveness that went through him, groaning when she bucked in his arms. His attention caught at the glint of light reflecting off of the rings that proclaimed to the world that she belonged to them.

The enormity of it hit him hard.

Her future lay entirely in his and Eb's hands.

He smiled down at her in awe, a surge of protectiveness washing over him. "Let go, sugar. Come for us." Fascinated by the look on her face and the sounds she made, he slowed the strokes to her clit, amazed that his cock stirred again.

He'd never seen quite that look before, especially on a woman in the throes of orgasm, and something powerful and hot swelled in his chest when he realized that he and Eb were the only ones who'd ever seen her this way.

Eb groaned, the tortured look on his face one that Jeremiah had never seen before.

Jeremiah had to move back out of the way when Eb collapsed on top of her, pulling her close. Running a hand over her golden hair, Jeremiah pushed some of the damp locks off of her face, his chest swelling even more when she turned her cheek against his palm.

He watched Eb and Maggie together, amused at the way they clung to each other before jealousy reared its ugly head again.

Which was just plain stupid.

He hadn't counted on this. He couldn't even blame it on Eb, who'd been amazingly generous.

He could do no less.

Not willing to ruin their private moment, he got to his feet, unsurprised that the muscles in his legs still trembled. Untangling the pants that he'd never completely kicked off, he pulled them back up again, looking away from the sight of Maggie nestled in his brother's arms.

Hearing their low murmurs, he felt like an intruder and planned to escape as soon as possible. Fastening his pants, he turned to look at them one last time, surprised to find them both watching him.

Maggie looked like she wanted to cry, and Eb looked mad as hell.

Fuck. Trust him to ruin something so incredible.

Eb kissed Maggie and rose, fastening his own pants. His low voice held more than a hint of anger as he approached Jeremiah, turning to frown as Maggie hurriedly covered herself. "Maggie needs both of us now. I've never known you to walk out on a woman like this before, and now you're going to do it to Maggie? If that's the way you're going to be, she's better off being with just me." He turned away in disgust, stripping out of his shirt and going back to sit on the sofa, pulling Maggie onto his lap and covering her nakedness with his shirt.

What the hell was he doing?

Meeting Maggie's tear-filled eyes, he smiled in apology and went to her, lifting her from his brother's lap and sat with her on his. Holding Maggie close to his heart, he felt guilty as hell. He owed her the truth, no matter how much it embarrassed him. "I'm sorry, honey. That was stupid. I didn't want to walk away from you, but seeing you in Eb's arms made me a little jealous. I thought both of you wanted some privacy." Meeting his brother's gaze, he rubbed Maggie's back. "It won't happen again."

To his surprise and anger, Maggie pushed away from him and got to her feet, staggering as she grabbed the shawl from a nearby chair and covered herself. "Get out, both of you. I can't believe I let you— just go away. I can't believe I actually let you talk me into this. I knew this would never work. Now you're jealous, and Eb's mad. How long will it be before one or both of you leave again? No. No. No. Just stay away from me! I'm not doing this again."

"We're not going anywhere. I don't think it's a bad idea, though, for each of us to spend some time alone with you." Eb settled back, apparently making himself right at home.

"I can't be with both of you. Didn't we just prove that?"

Jeremiah stood, frowning when she backed away from him. He couldn't remember anything ever hurting so much.

He'd made a mess of everything, and it was up to him to fix it. Hell, no wonder she always looked up to Eb. "No, we proved nothing except that I wasn't prepared to be jealous. It's my fault, not yours or Eb's." He tried to reach for her, but she backed away again.

Losing her virginity should have been a special occasion, and he'd ruined it for her. Full of self-loathing, he smiled apologetically. "I promise I'll make it up to you." His gaze went to her bare legs beneath the shawl. "You pack quite a punch, baby."

Readjusting the shawl, she inadvertently gave both of them an enticing flash of nipple. "This won't work."

Wondering if she knew how adorable she looked with her chin lifted and her arms folded over her chest, Jeremiah grinned, hoping her shawl slipped again. "Yeah, honey. It will. Make no mistake about that."

When Eb stood and started forward, Jeremiah recognized the determination in his brother's eyes even if Maggie didn't.

Sticking out an arm to hold off his brother, Jeremiah grinned and took another step toward Maggie. "Allow me."

Bending, he lifted her over his shoulder and started for the bedroom, ignoring her struggles and holding her in place with a hand on her lush ass. "Settle down, Maggie. It's time for bed."

"You're not sleeping with me, damn it. I want to be alone." She punched his back and then with a growl, sunk her sharp teeth into him.

Shocked at her aggression, he couldn't deny that the challenge of taming her had his cock hardening again. "Damn it, Maggie. Let go before I paddle your ass!"

Eb ran a hand under her shawl and over the naked cheeks of her bottom, stunning her into releasing Jeremiah. "You'll sleep between us from now on. Damn, woman, you're high-strung. I thought sex would settle you down."

Maggie came alive again, shrieking and beating on Jeremiah's back. "Stop touching me!"

Eb lifted the shawl over her head and slapped her naked ass in retaliation. "Behave, little girl. You've had a big day. It's time for bed."

"You can't tell me what to do, and I'm not a little girl, damn it!"

Chuckling, Jeremiah ran a hand up her leg, turning his head to nip her wiggling ass and grinning at his brother when she squealed. "Oh, yes, honey. We can."

Hell, at least she wasn't crying.

Continuing to the bedroom, Jeremiah couldn't resist caressing the bare bottom he held anchored over his shoulder, savoring the silky firmness. "Life's gonna be different for you now, Maggie."

Dropping her onto the bed, he lay on top of her so she couldn't move and looked into her eyes. "Now stay here so I can go get a warm cloth for your pussy. Let me take care of you."

He couldn't explain it—didn't understand it himself. He just knew that the need for intimacy had become so strong, he couldn't let her go.

Her blue eyes shot sparks at him. "You're not touching me there again. Just go back to Oklahoma, and leave me the hell alone."

Not bothering to hide his impatience, he grabbed her hands and raised them above her head. Angry at himself, his temper snapped. "We fucked you, Maggie. I took your virginity. You're going to be sore, and I want to take care of you. You could be carrying our baby even now. You're coming to Oklahoma with us, and if you give me any lip about it, I'll spank you good."

* * * *

Hours later, Jeremiah frowned into the darkness, running his hand over Maggie's soft hair.

She'd gone to sleep mad at him for threatening her yet again, and now he just couldn't settle.

Consumed by thoughts of her—her beauty, her sweetness, her passion, he couldn't relax and held himself stiffly next to her. He'd just taken her virginity, and the hurt look in her eyes was like a kick from a bull.

Thinking about her being pregnant with his child had sent such an overwhelming rush of emotion through him, tumbling him off balance, that he'd reacted in anger.

He'd calmed down since then but still felt off-balance.

The revelation he'd had filled him with awe as much as it scared him to death.

Why the hell hadn't he even anticipated falling in love with her?

Chapter Five

Aware that she did her best to ignore him, Eb watched Maggie during dinner the next evening, her delicate blush telling him that she was aware of his scrutiny.

She looked so small and confused as she sat there pushing food around her plate. She hadn't joined in the conversation except for one word answers when they'd asked about her packing this afternoon.

But he knew his Maggie from the past would be plotting revenge and had no reason to believe the woman she'd become would react any differently.

Because she'd been the darling of the ranch her entire life and had always been spoiled, it wasn't often that she felt the need for revenge, but when she did, she never let up until she evened the score.

The woman sitting next to him now would probably be even more intent on getting even.

Damned if he wasn't looking forward to it.

He hadn't seen her this morning, and he'd thought about her all day, a day spent in town after being shooed away by Esmeralda.

The two women had spent several hours loading the trunks he and Jeremiah had taken over to the small house. He'd wanted to stay and help, but Esmeralda had other ideas.

"Maggie needs to pack her things and gather what she wants to take of her father's. I want to spend some time alone with her before she leaves. You can come back to get the trunks later."

So he and Jeremiah had spent the day in town with several of the ranch hands, buying up as many supplies as he could. Blade, Hawke, and Phoenix would make sure that several of the men came with buckboards to the train station in Tulsa to meet them, and they would buy more supplies there before they left.

Getting supplies had always been a hardship, so they wanted to get as many as they could to take back to the Circle T. This time he'd simply bought out the store, not knowing what Maggie would like or need.

Or any of the other women he'd advertised for.

The thought of taking Maggie back home to a ranch filled with randy men set him on edge. He knew most of his men well and didn't believe for one minute that they'd be stupid enough to be forward with Maggie, but he'd seen enough shootouts over women that it made him uneasy.

His father nodded in agreement as Jeremiah finished telling him about advertising for women.

"Makes sense. Besides, Maggie'll be anxious for some female company. Just make sure you protect these women, or word'll get out and no decent woman will show her face there. Men will come to your ranch in droves looking for easy pickin's."

Esmeralda touched Maggie's arm from the other side. "That's right, and you'd better make sure Maggie's not surrounded by women with loose morals. If you want decent women, you're gonna have to treat 'em that way."

As Maggie's eyes lifted to touch on both him and Jeremiah, a blush reddened her cheeks, and she hurriedly looked away, reaching for her glass.

"I don't think they want decent women there, Esmeralda. I think warm bodies are enough for them."

Eb shared a look with his brother, amused and relieved at the return of Maggie's usual spunk. Still anticipating whatever her devious mind planned in retaliation, he sat back, confident he could handle her.

"Maggie knows better. Don't worry about the women that come there. They'll be looked after, protected, and provided for, but there'll be strict rules for them to follow, and it'll be up to their men to make sure they follow those rules." He paused for effect, waiting until Maggie met his gaze. "They'll be punished for disobeying them."

Esmeralda paused with her fork halfway to her mouth and lowered it again. "Punished how?"

Maggie stood, almost knocking over her glass. "Esmeralda, let's get dessert. My mouth's been watering all day for your apple pie."

Jeremiah didn't bother to cover his smile. "They'll have their bottoms paddled, but what'll be worse is that everyone else will know they've had a spanking."

Maggie plopped back into her chair, her eyes wide. "You don't mean that you'd—that the men who spank women would let other men watch?"

Eb wanted to laugh out loud at her horrified expression but settled for letting his lips twitch. "No, but since every woman can expect the same thing when they don't do what they're told, everyone will know."

Esmeralda shot a worried glance at their father. "What's gonna happen when you're out on the range? Who's gonna protect Maggie?"

Smiling to ease the housekeeper's fears, Eb turned when he heard a knock at the door and tossed his napkin on the table to stand. "Someone will be watching her at all times, and she'll just have to do what they say while we're away. If she doesn't mind them, we'll deal with her just as soon as we get back."

Hell, he would have to make damned sure he trusted whoever protected her. He trusted his men to be loyal to the brand and with his livestock, but there were damned few of them he would trust with Maggie.

He had an uneasy feeling that having women there would change all their lives in ways he couldn't even fathom. He'd been away from decent women for too long that he'd forgotten just how much trouble they could be.

The whores that passed through fawned all over the men and did whatever they wanted them to do, and got paid handsomely for it.

Having a wife appeared to be a whole different matter.

Cursing his short-sightedness, he opened the front door, surprised to find Hayes and Wyatt standing there.

Both men stood at his eye level, the aura of danger surrounding them a tangible thing. The only reason he could think of for them to come to his door was Savannah. "Is Savannah hurt?"

Hayes shook his head. "Not yet, and we want to keep it that way."

Wyatt removed his hat and rubbed a hand over the back of his neck. "We'd like to talk in private. It's kind of a delicate subject."

Wordlessly, Eb moved aside and gestured toward his father's study. "We can talk in here."

Seeing Jeremiah coming down the hall, he left the door to the study open and went inside, gesturing for the two men to take a seat. He waited until his brother came in and closed the door behind him, before moving behind his father's desk to sit.

"All right. What do you want to talk about?"

Hayes and Wyatt looked at each other, some silent communication passing between them before Hayes lowered himself into one of the chairs in front of their father's desk. "Are you really both married to Maggie?"

Stiffening, Eb narrowed his eyes, anger tightening his belly. He leaned back and eyed the other men coldly. "That's none of your concern."

Hayes nodded. "True, but I'm asking for a reason."

Jeremiah came farther into the room and took a seat on the sofa, crossing one foot over the other knee and smiling faintly. "Does this reason have anything to do with a dark-haired, dark-eyed niece of a preacher?"

Wyatt nodded and smiled grimly. "It does. We've heard you're taking Maggie back to that big ranch you have in Oklahoma. Will everyone accept both of you as her husbands?"

Eb folded his arms across his chest. "You seem to be taking a lot of interest in how we handle our wife."

Hayes mimicked his gesture. "Like I said, we have our reasons. We're wondering if there's a place we can live the same way with Savannah."

Shrugging, Eb smiled faintly. "We own the place and can live there any damned way we want. If you want to marry Savannah and move there, you should have no trouble with my men. I'm sure Maggie'll love having her friend so close. Savannah'll probably feel the same way."

Jeremiah turned from where he poured whiskey and grinned. "We've already advertised for mail-order brides for our ranch hands. Figured that if the men knew women would be coming, they'd leave ours alone."

Wyatt frowned into the whiskey Jeremiah handed to him. "I can't stand by much longer and watch Savannah's uncle mistreat her. She won't even admit it, but I've seen bruises on her arms."

Sharing a look with Hayes, he sighed. "She's up to something, too, but we don't know what it is. Has your wife said anything?"

Eb sat forward to accept the glass from his brother. "Not a thing, but the Savannah I knew years ago got real quiet just before she was about to make trouble. I don't know how well you know her, but she won't accept help unless it's shoved on her."

Wyatt's jaw tightened. "She won't even talk to us about leaving. We made it plain that we both want her and that scared her off. It's hard to get her to look at either one of us now, but, hell, we wanted to be honest straight off." He took a sip of his drink and leaned back. "You'd really sell us a parcel of your land and let us settle there?"

Hayes cursed and shot to his feet. "Christ. What the hell would we do there, Wyatt? I'm a lawman, not a fucking rancher." He scrubbed a hand over his face. "How the hell would we support her?" He shot a glance at Eb and sighed. "We chased an outlaw here and arrested him. That's when we met Savannah. We're bounty hunters, damn it."

Wyatt shrugged, eyeing his friend, before looking back at Eb. "We've taken some jobs close by, but roaming the country looking for outlaws lost its appeal once we met Savannah. We want to settle somewhere with her."

Jeremiah reclaimed his seat. "We need lawmen, too. We spend too much time fighting cattle rustlers and bandits who come across us and decide to help themselves to whatever they want. They think that since we're out in the middle of nowhere, we're defenseless. God knows you'd be busy enough, and it would be worth it to hire you. The way things are going, it'll be a damned town before long, especially once the women start arriving."

Eb nodded. "And if we're gonna get folks to move there, we need some kind of law, or they won't stay long. I'll be honest with you. I don't have the time or the patience to be upholding the law while I'm trying to run my ranch."

Hayes and Wyatt looked at each other, the silent communication between them obviously born of long friendship. Hayes narrowed his eyes, crossing his arms over his chest. "What kind of law?"

Eb chuckled at his wariness, more at ease with them than he'd been an hour ago. "Just the law. But we've got to do something about the women." Remembering the interest Maggie displayed, he shrugged. "I promised my wife."

Damn, it felt good to say that. *My wife.* Those two words filled him with a protective streak a mile wide.

He blew out a breath to relieve the pressure in his chest. "She'll be the only woman there for a while, and when the others come we've got to make sure they're protected until somebody claims them. I'd be glad to have that responsibility taken from my shoulders. I also think it would be a hell of a lot more effective if every man had an equal responsibility toward the women. Of course, their husbands would be the most directly responsible for them, but men are sometimes out on the range."

Wyatt nodded. "I see your point. But what woman is gonna want to move there? If it's as wild as you say it is, women won't come unless they're assured of protection."

Hayes shook his head. "We can't protect them properly *and* chase after cattle rustlers."

Jeremiah laughed softly and leaned back, resting his elbow on the arm of the sofa. "Maggie already gave us the lecture about that. We have to promise to see to their safety. If we can promise women that every man there will treat them with respect and protect them, they might come. Our women will be much safer and more secure if *every* woman is protected by *every* man.

Hayes stilled. "That's a hell of a plan, if you can pull it off." He swirled his glass, staring into it. "But it'll only work with men you really trust. Good men who want good women. A lot of them don't."

Eb nodded. "Any man who gives the women any trouble will be run off the place. We don't have the time to deal with troublemakers."

"What if the women don't wanna be claimed?" The frustration in Hayes' voice told Jeremiah that the two of them were having just such a problem with Savannah.

Jeremiah shared a look with Eb. "We can't force a woman to accept a claim she doesn't want, but we'd all be obligated to take care of all the women just the same. We can't make them do something they don't want to do or they'll leave in droves. But we made it clear in the advertisement that we wanted mail-order brides."

Hayes grimaced and stood, moving to the window. "How the hell are we going to handle all those women? What if they start trouble between the men? Hell, I'm sure we've all seen that more than once."

Eb's cock twitched at the memory of Maggie's firm ass wiggling on his lap. "Then they get their bottoms warmed to remind them to follow the damned rules."

Wyatt grinned. "Spank them?"

Hayes' brow went up. "What rules?"

Jeremiah stood, grabbed the whiskey bottle, and went to pour everyone another drink. "The rules we put in place to keep them safe when one of us isn't around. Our top priority has to be taking care of the women or we'll lose all control of everything. If they start putting themselves in harm's way, it'll make our job even harder. If they start pitting the men against each other, we'll have fights, shooting...you name it. No, these women have to be under control from the first day, and they have to know it. The men also have to know that there'll be no disrespect toward any of the women or they'll have to deal with every other man there."

Hayes sat back down, smiling for the first time since he walked through the front door. "You start turning women over your knee, and they'll leave for sure. They tend to frown on that kind of thing."

Eb frowned. "I'm not talking about beating them, but a warm bottom is a hell of a lot better than having them get kidnapped, raped, or worse. It's also a lot better than my men killing each other."

Jeremiah grinned, glancing toward the closed door and lowering his voice. "You just have to make sure they enjoy their spanking." At the other men's astonished looks, Jeremiah nodded. "Learned it from one of Trixie's whores."

Wyatt grinned, his eyes twinkling. "It sounds like a hell of a lot of fun, too."

Eb thought about the gleam in Maggie's eyes over dinner. "There's also another advantage to it. If all women are punished the same way then everyone'll know how they paid for their behavior. Hopefully, that'll be enough to keep them out of trouble."

Wyatt turned and hooked a hip over the corner of their father's desk. "Double the punishment with a little bit of play mixed in. That's good. But I don't think your woman would be real happy if you put another woman over your knee. No matter how hard you try to hide it, women talk, and your wife's gonna find out."

Jeremiah grimaced. "He's right." Shrugging, he stood and poured each of them another whiskey. "I don't want any other man spanking

Maggie, either. If someone else sees her do something wrong, they'll have to come tell one of us."

Hayes nodded. "And the single ones can have their bottoms paddled by one of the other single men. But it better be someone we can trust."

Wyatt drew a deep breath and let it out slowly, looking up at Hayes. "You do realize we're talking like we're really gonna do this? You'd better be sure. I'm not going all the way to Oklahoma only to have you decide you're not tying yourself to a woman, or you get all possessive and try to shove me out."

Standing, Hayes moved to the window, staring out. "We've got to get Savannah away from her uncle. She needs us. She's just a little thing and needs someone to watch out for her. She's too soft and sweet to be putting up with abuse like that. We both want her, and we'd all be better off somewhere that we can protect her and provide for her and where no one's gonna call her a whore for having two men."

Grinning, Wyatt sat back. "You really have blinders on when it comes to her. I can't wait until you find out that under all that soft sweetness is a little minx who's going to give us a run for our money."

Hayes clenched his jaw. "I don't think she even knows how to stand up for herself. She's just a helpless little thing."

Wyatt went back to his seat, not completely smothering his grin. "You're forgetting something, Hayes. She already told us to stay away from her. We can't claim her as ours if she refuses."

"We'll take care of it. She won't refuse. She needs us."

This time Wyatt didn't even bother to hide his grin, anticipation lighting his eyes. "We're gonna have a fight on our hands, but you're right. She needs us."

Shaking his head, Hayes stared out the window again. "I'm not making her do anything she doesn't want to do. She's had enough of that."

Jeremiah shifted in his seat. "We didn't listen when Maggie refused us. We just hustled her to the preacher and made her marry us." A muscle worked in his jaw as he made his way to the window, meeting Hayes' hard look. "What the hell were we supposed to do? She can't stay here, and we've waited for her long enough. You do the same with Savannah. You know what's good for her even if she doesn't. Believe me, she'll appreciate it in the end."

Surprised at his brother's defensiveness, Eb donned the bland expression he wore when playing poker, a little unsettled that his brother didn't.

Turning, Hayes regarded both Eb and Jeremiah, a thoughtful look on his face. "It sounds like you two have it all figured out for your woman. I don't know if the same thing'll work for Savannah, and I'm not about to force myself on her. Let's just leave it at that."

Eb shrugged and took a sip of his drink, the little kernel of guilt in his belly growing. "We didn't have much of a choice with hurrying Maggie. We told her father years ago that we both wanted to marry her, but she was too young. He got real mad and told us he wouldn't let his daughter be ridiculed by having two husbands. We left and spent the last five fucking years building a place we could live with her. Do you really think we would have taken 'no' for an answer?"

Wyatt nodded. "So you fell in love with her years ago?"

Eb bolted back his whiskey and turned to get another, hoping the burn would ease some of the guilt he felt at not giving her a choice, even though he knew that marrying her was in her best interest. "She was still a girl, for Christ's sake. But we've known we'd take care of her for a long time."

Jeremiah met his gaze before standing and starting to pace. "She's married to us now. She's coming home with us, and that's that."

Hayes and Wyatt gave each other another one of those looks. Hayes shrugged. "Like you said, she's married to you now. A woman's place is with her husband. But I don't believe in forcing a woman to do anything, and if that's the kind of law you're looking for in your town, I'm not the man you need."

Eb tossed back his whiskey, welcoming the burn. Being on the defensive pissed him off. "We're not trying to run roughshod over the women. We're trying to protect them. We've taken care of Maggie since she was a little girl. Nobody'll take care of her the way we will."

Wyatt inclined his head, not looking entirely convinced. "That's important."

Hayes started toward the door. "We'd better get going. We have a lot to do, and I'm sure you're anxious to get back to your bride. I'd like to talk to you again before you leave and go back to your town."

Staring out the window, Eb looked back over his shoulder at them, still irritated at himself for feeling guilty about the way he'd forced Maggie to marry him.

Damn it, he knew what was best for her.

"It's not a town yet. It would be nice to have a town, though, with a place we can get supplies. The only thing that's there is the Circle T."

Wyatt stood and joined Hayes at the doorway. "If you start bringing women, you get families. It'll be a town before you know it. Better come up with a name for it so you can tell people where the hell they're going."

Eb opened the door, stilling when he saw Maggie standing there with tear filled eyes.

"You ought to call it something like 'Arrogant City,' or 'Bossy Town,' or how about 'Any Warm Woman'll Do,' something that actually tells people what to expect. You'll have every roughneck and outlaw for miles camping there. You all should get along just fine."

Eb caught her arm when she would have turned away, his guilt growing, making his stomach knot and his tone harsher than he'd meant it to be.

"You listening at keyholes, darlin'?"

Jeremiah came forward, touching her shoulder, shooting a warning glance at him. "You're just tired, sweetheart. You know, you've got a point about the name. We don't want a name that'll attract unsavory characters, do we, honey?"

Maggie glared up at him. "Too late. From what I can see, two unsavory characters already own the place."

Eb stared down at Maggie, cupping her cheeks and using his thumb to wipe away the lone tear that trickled down her face, the knots in his stomach getting tighter. "Why are you crying?" A sudden suspicion hit him, knotting his stomach. "How long have you been standing here?"

Maggie kicked him in the shin, crying out and hopping on one foot. "Long enough. At least *they* care about Savannah. Good for her. At least *she'll* be happy." She leaned against the doorjamb, cradling her injured foot while trying to slap his hands away.

He picked her up, always surprised at how light and delicate she felt in his arms, and sat in the chair Hayes just recently vacated. Taking her foot in his hand, he rubbed it gently, searching for any sign of injury, frowning to find it ice cold. He took both feet in his hands to gently rub them, amazed at how dainty they looked in his hand.

Holding her little bare feet seemed extraordinarily intimate. He covered them possessively with his hand to warm them, but also to hide them, cursing his own irrational jealousy that Hayes and Wyatt might see her naked feet.

They were feet, for God's sake. It wasn't as though she'd bared her breasts for all of them to see.

Tightening his arm around her, he pulled her closer and bent to whisper in her ear. "I don't want to see you running around with bare feet anymore. Keep them covered unless you're in our bedroom."

He inwardly winced at how demanding that came out, especially when she looked so damned vulnerable.

Maggie stopped wiggling, obviously realizing he wouldn't let her go, and crossed her arms over her chest.

"What I wear on my feet is none of your business."

He wanted to laugh out loud at the return of her grit. Running his hand over her silky hair, he leaned down to brush his lips over her jaw, growling softly. "Everything about you is my business, little girl, including what you wear. Now stop wiggling that ass on my lap, or, newly opened or not, you're gonna get fucked again."

He didn't know what he'd do if she called his bluff. He had no intention of taking her again so soon and risking hurting her.

As his guilt grew, so did his possessiveness. What if she preferred men like Hayes and Wyatt? Did she feel cheated not to have men who fawned over her?

The best way to care for her was to protect her, damn it!

She froze, blinking up at him, and glanced at Hayes and Wyatt, as though to make sure they hadn't heard him.

He would swear he could almost hear her defiance snap back into place as her chin went up in that way that excited the hell out of him. Tamping down his jealousy, he smiled when she opened her mouth to speak, no doubt to rail at him, and slid a finger down her cheek. "Tell me something, honey. What do you think we should name the town?"

Knocking his hand away, she glared at him, her beautiful blue eyes shooting sparks. "I don't care what you name it. Tyler Town. How's that?"

Chuckling, Eb shook his head. He knew her hot temper came from hurt and exhaustion and only patience and indulgence would cool it. "God forbid. Then everyone'll hold us responsible for everything that goes wrong and come to complain to us about it. I'd never get any work done."

Taking in her flashing eyes and mutinous expression, Eb wanted nothing more than to strip her naked, lay her on the thick rug, and make a feast of her. He wanted to see those flashing eyes darken with passion, become wide with wonder, before closing on a moan.

The lips she pressed so firmly together would soften and part, allowing him entrance so he could swallow the sighs and gasps as he ran his hands over her slender, but surprisingly voluptuous, curves.

His cock stirred beneath her enticing bottom, surprising him again that he could become so aroused just being in the same room with her. He looked up at the other men, who stood watching them, and started rubbing her feet again.

"I think Maggie's right. We've got to give the town a name that won't sound so enticing to outlaws, but will make the women want to come. Any ideas?"

Hayes clenched his jaw, looking toward the window, but Eb got the impression he was seeing something entirely different. "What would you name a place started out of the desire to live somewhere the way you want without getting any trouble for it?"

Maggie looked up at Hayes, her expression softening. "How about Desire? You're thinking about Savannah, aren't you?"

A half-smile played at Hayes' lips as he watched Eb rub Maggie's feet. "It appears we'll need a map to your town, after all."

Wyatt glanced at his friend before meeting Maggie's eyes. "Do you think Savannah could be happy there?"

A pink-faced Maggie glanced up at Eb through her lashes before nodding. "I saw the way you looked at her. I'm sure you could make her happy. It'll be nice to have someone there to talk to."

Jeremiah's brows went up. "You can talk to us, you know."

Maggie shrugged and said nothing.

Furious that she seemed to think her friend would be happier than she would be, Eb stood and set Maggie on her feet, releasing her almost immediately. "Desire it is, then. Appropriate, since that's what the town was built on."

Smiling at her shock, he ran a finger down Maggie's arm.

"No self-respecting outlaw would want to hole up in a town named Desire, especially where the men'll watch each other so closely."

Maggie nodded and looked away. "And it's the only thing in the world you desire. Yeah, Desire's the perfect name for your town. Now, if you'll excuse me, I'm going to bed."

Not about to let her get away so easily, Eb grabbed her arm before she could escape, bending to whisper in her ear.

"What I desire most is you, Mrs. Tyler. Remember, the Circle T was built out of our *desire* to marry you. Now, go on up to bed, and think about that. We'll be up in a bit. And cover your feet. They're freezing."

* * * *

Eb and Jeremiah sat staring into their whiskey long after the other men left. Unable to get the image of Maggie lying upstairs in his bed out of his head, Eb reached for the bottle to pour himself another, hoping this one would settle him enough to sleep. He was used to hard work and being in the saddle all day and falling into bed dead tired.

Spending his days arranging for supplies hardly took any effort at all and left him feeling restless.

Wanting Maggie so badly he could taste it didn't help. Picturing her with her long hair draped over his pillow and her tiny frame warming his bed made it difficult to resist the urge to race up the stairs and join her.

It was too soon after losing her virginity to take her again, and he didn't know how he'd be able to lie next to her without wanting to sink his cock into her.

There was still much of that sweet little girl in her, something he tended to forget after the passionate way she fell apart in his arms. Her daring and boldness of the past had been tempered over the years, more subtle now than it used to be.

But it was there, and the enticing peeks he got of it made him want her even more.

He couldn't help but wonder of once she got over her father's death and the shock of being married to two men she probably thought she'd never see again, it would be back in full force.

God help him.

His cock twitched, making him grimace and shift his position again. He actually looked forward to her sassiness and definitely looked forward to taming it, readily admitting to himself that he hoped he never did.

Damn, he looked forward to getting her home, wondering if she'd realize just how much time and money he and Jeremiah had spent to make her feel at home right from the start.

His cock twitched again when he thought of just how she would thank him.

She'd look at him the way she used to, with adoration in her eyes.

He pushed aside the uneasy feeling he got when she talked about the way Hayes and Wyatt looked at Savannah.

Things like that weren't important. What mattered was that he and Jeremiah would protect her and provide for her and do their best to make sure she was happy. After living at the Circle T for a while, she'd understand that.

Hell, who was he trying to fool?

Maggie had already begun to soften him up, something he sure as hell couldn't afford once he got back to his ranch in Oklahoma. Knowing her, she wouldn't be happy until she had him and Jeremiah eating out of her hand.

Before long, they'd be spoiling her all over again, probably even more than they had in the past.

Well, no matter how much she got to him, he had a responsibility to keep her in line and keep her safe.

And he took his responsibilities very seriously.

Chapter Six

Maggie woke without opening her eyes, pausing mid-stretch as the warm, heavy band around her waist tightened and pulled her back several inches into an even warmer wall of muscle. The hand at her waist caressed her bare stomach, a sharp reminder that she lay naked between Eb and Jeremiah.

A memory of them coming to bed eased its way to the surface, along with their disgruntled groans when they found her wearing her warmest nightgown.

They'd quickly stripped her of it before nestling on either side of her again.

She'd still been mostly asleep when Jeremiah's lips circled a nipple before covering it with the blanket. "This is how you're supposed to sleep between us."

Eb's big hand at her waist slid up to cover her breast.

"Good mornin', darlin'." Eb's deep, gravelly voice in her ear made her shiver despite being warm and cozy between them. His hand moved lightly over her breast, his rough palm sending ribbons of tingling awareness through her as it slid back and forth over her nipple.

Stretching again, she arched her neck in invitation while pressing her bottom against the hard bulge that seemed to grow by the minute.

Realizing what she did, her eyes popped open, widening at the sight of Jeremiah's brown, muscular chest only inches away. Surprised to see that he held her hand even in sleep, she pulled it out of his grasp.

Jeremiah immediately opened his eyes and frowned like a little boy who'd had his favorite toy taken from him. He blinked twice, his eyes clearing before he smiled and lifted his hand to her other breast as he raised himself to his elbow and bent over her. "Damn, to think I get to wake up to this every morning for the rest of my life."

He ran his hand down her arm to her waist and beyond, sliding it over her hip to her thigh, pulling it toward him, his rough fingers tracing the tender flesh at the back of her knee before moving on again, sparking little showers of heat wherever he touched.

Eb lifted his head from the pillow and scraped his teeth over her shoulder. "How do you feel?" He slid a hand down her body and gently pressed a finger into her, pressing open-mouthed kisses over her shoulder and moving his finger just inside her. "You're always wet, darlin'. Are you sore?"

Finding it difficult to carry on a conversation while having a thick finger moving in and out of her pussy, Maggie moaned. "No, I told you I'm not."

Eb pushed his finger deep, at the same time touching his thumb to her clit. "Waiting to fuck you again is killing me, but as soon as I get my cock inside you, I just want to fuck you hard and deep, and I sure as hell don't want to worry about hurting you."

The deep morning huskiness in his voice increased the intimacy, delighting her. Smiling over her shoulder at him, she reached back to cup his jaw. "Then why do you keep touching me?" She turned slightly to her back to open her legs wider, rocking her hips in time to his strokes.

Jeremiah bent to uncover and kiss a nipple before lifting his head to smile down at her. "Because we like to touch you. We like to hear those sounds you make. We need to learn your body." His arrogant grin flashed. "We're also training you."

Maggie blinked, certain she'd misunderstood. "What did you say?"

Pinching the nipple he'd been licking, he laughed softly. "You heard me. We're training you. Your body's getting accustomed to pleasure, which makes you crave it. We're training your body to expect pleasure when we touch you, and it does. Look at you. You're not even fully awake yet, we've barely touched you, and already you're about to come."

Dumbfounded, Maggie could only stare at him, even as she grabbed on to his shoulders, the strokes to her clit making it nearly impossible to think. Kicking her legs and trying to shove Eb away got her nowhere at all. "Stop that. What do you mean *trained*? I'm not one of your horses. Oh!"

The scrape of Eb's teeth down her neck as he increased the strokes on her clit had her trembling on the edge of the release she now fought against.

Her breath came out in pants as she struggled to move his hand away, but her strength was no match for his.

Jeremiah traced her bottom lip with his finger. "No, not one of our horses. But taught to anticipate pleasure when we touch you, your body will expect it and automatically seek it whenever we get our hands on you. See how well it's already working?"

He applied pressure to her nipple, the sharp jolt of tingles to her pussy and clit making her clamp down on Eb's finger as the pressure inside her exploded.

Alarmed that they could do this to her without any apparent effort at all, Maggie cried out, her body tightening impossibly as the waves of ecstasy washed over her.

They made it last, their hands and mouths on her dragging out her orgasm until she thought she would die of it.

Her pussy tightened on Eb's finger, her heels digging in to the bed to lift into his touch.

Eb's strokes lightened enough to keep the jolts racing through her, making her body jerk in reaction, but not enough to release her from the erotic hold they had on her.

She could go on this way forever, this feeling so incredible she knew she'd never get enough of it.

Jeremiah released her nipple, bending to kiss it before leaning over her again. "A man's job is to provide whatever his woman needs. In all things. Safety. Discipline. Pleasure."

Maggie still trembled as Eb's strokes slowed, finally stopping altogether. She squeezed her eyes closed and held her breath, concentrating on not clenching on the finger he still held inside her. She moaned at his slow withdrawal and took several deep breaths before opening her eyes, inwardly wincing at their smug grins.

The desire to wipe those looks off their faces had her snapping at both of them.

"Is this the way you treated the women you fucked before?" Frustrated that she didn't see her dressing gown, she crawled to the foot of the bed and stood, yanking the quilt to wrap around her. She froze, gulping when she got a good look at what she'd revealed.

Neither Eb nor Jeremiah seemed the least bit disconcerted to be naked in her presence.

Eb jumped up and practically leapt for her, his eyes full of fire. Grabbing her by the shoulders, he shook her twice before lifting her to her toes. "I never want to hear language like that coming out of your mouth again. And what I've done with other women is none of your damned business."

Jeremiah stood slowly, moved in on her other side, and wrapped a hand around her hair. Pulling her head back, he leaned over her until their noses practically touched, his eyes glittering with gold and fierce as they held hers.

"We treat you just fine. Haven't we taken care of you since we came back? Didn't we marry you? Aren't we going around with our cocks so hard it hurts while we wait for you to heal?"

Maggie tightened her grip on the quilt, feeling small and defenseless in the face of such raw masculinity. Instead of being as scared as she probably should have been, she reveled in her femininity.

Remembering the almost effortless way they'd dealt with Fred, she knew their strength and bravado would be used to protect her and keep her safe.

It warmed her, gave her a sense of security and safety, and with that, a sense of freedom, despite their determination to rule her.

Eb set her back on her feet and turned away, running a hand through his hair. Standing at the window with his hands on his hips, he stared outside. "Damn it, Maggie. We're just trying to do right by you. I know this is all strange to you, and it's gonna be a big adjustment, but we'll help you, honey."

Maggie couldn't tear her eyes away from the muscular perfection of his body, a body made strong through years of hard work.

And a strength of will to match, one forged in the same fire.

With sudden insight, it all made sense—everything except the frustration she saw on Eb's face now.

Unless…

Was he starting to see her as a woman? Was he starting to care for her the way a man cares for a woman, not as an undisciplined child?

The vulnerability in his eyes filled her with a power that made her giddy, while the sight of their two hard, naked bodies, their cocks rising toward their stomachs, filled her with longing.

No matter how hard she tried to keep her eyes from the large cocks rising up from between their heavily muscled thighs, she just couldn't do it, finding it difficult to believe that anything that size fit inside her.

Their cocks looked so menacing, so hard and threatening, she wouldn't have believed she could have gotten so much pleasure from them.

"If you keep staring at me that way, I'm gonna take you again, newly opened or not."

Maggie took another step back, her eyes darting to Eb's as a shiver went through her at the threat in his low tone. The arrogance in his darkening eyes carried an indulgence that hadn't been there before.

Deciding that the only way to show them that she was more than woman enough for both of them, she hid her insecurities and lifted her chin, giving them her most scathing look. "Is that how you tell a woman you want her? You're both crude and vulgar."

Jeremiah laughed and turned to his brother. "I wonder which of us is crude and which is vulgar."

She couldn't look away from their bodies, and the knowledge of what it did to her shone in their eyes. She also couldn't help but notice the way both of them kept looking at her bare leg.

Filled with feminine power, Maggie loosened her hold on the quilt covering her.

Jeremiah's eyes flared when the quilt slipped momentarily, revealing her right breast.

Maggie fumbled with the quilt as though clumsy, taking her time to pull it back into place again.

Jeremiah stared at her nipple, his tongue coming out to lick his bottom lip, not meeting her eyes until she'd covered it again. Holding her gaze, he slid a hand down to his cock and began to slowly stroke it.

Maggie hid a smile. Her husband played dirty.

Stroking his cock with long, smooth strokes, Jeremiah held her eyes with his. "Honey, crude or not, we've barely begun. We're gonna have your body so trained for pleasure that as soon as we touch you, your pussy'll be soaking wet, and you'll be begging us to take you."

Mesmerized by the sight of his hand moving up and down his thick length and a little shocked at the way he ran his thumb over the head of his cock on each stroke, her stomach tightened, the low heaviness in her abdomen growing. She'd just had an orgasm, but the sight before her made her hot and quivery inside, and she involuntarily took a step toward him.

Eb came toward her, catching her easily when she tripped on the quilt. His fingers circled her upper arms and tightened, his eyes searching hers warily. "We *are* crude, Maggie. Life's a lot different in the wide open spaces in Oklahoma than it is in the crowded city. Especially on our place. It's survival of the fittest, darlin', and Jeremiah and I are both survivors."

Jeremiah sat on the bed and propped a pillow against the headboard before settling back and resuming his stroking. "We've been gentle with you, so you've got no call to complain."

The outer curve of her breasts warmed against Eb's hand. "Gentle? You spanked me." Running her fingers down her neck, she let them settle at the upper curve of her breast, hiding a smile when they both followed her movement.

Eb growled, ripping the quilt from her and tossing it aside. "We fucked you, something we're gonna be doing quite a bit once we get you back home. Now get ready. You're getting more belligerent every day, and we need to get back to the ranch. We're leaving today." Raising a brow, he ran a hand down her body, parting her folds and sliding a finger inside her. His eyes sharpened when she sucked in a breath. "You're ready, Maggie, in more ways than one. Keep fighting us, honey, and I'll show you how crude I can be."

Maggie couldn't hold back her moan as he moved his thick finger inside her. Her knees gave out, giving her no choice but to grab his shoulders for support, her breath quickening when he touched his thumb to her clit and began stroking.

His arm went around her to hold her steady. "That's it, honey. You're more than ready, aren't you?"

Dazed, Maggie stared up at him. "What have you done to me?" She seemed to have no willpower at all when either one of them touched her, something she'd have to remedy.

His smile, half devilish and half indulgent amusement, took her breath away. "Just proving to you just how crude we are. Don't try to deny you like it, darlin', especially when your juices are soaking my hand."

Fighting for the control she'd somehow lost, she tried to back away, but Eb merely tightened his arm around her waist and pressed his thumb to her clit, once again rendering her defenseless. Her body screamed for the release that they'd given her just moments ago, knowing she wouldn't be satisfied until they appeased this incredible hunger.

Jeremiah crawled to the foot of the bed and reached out to palm a breast. "When we get you home, we're gonna eat you alive, darlin'."

Eb kissed her shoulder and began to stroke her clit a little faster. "Yeah, I've got a hunger to do things to our Maggie that I never thought I'd do outside a whorehouse. First, we're gonna have to get her used to us seeing and touching her. That's a girl. Come for us again."

Grateful for Eb's strength, she dropped her head onto his chest, digging her short nails into his shoulders and giving herself over to them.

Did she have a choice? Did she want one?

The places they stroked burned and sizzled, creating a wild storm inside her that sent her hurling out of control. Something snapped, buckling her legs, and she cried out against Eb's chest, involuntarily pushing her breast more firmly against Jeremiah's palm. Her scream got muffled against Eb's hot skin, her frantic whimpers sounding desperate in the otherwise quiet room.

Jeremiah leaned close to kiss her jaw, running his thumb over her nipple and sending more ripples through her. "You're a wild little thing, aren't you, Maggie?"

His chuckle brought her to her senses.

With the hot pleasure still racing through her veins, she pushed out of Eb's arms, thankful that he released her. She stumbled and grabbed the wall to support herself. Having had the upper hand, even temporarily, gave her confidence and made her eager to experience it again. Locking her knees, she tossed back her hair.

"And yet you seem able to resist me."

Eb yanked her back against him and ran one hand down her back to settle on her bottom while the other covered a breast. "Oh, I want you, darlin'. Make no mistake about that. Once we get you home, you're gonna be loved and loved often. But the next time I take you, it's going to be in the bed Jeremiah and I made for you. Now get dressed. We've got to make sure everything's loaded in the buckboard."

As soon as he stepped away, Maggie bent to retrieve the quilt and wrapped it around her nakedness, unsurprised to see that her hand shook. She stared at both of them in disbelief.

"We can't go today!"

Jeremiah winced as he tucked his cock into his pants. "Of course we can. Once we get you back home, you'll stop bucking us at every opportunity." Finally managing to get his pants fastened, he took a step and grimaced. "If this ain't fucking uncomfortable."

"Too bad. Let's get a move on." Eb finished dressing and paused to look around the room. "We'll meet you at the house. Esmeralda's probably got a big meal waiting for us."

"She knows?" Maggie couldn't believe Esmeralda had kept it from her.

Jeremiah wrapped his arm around her waist from behind and pulled her back against his chest, running a hand down her back to her bottom. "She probably does now. I'm sure Dad told her this morning. She didn't keep a secret from you, Maggie."

Involuntarily tightening her buttocks, Maggie glared over her shoulder at him. "Like you did?" She yelped when he slapped her bottom.

His hand stayed there, holding the heat in. "It's for your own good, Maggie. Every day you're getting just a little more belligerent. We're gonna put an end to that before it gets out of hand."

Eb looked on, watching with hooded eyes. "You'll see that we're right. Get ready to go. We've got a few more things to take care of before we leave."

Maggie's stomach fluttered as she watched them go, a little surprised that both men paused to kiss her lightly on the forehead on their way out of the bedroom. They seemed more like the men who'd met her at the train station than the ones she'd woken up with only a short time ago, donning that cloak of ruthlessness and danger that surrounded them as easily as they donned their clothes.

Maggie watched them, unable to look away from the sight of their loose-limbed strides as they crossed the yard. She'd dreamed about them for years, never having a clue what intimacy with them would involve.

Now that she did, she was greedy for more of it.

She'd seen the looks on their faces and thought she understood just how hard it had been for them to walk away from her. If they felt anything like she had after her spanking, it explained their terrible moods.

A slow smile spread across her face as she realized that whenever they punished her, they would also be punishing themselves.

She'd seen their eyes when she'd bared a breast. What if she *accidentally* did something like that again?

She could use that against them. She'd just have to learn what else she could do to get to them.

Humming a tune, she crossed the room to get dressed. It seemed she'd finally found a way to get even with them.

* * * *

After a long day of travelling, Maggie stepped down onto the platform, amazed to find herself in Tulsa, Oklahoma. Grateful for Eb and Jeremiah's big bodies surrounding hers and their firm hold on her arms as they led her through the crowd, she struggled to keep up. Curious and intent on seeing everything, she whipped her head from side to side and probably would have tripped several times if they hadn't been holding on to her.

Despite her exhaustion after the long trip, her mind remained amazingly alert. Chills from nerves racked her body, which made her even clumsier. Straightening her spine, she forced herself to pay attention to her steps, determined not to fall and make a fool of herself, and raised her voice to be heard over all the noise.

"I thought you said there weren't that many people here."

Jeremiah pulled her closer to his side as they worked their way through the crowd, rubbing her shoulder as if aware of her trembling. "Tulsa's crowded. It's much better at the ranch."

"Don't you mean in Desire?"

Eb chuckled. "I can't wait to see what the men think about that."

As in Kansas City, the crowd moved aside to let them through. Even though they slowed their long-legged strides for her, she still had trouble keeping up with them.

Instead of being tired from the long trip, coming home seemed to energize them.

For Maggie, though, every step was a struggle, as though she walked through molasses.

Jeremiah caught her when she faltered. "Come on, honey. Let's get you to the hotel. You're done in."

"Hotel? I thought we were going to your ranch."

He didn't answer, the noise around them making it nearly impossible to have a conversation anyway.

Both men continued across the platform and down the steps to where several men gathered, straightening at their approach. To Maggie's horror, a very fierce-looking Indian came forward and headed straight toward them. Every smooth stride brought him closer, danger in every line of his body. Dressed as the other men, he wore a holster but also had a knife attached to his belt.

Scared now, Maggie tugged at Eb. "Oh, my God. Look, he's coming this way."

Jeremiah frowned down to where her hand fisted in Eb's jacket.

"It's all right, Maggie. He's one of ours."

As he gathered her against him, she released Eb, staring in fear at the Indian, her breath catching when he stopped directly in front of Eb and thrust out his hand. To her further amazement, when he spoke, he spoke in perfect English.

"Welcome home. Had enough of city life yet?" The grin that split his face stole Maggie's breath.

Eb grimaced, shaking his head. "I don't know how I lived there all those years. Maggie, this is Phoenix, one of our foremen. Phoenix, this is Maggie Tyler, our wife."

The other man didn't look even the least bit surprised at Eb's statement. When he took her hand in his and spoke, she understood why.

"It's about time I finally get to meet you. I understand the entire reason the Circle T was built is because of you."

He released her hand almost immediately, his smile disappearing when he turned back to Eb. "The buckboards are ready, and we'll watch them in shifts overnight. We'll have to wait to buy supplies from here until we see how much room we have left."

Jeremiah introduced her to the other men who came forward, each man just as hard and rugged looking as her husbands.

Feeling as though she'd somehow stepped into another world, Maggie moved closer to Eb.

Eb ran a hand over her hair, his smile distracted. "Jeremiah, why don't you go get Maggie settled while we start unloading?"

Jeremiah took her arm and pulled her firmly against his side. "I'll be back in a bit."

Away from the train station, the crowd thinned out, and for the first time since she got off the train, Maggie felt like she could breathe.

Looking around, she tried to take it all in. "I didn't know we'd be staying at a hotel. I thought we were going straight to your ranch."

Jeremiah led her down a street that still bustled with people at this late hour, most carrying bags as though they'd just come off the train, too.

Turning to look over her shoulder for a glimpse of Eb, she frowned when she didn't see him. Glancing up at Jeremiah, she reached out to touch his arm.

"Are they really going to unload all of that stuff you bought tonight?"

Jeremiah nodded once. "Have to. The train's got a schedule to keep, honey. We've got to get all of it off as fast as we can. That's why there're so many men. They'll also have to guard it all night so nobody steals it."

"Oh."

Feeling like an idiot for not thinking of that, Maggie walked alongside Jeremiah, grateful to see the sign for the hotel. Practically asleep on her feet, she leaned heavily against him as they stopped at the desk inside the hotel lobby.

"Well, if it ain't Jeremiah Tyler! It's been way too long since you've been in town."

The tall, heavily made-up woman behind the counter fluffed her dark hair and smiled flirtatiously at Jeremiah. Her barely covered full breasts almost spilled from her dress when she leaned over the tall desk and eyed Jeremiah like a treat she hungered for.

Straightening, Maggie wrapped her hand around Jeremiah's arm and lifted her chin, making sure the other woman got a good look at her wedding rings. Raising her brow, she snuggled against his side, fighting to hide her jealousy.

"Do you know that woman, Jeremiah?"

The other woman's smile broadened. "Jeremiah knows me intimately, don't you, honey? Where's that handsome brother of yours, and who's this little thing, your baby sister?"

His sharp glare at the woman had the smile falling, and she began to fidget with her hair. Before he could speak, Maggie leaned over from the other side of the desk.

"I'm Maggie Tyler, and I might be small, but I can shoot. Think about that before you make a play for my husband."

The other woman blanched. "Husband? Tyler? You're Jeremiah's wife?" Her eyes hardened and a calculated smile curved her lips as she ran her fingers over her décolleté as if to draw attention to her ample charms. "Well, perhaps now Eb'll be interested in my company. He's probably not as much fun as Jeremiah, but there's something about that dark broodiness that just makes a woman's heart flutter."

Maggie met the other woman's look squarely, while inwardly her confidence melted away. Knowing her husbands, how could she ever hope to compete with this woman's raw sexuality?

Tapping her finger where the two rings they'd placed there shone, she grinned. "He's mine, too."

Feeling plain and out of her element, Maggie kept her gaze on the other woman, too afraid of what she would see if she looked at Jeremiah.

The other woman's eyes went wide, her confident smile giving way to a look of astonishment. "You're married to both of them?"

Smiling smugly, Maggie straightened. "I am, so you might want to look elsewhere for your entertainment from now on." Irritated by her jealous insecurity, which Jeremiah would no doubt see as immaturity, her tone came out sharper than she'd meant it to.

Shooting a scathing look at Jeremiah, she turned away, still not looking at him when he joined her to cross the lobby.

As they started up the stairs, Maggie raised her chin again, trying to show bravado she didn't feel.

"If you or Eb even look at another woman, I'm going home." She turned away again, aware that the woman at the desk watched them.

Jeremiah jerked her arm, spinning her, and pinned her to the wall. The smug satisfaction in his grin made her want to smack him. "Why should we look at another woman when we've already got you, darlin'? You're already being trained for us, remember?"

Instead of rising to the bait as he obviously expected her to, she raised a brow, not about to let him intimidate her. "Careful, cowboy, that you're not the one being trained."

His grin widened. "You volunteering to train me, darlin'? Hell, that could be a lot of fun."

Maggie smiled secretly and looked around the lobby.

"There sure are a lot of men around here, aren't there? Are all the men at the Circle T, excuse me, in *Desire*, as rugged looking as the ones that met us at the train station?"

Jeremiah's smile fell, his lips thinning in anger. Gripping her arm, he hustled her the rest of the way up the stairs and down the hall to their room. He unlocked the door and ushered her inside none too gently, pushing her back against the wall and holding her there by pressing his body against hers.

With the only light coming from the hallway, it created a more intimate atmosphere, turning his threatening gesture into something entirely different, especially when his cock jumped against her belly.

Grabbing her hands, he held them on either side of her head, his eyes narrowed as he pressed the hard bulge against her belly. His voice deepened and softened, the soft growl in it oozing as much sex as it did anger.

"You even look at one of those men wrong, Margaret Tyler, and I'll tan your backside good. You're a married woman now."

Arching her back, Maggie pushed her breasts against him, thrilling at the flare of gold in his hooded gaze. "And you and Eb are married men. The first place we walk into, a woman practically throws herself at you. And you liked it. Do you expect me to share you the way you and Eb share me?"

She tilted her head back to brush her lips over his jaw, deciding to make use of the womanly charms she'd recently discovered. "Maybe you don't want me as much as you want that other woman. Maybe you're thinking about sharing me with someone else."

She hid a smile at his sharp intake of breath, the rush of feminine power making her dizzy. Intoxicated, she rubbed against him again, sucking in a breath when he pressed his cock against her.

Interlacing their fingers, he lowered their hands between them, the anger in the eyes holding hers adding a dark edge to the sexual tension. Brushing the back of her hands over her nipples, he rocked his narrow hips, thrusting his cock against her.

"No one but Eb and me will ever have you. I'll kill any man who tries. Clear enough for you, darlin'?"

Thrilled with his show of jealousy, Maggie looked up at him through her lashes. "So you won't be seeing any other women?"

He picked her up and carried her to the bed, tossing her into the center. "I'm married to you, Maggie." Leaning over her, he ran a hand possessively down the center of her body, pressing against her abdomen before straightening. "Isn't that what you told Dolly downstairs?"

Watching him light a lamp before kicking the door closed, Maggie sat up and gave him a scathing look. "Dolly? So I guess you and Dolly have been *friends* for a long time?"

Jeremiah turned up the wick on the lamp and turned, crossing his arms over his chest to glare back at her. "Dolly's a thing of the past and none of your business."

Maggie shrugged and scooted to the side of the bed to remove her boots. "So anything that happened before we got married doesn't matter?"

He reached the bed in two strides, tossed the hem of her dress up, and started tugging off her boots. "I don't know where you're going with this, but everything about you is our business. Now stop arguing and get into bed. You're too tired to fight with me tonight."

Now that she sat on the bed and her boots had come off, the fatigue had really started to set in. The events of the last few days, the emotional good-byes to Mr. Tyler and Esmeralda, and the long train ride all seemed to come together at once.

"I'm not arguing. You are." Not willing to give up yet and still jealous about the woman downstairs, she decided to stoke the flames of his temper. "At least Eb didn't sample her charms. Some men don't have to have every woman around."

After tossing her boots aside, he removed her stockings and impatiently knocked her hands away as she struggled to unbutton her dress to do it himself.

"You want to argue because you saw that woman look at me. I'm your damned husband every bit as much as Eb."

Lifting her to her feet, he efficiently stripped her out of her dress and tossed it onto a nearby chair, leaving her in just her chemise. Running his hands down her sides, he pulled her close and kissed her hard. "I don't know what you're getting so riled up about. You're the one who's gonna benefit from my experience with other women."

He moved ahead of her to pull back the covers, his jaw tight with suppressed anger. "Get in bed before you fall over."

Hiding a smile, she crawled tiredly into the big bed and closed her eyes. She could actually feel his frustration as he slid her to the center of the bed and tucked the covers all around her.

Jeremiah muttered the entire time he adjusted her to his liking and tucked her in. "One woman looks at me and you're talking about the men who came to meet us at the train station and asking questions about us sharing you with someone else. I'll tell you right now, Margaret Mary, you even think about making eyes at one of them, you're gonna get him run off or killed and find yourself in a heap of trouble."

Making herself comfortable under the covers, Maggie turned her face into the pillow to hide a smile.

"You're not jealous, are you, Jeremiah?"

The silence dragged on, but her eyelids were too heavy for her to open them and see his expression. His hand slid beneath the covers and felt warm and comforting as it moved over her back, a sharp contrast to his words. "You invite another man's attention and you'll get a spanking you won't ever forget."

He patted her bottom and bent to kiss her hair. "Go to sleep. We'll be back in a bit."

Too tired to do more than hum her agreement, Maggie listened to the door open and close again.

She wouldn't dare mix anyone else up in her plan to get even with Eb and Jeremiah, but if she could use their jealousy for each other, she just might be able to do a little *training* of her own.

With a smile on her face, she slipped into sleep.

* * * *

Exhilarated by the scenery, Maggie rode between Eb and Jeremiah and, with six other men, they made their way to her new home.

The men took turns driving the buckboard to give each other a break from riding on the hard seats. They'd ridden since morning, but none of them seemed to want to stop for longer than it took to rest and water the horses before they were on their way again.

They didn't even start a fire for coffee, instead just eating as they rode and drinking water from their canteens. Every single one of them seemed impatient to get home.

Although the other men didn't speak to her often, they were very solicitous toward her. Instead of asking her if she was all right or tired or hungry, they asked Eb or Jeremiah, who always stayed on either side of her.

The ranch hands answered her questions without hesitation and glanced at her often in concern as though checking to see if she was tired, but none of them looked at her in an impolite manner or seemed the least bit forward. Because of it, she relaxed and started asking questions about her new home.

"Are there really no other neighbors around?"

Eb grimaced. "Not yet, but something tells me there will be soon."

Phoenix's hooded gaze made him look even more threatening. "What do you mean?"

Eb sighed. "While I was in Kansas City, I talked to a couple of lawmen who have both taken a liking to my wife's best friend. They're trying to protect her from her uncle and want to marry her and bring her here to live."

He looked meaningfully at each of his men. "I told them they could come and that no one would give them any trouble. Anyone who doesn't like the way we live can leave anytime."

The man who'd introduced himself as Hart Sanderson and who drove the buckboard closest to them nodded thoughtfully. "Goes without sayin'. Does that mean we can get some law here to deal with those cattle rustlers? Even with those outriders you hired, it's a lot of land to cover."

Jeremiah nodded. "Yeah, they're gonna uphold the law." He glanced at Maggie. "There're also gonna be some laws regarding the women that we'll talk to you about later. We've advertised for mail-order brides, and every man's gonna have to do his part to protect the women. Once they're claimed, their husbands will be their closest protectors, but with some of us out on the range for days at a time, it'll be up to everyone to help protect all of them."

Phoenix didn't look too happy but nodded anyway. "Makes sense. As long as we're not required to claim any of 'em."

Hart shook his head. "Before you know it, there'll be a town here."

Eb grinned. "It's called Desire, and we've got to get a sign put up so Hayes and Wyatt can find it."

Phoenix blinked. "Desire? Where'd you come up with a name like that? You should have named it something with a little grit."

Jeremiah shook his head. "Never mind. That's the name of the town. We talked to a blacksmith who wants to get out of Kansas City and another man who was a Union soldier and dealt with supply lines. He's thinking about coming along to open a general store."

Hart's lips twitched. "You sure were busy in Kansas City. You going back there soon?"

Eb's look at Maggie made her insides flutter. "No plans to. I brought back what I wanted."

Embarrassed and inordinately pleased, Maggie smiled. "When's Savannah coming? It'll be great to have her here."

Shrugging, Eb looked away. "That's up to her men. Look, see that stream up ahead?"

At her nod, he straightened in the saddle and smiled, pride in every line of his body. "That's the border to the Circle T. Welcome home, Maggie."

Chapter Seven

Riding over the last hill, Maggie gasped and came to a stop between Eb and Jeremiah, almost afraid that she was dreaming.

Sitting on the next rising was an almost exact replica of their father's house back in Kansas City.

For some reason she didn't entirely understand, her eyes welled with tears that she hurriedly blinked away. She looked at Eb to find him watching her, his expression unreadable. Her throat had become so clogged with tears she had to swallow before speaking. "It looks like the big house."

Every one of the men brought his horse and the buckboards to a halt behind them, no one saying a word except Hart, who'd stopped on the other side of Eb.

"The *big* house?"

Eb nodded, not taking his eyes from hers. "That's what everyone calls the house at the Shenandoah. We built it for you, Maggie, so you wouldn't feel so homesick."

A sob escaped, and then another. Sensing Jeremiah's gaze, she turned toward him, blinking back tears.

"I can't believe you did that."

Despite the fact that the others looked on, Jeremiah moved closer and touched her thigh. "The furniture's as close as we could get it. Not every room has furniture yet, but we'll order some more for you as soon as you pick it out." Snapping the reins, he grinned. "Come on, let's go home."

She couldn't take her eyes from the house as they approached, the feeling of coming home forcing her to choke back even more sobs.

She could already picture sitting with them on the wide front porch and knew where she would plant the cuttings Esmeralda had sent with her.

Once they got near, the other men started around the house, looking away as Eb and Jeremiah paused with her at the bottom of the big front porch.

Eb slid from his horse and came around to lift her from hers, carrying her to the front door. "Take some time to look around while we unpack the supplies."

Jeremiah came up behind them and opened the door, running his hand over her hip as Eb carried her inside.

"We'll be in to get you as soon as we finish. Duke'll have supper ready soon, and I'm sure the men are all anxious to meet you."

Nodding as Eb set her on her feet, she let go of his shoulder, her gaze moving around the room, unable to take everything in fast enough. She took in the high ceilings and massive fireplace in the front room and immediately pictured sitting on the cowhide sofa on a cold winter night, warm from the fire and the arms of her two husbands. This is what she would have expected from the Eb and Jeremiah of the past. A sense of relief washed over her, and she turned to smile at both of them. "I can't believe you did this."

Eb patted her bottom and winked. "You can show your gratitude later. We'll be back in a bit."

Jeremiah stood watching her thoughtfully until Eb left, his tread light down the steps of the front porch. With a calculated gleam in his eyes, he approached her, looking more like a gunfighter than a cattle baron.

He whipped out a hand and yanked her back against him. "Hello, wife."

The thrill of being held so close to him, the firm muscles of the chest and legs pressed against hers, gave her that small, defenseless feeling again, one that excited her more each time she experienced it.

Now that she'd also had a taste of the power of being a woman and matching it against such masculine strength, she couldn't resist using it again.

Running a hand down his chest, she delighted in the feel of his warmth and strength as the muscles trembled beneath her caress. Looking up at him through her lashes, she rubbed her belly against the hard bulge pressing at her. She licked her lips, hiding a smile when his eyes flared. While he stared at her lips, she took advantage of his attention and gave him her best pout.

Standing on her toes, she brushed her lips over his jaw, her eyes closing as she breathed in the masculine scent of him. "Thank you for my house."

Jeremiah bent his head, forcing her head back and staring into her eyes, a half-smile playing at his lips. "You're very welcome."

His eyes darkened and became hooded as he lowered his head and covered the hand she flattened on his chest with his.

"Do you realize this is the first time you've ever touched me?"

Maggie blinked in surprise and gave him a slow smile and moved her hand over his chest again, thrilled that the muscles bunched and tightened under her hand. Staring at his lips, she licked hers again. "We've been intimate. Of course I touched you."

Jeremiah shook his head and released her hand to open his shirt, giving her a fantastic view of his very inviting chest. "We had sex, yeah, but you never reached out to touch me when you're awake. Only when you're sleeping. Men like to be touched, too."

Intrigued and more than a little nervous, Maggie allowed him to take her hand in his again and bring it to his chest, sliding it inside his shirt before releasing it. Marveling at the smooth heat beneath her palm, Maggie slid her hand over the hard muscle, her eyes shooting to his when he sucked in a breath.

Keeping his eyes on hers, Jeremiah smiled, making her heart beat even faster. "It feels real good when you touch me. Do it again." He opened his shirt the rest of the way, his movements hurried and stiffer than normal.

Delighting in the differences in their bodies, she lifted her other hand, using both to explore the magnificent sight before her. When she touched her finger to a male nipple, marveling at its texture, he jolted and hissed.

Intrigued, she did it again, her pussy clenching when he moaned.

"Does that feel the same to you as it does to me?"

The clearly defined muscles she caressed quivered as Jeremiah slid his hands to her hips. Yearning for his hands on her bare skin, she smiled and arched against him.

With a groan, he lifted her and carried her to the sofa she'd just been fantasizing about, positioning her to straddle him, settling her with her slit positioned right over where his cock bulged against his pants. "I don't know what it feels like to you, but I like it." Sliding his hands higher, he brushed his thumbs over her nipples poking at the front of her shirt.

Fisting her hands on his chest, she moaned and shifted on his lap, gasping when her clit made contact with the fabric of his pants.

Jeremiah groaned and used his hands on her hips to move her over his cock again. "Keep touching me." Sliding his hands up, he opened her shirt to expose her chemise, his eyes mere slits as they settled on her breasts.

Knowing he could see her nipples clearly through the thin material made them tingle with anticipation. She wanted him to see her, touch her everywhere.

She wanted to make him forget every other woman he'd ever touched.

With her hands braced on his chest, she arched her back, wordlessly offering herself to him.

Jeremiah accepted her offer, reaching out to cup her breasts and run his thumbs lightly over her nipples. His hooded eyes flared when she moaned. "I can't wait to have your hands on my cock."

Remembering when he'd placed her hand on him before, only to pull it away again, she nodded, wanting desperately to know how to bring him pleasure. "Yes, let me touch you there. Show me how to please you."

He sat up, supporting her weight with an arm across her back, and bent over her. "You're going to please me, all right. Lift your chemise out of the way and show me those nipples."

Trembling at his erotic command, she dug her fingers into his shoulders and moved against him, looking toward the large front window. "Somebody could see. Oh!"

Shuddering as a large hand moved to her throat and began its journey to the valley between her breasts, she threw her head back, knowing he would keep her from falling.

"I'll kill any man who sees you this way." He grabbed the front of her chemise and ripped it down the center, burying his face between her breasts.

The violence of his action startled her, but sent her arousal soaring. Her own needs were far from civilized, and the fact that he appeared to hunger for her the same way staggered her. Maggie slid her fingers into his hair, gripping handfuls of it and sucking in a breath when his lips closed over a nipple.

"I love these pretty little nipples, the most beautiful I ever saw."

Tugging his hair, she growled at him, feeling more primitive and earthy by the minute. "I don't want to hear about all those other women you took in the barn."

"You knew about—hell." Jeremiah scraped his teeth over a nipple in retaliation. "None of 'em was anything to me. They just made me appreciate you more." He took her nipple into his mouth and sucked hard, releasing it with a chuckle when she cried out and squirmed on his lap. "Besides, what good would I be to you if I didn't know what I was doing?"

Her clit swelled, becoming so sensitive that it burned. She leaned forward, touching her forehead to his, struggling to catch her breath when his hands slid under her skirt and up her thighs to her hips. "You'd better never do this with any other women ever again."

Running his hands in circles over her hips and buttocks, he nuzzled her jaw. "Just you, darlin'. There's nobody else."

Her stomach muscles tightened as he worked his way down to her breasts again, kissing each of her nipples and sending sharp ribbons of pleasure to her clit. A rush of moisture from her pussy dampened her thighs, and she couldn't help but rock her hips, pressing her slit against him. The feel of her naked pussy against the rough fabric of his pants made her gasp, the naughty decadence in it sending her arousal soaring.

Jeremiah sat back against the sofa, pulling her with him, his mouth hovering over hers. "Darlin', you're irresistible. You would tempt a saint." Squeezing the cheeks of her bottom, he grinned and teased her bottom hole. "In case you haven't noticed, darlin', I'm not a saint."

His mouth covered hers, forcing her lips open and sliding his tongue past them to tangle with her own in an erotic dance that made her head swim.

The incredibly erotic sounds of their gasps for air and low moans as they feasted on each other heightened the sexual tension, and before long, they both began ripping at each other's clothing. Pushing his shirt completely out of her way, she rubbed her breasts against his naked chest, wishing she could rub her slit against his nakedness instead of the coarse material of his pants.

His hands went to her bottom again and pulled her closer, moving her body against his with a groan. Without breaking off his kiss, he turned them both, lowering her to the rug and yanking her skirt up around her waist.

Having her pussy exposed made her even more desperate to have him touch her there, her folds tingling with anticipation. Maggie moaned and reached out for him, her eyes popping open in surprise when he took her hands in his and raised them over her head.

The effect it had on her shocked her to her core.

It lifted her breasts, leaving them vulnerable to him. The knowledge that she couldn't cover herself or stop him from doing what he wanted to do to her tender nipples sent a ripple of alarm through her, and she instinctively fought his hold.

"Easy, darlin'." The slash of his dimples and the wild hunger in his eyes made her heart race and eased some of her fear. He nudged her inner thighs with his knees, spreading them wider and eyeing her upraised breasts. "Now if this ain't a pretty sight. All pink and full and mine to enjoy."

Maggie shivered, her breath quickening when, still holding both of her hands in one of his, he began to explore her body with the other hand. Her eyes fluttered closed against the building need as his warm hand moved over her breasts. He pinched each of her nipples, teasing them until she whimpered at the sharp jolts to her clit. She drew in a sharp breath as he continued to her stomach, holding it, her muscles quivering. Knowing that he would move his hand lower, she found herself frozen as the seconds ticked by, seconds filled with tense anticipation.

A brush of his fingers over the slickness at her slit made her jolt, crying out at both his touch and in frustration when he moved his hand away. She tried to close her legs, but Jeremiah's thighs between them prevented it, holding hers wide, increasing the helpless feeling...and her arousal. Rocking her hips, she fought to get her hands free, cursing him.

Her pussy clenched with remembered pleasure. She already knew what it felt like when he entered her, what it felt like when his fingers teased her clit. And she wanted to feel it again *now*.

"Jeremiah, I can't wait, damn you. Do something, or leave me alone."

He laughed softly, the seductive sound vibrating through her. "You might as well stop struggling, honey. Now that I got you, I'm not about to let you go. I like you open this way. I get to play, and there's nothing you can do to stop me. Hmm, you like that, too. You like when I have my way with you."

He leaned over her, his overlong hair falling forward to partially shadow his face, the silky strands teasing her nipple. Watching her face while he slid a finger inside her, he smiled, a flash of white that made her heart beat faster. "Nice and wet. I'm a lucky man. I've got a wife who's got a body made for lovin', who likes everything I do to her, and who's got a heart as big as Oklahoma."

Maggie shook her head from side to side, arching her body and wrapping her legs around his thighs. "Jeremiah! Let go of my hands so I can touch you." Her inner muscles clamped down on the finger that slid deep, her breath coming in shuddering gulps when he slowly withdrew. She gasped when he curled it and pressed against something so incredibly sensitive it had her crying out in need.

He released her hands, slowly running his fingers over her arm as he made his way to her shoulder. "I'd love to have your hands on my cock, darlin', but not this time. I swear we'll get to it, but every time I touch you I go up in flames. Your little pussy's so soft and warm, and it's holding on to my finger, trying to pull me in. I'm ready to come just thinking about how tight and hot it's going to feel on my cock."

She thrashed as he teased that wonderful spot inside her, lifting her hips to hurry his strokes. "Jeremiah, I don't know what to do."

She only knew that she wanted more of it. That wonderful rush of sensation lured her, teasing her with those tingles that she knew would get stronger. Nothing in her experience had ever felt so incredible, and she still found it hard to believe that a body could experience such a wonderful sensation.

She knew instinctively that no other man could make her feel what Eb and Jeremiah could make her feel, and it scared her just a little to think she could have lived her entire life without ever knowing what she missed.

The intimacy in his silky tone flowed over her, filling her with an inner warmth. "You're doin' just fine, honey. Just feel, and let me take care of everything." Even the brush of his open shirt against her skin felt like a caress. The rough material of his pants on her inner thighs inflamed her and reminded her that he remained almost fully clothed while she lay there with every private part of her body exposed and on display for him.

She had no idea why that excited her even more, but it did. Her breath caught in her throat, making it difficult to draw enough air into her lungs. She gasped when his knuckles touched her inner thigh, his feather-light strokes sending streams of tingling warmth to gather at her clit and make her pussy clench with the need for his possession.

Bracing his weight on an elbow, he reached down to undo his pants, his eyes dark and wild as they narrowed on her face. "Damn, the list of things I want to do to you just keeps growing." His gaze swept over her body as he positioned himself at her entrance. "Starting with fucking this tight pussy."

Maggie reached for him, crying out when he thrust deep, the overwhelming sensation of being possessed never failing to startle her. She shoved his shirt from his shoulders, hungry to touch his bare skin.

His cock impaled her, the thick heat of it once again making her feel small and fragile against his strength. He slid a hand under her bottom, lifting her, and to her amazement, his cock slid even deeper inside her.

The difference in the way he took her now surprised her. She didn't realize that sex could vary from one time to the next. It was as though he'd loosened the reins on his hunger, driving into her with a purpose and desperation that brought her own baser needs to the surface.

She responded to it in a way that shocked her, clawing at him as she fought to get even closer.

It seemed her body knew what to do even if she didn't, knew what it wanted and made demands on Jeremiah, feminine, primitive demands that she didn't fully understand.

She dug her nails into his shoulders as he thrust into her, wrapping her legs around him to lift herself into his strokes and crying out each time he dug at that magical place inside her.

He seemed to welcome those demands, meeting them with a forceful determination that left her breathless, her own hungers seeming to feed his.

His thighs shifted, pushing hers even wider as he began to thrust faster, his face buried against her neck. "Maggie! So fucking good. Take more, darlin'." He nipped her earlobe, the slight sting like a jolt through her body, firing her need even more. She'd never realized sex could be so untamed and frenzied, the frantic turbulence just below the surface adding an animalistic element to it that alarmed her.

Overwhelmed by the riot of sensations and the strength of her own desires, she tucked her face beneath his jaw in a defensive effort to hide as much as she could from him, not daring to let him see her this way.

His knowledge of her body showed in every touch. The sureness of each bold move screamed of arrogant male, one who knew exactly what he did to her and the pleasure each caress gave her. He held her face pressed against his shoulder, murmuring softly to her as if understanding her insecurities even as his cock thrust deep.

Even the possibility that he could know her thoughts increased her sense of vulnerability.

She tightened her hold on him, brushing his shirt aside with her mouth and sinking her teeth into his shoulder. Whimpering, she held on to him as the pressure inside her built, her body tensing as he worked that special spot inside her with amazing accuracy.

Her clit throbbed painfully and she jolted each time his body came into contact with it. It began to burn, feeling swollen and far too sensitive, making each brush against it more intense than the last.

Jeremiah groaned, working the head of his cock with deliberate precision against the spot inside her, telling her that he knew more about her body than she did. "That's it, darlin'. Come. Now, damn it.

Come for me." His hoarse demand in her ear sent a shiver through her at the same time his cock hit that spot again.

A scream ripped from her as the pleasure seemed to explode. She grabbed handfuls of his hair, holding on for dear life as her world spun all around her.

Without warning, Jeremiah tensed and rolled to his back, keeping her head tucked against his shoulder, his hand on her bottom tightening and taking her with him. He held her there, rocking her against him, forcing her clit into contact with his body.

Wild now, Maggie took over, bracing her hands on his shoulders to take what she needed, her movements slowing as the pleasure crested and began its slow decent. Dropping her head back onto his chest, she struggled to breathe, soothed by the solid beat of his heart beneath her ear. Neither moved as she struggled for air, her body trembling helplessly against his.

With a soft chuckle he slid his hands beneath her shirt to wrap them around her.

"I love when you wiggle around. I think maybe next time I'm going to put you on top and let you ride me."

With a soft moan, she lifted her head, and despite feeling limp and weak, her pulse raced when she saw the look of tender affection in his eyes.

"Don't make fun of me. You know I can't be on top."

He nipped at her bottom lip before tangling his hands in her hair and giving her one of those kisses so hot it curled her toes inside her boots.

"Of course you can. How else do you think Eb and I can take you at the same time?"

He looked over her shoulder, his smile widening. With his hands at her sides, holding her, he used his thumbs to play with her nipples. "One of us will be inside you just like I'm inside you now. That leaves that tight little hole wide open and free for the other one."

The fleeting touch on her bottom hole made her jolt, her surprise giving way to alarm when Jeremiah applied pressure to her nipples again, and she realized that he couldn't have touched her there.

She tried to break away and sit up, but a hand pressed at the middle of her back held her in place. "Jeremiah!" Maggie pushed against him when she felt it again. "Someone's here!"

She wiggled around but Jeremiah caught her to him with a chuckle, not allowing her to look behind her.

He smiled, groaning when his cock slid from her. "I wonder who that could be."

Hot hands closed over the cheeks of her bottom as an equally hot body bent over her. "Looks like our woman ain't no shy virgin anymore. Something about a woman naked except for boots just turns me inside out, especially one with her ass spread wide and available."

Maggie shivered again at Eb's deep tone, the silky cadence of it both playful and threatening. Maggie closed her eyes, digging her nails into Jeremiah's shoulders as she fought for some semblance of control. "I'm not naked." Still weak from sex, she tried to straighten her legs, nervous at being caught with her bottom in such a vulnerable position. "Let me up."

Jeremiah held firm, kissing her cheek. "No, darlin'. Stay right where you are. I envy Eb right now. He's got that ass wide open and can do whatever he wants with it. She likes that, Eb. She likes being held down so we can have our way with her."

Eb pushed her hair aside and touched his lips to the back of her neck. "Figured as much. I got news for you, honey. That dress isn't covering anything important. It isn't every day a man walks into his house to find something like this waiting for him." He ran his hands down her sides as his lips slid to her back. He kissed his way across her shoulders, sending shivers through her each time he stopped to nibble at a particularly sensitive spot.

How could she not know about them when they knew just where and how to touch her to give her the most pleasure?

Jeremiah moved his hands to her shoulders to make way for his brother with an ease that spoke of experience, the thought filling her with jealousy. He slid his fingers through her hair again, pulling her down for another kiss as Eb's lips and hands made their way down her body.

Still trembling from her orgasm, Maggie lay defenseless under Eb's tender but thorough assault to her senses. She felt so naughty and decadent, with her dress hanging off of her, her breasts, slit, and bottom completely exposed. She wondered if she'd ever get used to being kissed by one man while another touched her most intimate places. It made it hard to think, and instead of being able to focus on one sensation, awareness raced through her everywhere at once.

Jeremiah broke off his kiss to look over her shoulder, his eyes darkening as he followed Eb's slow journey down her body. A moment later his hands tightened on her just as Eb's lips touched her bottom, stilling her automatic jolt.

"Easy, darlin'."

Maggie pushed against his shoulder to stare up at him incredulously, her toes curling as Eb scraped his teeth over her bottom. It made it hard to focus on what she was saying, her voice too raw and sounding nothing like her own. "Stop talking to me like I'm a horse you're breaking." She shivered as Eb's sure fingers worked magic over her still sensitive clit. "You can't—oh, God, Eb!" She fought Jeremiah's hold as Eb's hands slid to her inner thighs. "Eb, you can't kiss me there."

In a panic, Maggie tried to straighten her legs as Eb's warm lips moved over the cheeks of her bottom, working his way closer and closer to her slit. "What are you doing?"

She grabbed handfuls of Jeremiah's hair. "What's he going to do to me?"

It seemed nothing was off-limits to them, something that became more obvious each time they touched her.

Eb's hands went to the back of her thighs, circling them and lifting her to her knees. His leather holster brushed against her bottom, a sharp reminder of what a dangerous man he'd become, and adding a dark element to the hunger building inside her.

"I can kiss you wherever I want to. I can touch you everywhere, and I can fuck every one of your holes. You're my wife now, Maggie. I own you, darlin'. Don't you ever forget that."

Knowing how she must look with her bottom high in the air and her inner thighs coated with her juices and Jeremiah's seed, Maggie hid her face against Jeremiah's chest.

"I'm not one of your horses or your damned cows! You can't own me."

Jeremiah slid his hands lower and used his thumbs to tease her already sensitized nipples. "Yes, we can. We do. Every delicious part of you. I think one day soon I'm gonna start at your toes and lick my way all the way up your body."

Eb slid his thumbs up to part her folds. "Once you get to her sweet pussy, you're never gonna want to leave it."

On her hands and knees, Maggie couldn't stop rocking back and forth, needing the strokes on her nipples as badly as she needed the attention to her clit. Tilting her head back, she moaned, closing her eyes as Jeremiah fisted a hand in her hair and scraped his teeth down her neck.

She tried to speak, but her voice came out as a croak, and she had to clear her throat before trying again. "You talk about me like I'm not even here."

Eb slid two fingers into her soaked pussy, leaning over to kiss her ear and waiting until she stilled before speaking. "Get used to it. We know damned well you're here, darlin', but we're still gonna talk about what we're each doing to you. Wait until we both have our cocks inside you at the same time. Neither one of us wants to miss anything."

He withdrew almost completely before surging into her again. "When I take you now, I'm gonna stretch your ass a little more. Don't you think Jeremiah wants to know what I'm doing to his wife's tight ass?"

Maggie groaned as he withdrew again and coated her bottom hole with the juices he'd gathered, circling her opening, but drawing out the anticipation by not pushing into her. Missing the lips at her neck and shoulder, she opened her eyes to meet Jeremiah's.

He smiled and rewarded her by tweaking her nipples again. "That's a good girl. You're starting to understand that, even if only one of us is touching you, you belong to both of us at all times."

Eb gathered more of the juices leaking from her and, this time, pressed at her bottom hole hard enough to make her gasp, but not hard enough to enter her. "Did you come when Jeremiah fucked you?"

Helpless against his torment, she stayed as still as she could, not daring to move and inadvertently take his finger into her puckered opening. As much as it excited her when he did it, the anticipation of it still created a panic inside her at having her most private opening breached.

It made it difficult to concentrate on answering him as she held her breath, fearing that at any moment he would slide the two fingers devious into her.

Jeremiah cupped her jaw, stroking her cheek until she opened her eyes.

"What's Eb doing to you, honey?"

Her hands tightened in his hair as Eb's fingers collected more of her juices. She groaned when Eb lightly tapped her clit before sliding back to press at her puckered opening.

Jeremiah tugged at her hair. "Maggie, I asked you a question. Tell me what Eb's doing. I'm your husband, and I want to know right now what your other husband's doing to you."

He pinched her nipple, not releasing it until she gasped. "Tell me right now, Maggie, or you'll regret it."

She couldn't look away from Jeremiah's face as the sharp pain in her nipple made her pussy clench and leak even more moisture. "He—he's touching my bottom hole."

Jeremiah slid a thumb over her bottom lip. His incredibly soft voice added a comforting warmth to the heat raging inside her. "Do you like it?"

"I don't...yes...no...I don't know. Oh, God."

"Is he inside you?"

"No. He's teasing me. Oh!" She sucked in a breath as Eb applied more pressure, making her bottom hole sting.

From behind her, Eb ran a hand over her back as he pressed both fingers at her tight opening. "She loves this. Her pussy and ass keep clenching. She's afraid, but she wants it."

Cupping her breast, Jeremiah stroked her nipple, his fingers gentle, but with all the attention he'd already given her there, it was more than enough to have her writhing against him. "Is that true, Maggie? Do you like having something filling that tight bottom?"

Breathing in gulps, she struggled to adjust as Eb applied more pressure.

He didn't pause, not easing up on the pressure at all until he breached the tight ring of muscle, forcing it to give way under his relentless insistence.

Maggie gasped, fighting the chills that raced through her. She couldn't believe anything could feel more intimate than having a cock in her pussy, but the feel of his fingers inside her bottom felt even more deliberately decadent.

"It burns. Oh, God. It's inside me. I can't believe you're doing this to me."

Her head spun, her mind taken over completely by an act so erotic it tore past all her defenses as though they weren't there. She hadn't recovered completely from her last orgasm, and already she trembled with need for another.

Jeremiah's expression softened, his eyes steady on hers as though gauging her reaction. "Don't tighten up, honey. Eb, maybe we should do this another time. Maybe our little darlin' isn't quite ready for this."

Entranced, Maggie stared at him in wonder, hardly able to believe that Jeremiah, *her* Jeremiah looked at her in that way.

The way Hayes and Wyatt looked at Savannah.

Mesmerized by it, she let out a startled whimper as Eb slid his fingers deeper.

"Jeremiah." She breathed his name, thrilling at the flare of possessiveness in his eyes.

The knuckles of Eb's other hand brushed the back of her thighs just seconds before his holster hit the floor.

While pushing his fingers a little deeper into her bottom, he pressed another into her pussy.

Maggie cried out, the burn in her bottom and chills racing through her growing stronger by the minute. The feeling of his finger moving in her pussy at the same time he stretched her bottom was like nothing she'd ever imagined.

Eb's tone sharpened. "No, Maggie can take this just fine. A little more each time, Maggie, until we can both take you together. You want both of us filling you up with cock, don't you, honey?"

Right now there was nothing on earth she wanted more. This hunger inside her raged out of control, leaving her shaking with a desire for them to take her, to take everything she had to offer, while giving her all they had to give.

Maggie groaned as his fingers slid from her pussy with a speed that left her clenching at emptiness.

Almost immediately, his cock touched her folds, and hot and hard as iron, it began to press into her pussy.

His voice lowered seductively. "A cock filling you is just what you need, isn't it, Maggie?" He moved his fingers in her ass as he pushed his cock a little deeper.

Maggie gasped, throwing her head back and pushing her hands flat on the floor on either side of Jeremiah's chest. She panted through the erotic burn in her ass and the too-full feeling of his cock in her pussy.

Smoothing gentle hands over her shoulders, Jeremiah gathered her against him.

"Easy, baby. Eb, be gentle with her. This is Maggie, remember?"

Eb wrapped an arm around her from behind and yanked her back against him, sliding his fingers another inch into her ass. "I know damned well who I'm fucking."

Maggie bucked in his arms, taking more of his fingers and another inch of his cock inside her, throwing her head back again when Jeremiah palmed her breasts. "Oh, God."

She held on to Jeremiah with one hand and, with the other, reached up to grip Eb's sinewy forearm, crying out repeatedly as both men continued their decadent assault. Unable to keep from gripping Eb's cock and fingers tighter, she whimpered through her panting breaths as the burn created the most amazing sizzles to her clit.

Eb's cock slid deep, making the fingers he curled in her bottom feel even thicker than before.

Below her, Jeremiah sat up, taking a nipple into his mouth.

Her entire body shook, caught in an erotic hold she never wanted to escape. Her nipples tingled as Jeremiah gave his attention to first one and then the other, the tingles racing through her and settling at her center, encompassing her entire slit from her bottom hole to her clit. The stretch of her ass, the slow, shallow strokes in her pussy that kept getting deeper, and the throbbing in her clit combined into a powerful surge that she had no hope of fighting.

She couldn't stop clamping down on the cock in her pussy or the fingers that stretched her bottom, feeling fuller than she ever thought possible.

Bucking in Eb's arms, she took even more of his cock, groaning when he slid deep, a groan that got deeper when Jeremiah slid his hand down her body.

Her stomach and abdomen muscles tightened when Jeremiah's fingers brushed them, quivering with anticipation.

Suddenly, the fingers inside her ass moved, and Eb slid deep.

Maggie whimpered in her throat, overwhelmed at the feeling of fullness and the unreal sensation of having surrendered. With her ass and pussy filled, she felt taken over, his possession both firm and controlled.

Jeremiah let his head fall back, letting his fingers trail lightly over her folds as he watched her with hooded eyes.

Her body tightened unbearably, the pressure inside her building to near pain.

"Please!"

Oh, God. If only Eb would move faster, push his fingers in a little deeper.

If only Jeremiah would touch her clit...

Jeremiah cupped a breast. "Please, what? What do you want, Maggie?"

Eb withdrew his fingers slightly, holding them just past the tight ring of muscle, and pulled his cock almost completely from her before sliding it deep once again. "This is what it'll be like when we take you together. One of us under you, one of us behind you. Your pussy and ass both filled with cock."

He began to thrust faster now, his breathing ragged, his arm tightening around her to hold her in place. "Tell Jeremiah what you want, Maggie." His commanding tone sent another shiver through her.

Clamping down on him, she felt those hot little sizzles that warned her she was about to come. Desperate for release, she ignored their questions, squeezing her eyes closed to escape into her own world of pleasure and thinking about nothing except ending this delicious torment.

Amazed at the feeling of fullness, she began to rock her hips again, a naughty thrill racing through her when her movements took Eb's fingers a little deeper.

With her head back, she cried out with every thrust, lost in her own world, a world where nothing existed except the race to orgasm. The delicious pressure inside her kept building, each thrust, each caress bringing it even closer. So close she could practically taste it, she let herself go, blocking out everything except the delicious sizzles that she knew would send her flying.

Without warning, Eb and Jeremiah stilled.

"No!" Maggie's eyes flew open and she fought Eb's hold, but she was no match for his strength.

She was so close that her need had become one of frenzied desperation, bringing tears of frustration to her eyes. "Don't stop. Please. Oh, God. Please don't stop." She tried to buck but couldn't move on him fast enough to get the relief she needed.

Eb moved his fingers, the firm pressure making her bottom burn. "What do you want, Maggie?"

Staring down at Jeremiah, Maggie groaned at the burn of her bottom hole being stretched, pushing back when Eb thrust deep into her pussy again. "I want you to move. I want Jeremiah to touch me."

Chuckling, Eb thrust once, twice and stopped again, holding himself still inside her. "Jeremiah *is* touching you. Isn't he playing with those pretty little nipples?"

She threw back her head when Jeremiah pinched them again, arching her back to thrust her bottom at Eb and her breasts at Jeremiah. Inhibitions fled in the presence of such need, where in her world right now, nothing existed except satisfaction.

"Damn it, Eb. That's not what I mean, and you know it." Squeezing her eyes closed, she whimpered, her voice husky and raw. "Stop teasing me, damn you. Make me come."

Her eyes fluttered open when Jeremiah sat up again, his hard chest brushing against her nipples as he kissed her jaw. The look of wonder in his eyes and something else, some other emotion she'd never seen in them before, enthralled her. She cupped his jaw, running her thumb over his bottom lip, the closeness she felt with him at that moment much stronger than ever.

Hoping he felt the same, she stared into his eyes. "Please help me."

Jeremiah's eyes flared. "Maggie, I'll give you whatever you want. All you have to do is ask." He brushed her hair aside, smiling faintly. "Do you want me to touch your clit?"

Almost giddy with relief that he understood, she nodded, moaning as Eb began to move inside her again. "Yes."

Sliding his hand down her body, Jeremiah smiled tenderly. "All you have to do is tell me what you want and I'll do it. Say it, Maggie."

Too far gone to feel any embarrassment, Maggie threw her head back again and rocked into Eb's thrusts.

"Touch my clit."

Eb used his arm to move Maggie on his cock and fingers. "She's ready, Jeremiah. She's already milking me."

Could they know how much it excited her when they said things like that?

Jeremiah tweaked a nipple, sending a sharp arrow of need to her already throbbing clit. "Open your eyes, Maggie. I want you looking at me when I play with your clit."

Maggie did as he demanded, willing to do anything to get him to touch her there. "It burns everywhere. Help me."

Jeremiah smiled. "Let's take care of that, honey. Hold on to my shoulders and don't let go."

Eb growled, his fingers sliding from her bottom as he began to thrust in earnest.

At the first touch of Jeremiah's callused finger on her clit, everything inside her seemed to explode, the ripples like waves of electricity racing through her. Screaming Jeremiah's name, she tightened on Eb, her bottom still burning from his possession.

Eb groaned, the hand around her waist yanking her back against him as he surged deep and pulsed inside her. Burying his face in her hair, he groaned again, a low, husky sound that sounded as though it came from deep inside him.

But it was the look in Jeremiah's eyes that held her attention. So dark and intense they seemed to bore into hers as though he could see into her soul, holding hers as Eb wrapped himself around her from behind and buried his face in her neck.

She stared at Jeremiah as Eb's hand covered a breast and caressed lightly, his big body trembling against hers. She couldn't look away as she started to come down, her body still trembling in the aftermath. Thankful that Eb held her steady, she leaned back against his shoulder, her gaze still held in Jeremiah's.

Jeremiah smiled slowly, threading his fingers through her hair. "Do you know how damned beautiful you are?"

Maggie's tremulous smile melted under his kiss, a kiss as soft as butterfly wings. Still trembling and breathing heavily, she welcomed his gentleness and began to calm under his and Eb's soft caresses.

"Jeremiah."

His name came out on a breath against his lips a second before they covered hers.

Eb stilled behind her, earning a whimper from her, a whimper Jeremiah swallowed before lifting his head.

"Shh, honey. That's a girl." Jeremiah's words came out as a warm breath against her cheek.

Despite having Eb's arm between them, he gathered her close and started to rub her back.

Eb yanked his arm from between them and withdrew from her pussy, running his hands over her hips before standing.

"I've got some things to check on."

Hurt at his brusque tone and the fact that he would leave her so soon after taking her so completely, Maggie turned her face away from him and tried to sit up, but Jeremiah held her close.

Determined not to cry, she stared at the stone fireplace, the vision in her mind of sitting in front of it with a naked Eb and Jeremiah blurring until only she and Jeremiah sat there.

"I understand. This ranch is the most important thing to you. Desire's a good name for your town, since it seems to be the only thing you really care about."

Jeremiah stilled for several seconds before his hand started to move up and down her back again. "That's not true, Maggie. This place was built because of our desire for you."

Forcing a smile, Maggie sat up, not looking in Eb's direction. "That's a nice thing to say."

Standing, she righted her clothing, still avoiding the stare she could feel coming from Eb. "If you'll excuse me, I have some things to take care of, and I'd like to look around my new home."

She smiled once more at Jeremiah, who glared at his brother. "Thank you so much for my new home."

Without looking in Eb's direction, she headed for the stairs, her steps faltering when she heard the sound of glass breaking. Determined not to show any emotion, she continued up to the second floor and into the only room with furniture.

Closing and locking the door behind her, she heard words flung in anger from below but couldn't make out what was said.

She turned away and went to sit in a chair by the window, gathering her shirt around her as she looked out at what appeared to be the only thing in the world Eb would ever love.

Chapter Eight

Hearing the back door slam, Maggie looked down to see both Eb and Jeremiah crossing the yard, their stiffer than normal movements making their anger apparent.

She forced back the hurt, knowing she could do nothing about it anyway. She loved both of them so much she wouldn't, *couldn't* ever walk away from them and just hoped that over time, Eb would allow her to get close the way Jeremiah seemed to want to.

Deciding to go on as though nothing had happened, Maggie spent the next hour wandering through the rooms, hardly able to believe that she would now be mistress of such a fine house. She'd helped Esmeralda with her chores often enough that she was confident in her ability to make it a home.

A home even Eb would have to appreciate.

Gradually, she made her way to the kitchen, her heart leaping when she glanced casually out the window.

Eb approached, his long strides eating up the ground as he crossed the yard toward the back door, the look on his face telling her he was in no better mood than he'd been in when he left.

Determined not to let him see how much he'd hurt her, Maggie looked up with a smile as he stormed through the door. "Did you get everything put away?"

He strode across the room like a warrior on a mission. "Yeah. Everyone wants to meet you, and Duke has supper ready in the chow shack. Come on, and don't even think about making any comments about the 'rugged- looking' ranch hands, or I'll paddle your ass."

Maggie's welcoming smile fell, while inside a kernel of hope took root.

Eb nodded at her startled look, gripping her arm and leading her to the door he'd just come through. "Yeah, I heard about that from Jeremiah. Did you think he wouldn't tell me? You've got a lot to learn about having two husbands."

You've got a lot to learn about having a wife.

Delighted with his show of jealousy, she smiled again, not giving him the satisfaction of trying to pull away.

Besides, she liked it when he held her.

Smiling in the direction of the ranch hands who also headed toward the outbuilding, eyeing her curiously, she shrugged. "I didn't say anything wrong. It was just an observation. The men who met us at the train station looked capable of handling anything. You don't see men like that too often in Kansas City."

Eb slid a hand over her bottom, patting it threateningly, the warmth of his hand sending a wave of longing through her. "Don't observe anymore. I don't want you causing trouble with my men."

Insulted that he would think such a thing, Maggie spun and pulled out of his grasp, knocking his hand away when he reached for her. "I'm not about to cause any trouble with your men." Hurt that he had so little trust in her, she started toward the long, wooden outbuilding, unsurprised when he caught up with her and grabbed her arm again.

"Listen, you little brat! I'm not going to have you swishing your skirts at any other men just because you want to lead me around by the nose. You behave yourself, or by God, you'll regret it."

Maggie looked down to where his hand circled her arm before lifting her gaze to his again, carefully keeping her face blank. "You know, you really have changed. I remember when all the girls in town would fall all over themselves to be with you. Too bad you're not as charming as Jeremiah."

Eb's jaw clenched. "Thank God."

Shaking her head, she stared straight ahead. "I don't know what those women ever saw in you if you were as mean to them as you are to me. Even the woman in Tulsa asked about you."

"Did she, now? They liked the same things you do. My cock and how good I can make you feel. My ability to provide for you. None of the rest really matters, does it?"

Before she could answer, he led her inside the crowded building, leading her to where the biggest, meanest looking men she'd ever seen in her life stood cooking and handing out food behind several scarred wooden tables.

Duke had a long scar, which ran from below his left eye to his prominent chin, making him look even more menacing.

He looked up, grunted what she assumed was a greeting, and immediately fixed her a plate. He handed it to her, his scowl never faltering.

"Ma'am. You come by tomorrow and we'll get you set up with supplies."

He spoke softly, but she doubted a man that size ever had to raise his voice. He turned away and picked up a large, sinister-looking knife, wielding it with expert precision on the huge slab of meat he'd obviously been cutting.

Enthralled, she couldn't take her eyes from him as he sliced through the meat as easily as if he sliced melted butter, his bulging muscles shifting with every swipe of the knife. Transfixed, she jumped when Jeremiah came up behind her and bent to whisper in her ear.

"You should feel honored. As long as I've known him, Duke's never fixed a plate for anybody."

Phoenix came up on her other side. "Whatever you do, don't *ever* say anything bad about his food."

Amused and no longer afraid of the fierce-looking Indian, Maggie grinned and glanced up at him over her shoulder.

"Did *you* ever criticize his food?"

Phoenix grimaced and reached for his own plate. "Once. He nearly scalped me with that knife of his. Duke's deadly with that knife."

Taking in the long, dark braid that fell down his back, Maggie laughed softly, her laughter dying when two other fierce-looking Indians stepped up beside Phoenix. Their impossibly black eyes narrowed, their expressions forbidding and cold.

Both had the same dark skin and the same ink-black hair as Phoenix, and their lean, muscular builds emanated power. Unlike Phoenix, both Indians wore buckskins, and their feet were covered with moccasins instead of the boots the other men wore.

The most menacing looking of the two had shoulder-length hair, and when he spoke, his words came out gravelly and so low she had to struggle to hear him. "If you're gonna talk—move. Some of us worked all day and are hungry."

Alarmed, Maggie took a step back, pressing against Jeremiah and probably would have dropped her plate if Eb hadn't reached out and caught it in time.

To her surprise, Phoenix grinned, the transformation of his harsh features remarkable. Her eyes darted back and forth between him and the other Indian, blinking when Phoenix's nearly black eyes twinkled and met the other man's glare unflinchingly.

"One of us had to go, and neither one of you ever want to go to the city."

The Indian with the long, flowing hair who'd walked up with the other shot her a glance and grunted, using a broad shoulder to knock Phoenix aside so he could start piling food on his plate. "Is anyone going to introduce us to the lady?"

Maggie automatically looked up at Eb to find him watching her, a faint smile playing at his lips. "Maggie, this man doing his best to intimidate his little brother is Hawke Royal. The one behind him piling enough grub for three men on his plate is his other brother, Blade. Hawke, Blade, this is Maggie Tyler, our wife."

Hawke spared one last glare for Phoenix and turned to her. His expression softened somewhat, but he still looked like a man no one in his right mind would want to go up against. "It's a pleasure to meet you, Mrs. Tyler."

Maggie smiled, for the first time realizing that only the harshness of his features prevented him from being truly handsome. Because of her nervousness, she said the first thought that popped into her mind. "Your name is Royal?"

Blade paused in the act of filling his plate and looked around his brother at her, flashing a cool smile. "Strange name for an Indian, isn't it? Nice to finally meet you, Mrs. Tyler."

Maggie's face burned. "No. I mean...I'm just surprised—" She stopped abruptly when she found herself talking to his back.

Phoenix took pity on her and smiled, shaking his head. "My brothers are a little sensitive. Our mother and father were never married. Royal was our mother's name."

"Oh." Afraid of offending anyone further, Maggie nodded, thankful for the supportive hand Jeremiah placed on her shoulder.

Hawke set down his plate on the scarred wood surface and turned to scowl at Phoenix. "Sensitive? About being a bastard or about being a half-breed?"

Phoenix shook his head. "Our father's tribe never would have accepted us, anyway."

"Neither do the whites."

Maggie watched out of the corner of her eye as Blade turned back and helped himself to the big piece of meat Hawke had plunked down on his plate.

Turning his head, he caught her watching and winked at her before turning away and heading toward one of the long tables.

Relieved that he'd apparently forgiven her, she giggled before she could help herself. Slapping a hand over her mouth to prevent another one, she hurriedly looked away, her eyes caught by Hawke's.

Hawke's icy eyes held hers for several long seconds, as though he thought she'd laughed at him, before he followed her brief glance behind him and sighed in resignation. "He took my food, didn't he?"

Her laugh burst free, a combination of amusement and relief. "I'm afraid so. Is that something that happens often?"

"Often enough." He stared down at his plate, shaking his head before looking over to give Blade's back a menacing look.

Jeremiah nudged Maggie. "Let's get out of the line of fire."

Feeling more at ease, Maggie followed Jeremiah to a table, where he placed both of their plates, and glanced over her shoulder to watch Hawke approach Blade. "They won't fight, will they?"

Jeremiah shook his head. "I'd be surprised. There are only a few of our men who seem to like fighting." He shifted his gaze and inclined his head.

She followed his gaze toward another table where several men watched Hawke, the mixture of nervousness and anticipation on their faces making her uneasy.

Eb took a seat on her other side. "We've got enough to fight the weather, outlaws, and cattle rustlers. We don't have the time or the energy to fight each other." He looked at her meaningfully. "Unless we have to. Don't worry about those men over there. They're just looking for trouble. They'll have to lose that habit or find themselves another job. The other men can handle them, but with you here, I'm going to have to watch them."

Nodding uneasily, Maggie started eating, looking up at Jeremiah's low growl.

He stared toward the other table again. "They're going to find more trouble than they bargained for if they don't stop staring at Maggie."

Not wanting to be the cause of any violence, Maggie touched Jeremiah's arm and leaned into him, hoping to distract him.

"Jeremiah, I wandered around the house before Eb came to get me. It's beautiful. I can't believe you built one just like the big house. That must have been a lot of work."

Setting his fork aside, he wrapped an arm around her waist and pulled her close. "It was worth it to see that look on your face. We wanted you to feel at home." Running a finger down her cheek, he bent close.

"I want to fill it with all the babies you're going to give us."

Her face burning, Maggie tried to look away, but he captured her chin.

His eyes twinkled the way they used to when he'd teased her in the past. "I always want you, but when you blush, my cock gets hard enough to pound nails. It makes me want to make you blush all the time."

Bending closer, he bit her earlobe. "Those sounds you make when we're taking you drive me crazy. I can't wait to hear the sounds you make when I take your ass."

Shivering, she looked around to make sure no one else had heard him. "I can't believe the way you and Eb talk. Do you talk that way because it's only…you know, physical for you?" Shrugging, she felt her face burn even hotter. "I've never heard a man talk to his wife that way before."

Sighing, Jeremiah laced her fingers with his. "We're blunt, Maggie. Just because I use coarse words, doesn't mean I think less of you. I've always had a soft spot for you, Maggie. When you looked up to me with so much trust in your eyes…" He blew out a breath. "I always cared about you but now…eat your supper."

Looking down at her plate, Maggie moved her hand in his work-roughened one. "I wish you'd never left. It changed everything."

Sighing again, Jeremiah released her hand and started eating again. "We had to, Maggie. We both wanted to marry you and could never have lived that way in Kansas City. I thought you understood that."

"Understanding it doesn't make the hurt go away. If you really cared about me the way a man should care about the woman he wants to marry, you never would have been able to leave."

Jeremiah chuckled. "You were only a kid when we left, honey. How could we think of you as a woman? Now eat your dinner so we can get back to the house. We've got water heating for baths for all of us, and then we can go to bed."

With a sinking heart, Maggie set her fork aside. "I want us to be the way we were before."

Eb must have heard her because he leaned close from the other side.

"Get that out of your head right now. We'll never be the way we were before. You were a little girl, and we were friends. I'm not your friend anymore, Maggie, no more than you're mine. You're my wife, and that's an entirely different thing."

She'd noticed his arrogance seemed to have grown now that he'd come home to his ranch, the set of his jaw just a little tighter, his stride just a little more self-assured.

His tone even harsher than before.

Leaning toward Eb, she kept her voice low enough so that Jeremiah couldn't hear her.

"Then why did you give away my virginity so easily to Jeremiah instead of taking it yourself?"

Eb looked surprised by her question, but quickly recovered. "I have my reasons." Leaning closer, he ran a finger down her arm, his eyes coldly possessive.

"Besides, when the time comes, I'm the one who'll be taking your ass."

Aware that the others looked on, she smiled adoringly, but kept her tone cool. "You used to treat me like a person. You used to talk to me."

She deliberately turned away, ignoring the bit off curse from Eb, and listened attentively to Jeremiah's conversation as though hanging on to his every word.

Next to her, Eb banged his cup down so hard she jumped, and it took tremendous willpower not to turn back around.

Because she'd grown up on their father's ranch, she had enough knowledge to participate in Jeremiah's conversation with another man, delighted to be included, while Eb remained notably silent.

Without warning, Eb grabbed her arm and stood, nearly yanking her from her seat. "You're finished eating. Come with me."

Maggie shook her head in warning when Jeremiah spun, a shocked look on his face and several of the other men's as Eb practically dragged her from the outbuilding.

Digging her heels in, she tried unsuccessfully to tug her arm from his grip. "Stop dragging me. Where are we going?"

Eb slowed his steps some but didn't release her arm.

"I wanted to show you how the supplies are sorted so you can find what you need."

She looked up at him in surprise. It didn't make any sense, especially when he'd already told her that Duke would take care of getting her whatever she needed tomorrow.

His features appeared to be carved in stone, not the look of a man who wanted nothing more than to show his wife around a supply building.

Her heart beat faster, though, as they walked across the yard. No matter how much he'd changed, she couldn't quite get used to the fact that after all these years, her childhood hero was back in her life.

As her husband.

Would she ever get used to it? Would it ever really feel like she was married to him instead of being just a guest here, one that he felt obligated to take care of?

Determined to do everything she could to make him see her as his wife, to get his attention as a woman, she tried to pull away. She'd made it too easy for them so far and thought it was time they had a little bit of a challenge.

"That's all right. Duke said he'd show me tomorrow."

Eb's jaw tightened. "*I'll* show you where the supplies are kept."

That possessiveness in him seemed to grow with every passing day. Suspecting that the anger and callousness was caused by jealousy, she hid a grin and allowed herself to be led to the outbuilding where they kept all the supplies. She knew damned well he had to have had a hand in the decision to build such a house for her, which meant that he had to care for her at least a little, despite his determination not to let her see it.

She just hoped she was right. If not, he'd break her heart for sure.

She waited while he lit a lantern, her jaw dropping when she saw the large number of shelves, every single one of them completely filled. Barrels stood in two of the corners, bags stacked high in another. The amount of supplies they stored staggered her, and it hit her all at once just how isolated they were.

"I never realized…"

Holding the lamp high, Eb gestured her inside and pointed to a shelf on the side. "There's material there for you. You don't have to worry about making shirts for us. I bought as many shirts and pants as I could find in Kansas City and Tulsa." He pointed to another shelf that held stacks and stacks of them. "You can take whatever you need from them, but I thought you might want to make yourself a new dress or two."

Stepping away from him, she walked down the racks and racks of shelves. Maggie shrugged again, trembling with awareness when he closed the door behind them. "I usually wear pants. They're more comfortable and don't get in my way as much."

As she continued on, she looked over her shoulder at him in time to see him set the lantern on one of the barrels. The look of determination in his eyes as they raked over her made her nipples tingle and pebble and sent an answering surge of need through her.

Not wanting him to know how quickly she fell under his seductive spell, she turned away and continued to inspect the shelves, not remembering half of what she looked at. "Are you sure we shouldn't be getting back to Jeremiah? He might not like us going off alone like this."

She knew a man like Eb hated to answer to anyone, but she hadn't counted on his reaction.

With a curse, he caught her waist from behind, pulling her back against him, his teeth scraping over her neck at the same time he pressed his cock against the small of her back.

"Right now I don't give a damn what Jeremiah wants. All I care about is getting inside you. I want my wife."

Holding on to the arm at her waist, Maggie leaned back against him, not even bothering to fight the need he stirred so easily. "You want a woman, or you want me?"

His other arm came around her and immediately covered a breast, massaging gently while the hand at her waist slid lower. "I want you. Right here. Right now."

Her knees gave out when he started to nibble at her neck. "I don't want a husband who doesn't care about me, one who only wants to be my husband when he wants sex."

The hand over her abdomen gathered the front of her dress, raising it inch by inch. "I'm your husband *all* the time—even when Jeremiah's inside you and I'm not around. Don't ever forget who you belong to, Maggie."

The hand at her breast shifted slightly, and she gasped at the sting when he pinched her nipple and let her head fall back. "Never."

Without hesitation, she let him support her weight, leaning back against him as his fingers teased a nipple and the other hand worked her skirt out of the way and covered her mound, his strong fingers pressing insistently between her thighs.

Maggie's head fell to the side, her neck no longer strong enough to support it. A languorous heat flowed through her, weakening her everywhere, allowing him to position her any way he wanted.

"Don't you ever forget that I'm your wife."

Eb took advantage, running his lips over her neck. "You're my wife, all right, and this time I'm going to have you all to myself."

He opened her shirt and slid his hand inside with a sureness that weakened her even more. "My grown up Maggie. My wife."

The silky possessiveness in his tone and gentleness of his touch contrasted sharply with the cold demeanor he usually displayed, and the contrast captivated her.

Covering his hand with hers, she arched her neck to give him better access. "I need you, Eb. I need us to be close the way we were before."

Her stomach quivered under his hand, her nipple pebbling against his palm as he caressed her. Crying out when his fingers teased her slick folds, she grabbed on to his sinewy arm as her knees buckled completely.

He caught her with no apparent effort, lifting her until her feet no longer touched the ground.

"We'll be even closer in a few minutes. You're all wet again, sweetheart. I can't wait to teach you some of the other ways we can give each other pleasure."

Moaning, Maggie licked her lips and arched against him. "Do you mean besides you and Jeremiah taking me together?"

Her breast felt hot and swollen in his hand, her nipple tight and tingling with an ache that sharpened with each pass of his work-roughened thumb. Fisting her hand in his shirt, she turned her face against his shoulder to muffle the cries she couldn't contain.

"There's a lot more that we can do together, just the two of us, honey. That's it, Maggie. Just let me make you feel good. You want this as much as I do, don't you?"

Eb's attention centered at her slit, tracing her folds until they felt swollen and heavy, the random taps to her clit making her jolt in his arms. His arms tightened around her, absorbing her shudders, and, catching her earlobe with his teeth, he thrust his finger inside her.

Her pussy clenched on him as though trying to suck him in, her juices easing the way for his slow thrusts. Tilting her hips, she tried to take him deeper, gasping when he slid his thumb over her clit and held it there.

Maggie cried out, bucking against him, trying to get the friction she needed. Her clit felt swollen and heavy, throbbing against his thumb, so hot she could hardly stand it. Too to control her movements, she whimpered in frustration and kicked at him.

With a string of curses, he withdrew his finger and strode to where several bags had been stacked. Before she knew what to expect, he turned her to face him and placed her on top of them, tossing her skirt up and out of the way.

Making a place for himself between her thighs, he slid a hand under her neck and lifted her. "You want my cock, don't you? I can make you forget all of that other shit and make you feel so good you don't care about anything else."

Moaning, she let her head fall back, trembling when his hand covered her mound. "No, I want more."

Eb scraped his teeth down her jaw, ripping open the front of her shirt to reveal her breasts. Fisting his hand in her hair, he pulled her head back until he could reach her nipples with his mouth and held her there.

"That's it, baby. I'll take care of you. Part of being your husband is satisfying all of your needs, including this. You're in good hands, baby. I'm gonna make you come so hard you'll scream."

Maggie cried out as he closed his mouth over her nipple, her eyes drifting closed as her head fell back against one of the sacks. So he did understand what she wanted and still continued to deny her. She couldn't let him get away with it, but right now, as he took a nipple into his mouth and swirled his warm tongue around it, she didn't need any words at all.

He flicked a thumb over her clit. "I've got better uses for my mouth than spouting a bunch of pretty words. Let me show you."

Fighting the rising hunger, Maggie kicked her legs, needing to be more to him than just a woman to fuck. Determined to get closer to him, she wrapped her legs around him and tried to pull herself up, but the hand in her hair prevented it.

Meeting his eyes, she smiled tremulously, moaning as the strokes on her clit became more deliberate. "Yes, Eb, please kiss me."

He smiled coldly, despite the warmth simmering in his eyes. Both hands went to her thighs, lifting them high and wide. "Demanding, aren't you. Well, never let it be said I didn't satisfy my wife."

Lifting her, he slid his hands under her bottom and buried his face between her thighs, his thumbs threateningly close to her bottom hole as he closed his lips over her clit.

The heat and pressure as he sucked was immediate and all consuming. She only had time to suck in one breath before a scream escaped, one of overwhelming desperation.

With no warning, he shot her into a place where nothing existed except her burning clit, and controlled her entire body with nothing more than the sweep of his tongue.

She threw her hands over her head in an effort to hold on to something solid, so lost in sensation she could no longer even feel the bags beneath her. Digging her heels into his back, she fought to get away from him, the euphoric sensation too strong to bear.

Her orgasm crashed over her with no build-up at all, the huge wave crashing over her with such intensity she froze in the throes of it. She couldn't even scream, the pleasure so powerful it struck her senseless.

His warm tongue stroked her clit with a cold precision and ruthlessness that left her shaking helplessly, that no amount of writhing could escape.

Eb held her there, not releasing her from the almost unbearable pleasure, mercilessly holding her there with his mouth and the thumbs he used to apply enough pressure outward on either side of her bottom hole to make it sting.

When her pleasure crested and finally began to release her from its erotic hold, she desperately sucked air into her lungs, each breath followed by a whimpered moan.

She'd just experienced more pleasure than she'd thought herself capable of, but the cold calculation in his touch left her feeling sad and disillusioned. Still shaking and weak, she whimpered again when his head shot up and he spun away from her.

"Come out and show yourself."

The cold menace in his tone hit her like a splash of ice water in the face. Still trembling, she struggled to sit up, unable to make sense of why Eb sounded so furious or who he was talking to.

But it did register that someone was there and it wasn't Jeremiah.

She hurriedly gathered the ends of her torn shirt as Eb reached back and tossed her skirt down to cover her legs.

Hearing the scrape of a boot on the wooden floor, she turned her head to see one of the men who'd been staring at Hawke and Blade in the chow shack move closer, making his way around one of the shelves until he stood in the open.

"Sorry, Boss. I thought I heard screaming."

Maggie scrambled behind Eb for cover, mortified that someone had heard her and had probably seen her naked and in the throes of passion.

With her hand on Eb's back, she felt his muscles tighten, the fury emanating from him reminding her just how lethal he'd become. For the first time she realized he held a gun on the other man, a gun that remained steady and aimed at the man's chest.

Eb's soft, deadly tone made her shiver. "You couldn't tell it was a woman's scream? You didn't know that the only woman on the place is my wife?"

The other man shifted his feet, his eyes darting from the gun to Eb's face and back again. "Uh, yeah, boss. I knew it was a woman and thought maybe Mrs. Tyler was in some kind of danger." He glanced at her, his gaze obviously lingering a little too long for Eb's taste.

Eb's body shifted, and with his free hand, he reached back and pushed her none too gently behind him, but she still managed to peek around his arm, prepared to try to stop him if he tried to kill the other man.

He wouldn't really kill him, would he?

Remembering what they'd said about a man not pulling a gun unless he meant to use it, Maggie feared for the other man's life, not daring to look away from the scene playing out before her.

With a voice like iron, Eb shoved her back again.

"If you thought my wife was in danger, why did you sneak in instead of running in to help?"

Maggie looked around Eb, running what she hoped was a calming hand down his back.

The other man gulped and eyed the gun again. "I...uh...once I heard your voice, I didn't want to interrupt. I was gonna sneak back out again without you knowing I was here." He shrugged his shoulders and looked away. "I figured you'd be mad if you saw me in here, but I didn't mean no harm, boss. I swear it."

Maggie had already righted her clothing and no longer saw the need to hide. As mistress of the Circle T, she would show no fear and make Eb and Jeremiah proud.

Pushing at Eb's arm, she started to step out from behind him, lifting her chin and meeting the other man's eyes squarely.

Eb growled when the other man looked in her direction, his eyes razor sharp as he yanked her back behind him.

"Get out of here, Stockney, and stay the hell away from my wife. I catch you looking at her again, you're dead."

The snap in his tone was more effective at keeping her in place than his grip on her arm. As soon as she heard the click of the door being closed again, Eb stuck his gun back in his holster and turned slowly, his body trembling in rage, his eyes narrowed to mere slits.

"When I put you somewhere, from now on, you stay there. Or were you trying to give Stockney a peek at those breasts?"

He lifted her by her arms and plopped her back down on the stack of bags, getting right in her face. "You like having men panting for you? You like making them crazy to have you? You trying to be like every other damned woman?"

Grabbing a handful of her hair, he pulled her head back, his face tight with anger as he loomed over her. His free hand roamed over her breasts and, with cold deliberation, tugged a nipple until she cried out.

"Don't you ever forget that these are mine. So's your pussy and ass. If I ever catch you teasing anyone, I'll beat your ass raw and then fuck it until you beg for mercy. You can't play with these men like you played with your little friend Fred back home. These are *men*, not little boys, and I won't have my *wife* offering her favors to anyone else."

Maggie pushed at his chest, ignoring the sharp pull of her hair. "Listen, you sidewinder! I never played with Fred's feelings, and you know darned well I was never free with my favors. I don't tease other men, and I never have."

Smirking, she didn't let her fear or hurt show even when he tightened his grip and lifted her to her toes, his eyes glittering coldly.

"I never even wanted to marry you, if you remember. As far as I'm concerned, men are more trouble than they're worth. Every one of you thinks a woman should fall all over themselves with gratitude whenever you give them some attention."

For him to think that she would do anything like that cut her like Duke's knife.

She poked him in the chest, her anger overriding her fear.

"You don't want a wife. You want one of the whores that pass through here, who'll follow your every command and see to your every desire. I'm not one of them, and I'll be damned if I'll let you treat me like one!"

She twisted from his grasp and actually managed to take two steps before he caught her around the waist from behind and lifted her several inches off the floor. She cried out in surprise, biting her lip to keep from giving him the satisfaction of crying out again when his free hand came down hard on her bottom.

"You're my wife. Mine. That means, sweetheart, that I can do whatever I want to with you, and there's no one who will lift a hand to stop me."

She found it hard to believe that just minutes ago she'd been falling apart in his arms.

Lifting her chin, she glared over her shoulder at him. "Jeremiah will. Let go of me. I need some air."

Eb's temper snapped, something she'd seen only a handful of times in all the years she'd known him, the ice in his eyes turning to searing heat in a heartbeat. Curses poured from him, each a little more vicious than the last as he strode to the nearest barrel and sat on top, throwing her over his lap. He overcame her struggles with remarkable ease, tossing her skirt out of the way and blithely ignoring her screams and threats.

"Don't you ever, *ever*, try to pit me and Jeremiah against each other again!"

His hand came down hard on one cheek of her ass and before she could draw breath, on the other. "Never, Maggie."

Hanging upside down over Eb's lap, Maggie screamed in outrage. "That hurts, damn you! I didn't do anything wrong. Wait until Jeremiah hears about this."

"Hears about what, darlin'?"

With a gasp she twisted, grabbing Eb's leg for leverage and facing a grim-faced Jeremiah. Counting on him to show her the tenderness he had earlier, she reached out for him, pouting her best pout.

"Eb's spanking me for no reason. He's just mad because that man came in here and saw me naked."

He shot a look at Eb and stepped closer.

"What man saw you naked? What the hell happened in here?"

Eb slapped her ass again, leaving his hand over it this time. "Stockney snuck in here, and I was too distracted eating Maggie's pussy to notice at first. I don't know how long he was here, but when I turned, he was watching us through the shelves. I think I was blocking his view of her, but I just don't know. Fucking asshole."

Alarmed when Jeremiah moved closer to her feet and disappeared from view, Maggie tried to shove her skirt away to see him again.

"That's not my fault. I didn't know he was here. You can't blame me because you decided to take my clothes off in the damned storage shed!"

Eb slapped her ass again, making it even hotter, but what startled her the most was the feel of another set of hands moving slowly up and down the backs of her thighs.

Instead of holding the heat in the way he had before, this time Eb pushed his hand between her thighs, shocking her into immobility.

"What are you doing?"

Ignoring her question, he slid his fingers through her slick folds and spoke to his brother.

"She isn't being punished for that, and she knows it. No, letting Stockney see her was my fault, a mistake that won't be repeated. But she kept peeking out from behind me when I was trying to keep her covered, despite the fact that I kept pushing her back there."

Maggie kicked at Jeremiah. "*Shoving* me back there."

Avoiding her kicking legs, Jeremiah slid his hand down her legs and back up again. "She shouldn't have done that."

Maggie bit back a moan, hoping Eb assumed that the juices he slid his fingers through came from her orgasm only minutes ago. She couldn't stand for him to know how much being helpless and over his lap, with her bottom bare and vulnerable, excited her and that even now her pussy and bottom hole tingled with anticipation.

She had to swallow before speaking, careful to keep her voice firm.

"I'm mistress here. I can't cower in front of the men who work here."

Eb teased her pussy opening, his big hand between her thighs preventing her from closing them, and went on as though she hadn't spoken.

"When I accused her of trying to let Stockney get a look at those pretty pink nipples, she told me that men are more trouble than they're worth and told me to stay away from her. She also accused me of treating her like a whore and threatened me with you."

"You were being mean!"

"So, I decided to teach her a lesson about trying to pit the two of us against each other."

Jeremiah laid his hand over the cheeks of her bottom, sliding his thumbs threateningly down the crease.

"She's so sweet, you know, but you're right. I keep thinking about the conversation we had back in Kansas City. She can't try to play one of us against the other."

Eb slid a finger into her pussy, laughing softly when she moaned. "That's exactly what I was about to teach her."

It excited her that his anger had apparently changed into something erotically sinister. It aroused her unbearably to be in such a vulnerable position, the slight fear adding to the sexual tension, but she was scared to death to admit it or let them see it for fear they would think badly of her.

It got harder to hide it, though, as their devious attention continued.

Jeremiah squeezed her bottom, pulling her cheeks apart until she felt cool air brush against her puckered opening, sending her excitement and fear both soaring.

Jeremiah paused, holding her open as he spoke to Eb. "You're doing your best to keep her at a distance, though, and that's not fair to any of us. She's not Emily. She's not the woman you walked away from. This is Maggie, Eb. Don't do anything you might regret."

Maggie stilled, a shiver going through her when a thumb slid over her forbidden opening at the same time the finger in her pussy started to move.

Eb stilled, his finger pressed deep.

"What the fuck are you talking about?"

Lying in such a vulnerable position while Eb and Jeremiah fought wasn't something she wanted to do.

"Just let me up and you two can fight all you want to."

Jeremiah's laugh filled her with foreboding. "We would never fight about you in front of you. Oh, no, Maggie, if we did that, you'd just find a way to pit us against each other again. I just want Eb to stop fighting the love I saw on his face when I walked in here."

A slap on her ass had her kicking her legs again.

"And you need to stay out of it."

"Damn you. Let me up."

Both men spoke in low murmurs, and she stilled, struggling to hear what they said.

Another slap landed, making her shriek.

Jeremiah came to kneel beside her head.

"Behave yourself." He brushed her hair back from her face, his smile somehow tender and devious at the same time.

"Let's go back to the house. I don't want to chance anyone else walking in here."

Eb lifted her so fast it made her dizzy, rubbing her warm bottom once more before letting her skirt drop into place.

"You can take your bath and wait for us in bed."

Furious, aroused, and more than a little shaken by the devious smiles on both their faces, Maggie swiped her hair back, hurriedly stepping back out of their reach.

"I'm not going to bed with either one of you. You can both sleep with the horses!"

She stormed out of the shed, her skirts flying as she ran across the yard toward the house, intent to get away from them as fast as possible. Angry at herself for letting Eb hurt her again and hurt by Jeremiah's betrayal, she couldn't face either one of them right now.

Of course, they both caught up with her right away, flanking her and keeping up with her with no apparent effort.

Fighting the stitch in her side, she kept staring straight ahead. "I can't believe I thought you could both take me seriously."

Jeremiah grabbed her hand and spun her, and before she knew it, she found herself over his shoulder.

"Come on, honey. Let's get ready for bed and calm you down."

For the first time, Maggie noticed that several of the ranch hands stood around, amused smiles on their faces as they watched the scene playing out in front of them.

Maggie cringed, not knowing how much they'd witnessed, or what they'd heard, and hid her face in embarrassment.

"Stop treating me like a child, damn it. Put me down."

Jeremiah opened the back door and strode inside before setting her on her feet. "Believe me, Maggie. I don't think of you as a child at all."

Maggie backed away as he stepped closer, jolting when she backed straight into Eb. "You lied to me. I thought you'd started to care about me."

Taking the final step closer, Jeremiah reached out a hand and with one finger traced the curve of her breast.

"I've cared about you since you were a little girl, Maggie. Just not the same way I do now."

Eb's arms came around her from behind, one hand lightly rubbing her stomach. "You're a woman now, Maggie. Not a little girl. You're gonna have to learn how to behave like a woman, one who has two husbands. There's a whole new set of rules you'll have to live by in order to make this work."

Bending to scrape his teeth over her neck, he lowered his voice. "And you'll abide by those rules whether you like it or not."

Jeremiah bent and tugged off her boots before removing his own. "It's been a long day. Your bath is ready in the kitchen, and then I want you to go up to bed. We'll be right up."

Pulling out of Eb's arms, Maggie shot each of them a dirty look. "I don't think it's fair that I have to live by your rules, but both of you can do whatever you want."

Eb reached out and ran his finger over a nipple. "Fair or not, you'll do what we say. Now, are you going to go get your bath, or do you want me to strip you and bathe you myself?"

Maggie lifted her chin. "I'll do it myself, thank you. Don't get mud on my floor."

She turned and strode away, smiling at the stunned silence behind her.

Chapter Nine

Maggie could hardly keep her eyes open as she stared out into the darkness. Determined not to be waiting in bed when Eb and Jeremiah came up, she sat in the window seat wearing her thickest nightgown and the shawl Esmeralda had given her.

She found it hard to believe that she'd only arrived at the Circle T today, and already her life had changed so much.

Hearing their low conversation as they came up the stairs, Maggie stiffened.

"I thought I told you to get in bed. You're gonna catch a cold."

Maggie turned her head, a little surprised at Jeremiah's arrogant tone. "I'm warm enough. I wanted to sit up a bit. You two go ahead."

Eb strode straight toward her, plucking her out of the window seat and holding her high against his chest.

"We're not going to argue with you, Maggie. You'd better get into the habit of doing what you're told, or I'll have you over my knee again."

Jeremiah laughed softly as he turned the bed down. "I'll bet her ass is still warm from the spanking you just gave her."

Eb laid her in the center of the bed, and between the two of them, they efficiently stripped her. "Maybe we'd better check."

He rolled her to her stomach, keeping her there with a hand on her back, and ran his other over her warm bottom.

"Hmm. She's still nice and warm."

Maggie groaned, finding it hard to believe they could get a response from her with so little effort.

Jeremiah bent over her from the other side, spreading her thighs and lifting her until her ass was in the air before sliding a finger into her pussy. "Wet, too. I think our wife likes her spankings a little too much. We'll have to do something about that." He sighed heavily. "But she's tired and cranky. As soon as she comes, she's gonna fall right to sleep."

Maggie buried her face in the pillow. Two minutes ago she'd been alone and shivering, and now, completely naked, with Eb holding her down and his hand on her bottom and Jeremiah slowly stroking her pussy, she burned everywhere.

She hid her face, embarrassed that they knew her shameful secret. How could a woman get sexually excited while being punished?

"I'm right here, you know. Stop talking about me."

Eb slapped her ass in warning. "Quiet." He held his hand over her bottom, once again appearing to know how it held the heat in and made her entire body burn.

"Get the salve. I think we should give a little more attention to this ass while we're making her come."

Jeremiah slid his finger from her pussy. "Good idea, but I get to eat her pussy this time."

Eb moved his hand over her bottom. "While I finger fuck her ass."

Maggie froze, automatically clenching the cheeks of her ass in denial. It was one thing to have them play with her there while in the throes of passion, but it was entirely different to have them focus their attention there with no apparent plans to take her.

"Just take me. You know you want to. Leave my bottom alone and just make love to me."

Eb delivered one hard slap, and then another. "Don't ever try to tell us what to do to you, Maggie. I need to stretch this ass a little more, and you need to learn how much pleasure you can get by focusing on that tight little hole. You're tired and lethargic from your bath, so your resistance is down and you'll relax that bottom a little more."

"No, I won't."

Maggie shuddered when the bed dipped as Jeremiah got up. Turning her head, she watched him undress before collecting a tin of salve.

He turned toward her, his cock hard and standing at attention. Its purplish head glistened with moisture, and she involuntarily licked her lips.

His eyes stayed on hers as he opened the tin and held it out to his brother. "You always trusted us before, honey. Trust us with this. I'm going to watch Eb grease you up, and then I'm going to lap up all your juices."

With a knee on the bed, he leaned closer, running his lips over her shoulder. "And don't lick your lips like that unless you want your mouth filled with my cock."

With a moan, Maggie stuck her face back into the pillow as Eb's strong hand lifted and parted the cheeks of her bottom, exposing her puckered opening.

"You would put it in my mouth?" Her words came out muffled, and, unable to breathe, she turned her head again to repeat them.

Jeremiah replaced Eb's hand on her back with his own, leaving Eb holding her bottom cheeks parted with one hand and his other free.

"Damned right, and I will. Sometimes one of us will fuck you while you please the other with that mouth."

Maggie sucked in a breath as Eb touched her bottom hole, arching her head back as far as she could when he began to push his slick finger into her. Chills raced through her as the salve made it easy for him to push his finger through her tight opening and deep into her.

"Oh, God. It's in there."

Eb parted her cheeks wider. "It sure as hell is. Look at this, Jeremiah. She's squeezing my finger so damned hard she's gonna break it off. I've got to have her."

Jeremiah groaned. "Let me feel."

Eb's finger slid out. "Here, work some more of the salve in her." He released his hold on her bottom. "Lift her higher."

Maggie buried her face again as they lifted her and parted her legs even wider. She knew they could see everything, the cool air blowing over her folds and bottom telling her just how exposed she'd become.

Kicking wildly, she swore at them, alarmed at how quickly her arousal grew.

They were turning her into a woman she no longer recognized, and it scared the hell out of her. How could she respond so completely to something so naughty, so breathtakingly intimate?

Jeremiah kept a hand pressed to her upper back, holding her down as Eb threw off his clothes.

A few seconds later she felt the hair on his thighs against the backs of hers, increasing her panic.

"Ain't that a pretty sight. This little pink hole all greased up and just waiting to be fucked."

Maggie kicked at him, scared that she wouldn't be able to take his cock inside her, but more scared that she would like it and they would use it against her.

"Once you get inside her, sit at the edge of the bed so I can eat her pussy. I'll bet she bucks like a bronco on your cock."

Hiding her face again, she moaned as more of her juices coated her thighs. Her clit throbbed so badly it hurt, and she bit her lip, scared that she would be reduced to begging to get them to touch her there.

Eb chuckled. "Yeah, I'll have to return the favor. Make sure you've got enough salve. I want her greased up real good."

Maggie couldn't believe she was lying there while Eb and Jeremiah talked about her bottom hole and how they planned to take her there. She couldn't believe how much hearing them talk excited her, the anticipation of knowing what they were going to do to her heightening her arousal even more.

Jeremiah's hand tightened on her back. "Easy, Maggie, I'm gonna slide two fingers into you this time."

Maggie reached above her, holding on to the bed rails for support, a whimper escaping as Jeremiah used a twisting motion to press two thick fingers into her. She stilled, breathing in shallow gulps as she tried to adjust to such an intimate and primitive sensation.

It burned, the ring of muscles stretching to accommodate his slow thrusts. Her inner muscles gripped him, making the burn even worse as the chills and tingles that raced from there overwhelmed her.

With slow thrusts, he worked his fingers deep. "Takes all the fight right out of her, doesn't it?"

Eb laughed softly. "Sure does. Now we know how to get her to behave. The piece we had made for her before we left Kansas City's gonna be perfect for her. I almost can't wait until she's bad again so we can punish her with it."

Turning her head again, Maggie whimpered as Jeremiah slid his fingers almost all the way out of her and then thrust them back in again.

"What piece? What are you planning to do to me? Oh! Oh, my God. It burns. It's tingling all over."

Jeremiah chuckled and did it again. "Poor baby. I'll bet your little clit is all swollen. Once Eb gets his cock in you, I'll lick it, but only if you ask me nicely."

Eb growled. "That's enough. I want my cock in her. You should make her suck your cock before you let her come."

Sliding his fingers from her, Jeremiah bent until his head was next to hers. "Hmm, that sounds like fun. I'm gonna love sticking my cock in that hot little mouth."

Pushing the damp tendrils from her forehead, Jeremiah grinned, showing his dimples. "You ready to learn how to use that tongue on my cock, darlin'?"

Unable to prevent it, Maggie looked down, eyeing his cock as Eb pressed his against her puckered opening.

"I don't…oh, God. He's going to put it in me, isn't he?"

Her fear must have shown because Jeremiah's eyes gentled as he lay down beside her.

"Easy, darlin'. Relax that tight ass so Eb can work his cock inside. It's gonna be tight."

Maggie tried to turn away again, but Jeremiah held her head in place with a hand fisted in her hair. "No, don't look away from me. I want to watch your face when he takes your ass."

If there was anything more intimate and intimidating than this, Maggie couldn't imagine it. She groaned as Eb pushed his cock against her, the unrelenting pressure forcing the tight ring to give way. With her bottom up in the air and her thighs spread wide, she had no way to stop him or even slow him down.

"Ahh! Oh, God. Oh, God. It's in me. He put it in me. Oh, God, it burns."

With his hands firm on her hips, not letting her move at all, Eb let out a deep growl. "Fuck. I've only got the head inside her. So damned tight. Fuck, Jeremiah. Play with her nipples or something. Distract her. I've got to get inside her, and she's got a fucking death grip on my cock."

Did they realize how their talk excited her?

Did they have any idea how powerful it made her feel to know that she was responsible for that desperation in Eb's voice?

The chills grew stronger as Eb pressed a little more of his cock into her, the stretching sensation even stronger now than it had been when they used their fingers. She tightened her hands on the bars of the headboard, her toes curling when Jeremiah slid a hand beneath her to stroke first one nipple and then the other, using the other hand to caress her back.

Her clit felt as though it was on fire, swollen and aching with the need to be touched. The strokes to her nipples just made it worse, but no matter what Eb said, nothing could distract her from the burning, too full feeling of her bottom being slowly but deliberately taken.

Eb paused, his hands smoothing over her hips. "That's it, darlin'. We'll take this nice and slow."

She couldn't remember hearing such tenderness in his voice since the night he and Jeremiah comforted her and helped her bury her kitten. To hear it now eased the last of her inhibitions and made her want to give him everything.

"Eb." His name came out on a breath as he began stroking again, each time pressing just a little bit deeper.

She could feel herself open to him, her inner muscles massaging his cock with every thrust. Each time she tightened on him, the burn stole her breath, but still she pushed back against him, needing more.

Jeremiah stayed next to her, and it was his eyes she stared into, but right now she felt more of a connection with Eb than she had since he left all those years ago.

Eb continued to murmur to her, encouraging her and telling her just how good it felt to be inside her.

"That's it, baby. Let me in. Just a little more. No, don't push back. I can't give you all of my cock tonight. You're too damned tight."

Maggie's harsh moans and high pitched whimpers drowned out whatever else Eb said, but the gentleness in his hands and in his tone was more than enough for her.

Being taken by him this way emphasized the difference in them and made her feel even smaller and more feminine than ever before. Instinctively understanding how cruel and demeaning such an act could be, she focused on the sound of his voice. She reveled in the fact that she gave him the ultimate gift, and was confident that he considered it as such.

"Eb?"

Eb paused in his stroking, running his hands up and down her back. "What is it, baby?"

Maggie threw her head back, caught up in the sound of Eb's voice and moaning at the caress of Jeremiah's hand over her breasts.

He'd never called her 'baby' in the past, and the word from his lips now nearly sent her over the edge.

Arching her back, she tilted her bottom higher. "Please. I need you inside me. I need you to hold me."

Wrapping his arms around her from behind, Eb nuzzled her neck.

"Slow and easy, baby. I'll help you, and I'll hold you all you want."

He slid his hand lower over her stomach and down to her mound. Placing a rough finger over her clit, he kissed her neck.

"You do it, honey. Take what you want. You're so fucking tight, you're killing me."

His slow, smooth strokes in her bottom threatened to steal her sanity, as did the infrequent but potent caresses to her clit.

Her entire body shook, every nerve ending alive with need, but she hadn't expected the effect it would have on her mind.

No matter what Jeremiah did or said, her main focus remained on Eb.

He controlled her completely, every smooth thrust of his cock stealing a little more of her and making her truly his.

The tortured moans coming from him between the soft, gravelly words of praise made her heart soar, convincing her that right now, more than ever before, she had just as much of him.

Her cries of pleasure mixed with whimpers of vulnerability both seemed to have extreme effects on him, making him both primitively sexual and breathtakingly tender.

The combination overwhelmed her.

With a hoarse growl, Eb sank into her, removing the hand over her mound to brace himself against the headboard. Leaning over her, he tightened the hand around her waist and used his teeth to scrape the back of her neck.

"I'm in. Don't move, baby. Just breathe, and don't fucking move."

Jeremiah kissed her other shoulder. "Tell me."

Eb hissed when she inadvertently tightened on him. "Nothing ever better. She's drenched and close to coming."

He hissed again, his body trembling against hers. "Her ass is milking me and she's shaking all over. Let me get to the edge of the bed and you can put us both out of our torment. Don't even think about having her suck your cock now. Neither one of us can wait."

Maggie swallowed a sob. "Hurry. I can't—it's too much."

Jeremiah slid from the bed to kneel beside it. "I'll take care of you, honey."

She couldn't believe how full she felt, couldn't believe she'd actually taken his cock into her, but it wasn't easy.

She wouldn't have missed this for the world.

With a groan, he adjusted her, lifting her slightly and settling her on his lap at the edge of the bed. "Easy, baby. I've got you. Just trust me and let me take care of everything. Jeremiah, I've got to hold her up a little. My cock'll go too deep if I don't."

His cock shifted inside her as he moved both of them, the thick heat so hard and solid she couldn't hold back her cries as she struggled to adjust to it.

The concern in his tone and the gentle way he handled her made her feel like something precious, and she never wanted this feeling to end.

Jeremiah held out his hands to help his brother, holding her while Eb got them both in place. Once she was positioned on Eb's lap, Jeremiah spread her legs to hang on either side of his brother's. "She *is* soaked. Jesus."

With a thumb, he pushed back the hood of her clit and whistled. "Damn, all red and swollen. She won't last but a stroke or two."

Leaning back against Eb's shoulder, Maggie turned her face toward him, lifting her hand to hold on to his neck, sinking her fingers into his dark, silky hair. Impaled on his cock, she shuddered as the chills continued, her entire body shaking with the force of them. Her ass burned as it stretched to accommodate his thick cock, grasping at it greedily in an effort to take more.

She kept her body stiff, afraid that she would inadvertently take his cock too deep. "Eb, it's so deep inside me. Oh, God. Help me."

Jeremiah settled himself between her thighs, licking his lips as he parted her folds. "Hold on to her, Eb."

Eb's hand tangled in her hair, keeping her face turned, his eyes hooded and indescribably gentle as they held hers, despite his tortured expression. Tightening the arm he had wrapped around her waist, he smiled tenderly, his voice as soft as a breeze. "I've got her."

Maggie whimpered when his cock jumped inside her, her thighs trembling so hard she curled her feet around his calves.

At the first touch of Jeremiah's mouth on her clit, she screamed, squeezing her eyes closed. Her bottom burned as it clamped down on Eb's cock, the muscles in her abdomen tightening to the point of pain.

Without meaning to, she started to move, using her stomach muscles to rock on Eb, taking more of his cock inside her. She couldn't stay still as the erotic feel of having such thick heat stroking her most intimate opening was too irresistible to deny.

Eb cursed, holding her tighter. "Easy, baby."

Nearly frantic now, Maggie growled at him. "No. Move. Oh, God. It burns everywhere. Help me move. I need to—Oh!"

She'd managed to take Eb's cock deeper as Jeremiah sucked her clit hard. Everything inside her exploded at once, her body stiffening impossibly as the most incredible feeling washed over her. She bucked once, twice, her body jolting with every movement of Jeremiah's tongue, her body arching toward him and wiggling on Eb's lap.

Eb's loud groan in her ear was like no sound she'd ever heard from him before. His body stiffened, his arms like iron as they held her to him. His cock pulsed deep inside her, matching the hot pulsing of her clit.

Both sent her higher, her hoarse screams melding with Eb's deep baritone into a sound both tortured and ecstatic.

The pleasure crested and began its slow descent and she squirmed restlessly to get away from Jeremiah's devastating mouth, gasping at the feel of Eb's cock moving inside her. "Please. No more. No more."

Eb shuddered, his hands gentle as he gathered her against him and Jeremiah lifted his head. Cupping her jaw, Eb tilted her head back against his shoulder. "No more, baby."

Covering her mouth with his, he brushed her lips. "You are so beautiful, baby. That's a girl. Shh. That's my baby."

His kisses were as soft as butterfly wings, and the slow, gentle caresses as his hands moved over her body were like nothing she'd ever imagined and stole her heart completely.

She was his, and no matter what happened in the future, she would never forget this.

She slumped against him, soft moans escaping as he sipped from her lips, moans that he readily swallowed.

Jeremiah straightened and, still on his knees, kissed her shoulder, lightly cupping her breast. "Hell, honey. I never saw anything like that in my life. The way you went wild…My cock's so hard I think I could break stone with it."

Eb nuzzled her jaw, still caressing her as he held her against him. "Too bad. She's had enough. I'm gonna get her cleaned up and into bed."

He lifted her slowly from his cock, smiling when she gasped as it slipped from her. "Poor baby."

Maggie could barely keep her eyes open, so lethargic her movements were clumsy and uncoordinated. "I can do it." She started to rise from Eb's lap, smiling tiredly at Jeremiah as he stood.

Eb clicked his tongue, male satisfaction and indulgence twinkling in his eyes. "No. I'll take care of you."

Standing, he turned and placed her gently in the middle of the bed, bending to kiss her lightly. "Stay put."

Jeremiah sat next to her on the bed, running his hands over her and bent to touch his lips to hers. "You were incredible. I can't wait to get my cock into that tight little ass and feel you clenching on me the way you did with Eb."

She felt guilty for not seeing to his pleasure and wanted to make up for it. She reached for him, lifting her hand to his shoulder. "Jeremiah—"

He caught her hand, kissing her fingers. "No, honey. I'll take care of it myself. Next time, though…" His stiff grin told her just how badly he suffered, making her feel even worse.

"But Jeremiah, it's not fair. Show me what to do."

Eb came back to the bed with two cloths, one damp and the other dry. "No. He can suffer a little. Now be still, so I can get you ready for bed."

Guessing his intention, she started to sit up, her face burning. "Eb, no. I can—"

Eb toppled her back. "I said no, Maggie. Now lay back and be still. Jeremiah, hold her down if she starts to fight me."

Not wanting to be involved in a wrestling match she had no hopes of winning and too tired to try, Maggie held her breath as Eb approached.

To her surprise, he swiped the cloth all over her arms and chest, even under her arms before spreading her thighs.

Jeremiah took the dry cloth to dry what Eb had already washed, running the cloth gently over her skin and frowning when she shivered.

"Hurry up, Eb. She's getting cold."

"She'll be warm enough in a minute."

Eb cleaned their combined juices from her thighs and pussy before raising her legs higher, ignoring Maggie's struggle when he touched the cloth to her puckered opening and began to clean her there.

"Be still, Maggie. I'm your husband, and it's my job to take care of you."

Maggie groaned as he thoroughly cleaned the entire area between her legs, hardly believing that he would do such a thing. "But not this way."

Eb finished with the cloth and tossed it aside, his eyes thoughtful as he watched Jeremiah dry her. Reaching for the tin of salve, he paused to glance at her, his brows going up. "Taking care of you in every way. Now be still so I can use some of this salve on your ass."

Sitting up, she slapped Jeremiah's hands away, staring up at Eb in alarm. "Again?"

Both men started laughing, and insulted, she kicked at them. "Leave me alone."

Eb tumbled her back, his playfulness shocking her. "Nope. You're all ours, and we're never leaving you alone. Now, do you really want to have me wrestle you to your belly and hold you down while I apply the salve, or would you rather lie still and let me rub it in gently and crawl into bed beside you and hold you while you fall asleep?"

Suspicious, she looked from one to the other, eyeing Jeremiah's erection. "Are you sure that's all you're going to do?"

Jeremiah threw back his head and laughed, gesturing toward his cock. "You afraid I'm gonna fuck that tight little bottom? I already told you I'd take care of this myself."

Eb kissed her nose. "Come on, honey. You're too sore for anything else. Breaking you in takes as much patience as breaking in a new horse." He sat up, making a place for himself between her thighs, lifting them over his.

"But you're a hell of a lot softer and smell a hell of a lot better. Now, be good while I work some of this into you. It's for your own good."

Maggie shook her head, her face burning again as he worked the salve into her slightly sore bottom. She sucked in a breath when his finger went deep. "Are all husbands this intimate with their wives?"

Eb grinned. "If they're not, they should be."

Jeremiah grimaced. "I'll be back in a few minutes." He moved the lamp to his side of the bed before he left the room, stroking his cock on the way out the door.

Apparently finished, Eb went to the bowl and washed his hands before coming back to crawl into bed with her.

"Come here, honey."

Maggie's eyes popped open, and she hadn't even realized when they'd closed. She let out a soft moan when Eb pulled her against him, curling into his warmth.

"Go to sleep, baby."

With an arm wrapped around her, he pulled her close and kissed her hair.

Maggie laid her hand on his chest, incredibly touched when he laced her fingers with his.

"Good night, Eb." Not sure if he'd heard her whisper, she closed her eyes and cuddled into him.

The hand on her back moved, caressing her. "Good night, baby."

Despite her exhaustion, Maggie's eyes opened again at the groggy satisfaction in his voice and the fact that he called her "baby" once again. Smiling, she closed her eyes again, filled with hope for their future.

Chapter Ten

"Margaret Tyler! Where the hell are you? You'd better answer me, damn it."

The warm inner glow she'd experienced since waking up to Eb and Jeremiah on either side of her, with their deep "good mornings," tender kisses, and intimate caresses, cooled in an icy breeze.

Maggie straightened from where she'd been gathering supplies, shocked at the temper and slight trace of panic in Eb's tone.

"I'm in here!"

Struggling to hold on to the items she'd gathered, she hurried outside, squinting against the drizzling rain. She stopped abruptly, her pulse tripping when she saw him striding toward her, his long legs eating up the muddy ground. A few ranch hands in the distance looked up in their direction.

Phoenix stood out because of his braid, but because of their slickers and hats pulled low against the cold rain, she didn't recognize the others.

She turned back to watch Eb's approach, wondering what sparked his temper this time.

His hat, positioned low over his forehead, dripped water and kept her from seeing his face clearly, but what she could see didn't bode well for her. Not even the slicker he wore could hide the powerful lines of his body, a body that only hours earlier had been naked in bed beside her, keeping her warm.

"What the hell are you doing out here? Why did you leave the house without telling anyone?"

Blinking against the rain, Maggie stepped back into the shed, not wanting to risk getting everything wet.

"Eb, what are you talking about? I just came out here to—"

He took the last few steps, ripping the things out of her hands, his impatience evident as he tossed them none too gently onto a nearby barrel. Without pausing, he whipped an arm out to catch her around the waist and yanked her against him.

"You scared me."

Not understanding the flash of concern in his eyes, she opened her mouth to ask him about it, only to melt under the heat of his kiss, a kiss that still held the hard edge of anger. His rain-soaked slicker dampened the front of her shirt, making her nipples pebble.

Wrapping her arms around his neck, she no longer felt the cold. The heat from his body penetrated her clothing, warming her from head to toe as one kiss melded into another. With her hands on his shoulders, she pressed herself against him, reveling in the feel of his hard body against hers.

Warming her body was one thing, but what warmed her heart was the underlying tenderness in his kiss, apparent even through the desperation and need, so tangible she could taste them.

He swallowed her moan, brushing her lips with his as he lifted his head, his arms around her steadying her when she swayed. He cupped her jaw, his eyes hardening.

"Don't do it again."

Maggie blinked, his cold tone like a slap to the face.

She pushed at his chest, grimacing when she realized how wet she'd gotten from his slicker.

"What the hell's wrong with you? I came out here to get some supplies, and you act like I did something wrong."

Eb held her away from him and cursed. "Look at you. You're soaking wet. Where the hell's your slicker? What the hell are you doing out here in the rain? Damn it, when I left the house, you were nice and warm in bed, and now look at you. I swear, I have half a mind to turn you over my knee."

Pushing out of his arms, Maggie glared at him, pointing to another barrel. "My slicker's over there, you baboon! And you're right about one thing. You do have half a mind. I took it off because I didn't want to get the bolts of fabric wet when I was looking through them for material to make myself a new nightgown."

Eb's eyes narrowed. "You don't need any damned nightgowns."

Stomping her foot, Maggie put her hands on her hips. "Grr! You make me so damned mad."

"Stop swearing."

"You *told* me to come out here when I need something."

"What the hell did you need that was so damned important?"

"—and I wanted to make some coffee at the house so I didn't have to keep going to the chow shack to get some. I also thought it would be nice to have some ready when you and Jeremiah came in later."

Eb inclined his head. "That would be nice, but we could have gotten it for you."

"I also thought if I got some cloth, I could make a pretty nightgown. It'll give me something to do on days like this."

"You have that big house to take care of. You've got plenty to do."

"I can't do the laundry because it's raining. I wanted to work in the vegetable garden, but I can't now, and I don't know who takes care of it anyway to ask if they'd like my help."

"You don't have to work in the garden. Duke supervises that."

"Duke has enough to do."

"So do you."

"I want to be able to work in the garden. I want to can some of the vegetables for winter."

"We buy them in Tulsa."

"We don't have to. I can do it."

Eb shook his head, taking a step toward her for each one she took back. "It's too much work, and you have enough to do."

"I'm doing it, and that's that. Stop stalking me. You're being mean and contrary, and I don't like it one bit."

"Tough."

"I don't know what you're so mad about. I came out here to get supplies and I'm not going to apologize for that."

Inclining his head again, Eb moved in closer. "Maybe not. But you *are* going to be more careful in the future, or I'll teach you a lesson you'll never forget."

Grabbing her arm, he led her back to the barrel with her slicker and bundled her into it like he was dressing a child.

"Damn it, Eb. Stop manhandling me."

"I'll handle you any damned way I want."

He proved it by dragging her over to the open doorway, holding her upper arm in his tight grip while pointing with the other hand.

"What do you see?"

She snapped her mouth shut, swallowing her retort, and stared in the direction he pointed. "Rain, it's letting up some. That's Phoenix out there and a couple of other men. I don't know who they are. Cows. Horses. Trees. Grass."

She turned to him, frowning. "It's a ranch, Eb. What am I supposed to be looking at?"

Eb's lips thinned. "What was out there when you came outside?"

Surprised, Maggie stared back out into the yard. "I don't know. The same thing that's out there now, I suppose."

Eb nodded, his jaw clenched. "That's what I thought. Damn it, Maggie. Do you see the man on the right?"

At her nod, he continued. "That's Stockney, the man who snuck in here trying to get a look at you naked."

Not understanding what had him so upset, she shrugged, still embarrassed by the entire incident. "We don't know that's what he was doing. He could have been telling the truth. Maybe he heard me cry out and came to investigate."

The thought of the other man hearing her cries of passion still made her feel dirty.

Eb dropped the hand he used to point and turned toward her. "Do you think I like that another man heard what you sound like when you come?" He waved his hand. "But that doesn't matter right now. I know Stockney. You don't. He wouldn't lift a hand to help anyone but himself. And he's violent. The whores won't even let him come around them anymore."

Maggie shuddered with revulsion. "Why do you have someone like that working here?"

A muscle worked in Eb's jaw. "It never mattered before. There's not a man on the place who can't handle him. But now that you're here, he has to go."

Aghast that a man would lose his job because of her, Maggie gasped and reached out to grab Eb's arm.

"But that's not fair. He shouldn't lose his job because of me."

Eb looked down at her arm, his face lined with fury when he met her eyes again. "Do you know what he was doing when you walked in here? Following you. He was peeking into the house and followed you out here. Phoenix saw him and followed *him*, making sure Stockney knew it."

"What do you mean, made sure Stockney knew it? Of course he would know if someone was following him."

Eb's brow went up. "If Phoenix, Blade, or Hawke didn't want you to know they were there, you wouldn't. But that's beside the point. I'd bet my prize bull that Stockney would have come in here offering to help you and then would have attacked you."

He pointed in the distance again where another rider approached Stockney. "Jeremiah's giving him his pay now."

Stunned, Maggie stared up at him, the knots in her stomach getting tighter as the implications set in. "Do you mean he would have...?"

Eb crossed his arms over his chest, watching in the distance. "That's exactly what I mean. That's the kind of thing I've been trying to warn you about. Any man who wouldn't give his life to protect you isn't welcome on the Circle T."

Maggie stared up at him, her jaw dropping. "You can't expect that."

Eb glanced at her before looking out again. "I can, and I do. So do the other men with the women who'll be their wives. It's a dangerous place out here, Maggie, and the women have to be protected at all costs."

His voice lowered, becoming thoughtful. "It's really no life out here without women, something I think we've all come to understand. No civilization, no children, no reason to go on."

Turning to face her fully, he gathered her against him. "A woman makes a man a better man. We talked to Hayes and Wyatt about this before we left, and I think they understood it even better than we did at the time."

Amazed to hear such a thing from his lips, she snuggled against him. "I want to be good for you, Eb. For both you and Jeremiah."

Eb patted her bottom, the underlying threat in his voice giving her pause. "Then start paying attention, Maggie. If you do anything to put yourself in any kind of danger again, I'll beat your ass raw."

* * * *

Thrilled with the new level of closeness between Eb and Maggie, Jeremiah watched them both as they cuddled.

Sitting on the sofa in front of the fire, Maggie lay against Eb watching the flames, her bare feet tucked beneath her. She wore the nightgown they'd taken off of her the night before and the shawl

Esmeralda had given her, her hair loose and lying in shining waves to her hips.

Eb played with the ends of her hair now as he and Jeremiah spoke, his eyes going with increasing frequency to Maggie. His brother didn't seem able to tear his eyes away from her during dinner, the underlying threat in his indulgent gaze amusing Jeremiah no end.

He'd been that way ever since he'd taken Maggie's ass, and Jeremiah knew his brother well enough to understand it.

Her complete surrender had satisfied Eb's dominant nature. Giving herself to him that way, she'd made herself truly his, especially when she responded so completely.

Eb showed a tenderness Jeremiah hadn't seen from his brother in a long time, certainly not since the night they buried Maggie's dead kitten. Eb felt a deep responsibility for anything that belonged to him, and Maggie's submission and sweet response put her at the top of his list.

It wouldn't surprise Jeremiah at all to see Eb fall the rest of the way in love with her, and when that happened, God help anyone who dared to hurt her in any way.

A small seed of unease planted itself in his gut. He couldn't help but wonder what would happen if he inadvertently hurt Maggie and what it would do to his relationship with his brother.

Irritated at himself for the jealousy that came from Eb having established himself so clearly as Maggie's protector, Jeremiah decided it was time to reestablish his own place in this marriage and remind her that she belonged to him just as much as she belonged to Eb.

Sitting in the chair across from them, Jeremiah set aside the small whiskey he allowed himself and rose, crossing to sit on the other side of Maggie.

"Come here, honey."

Relieved when Eb kissed her forehead and lifted his arm resting on her hip, Jeremiah grinned at her sleepy frown and reached for her, sliding his hands under her and pulling her onto his lap.

"I just want to hold you for a while." Settling her more comfortably against him, he smiled when her head fell back against his arm, her blue eyes already clouded with sleep.

She nodded, her eyes already closing.

Running his hands up and down her thighs, he watched her slip into sleep, waiting until her breathing evened out before looking up at his brother.

"Stockney's dangerous. He's made a few friends while he's been working here. Lee, Willy, and Stick always followed him around and did whatever he said. I'd like to get rid of them, too, but they haven't given us cause."

Eb touched Maggie's feet, frowned, and took them in his hands, rubbing them. "I talked to them today. Believe it or not, they're as happy as everyone else to see him go. Turns out he bullied them."

Jeremiah smoothed a hand over her hair. "The thought of Stockney following her today makes me want to hit something. She's gonna have to learn to be more careful."

With a sigh, Eb stared into the fire. "She's not as prepared for life here as I thought. She didn't have a clue anyone was watching her. Hell, she grew up being the darling of the Shenandoah. Everybody there looked out for her."

Jeremiah ran his fingers through the ends of her hair, enjoying the silky texture. "We'll have to make sure the same thing happens here. If anyone like Stockney hurts one of the women, there'll be violence for sure. With all the women we hope to bring here, it could turn into a bloodbath. Trixie told me it took one of her girls two months to recover when Stockney got done with her."

Eb nodded grimly. "Yeah."

Silence fell as both men watched Maggie sleep. Jeremiah slid his hand from her stomach to her breast, smiling faintly when she moaned and turned toward him, pressing her breast more firmly into his hand.

"She's a weakness." Unable to resist, he flicked a thumb over her nipple, his cock stirring impatiently when she moaned again and shifted her legs.

"It scares me. Hell, she could get hurt so easily, and we're not always within shouting distance."

Beneath her nightgown, Eb slid his hands up Maggie's legs. "I know. That's why it just makes sense to have all the men watch out for her and for any other women who come along."

Maggie moaned again, her eyes fluttering open. "That feels good."

Jeremiah bent to kiss her, a bare whisper of his lips over hers, slipping his hand between her thighs, his cock coming to life to find her warm and wet. He slid a finger over her folds and teased her opening before pressing it into her.

The velvety smoothness of her lips rivaled that of the tight pussy he stroked, and swallowing her moan, he sank into both.

Holding her in his arms, hearing the surprise and pleasure in her moans, breathing in the sweet scent of her, he knew he would die before he ever let anyone hurt her.

She opened readily, her lips and thighs parting for him, and he eagerly took advantage of both.

He'd already become addicted to the taste of her, the feel of her in his arms, and each time he touched her, the addiction grew even stronger.

Needing to hear those erotic sounds she made when she came, Jeremiah flicked a thumb over her swollen clit and swallowed her whimper.

Half asleep, she would be too tired to be taken, but he wanted to give her pleasure anyway. A selfish part of him wanted to sink into her, but he would settle for hearing his name on her lips, the need to establish a bond with her again nearly overwhelming.

To his surprise, she pulled at his hair until he lifted his head.

"I want you to take me."

The soft plea in her voice went straight to his cock. The painful press of it against her hip got even worse when a fresh rush of her juices coated his fingers.

Bending again, he brushed his lips over her cheek. "You're tired, honey. Just keep those thighs open, and I'll make you come."

She closed her thighs on his hand and pulled his hair when he attempted to lower his head again. "Don't you want me? Are you mad at me because of that Stockney man?"

The distress and arousal in her eyes both pulled at him on different levels.

He could have overpowered her and continued to stroke her clit, but he held that hand still, while with the other he lifted her higher against his chest.

"Stockney has nothing to do with it, but if you're ever so careless with your safety again, your ass is gonna be bright red. The way you were squirming, I thought you needed to come. Be still, and let me take care of it."

Maggie wiggled again, pulling herself up and rubbing her breasts against his chest. "I want you to be inside me when I do."

Unable to resist her, he slid his hand from between her thighs and with no finesse at all, lifted her higher and freed his cock.

Eb gathered her in his arms and stood, repositioning her until she straddled Jeremiah's lap, meeting his eyes as he cupped Maggie's breasts from behind.

Caught up in his desire for her, he watched her eyes as he lifted her and slowly lowered her onto his cock. He groaned at the hot, slick warmth that surrounded him, holding his breath as her tight pussy clenched on him in time to the flick of Eb's thumbs on her nipples.

He watched in fascination as Eb lifted the hem of her nightgown up and then the garment completely off of her, leaving her naked.

He'd taken a lot of women over the years, but he'd never been so entranced by a woman's body.

Maggie's tiny waist emphasized the voluptuousness of her breasts and hips, making them more exciting to fondle than any other woman's had ever been. Her nipples enticed him more than any other woman's.

Her pussy tasted sweeter.

Her round, firm ass made his hands itch to touch it.

He could have spent all day just sipping from her lips.

Even the sounds she made turned him inside out, each cry, each sigh like a stroke to his cock.

The memory of every other woman he'd ever fucked faded more each time he took her.

Circling her waist, he lifted her now, teasing them both by lowering her slowly onto his cock before raising her inch by inch back up again.

The tight feel of her pussy surrounding him almost made him come on the spot. Watching her closely, he took several deep breaths in an effort to hold back his orgasm.

Eb made it more difficult by nuzzling her neck while cupping her breasts and closing his thumbs and forefingers over her nipples, holding them there.

Maggie squirmed on his cock, gasping when Eb pinched her nipples and tugged.

With a smile and meaningful look at Eb, Jeremiah helped his brother adjust Maggie on the sofa between them with Jeremiah kneeling between her thighs and Eb on his knees above her.

Eb released Maggie's nipples and freed his cock, fisting it in his hand and touching the head to Maggie's cheek. "Open your mouth, baby."

Maggie reached for Eb, crying out when Jeremiah almost completely withdrew from her and slid deep again.

Eb took advantage of her cry and slipped the head of his cock between her parted lips.

"Suck, Maggie."

While Eb moved slowly in and out of Maggie's mouth, he teased her nipples, making her squirm.

Not releasing his hold on her hips, Jeremiah pinched her clit between his thumbs and kept moving her on his cock while Eb fucked her mouth.

Maggie's reaction startled him. She went wild, kicking her legs and grabbing on to Eb's thighs. She took Eb deeper and rocked her hips, her wild cries becoming louder and more desperate with every thrust.

Her pussy clenched on him, the tight hold she had on his cock sending him racing to come.

He wouldn't go without her.

He used one thumb to pull back the hood, used her own juices to lubricate her clit and flicked it, not giving her what she needed, but enough to make her clit burn. It took both of them to hold her when she started bucking, twisting, and turning to get the strokes on her clit she needed and to get Eb to touch her breasts again.

Avoiding her became a challenge, and it wasn't long before both he and Eb laughed at her antics. Between groans, he chuckled when she sucked Eb with an enthusiasm that made his brother curse up a storm, his face a tortured mask as he attempted to slow her down.

"Damn it, Maggie. Slow down. Fuck." His head went up at Jeremiah's laughter. "Wait until your cock's in her mouth. Then we'll see how fucking funny it is."

Bending, he cupped her jaw. "Baby, ease up. Gently." His touch remained tender even though his words came out raw and gritty.

Jeremiah understood his brother's dilemma, doing his best to keep his own hands gentle on her hips even though he felt like his head was about to explode.

Her tight pussy kept clenching on his cock, covering it with her juices.

Working that place inside her took extreme concentration, the texture of her driving him wild.

He closed his eyes, focusing his attention on hitting that spot with every thrust. Holding her trembling body, he kept her folds parted, knowing how much she liked having them exposed, which gave him another idea.

A few more thrusts and he would begin stroking her clit. When her hand touched his, his eyes flew open in shock.

"No!"

Without hesitation, he slapped at her hand, inadvertently hitting her clit with his fingers. Her reaction turned out to be even more of a shock.

She froze, her body drawn tight, and she screamed around Eb's cock. Her body bucked. She kicked her feet, and her knuckles turned white where she grabbed on to Eb's thighs.

Horrified that he'd hurt her, he shared a look of alarm with his brother before reaching for her.

Eb doubled over, bracing a hand on either side of her tiny waist as he groaned his completion.

"Fuck. Baby, let go. Shit. I'm sorry. Fuck. Let me make it better."

He withdrew from her mouth and straightened, scrambling out from under her and dropping to his knees on the floor beside her.

Jeremiah hurriedly withdrew and reached for her. "Honey? Oh, hell, I'm so sorry." He froze at Maggie's cry of outrage.

"Don't you dare stop. Oh! I'm coming. Don't stop. Don't stop."

Whipping his head around, he shared another look of shock with his brother. "Hell, I think she liked that."

Sliding his cock into her again, he groaned at the feel of her pussy grabbing at him and began thrusting in earnest.

Eb bent over her, running his hands up and down her body, his eyes nearly black as he watched her arch and reach for her clit again.

This time Eb was the one who slapped her hand. "No. I'll do it. Put your hands over your head and keep them there."

Jeremiah watched in disbelief when she readily complied, her pussy quivering all around him. As soon as Eb touched her clit, she froze for an instant and then began, screaming and twisting on the sofa, fighting their restraining hands as she came.

Both Jeremiah and Eb cursed, and it took both of them to hold her down for Jeremiah's thrusts and Eb's strokes to her clit.

A deep groan escaped, one that felt like it originated in his toes, the rumble of it consuming his entire body. He came hard, his seed bursting from his cock into her hot pussy with a force that left him weak and trembling.

Breathing heavily, he couldn't take his eyes from her, mesmerized by the sights and sounds of her in the throes of orgasm.

She arched, jolting and clamping down on Jeremiah's cock with every one of Eb's strokes to her clit. Her legs wrapped around his hips, her heels digging into him in an apparent effort to hold him deep.

When she slumped, he shared another look with his brother, all amusement gone.

He couldn't keep his eyes from Maggie for long and, with an indulgent smile, slid his hands beneath her and, still inside her, lifted her limp body against his. Dropping back onto the sofa, he gathered her against him, running his hands up and down her back in an effort to calm her trembling body.

With a hand in her hair and the other on her back, he met Eb's gaze over her shoulder, unsurprised to see the longing in his brother's eyes. "It always takes her so long to settle."

The softness of her creamy skin under his hand never ceased to delight him.

Eb kept his eyes on Maggie as she cuddled into Jeremiah and sighed. He nodded soberly, running his hands up and down her arms while bending to kiss her shoulder. "And then she falls asleep. Give her to me so I can put her to bed."

Jeremiah stood with her, holding her with a hand on her bottom and the other on her back, smiling when she let out a disgruntled moan. "I've got her."

Eb stood with him, holding out his hands as though afraid Jeremiah would drop her, his whisper full of impatience. "Easy with her. Give her to me before you wake her up."

Jeremiah laughed softly, bending to kiss Maggie's cheek when her head fell to his shoulder. "Can you believe how hard she came this time? Hell, I never even heard of a woman coming when she had her clit slapped. I'm gonna have to do it again."

Eb cursed as Jeremiah passed him with her and followed them to the bedroom.

"You didn't hit her hard, did you? Hell, if she's sore because of it—"

Frowning, Jeremiah strode into the bedroom and laid Maggie gently in the middle of the bed, the pale moonlight coming in the window affording enough light for him to watch her immediately curl into a ball.

"Of course I didn't hit her hard. I was only trying to slap her hand away from her clit."

Eb hurried to get in beside her, tucking the covers around her and pulling her close.

Jeremiah watched Maggie curl into Eb and, listening to her satisfied sigh, suddenly felt the cold. "How come you get to hold her?"

He climbed into bed, cuddling into Maggie's warmth. "I took her. I should get to hold her."

Eb opened one eye. "You did, on the way here. It's my turn. Now shut up before you wake her."

* * * *

Hours later, Jeremiah woke as Maggie turned in her sleep and cuddled against him.

"Hmm. Jeremiah."

Her soft whisper eased a knot inside him he hadn't even been aware of until then, but one which must have stayed with him even in sleep.

Wrapping an arm around her to pillow her head on his shoulder, Jeremiah kissed her hair and waited until she settled once again.

Eb grunted from beside him. "What the—? Damn it."

In the darkness, Jeremiah smiled and, with Maggie in his arms, let sleep overtake him again, the tightness in his belly gone.

Chapter Eleven

After washing clothes and putting them on the line, Maggie did her housework and started making pies with the dried apples she found in the supply shed. She'd promised all but one to Duke, who seemed to be softening more toward her every day.

While rolling them out, she'd gotten so caught up in memories of making pies with Esmeralda and thinking about Eb and Jeremiah's reaction to having their favorite dessert that she hadn't even noticed when the clouds started rolling in.

A dangerous thing when living on a ranch.

She heard the rain hit the window and looked outside just as the wind picked up and blew several freshly washed pieces of laundry across the yard.

With a curse, she raced to the back door, pulled on her boots, slicker, and hat, and raced outside. Fighting the wind, she hurried across the yard, her pants becoming soaked within seconds. Several of the things she'd had on the line had already fallen off and were now muddy and would need to be rewashed.

Using some of the more inventive cuss words she'd overheard at the Shenandoah, she stripped the clean items from the line as quickly as she could, not even bothering to chase her hat when it blew away. Wadding them up in a ball, she ran for the back door, eyeing the dirty clothes in resignation.

She'd have to make another trip or risk getting the rest of the clothes dirty.

A flash of lightning came out of the darkening sky, the electricity in the air making the hair on the back of her neck stand on end.

Hearing a loud crack, she spun, watching in horror as smoke came from a nearby tree and a large branch broke from it, falling to the ground.

The deafening thunder that followed had her feet moving again, racing toward the back door. Once inside, she dropped the clothes in an empty basket and ran back out again.

In the two weeks she'd been here, she'd learned how hard it could be to get supplies, and several items of Jeremiah's and Eb's work clothes were about to blow away.

They worked their asses off every day, and she couldn't bear to see the disappointment on their faces if she just ran inside and let their things go.

Surprised at the strength of the wind, she tried to brace herself but fell to the ground several times anyway. The wind had gotten so strong that the rain came down sideways, the force of it stinging her face.

Her knees stung from falling down so many times, but she'd finally gathered every single item she could find. With her arms loaded down with the muddy clothes, she turned to hurry back to the house just when the hail started.

It hit hard, stinging everywhere. The force of the wind knocked her down again, blowing her sideways. Holding on to the clothes with one hand, she dug the fingers of the other into the wet grass and managed to raise herself to one knee, wincing as a large hailstone hit her on the back of the head.

Another hit her shoulder, and then another.

The flashing of light seemed to come from everywhere, followed by thunder so loud it terrified her.

The noise from the wind and the thunder was deafening as she struggled to get to her feet once again. Loud sounds that sounded like crashing came from somewhere behind her, and lightning hit another one of the nearby trees, the sound like that of a gunshot.

Her face was wet with both rain and tears as she got to her knees again, ducking her head against the sticks and leaves that hit her with a force that staggered her.

The sound of thunder grew louder. The snaps and cracks came from all around her now.

A sob broke free as she got to her feet and fought the wind in her determination to get back to the house.

Where were Eb and Jeremiah?

Daring to pause, she looked over her shoulder, sending up a prayer that they'd found shelter. Assuring herself that they knew this terrain and would find a place to stay safe, Maggie couldn't help wishing they were with her.

She'd never been so scared in her life.

She could do this. She would light lanterns and be ready for them when they came in with hot coffee and pie, and everything would be all right.

They counted on her to know how to handle this, and she wouldn't let them down.

She wouldn't let herself down.

The sound of whistling puzzled her and she looked up, horrified to see that a piece of wood from the side of the chow shack broke free. And then another. And another.

One after another, as if a giant hand flicked them away, the entire side of the chow shack came toward her one board at a time. Horrified, she stood rooted to the spot as several of the pieces came hurling in her direction.

They came so fast she didn't even stand a chance of avoiding them.

One hit her hard in the side, another in the shoulder. She didn't even feel any pain as her knees gave out.

And everything went black.

* * * *

Eb watched in horror as the wood sailing across the yard hit Maggie and she fell to the ground, unmoving.

He'd been in the far pasture when he saw the storm coming and raced to get back to the house, realizing that he'd never showed Maggie where the tornado shelters were.

How could he have been so stupid?

He should have been taking care of her and seeing to her safety instead of spending the last month just trying to get inside her whenever he could.

Panic set in, fear like he'd never known pumping wildly through his veins.

Furious with himself and his failure to protect her, he rode faster than ever before in his hurry to get to her. He knew she'd never been afraid of storms in her life. Hell, they'd all had to get her when she got caught in a storm because she would just stand there with a big smile plastered on her face, watching the lightning.

Why hadn't he remembered that until just now?

He didn't bother saying anything to Jeremiah, who rode grim-faced beside him. With all the noise, his brother wouldn't be able to hear him anyway, but they shared a look that said everything.

Maggie was hurt. Nothing else mattered.

Calling her name until he was hoarse, Eb raced to her side, not even waiting for his horse to stop before he flung himself out of the saddle in Maggie's direction.

Alarmed at the blood that ran into her hair, he gathered her against him, leaning over her to protect her from the storm and the flying debris.

Jeremiah leaned over her from the other side. "Maggie! Damn it, Maggie, open your eyes right now."

"Come on! Let's get her to the shelter."

Eb glanced over his shoulder at Duke's mighty roar and nodded. He started to lift her against him, for the first time noticing the dirty clothes all around her. Impatiently throwing them out of the way, he gathered her in his arms, bending over her the best he could to protect her.

Jeremiah leaned over her from the other side, using his body as a buffer as they raced toward the shelter.

Duke strode in front of them, using his big body to deflect the debris that flew toward them.

It seemed to take forever to get across the yard to the shelter situated beside the house, but they finally managed it.

Hawke fought the wind to rush forward while Blade held the door open for them.

"How bad is she hurt? Hell, I'm sorry. I should have gotten here sooner."

Eb shook his head, tightening his arms around her and fighting his panic that she didn't come to. "It's my fault. She's my responsibility."

Several of the other men stood aside, all grim-faced as they watched Eb start down the steps with his precious bundle.

Jeremiah whipped off his slicker and spread it on the dirt floor, and Phoenix immediately covered it with one of the dry blankets they stored there.

Choked with fear and emotion, Eb laid her on the makeshift pallet, swallowing the lump in his throat when she moaned.

"It's all right, baby. We're here. We'll take care of you."

Jeremiah started running his hands up and down her legs and under her slicker. "Just stay still, darlin'."

Hawke and Blade each held a lantern above her and Phoenix hovered over them with yet another blanket.

Duke crouched next to them, lowering the huge knife he always carried toward Maggie.

Eb reacted without thinking, grabbing Duke's arm. He and Jeremiah each swung a fist toward the larger man's face.

Ducking one and blocking the other with a speed unusual for such a large man, Duke glared at both of them.

"I wouldn't hurt your woman."

He looked away, dismissing them, and slid his hand into the waistband of her pants, keeping his hand against her skin to protect it as he slid the knife through the material with alarming ease.

Eb pushed her slicker the rest of the way off of her, wincing at the angry looking red mark on her hip which had already started to bruise. "Hell and damnation."

Duke nodded, removing his hand. "In the chow shack when the side blew off and saw the plank hit her. Tried to yell a warning, but don't think she heard me. Another one glanced off her shoulder and hit her head."

He stood and moved away, but Eb only had eyes for Maggie.

Ripping off his wet kerchief, Eb wiped the blood running far too freely from her temple. "Damn it, Maggie. Wake up." He didn't remember ever being so scared.

Jeremiah used his own kerchief to wipe her face, leaning down to whisper to her.

The sound of the howling wind got louder then quieted again, and for the first time, Eb looked around. Several of the other men stood around them, worried looks on their faces as they lit lanterns and offered bandages and advice. Others stood on the stairs while someone held on to the door.

The sound of the hail hitting the door stopped suddenly, allowing Eb to hear what Jeremiah kept saying to Maggie.

"I love you, honey. Open your eyes."

Eb spun back, hardly able to believe he heard those words from his brother's lips.

Jeremiah brushed Maggie's hair back from her forehead, holding the wet kerchief over her injured hip. "Come on, honey. Open your pretty blue eyes for me. I love you, Maggie. I love you."

Maggie moaned, her eyes fluttering just as Duke pushed his way back to her side, his huge hands full of hailstones.

"This should help." He dropped them into a kerchief another man offered and started to put it on her hip and paused, his eyes meeting Eb's.

Without a word, he handed the ice-filled kerchief over. "You should do this."

Eb accepted the kerchief, his eyes meeting Hawke's as Duke turned and walked away.

Hawke shrugged and whipped the blanket from a preoccupied Phoenix and started to cover Maggie's legs. "I hope you ordered a pint-sized woman for him. I never would have believed Duke had a soft side, but it looks like any woman of his would have to fit in his pocket."

Phoenix grunted. "That wouldn't be hard to do."

Maggie groaned, her eyes fluttering open again, widening when she saw everyone staring down at her.

"What happened?" A look of horror crossed her face. "The laundry!"

"The laundry?" With a sigh of relief, Eb bent over her, keeping the ice on her hip and cursing when she tried to sit up.

Wincing, she fell back.

Jeremiah caught her, lowering her to the blanket. "You went back out in that to get the laundry?"

Maggie shrugged, wincing again. "It was only a storm."

Eb took the ice from her hip and put it to her temple, where a knot had already started to form. "If I don't miss my guess, that was a tornado."

"A tornado?" Maggie leaned into Jeremiah, smiling up at him. "Did you say you love me?"

Jeremiah gathered her against him, kissing her forehead and taking the kerchief from Eb to hold it to the bump on her head. "I did."

Several men chuckled, their relief evident as they turned away. The sounds of the storm outside lessened and dwindled while Eb watched Jeremiah and Maggie cuddle together. Instead of making him jealous, it gave Eb a deep sense of relief that Jeremiah could comfort her while he tended to her injuries and checked for others.

Aware of her scrutiny, Eb took advantage of it while checking her over. "You risked your life for laundry?"

Maggie sighed. "I know how precious supplies are and that it's hard to replace them. Besides, it was just a little wind and rain when I went out there. What kind of ranch wife would I be if I was afraid of going out in the wind and rain?"

Jeremiah held her away, inspecting the injury on her head that had finally stopped bleeding. "You're more precious to us than any supplies. No more risking your safety, you hear me, Maggie Tyler?"

"Boss, the storm's over. Looks like we lost most of the chow shack. We're gonna go check on the livestock."

Eb nodded, not bothering to look over his shoulder at Hart Sanderson. Keeping his eyes on Maggie, he laid a hand over her stomach. "Some things can be replaced. Some things can't."

Maggie sighed, glancing over her shoulder as the men all filed out, chuckling and slapping each other on the back in relief that the damage hadn't been worse and moaning over all the work that needed to be done.

"Ebenezer Tyler, are you saying you love me, too?"

Overcome with emotion and still shaken, Eb took her from Jeremiah, gathering her against him and burying his face in her neck.

"Yes, and if you ever scare me like that again, I'll paddle your ass."

Maggie giggled, the sound like music to his ears. "I'm going to have to work on teaching you to be a gentleman."

Eb placed the kerchief over her hip again, letting his fingers rest on her mound. "You do that. Now tell us both that you love us, too, and we'll carry you to the house."

Maggie sat up, holding her head, but spreading her thighs a few more inches apart, moaning when Eb slid a finger over her clit. "That's blackmail."

Eb nodded and did it again, loving the way her beautiful blue eyes darkened. "Like you said, I'm no gentleman."

Reaching out a hand to each of them, Maggie smiled, her eyes welling with tears. "I've always loved both of you. When you left me, you broke my heart."

Jeremiah slid a hand around her shoulders, smiling down at her when her head fell back to his shoulder. "We'll make it up to you. Now let's get you inside so we can strip you down and check for other injuries. Do you hurt anywhere else?"

"No." Maggie's smile made Eb's heart trip. "Now that I know that you love me, I don't hurt anymore."

Chapter Twelve

Maggie groaned, disgruntled to have the covers pulled away. "Give that back. I'm cold."

Not bothering to open her eyes, she reached out for the quilt, smiling when her hand encountered warm, bare flesh, moaning when an equally warm hand slid gently over her hip.

"Or you can come back here and keep me warm."

Eb chuckled and spread her thighs. "I think I can manage that. Your bruise is all gone."

Maggie's eyes flew open when her wrists were gathered in one strong hand and lifted over her head, her eyes widening to see Jeremiah lowering his mouth to her breast.

They'd delighted her by touching her frequently in the two weeks since the storm, their touches loving and gentle, nothing like the way they'd been before.

She missed it.

She missed the raw passion and fierce determination in their lovemaking more than she'd ever thought possible.

Of course, she loved the tenderness they'd showed since she'd been injured and thrilled at their hushed conversations in the dark.

Both still had hard edges she knew she'd never completely get rid of, but she loved that part of them now. They'd worked tirelessly since the tornado, sending men to town to get supplies and building a new outbuilding, one even larger than the old one.

Jeremiah laughed when she commented on it. "With all the new women coming, they'll have to eat somewhere, at least until they're claimed. Men have already started scooping up the land adjoining the ranch to build houses for their new brides."

Working all day, rebuilding the chow shack, along with fence and rounding up horses and cattle, they still came home several times during the day to check on her. When they found her out in the yard helping Duke cook the never-ending meals he supplied, they'd gone crazy, carrying her back into the house and putting her in bed.

Eb stood over her, his hands on his hips as he scowled down at her. "Stay put, damn it. You're still sore, and what about that bump on your head? What if you get dizzy and fall down?"

Maggie had stared up at him in astonishment. "You really don't think I'm going to stay in bed all day, do you? I haven't stayed in bed all day since Esmeralda put me there when I had a bad cold. I'm not sick, and I'll go crazy here. I'm just helping Duke cook. I helped Cookie enough times to know what to do."

Glowering, Eb shook his head. "No."

She'd done it anyway, ignoring his and Jeremiah's glares, and they'd eventually calmed down, but still checked her injuries every day.

Now that she'd finally recovered, she couldn't wait to see what they had in store for her.

Arching, she sucked in a breath when Eb ran his tongue through her slit. "I told you that last night. Oh, God. More."

Jeremiah sucked a nipple, scraping it with his teeth before raising his head to smile down at her. "You've been telling us that every night for a week, but it was still there."

He nipped at her bottom lip, his eyes hooded. "You've been lying."

Eb's mouth on her slit made it nearly impossible to form a coherent thought. "Oh! No, I wasn't. Ahhh! Lying. You think I'm too fragile to—oh, God—touch me anymore and I want you to—Eb!"

The pull on her clit sent her right to the edge with a speed that left her breathless. Digging her heels into Eb's back, she fought

Jeremiah's hold on her wrists, screaming in frustration when Eb lifted his head. "Damn you. Finish it."

"No." Eb held her legs, his smile devious. "You're all better now, and it's time for you to pay for a few things."

Maggie's pussy clenched at the silky decadence in his deep tone. Her temper flared, her unsatisfied lust adding fuel to the fire.

"There's nothing for me to pay for. Stop teasing me, and make me come. Besides, you said you love me."

Eb blinked. "What's that got to do with anything? We've just been waiting for you to recover to give you the punishments you've been earning."

Shifting restlessly, Maggie tried to get Jeremiah to touch her breasts, rubbing her thighs together in an effort to relieve the ache that settled there. Her clit throbbed, still moist and warm from Eb's tongue.

"Damn it. You said you love me. You can't spank me anymore!"

Jeremiah chuckled. "If we didn't love you, we wouldn't have spanked you in the first place."

Maggie shivered as his fingers traced over her nipples. "That doesn't make any sense. You're only mean to me if you love me? Oh, God. Do that again."

Eb parted her folds and blew lightly on her clit, chuckling when she moaned and kicked her feet.

"If we didn't care about you, we wouldn't care what you did. Your health, safety, and happiness are the most important things to us, and anyone who jeopardizes any one of them will have to pay." Sliding his thumbs lower, he ran his thumb over her puckered opening, his eyes narrowing threateningly. "Including you."

The touch to her bottom hole filled her with trepidation, especially combined with their hooded gazes and Jeremiah's devious smile.

It also sent a wave of longing through her that had her nipples pebbling even tighter, tingling with anticipation. She rocked her hips, her pussy clenching in desperation and releasing even more of her juices.

"I didn't do anything wrong, damn it."

Eb touched her clit, making her jolt at the sharp pleasure. "You went out in a storm when you should have stayed inside where it was safe."

Maggie stared up at him in disbelief, cursing the fact that her clit burned. "Why don't you stay inside safe instead of doing the dangerous work you do? You think I don't know about those cattle rustlers you chased down?"

Jeremiah paused and shot a glance at Eb before narrowing his eyes at her. "How did you know about that?"

Eb tapped her clit. "She's been eavesdropping again. That's how she learned to cuss. Maggie, it's our ranch and our responsibility to protect it. And you."

Maggie bit her lip to keep from crying out at the tap to her clit, not wanting to give them the satisfaction of knowing how effective their teasing was. "And my job is to take care of other things. Like the laundry and cooking. You can't punish me for that."

It sounded like a good argument to her, and she hoped they agreed. She couldn't take much more of their play, not when her body already burned this way, the warning signs of an impending orgasm growing stronger and stronger.

To her frustration, Jeremiah smiled and teased her nipples. "Not when it endangers you unnecessarily, like gathering laundry in the middle of a thunderstorm, and not when it's something we've already told you not to do, like being outside cooking when you're recovering from a head injury."

Having her wrists still clasped in his hand and held over her head left her breasts far too vulnerable, something Jeremiah obviously intended to take advantage of. As hard as she tried, she couldn't remain still while he ran his fingers back and forth over her nipples, the little electric shocks shooting one after another to her slit.

Her pussy leaked even more moisture, coating the fingers Eb teased her with, his knowing smile thrilling her. Her clit throbbed in time with her heartbeat, making it feel swollen and heavy.

The more they played with her body this way, the more she had trouble concentrating on their words. "If I passed out around Duke, he would have helped me."

Eb pressed a thumb against her bottom hole, applying enough pressure to steal her breath. "We told you not to. You've also been getting away with quite a bit the last few weeks, like telling lies about not hurting when you were. You can't lie to us about things like that, Maggie. We can't keep you safe if you don't tell us the truth."

Jeremiah bent, licking a nipple and then blowing on it. "Besides, after the way you responded when I slapped your clit, we're anxious to use the leather piece we bought on you. You seem to be getting a little cocky since we told you we love you."

Maggie closed her hands into fists, her body stiffening when Eb applied a little more pressure, pressing the tip of his finger into her and making her bottom hole sting.

Eb moved his finger, his smile wicked and arrogant. "You seem to think that because we love you, you can get away with anything. We're about to show you differently. Because we love you, you're going to be watched constantly. By everyone."

She opened her mouth to object but forgot what she was about to say when Jeremiah pinched a nipple.

Leaning close, Jeremiah brushed her lips with his. "You wanted us to assure you that all the women would be protected, remember? That includes you, darlin'."

Eb slid from the bed to stand beside it at the same time Jeremiah straightened to kneel on the bed next to her on the other side. In a move so fast she never saw it coming, Eb flipped her to her stomach, even now not putting any pressure on her recently healed hip.

His lips touched her ear, his voice soft velvet layered over strong iron. The firm hand on her lower back held her down, and all the squirming in the world couldn't free her hands.

"The only way to protect you is to get you to obey us. It appears the only way to get you to obey us is to teach you that we mean what we say. To do that, we need to get your attention."

Jeremiah kissed her shoulder on the other side. "A lesson you'll never forget. Remember how wet you got when we spanked you?"

Unable to stop herself, Maggie pressed her mound to the bed. How could she forget? The promise of experiencing that kind of pleasure again had her pussy leaking moisture, but at the same time filled her with a sense of failure.

Closing her hands into fists again, she turned her head to Eb, shivering again when his lips caressed her neck. "I don't understand. I thought you cared about me. I didn't think you'd be mad at me anymore."

Both men stilled, their hands unmoving on her, and a tense silence filled the room. The seconds seemed to drag on forever when the only sound she could hear was that of her own heart.

Keeping her eyes closed, she waited, hardly daring to breathe.

She'd thought they'd finally begun to care for her as a wife. She thought she'd finally earned their respect as a woman, one who could face the hardships of the life they lived.

The silence and stillness ended in a rush as Eb flipped her to her back and gathered her against him, a grim-faced Jeremiah on her other side.

Eb cupped her jaw, turning her to face him. "Not care for you?"

His hand tightened, his face a mask of fury. "I'd give my life to keep you safe. Without question. Without hesitation. Do you know what it felt like to see that board hit you? Do you know that my heart stopped thinking you were dead? Do you know what it felt like to watch you crumble to the ground, or that I prayed the whole time I raced to you? Do you know what it felt like to have you in my arms and you wouldn't open those blue eyes for me?"

Eb gathered her close, burying his face in her hair. "I'd die for you, Maggie. I love you so much I can hardly stand it."

Stunned, Maggie lifted her hand to his hair, holding him against her. "Oh, Eb. Really? You love me that much? You really love me that way?"

He lifted his head, a look of shock and disbelief twisting his features. "I swear, woman, one of these days you're going to push me too far."

A thrill went through her at the "woman," as Jeremiah shot his brother a look and reached for her, wrapping his arms around her. Eb cursed heatedly and shot up from the bed to pace back and forth in front of the window.

With a hand in her hair, Jeremiah lifted her against him. "Maggie, of course we love you. We thought you understood that. When you got hurt, it scared us to death."

Amazed at the remembered horror on his face and the fact that Eb still cursed and paced, Maggie lifted a hand to Jeremiah's cheek, wanting nothing more than to spend her life showing these two remarkable men just how much she loved both of them. "Love me, then. All I ever wanted was for you and Eb to love me. I can't believe you're both really mine. I've loved you both for so long. After all these years…"

Jeremiah smiled, his fingers trailing down her cheek. "Darlin', you scared the hell out of us. We already knew we'd have to keep you in line in order to keep you safe. You've always been too headstrong, which was fine when you were back on the Shenandoah. You had plenty of people to look out for you from the time you learned how to walk. But it's different here, and although you're still going to have people looking out for you, there are dangers here that you never faced back home."

Eb paused next to the bed, his hands on his hips as he scowled down at her. "At home, no one would have left you outside when a damned tornado was brewing. Damn it, Maggie, what the hell were you thinking?"

Maggie blinked. "I was trying to be a good wife. The laundry—"

Jeremiah's eyes flashed in a rare show of temper. "Fuck the laundry! If that board had hit you in the head instead of hitting your shoulder first—"

His hands tightened on her as he rocked her against him. "Christ, when I think about how easily you could have died—hell."

Eb touched her hair. "You're going to learn in a way that makes a hell of an impression just how important your safety is to us. You might get mad, but I don't give a damn."

In a voice as soft as it was menacing, Eb slid a hand over her bottom. "Jeremiah, let's show our darling little wife what will happen to her the next time she decides to risk herself."

Jeremiah tangled his fingers in her hair, tilting her head back to face her fully. The flash of heat in his eyes was her only warning before he flipped her effortlessly over his lap.

Two sharp slaps landed before she could draw a breath, followed quickly by another two.

"You keep yourself safe and out of harm's way no matter what, do you hear me, Margaret Mary?"

Maggie squealed, covering her burning bottom with her hands. "Of course I can hear you. Damn it, stop spanking me."

Jeremiah caught both of her hands in one of his and held them securely at the small of her back. "No." Several more slaps landed in rapid succession.

No matter how much she tried to twist and turn, she couldn't escape her spanking. Cursing and squealing the entire time, she froze when he stopped abruptly and strong hands grasped the cheeks of her ass, spreading them wide.

"What are you doing?" The panic in her voice couldn't be hidden as she tried to clench her buttocks.

Another slap landed before his hands went to her inner thighs, spreading them. Jeremiah rested a forearm across her back, effectively holding her down. "Be still. You're not going anywhere until we're through."

Although the slaps to her bottom burned, the heat from them did more to arouse than to hurt, something she suspected they knew.

With her thighs and bottom cheeks spread, she knew they could see her juices coating her thighs, made worse by the tremendously vulnerable feeling of having her forbidden opening revealed.

Kicking her feet, she tried to look over her shoulder at them. "Why can't you leave my bottom alone?"

Eb chuckled, a devious sound that had her bottom hole clenching defensively. "Because you respond so well to attention there. Playing with your ass and clit gets your attention like nothing else."

Jeremiah ran a hand down her back. "But playing with your clit doesn't scare you. Hell, you even like it when we slap you there. But inserting something into your ass, well, that's another story. That consumes you, doesn't it, darlin'?"

The open tin of salve hit the floor right under her, and she knew they'd done it on purpose so she would know what they intended.

Eb laid a hand low over her bottom, lifting and parting her bottom cheeks again, while at the same time holding in the heat from Jeremiah's spanking.

"Tonight, baby, you're getting fucked by both of your husbands at the same time. By the time tonight rolls around, you'll be begging for it."

Jeremiah rubbed her back at her involuntary shiver. "After you have some time to think about putting yourself at risk again. You won't be able to stop thinking about us for one minute. You'll remember all day not to do anything we wouldn't want you to do."

Bending close, he reached beneath her to pinch a nipple, chuckling when she cried out and tried to rub against him.

"We can do this to you every single day until you learn to remember our rules for you and learn to keep out of trouble, no matter what."

Maggie trembled, crying out when a thick, salve-coated finger slid right through the tight ring of muscle and into her bottom. "Oh, God. I can't believe when you do that to me."

She clenched on it, loving and fearing having that part of her body invaded. The fear added an element to sex she doubted if she'd ever understand, but that took her to another place, a place where nothing existed but sensation.

Another pinch to her nipple and a stroke to her clit had her writhing on Jeremiah's lap, crying out and fighting to get the release she so desperately needed.

Her clit was on fire, the swollen bundle of nerves throbbing endlessly and driving her wild. Her ass wouldn't stop clamping down on the finger moving inside it as it withdrew and came back with even more of the slippery salve.

Suddenly, the finger withdrew, leaving her bottom hole grasping at emptiness.

Through her cries, Jeremiah stood, holding her in front of him with a strong forearm wrapped around her waist. When Eb moved to stand in front of her, she automatically reached out for him, her arms dropping when he smiled and held up a piece of leather.

"This is for you, baby. You'll wear this until we take it off of you. See this little piece of smooth metal in the back? It was made to go up your ass where it'll stay until I take it out."

Jeremiah turned toward the bed, forcing her to her knees at the edge of it and standing between her thighs to keep them spread wide. "You should be thanking us, darlin'. We had that specially made for you."

With her ass in the air and her thighs coated with her juices, Maggie strove for dignity. "Go to hell. Ahh!"

Something hard and cold slid into her ass, not far, but it was wide enough to stretch her, making her feel full and possessed. Before she could adjust to it, Jeremiah lifted her to her feet again, holding her steady as Eb brought the piece of leather up between her legs.

To her shock, he parted her folds and slipped the narrow band of leather between them. From the back, Jeremiah pulled another strip of leather between the cheeks of her bottom.

The leather was pulled tight, pushing the ball of metal a little deeper into her bottom, and both men worked to secure the straps.

Eb stepped back to view his handiwork, an unholy grin spreading across his face. "The leather over your clit was left just a little rougher so it would rub against it as you move today. I'd advise you to wear a dress today instead of your pants, or you're going to be even more uncomfortable."

Taking her nipples between his thumbs and forefingers, he squeezed none too gently, making her knees buckle at the rush of lust that raced through her. "You be good today. We'll be home at lunch to check on you."

He turned and walked out of the room, whistling as he went down the stairs.

Held back against Jeremiah, Maggie let her head roll back to his shoulder. "Jeremiah, please don't leave me this way. Take me."

Cupping her breasts from behind, he scraped his teeth over her neck. "You need to come, darlin'?"

Maggie covered his hands with hers, moaning as his callused palms provided an amazing friction to her nipples. "God, yes."

The metal ball in her bottom felt so decadent and naughty, more overwhelming by the minute. She couldn't stop tightening on it and could already feel her juices dampening the leather between her legs. Rocking her hips, she could feel the leather rub against her clit, and although it had been pulled too tightly for her to get the friction she needed, it didn't hurt, just threatened to drive her insane.

"So you think I should go behind Eb's back and satisfy you?"

Moaning as his hands moved over her, she leaned into him. Wearing nothing but the leather made her feel like such a sexual being, she had trouble thinking of anything else. "Yes. I won't tell him. Jeremiah, please. Take me. Any way you want. You can even take my bottom. Just make me come. I can't stay this way."

The pinch on her nipples was harder this time, and she cried out, but he'd already released her. Bending her over his arm, he slapped her ass several more times, punctuating each slap with a curse. After delivering about a half-dozen of them, he spun her to face him, his eyes cold.

"Look at you." He dragged her to the mirror, meeting her look of shock with a cold stare.

"You're being disciplined, and still you try to pit one of us against the other. Haven't you heard a word we've said to you? Part of being able to protect you is trust. For all of us. If any one of us betrays that trust, we risk everything."

Maggie stared in the mirror, hardly able to believe she was looking at herself. Her hair hung wild and tangled around her shoulder, her eyes darker than she'd ever seen them before. Her nipples, now red because of their attention, stood out as though begging for more.

But the leather piece that went between her legs and attached at the waist attracted her attention even more. It looked sinister and primitive as did the man running his hand over the soft leather and tapping her folds.

"When we come home to eat, be wearing this and nothing else. I want to see this better. Have my razor and soap ready."

He slapped her ass again, smiling coldly at her low moan. "I'm going to shave your pussy while Eb watches. Now get dressed, and don't forget to be ready when we get back."

Chapter Thirteen

Maggie couldn't stand still as she waited for Eb and Jeremiah to come home to eat.

She'd spent the better part of the morning trying to undo the straps that held the leather in place, desperate to rub her clit to release herself from this torment.

She'd come close, too close, to cutting it, but feared their reaction to that too much to take a chance.

Standing in the kitchen wearing nothing but the dreaded leather, she eyed the razor and soap she'd placed next to Jeremiah's plate at the table.

He wouldn't really shave her pussy hair, would he?

If he was trying to scare her, he was doing a hell of a job.

The sound of horses approaching had her spinning back to the window, her heart leaping to her throat to see Eb and Jeremiah crossing the yard toward the house.

They'd gotten into the habit of eating here now instead of the new chow shack, so no one appeared to notice anything amiss.

But Maggie saw their expressions as they approached and knew this would be no ordinary meal.

Not sure where to stand or what to do, she sat at the table where the food waited and crossed her arms over her breasts, sucking in a breath when the knob moved inside her ass.

The sound of the back door opening sent a wave of fear and longing through her, her juices wetting the leather even more. Closing her eyes, she listened to the sounds they made and pictured them removing their jackets and boots. Feeling their presence, she slowly opened her eyes to find them standing in their stockinged feet in the doorway.

"Come here."

Maggie shivered at the ice in Eb's demand and reluctantly stood, her knees shaking as she stepped toward him.

Folding his arms across his chest, he glared down at her. "Put your hands at your sides."

Maggie shot a look at Jeremiah, who simply raised a brow and stared back at her.

Finding no help there, she lowered her hands, and to her consternation, her nipples grew tighter under Eb's gaze.

"Did you try to get Jeremiah to fuck your ass after I left the room?"

Maggie's eyes slid to Jeremiah's again, the sharp edge of betrayal cutting deep. Shrugging, she looked at Eb's belt buckle. "Yes, but—"

"What did I tell you about trying to pit one of us against the other?"

Shrugging again, Maggie glanced up, but the look in his eyes had her staring at his belt buckle again, intrigued that the bulge beneath it continued to grow.

"You said not to."

He reached out a hand and ran a finger down the front of the leather strap between her legs, pausing to tap her folds. "And even wearing this wasn't enough of a reminder about the rules you've been told to obey?"

Not knowing what to say and scared of getting into even more trouble, Maggie shrugged again. "I have to use the necessary."

Jeremiah chuckled, and Maggie looked up in relief, only to encounter Eb's grim expression and Jeremiah's cold smile.

Turning her around, Jeremiah undid the straps from behind. "This had to come off anyway. Go put on my jacket. I'll come with you and stand right outside. Don't be too long. I don't want you touching that clit."

He whipped a drying cloth from a hook and spun her around, wiping the excess salve from her before slapping her bottom. "Go."

Once they returned, Maggie washed her hands as Eb and Jeremiah sat at the table. When she came back and sat down, Eb paused in the act of dumping a spoonful of potatoes on her plate.

"Go take the jacket off."

Damn. She'd hoped to keep it on while they ate. She should have known better.

While she removed it, Eb stood and tossed more wood on the fire, making the kitchen almost uncomfortably warm.

Usually Eb and Jeremiah talked while they ate, including her in the conversation, but today the only sounds came from forks scraping plates and the soft sounds she made when they reached out to touch her.

Which they did often.

She never knew when one of them would reach out and stroke her nipple, caress her shoulder, or run a hand up her thigh. Being on fire made it difficult to eat.

The hard chair beneath her bottom felt strange. She'd never eaten naked before, and the only times she'd ever been naked in the kitchen were during her baths. Embarrassed that her juices wet the chair she sat in, she squirmed, only to moan again when Jeremiah reached out to cup a breast.

"Clear the table so I can shave you."

With a start she realized they'd both finished eating and sat staring at her.

Eb leaned back in his chair, watching her expectantly as he sipped his coffee.

"Hurry up. You've got another spanking coming for what you did after I left this morning, and we've got to put your harness back on."

"Harness?"

Eb shrugged. "It's as good a name for it as any other."

Maggie stacked the plates, inadvertently eyeing the leather piece which hung on Eb's chair. "I don't like it."

"Too bad. Hurry up, so Jeremiah can shave that pussy bare."

As Maggie cleared the table, Eb spoke to his brother as though she wasn't there. "Shaving her pussy's a good idea, especially for her clit spankings. She'll feel it even more."

Ignoring her gasp, Jeremiah nodded and sipped his own coffee. "I've heard it makes a woman more sensitive there. There'll be no hiding from us now."

He got up and added water to the soap to build a lather. "You might have to hold her down so I don't cut her."

"Cut me?" Maggie hurriedly set the dishes aside and raced back to him, aware that both men stared at her breasts. "Jeremiah, please don't do this."

Jeremiah grinned, showing the dimples the women in Kansas City went wild over, and tapped a nipple. "Oh, I'm shaving your pussy, darlin'. You'll just have to stay real still. Consider it part of your punishment."

He set the cup of lather aside and reached for her, his hands circling her waist as he lifted her to sit on the table in front of him. "Lie back."

Holding on to his shoulders, Maggie stared at him in dismay. "On the table? Jeremiah, please don't do this to me."

More scared than she'd like to admit, Maggie hoped to talk him out of it, but Jeremiah remained adamant.

"Lie back or I'll tie you down."

Eb took the decision out of her hands by pulling her back to the edge of the table from behind and lifting her hands over her head. To her astonishment, his cock touched her cheek. "Suck."

His hands went to her breasts as Jeremiah's shaving brush spread lather all over her mound. When she paused, Eb pinched her nipples. "I said, suck. Now, Maggie."

Maggie opened wide, her arousal flaring to life all over again. She didn't know what it was about their high-handedness that excited her so much, but she couldn't argue that it didn't.

The hands at her breasts manipulated her nipples with alarming expertise as the head of Eb's cock passed her lips.

"Stop fidgeting, Maggie. I don't want to cut you."

Reveling in the taste of Eb as his cock slid a little deeper into her mouth, Maggie grabbed on to his hips, forcing herself to remain motionless as Jeremiah's blade slid over her mound.

She couldn't believe they would actually do something to embarrass her this way, but even through her embarrassment, her excitement soared.

She concentrated on sucking Eb, loving the sounds he made as she pleased him, finally understanding why they worked so hard to draw the sounds of pleasure from her.

He groaned, his hands becoming a little rougher on her, roaming over her with abandon as she sucked him as deep as she could to her throat. His firmer touch drove her lust even higher, as it always did when his control slipped.

The blade kept swiping over her mound, the air touching her newly bared skin, adding to the number of sensations bombarding her.

She moaned when Jeremiah lifted her knees and spread her, and the shaving brush swirled over her folds.

"Stay really still now, darlin'. Hell, Eb, don't let her move."

Eb bent farther over her, his cock pushing deeper as he lifted her by the ankles, spreading her legs high and wide.

Maggie sucked frantically, gulping in air through her nose as the sharp razor swiped repeatedly over her folds. Her pussy clenched with the need to be taken by these strong men, men who had a dark side she found irresistible.

She'd never have thought herself capable of the passion that ignited inside her, the passion that seemed to grow stronger with every decadent thing they did to her. She shivered again when

Jeremiah wiped her folds clean, the cool air hitting them almost more than she could stand.

Eb shuddered from above her, the muscles in his thighs becoming rock hard. "Jesus. Look at that. Is she as soft as she looks?"

Maggie wondered if she'd ever get used to them talking about her this way.

She hoped not.

It gave her a glimpse into what they were thinking that she'd probably never get otherwise.

Maggie jolted when fingers traced over her folds, the sensation so strong and strange she automatically started to lift up to see.

Eb released her ankles, one hand under her chin and the other tugging a nipple as his eyes met hers and held them. "No. Keep sucking."

Remembering the last time she'd done this, she kept her legs spread wide for Jeremiah, waiting expectantly for him to plunge into her.

His touch on her too sensitive slit never faltered, but no matter how much she twisted and turned, she couldn't get him to touch her clit.

She sucked Eb harder, her lust not allowing her to be easy on him and determined to get him to come. The last time he'd released into her mouth had surprised her, but this time she knew what to expect.

She knew his taste, knew the deep, tortured sounds he would make, knew how his thighs would tremble.

Maggie wanted it as much as she wanted her own orgasm.

Striving for both, she sucked harder, releasing her hold on his thighs to touch her clit herself.

Eb reacted instantly, slapping her hand away from her clit. "No coming." Sighing, he groaned again. "For either of us."

He withdrew from her mouth, chuckling when she tried to suck him back in. Bending close, he dropped a kiss on her parted lips.

"Which is something you'll regret tonight—I'll be starving for you then the way I am now when I take that tight ass."

He straightened and helped her up, straight into Jeremiah's arms.

Jeremiah smiled faintly, running his fingers over her folds again. "How does it feel?"

Feeling far too exposed, Maggie looked down at herself, her face burning to see how much of her slit showed. Slapping a hand over her mound to cover herself, she lifted her chin and started to scoot to the edge of the table.

"I can't believe you would humiliate me this way. Why would you do this to me?"

Eb seemed content to sit back in his chair, holding the piece of leather loosely in his hand while sipping his coffee.

Jeremiah lifted her from the table, holding her to stand next to him. He ran his fingers through her slick folds again, smiling when she shivered.

"Are you going to tell me you don't like the way this feels?"

Maggie stood stark naked in the kitchen with both of them staring at her, so aroused she had to lock her knees to stay upright.

Holding on to the edge of the table for support, she held a hand over her mound.

"I'm not here for your amusement. I'm your wife, and you can't treat me this way."

Expecting Eb to react, she made the mistake of not paying attention to Jeremiah.

He swatted her ass with a slap that startled her, making her bottom sting. "You are our wife and we damned well treat you like one. You just don't want to act like one. But you'll learn, little girl." He stood, moving behind her and running a threatening hand over her hot bottom.

"You'll learn."

He bent her over the table, spreading her thighs with his and forcing her to face Eb.

Eb smiled, leaning forward to cup a breast while handing the leather piece to Jeremiah over her shoulder.

"Looks like that mouth got you in some trouble again."

The open tin of salve hit the table next to her harder than necessary, bouncing twice before settling.

Eb picked it up, eyeing it thoughtfully. "It looks like we're gonna have to get a good supply of salve stored." Setting the tin aside, he cupped her cheek. "Between you and all the other women we advertised for, we'll be using more salve than flour on the Circle T."

Maggie shivered at the touch of Jeremiah's finger on her bottom hole. "Don't you mean *Desire?*"

Eb caught her nipple, tugging it. "Oh, baby. I mean desire very much. My cock is hard and hot and full of desire to fuck that ass."

Maggie's shriek of outrage turned into a gasp when Jeremiah slid his finger deep. She could never get used to being invaded there, the sensation of helplessness taking her over yet again. Each time felt like the first, the too intimate caress so decadent and forbidding that she could never stop fighting it no matter how much pleasure it gave her.

With a hand on her back, Jeremiah moved his finger inside her. "She's still pretty slick from the other salve. Give me that harness."

Maggie gritted her teeth. "Stop calling it that. I—oh, God."

The ball was forced into her again, the sensation of having her ass plugged never failing to steal her self control.

Eb caressed a nipple, sending another surge of lust racing through her. She hadn't known it would be possible to be this aroused for so long, the strength of it varying, but as long as Eb and Jeremiah kept teasing her and not allowing her to come, it never went away completely.

Her temper sparked and she tried to pull away from Eb, but he must have anticipated it because he held her, his grip unbreakable.

"I wondered how long it would take you. I knew when we came in you weren't aroused enough to have learned your lesson. You'll be good and mad before we get back."

She fought as Jeremiah attached the leather to her again, kicking and screaming, calling them every name she could think of, but nothing seemed to affect them.

When Jeremiah finished, they both released her, standing back and eyeing her naked form smugly.

Hurriedly straightening, she twisted away from both of them, pushing her hair back from her face. "I hate you. I hate both of you. I hope you fall off your horses. I hope you get kicked by a bull. I hope—"

Eb shot to his feet. "We get the picture." Yanking her to him, he ran a hand over the bare cheeks of her bottom and pushed at the leather between her legs, forcing the ball inside her deeper.

"But you'll think of your husbands for the rest of the day, which is what a nice little obedient wife should do. Now go get dressed."

Furious, aroused, confused, Maggie stomped her bare foot. "I'm not going to be waiting here naked for you to get back."

Jeremiah picked her up and set her on the table, shifting the small ball inside her bottom and making it feel huge. "Of course not. We're eating in the chow shack tonight. Can't have all those other men eyeing my property."

Maggie gasped in outrage, which Jeremiah took advantage of, dropping a quick kiss on her parted lips before grinning and walking away.

With her hands fisted at her sides, Maggie listened to them go out the back door, the door slamming shut on their laughter.

One day soon, she'd get the better of them. Both of them.

Going to the pump, she filled a bowl with cool water and splashed her face with it, hoping to quell the heat raging inside her. It helped temporarily, until she started to walk again and the ball shifted inside her and the leather moved over her clit.

Pausing on the stairs, she lifted her hands to her breasts, tugging at her nipples, but it only made things worse. By the time she got to the bedroom and donned her dress, her anger had grown and she'd started muttering to herself.

"I'll show them desire. Trying to control me by using my body against me. When they take me tonight, they're not going to know what hit them. Bastards."

She ran down the stairs to burn off some of the restless energy flowing through her veins, cursing Eb and Jeremiah as much as she longed for them.

After cleaning up the dishes from their mid-day meal, she stared out the window, easily picking them out of the men surrounding them.

She didn't quite know how she did it, but she could always pick both of them out of a dozen ranch hands at a distance, something that had always amused both her father and theirs.

Smiling, she shook her head, wondering what the mail-order brides would think of the men here.

She just hoped the women here would find the love that she had.

That led her to thinking about Savannah. She couldn't wait until her friend got here and wondered what she'd think of Desire, Oklahoma.

Narrowing her eyes toward the stable Eb, Jeremiah, and several other men just entered, Maggie touched her waist where the leather shifted beneath her dress.

She couldn't let her friend, Savannah, see her so easily controlled, especially after all the times she'd lectured her about standing up to her uncle. The more she thought about it, the more determined she became.

How dare Eb and Jeremiah use her weakness for them against her?

She couldn't prevent a smile as she ran her hands over her breasts and shifted slightly, moaning at the feel of the leather moving against her. Of course she wouldn't want them to stop doing things like this to her, but she didn't have to give in quite so easily.

God, she burned.

She couldn't let them just blithely walk away from her when she needed their attention so desperately.

Filled with determination and frustration, she headed toward the back door to slip on her boots. Slamming the door behind her the way they had, she started across the yard, wondering what she'd have to do in order to get them to come back to the house and give her some more of their erotic attention.

Each step took her closer to her destination, and each shifted the leather she wore, stoking her lust.

And her temper.

* * * *

It took Eb far too long to calm down after walking out on Maggie, every instinct screaming at him to go back to the house and finish what he and Jeremiah started.

Leading one of the horses into the stable, Jeremiah tossed the reins aside to a waiting ranch hand. "You don't think it's too much? I mean, for her to be aroused like that all day?"

Eb scrubbed a hand over his face. "Hell, I don't know. I never teased anyone like this before. I played. I fucked them, and that was the end of it. How the hell are we supposed to teach her a lesson if we don't get her damned attention?"

Jeremiah sighed, leaning over one of the rails. "I don't know, but the poor thing's got to be in agony. I know I am."

Eb's temper snapped. "What the hell are we supposed to do? Give in? Go back to find her sewing or something and tell her we think she's had enough?"

"When she's had enough, you'll know it."

Turning his head at the softly spoken words, Eb met Blade's eyes. "Is that a fact?"

Blade shrugged, not looking the least bit repentant at butting into their conversation. "Don't mean to meddle in something that's none of my business, but I couldn't help overhearing. Sometimes I wonder if women are more trouble than they're worth."

He grinned, a flash of white against his dark skin. "Then I get between a set of creamy thighs and remember why I put up with them."

Hawke came up behind him, his tread silent as he crossed the stable, but Blade looked over his shoulder at his approach. "No decent woman is ever gonna let a bastard half-breed in her bed, so don't start on the bosses about the mail-order brides. Just be happy Trixie and her girls let you touch them. Now stop thinking about your cock, and get back to work."

Eb grunted. "I can't wait to see some woman get under Hawke's skin."

Blade shrugged and started to walk away, but Eb stopped him with a hand on his shoulder.

"What did you mean, 'when she's had enough, you'll know it'?"

Blade shrugged, looking uncomfortable for the first time since Eb met him. "I didn't mean to intrude on your business with your wife, but I saw your face when we had the tornado. I know if it was my woman that was hurt—hell, I would have gone crazy."

Eb nodded, shooting a glance at Jeremiah. "Yeah, well, we might have gone too far."

Blade shook his head. "Nothing's too far if it'll make her think twice about putting herself in harm's way again." He shrugged, looking away. "It's hard not to know what's going on at a ranch like this when we're all watching out for each other. And we all watch out for Mrs. Tyler. Women will always let you know when they've had enough of something—or when they need more. Fascinating creatures, aren't they?"

Eb watched him walk away before turning his head to meet his brother's gaze.

Jeremiah's brows went up. "You ever hear him talk so much?"

Phoenix came up beside them without making a sound. "When it comes to women, Blade is very opinionated. Speaking of women, it looks like yours is headed this way, and she doesn't look too happy."

Eb looked up in time to see Maggie crossing the yard to the stable, her skirts flying and looking mad as hell. Aware that the other men watched in amusement, apparently prepared to sit back and enjoy a show, Eb crossed his arms over his chest and waited.

Jeremiah's amused tone came from beside him. "Maggie sure looks like she's wound up some, doesn't she?"

A grin spread on Eb's face, one of anticipation and of love for the tiny bit of dynamite coming toward them with fire in her eyes and fury in every stride.

"Looks mad as a rattler, doesn't she? You looking forward to this as much as I am?"

Jeremiah laughed softly and straightened. "More. Maggie in a temper was always a sight, but now..."

Distracted by the sight of his wife striding toward him, Eb almost missed a move that could have ended in tragedy.

As Maggie passed, Stockney stepped out from where he'd obviously been hiding in the supply shed, gun in hand, and ran toward her.

Stockney grabbed Maggie's arm and yanked her around to face him, stepping squarely into the fist she swung at him. He went down like a sack of flour without a sound.

Maggie didn't even pause to look at him, but kept coming toward the stable, anger coming off of her in waves.

It all happened so fast Eb hadn't been able to react, something that might have cost Maggie her life.

Men paused in their tracks, turning to look at each other, before racing toward Stockney, Hawke out in front.

Phoenix turned from where he'd paused in the doorway, his eyes wide. "Did you see that?" He started laughing and didn't seem able to stop. "You've got yourself a hell of a woman there. Hell, I'm getting out of the way."

Eb strode past him on his way to confront his wife, his heart pounding furiously. Out of the corner of his eye, he saw Hawke and Duke each holding Stockney up by an arm, the other man's gun tucked safely into Hawke's belt.

But Eb had eyes for no one but his wife.

With her hair flying out behind her, she approached him, raising her fist. "Listen, you sidewinder, I've got a few things to say to you."

Eb stopped, nodding soberly, aware of the audience they'd attracted. "Looks like you're a little upset."

Standing next to him, Jeremiah coughed. "Uh, honey, did you see Stockney, or did you just run him over?"

Chuckles of relief and amusement came from all around them, stopping abruptly and turning to coughs when Maggie spun.

Several of the men held their hands up in surrender, a few even taking a step back.

Maggie snorted once and turned back to face him and his brother, her hands on her hips and glaring at them. "He got in my way. I have a few things to say to both of you."

She looked so damned adorable with her hands on her hips, her hair loose and her lips pursed in a pout he could spend the rest of the day kissing.

Eb strode toward her, not about to be chewed out in front of his men and desperate to take his hot little wife. Not pausing when he reached her, he bent and lifted her over his shoulder in one movement and kept going.

Turning his head, he raised his voice. "Jeremiah and I are unavailable for the rest of the day."

He caught Blade's gaze on him, the grinning Indian raising his hand in salute as he passed.

"Yes, Boss. Good luck with that one."

"Hell of a woman."

Eb smiled at Phoenix's words, which could barely be heard over the temper tantrum his wife threw while beating his back. A sharp slap on her ass shut her up long enough for him to be heard.

"They're right, you know. You are a hell of a woman." And he couldn't wait to get inside her.

Maggie hit him again. "Then why do you keep stirring me up and walking out on me, you bastard?"

Walking beside them, Jeremiah ran a hand over her the backs of her thighs. "You've certainly got our attention now, darlin'. Why don't we see what we can do about getting rid of some of this energy you got stored up?"

Maggie beat Eb's back again. "I don't want either one of you. I hate you."

Eb's cock was so hard, walking became almost painful. "We've got all day and all night to change your mind about that."

Chapter Fourteen

Maggie bounced once on the bed and hurried to scramble off the other side. "You can't just pick me up when you want to play with me and ignore me the rest of the time."

Jeremiah turned from hanging his holster, pausing to scowl at her. "We never ignore you, darlin'. We love you."

Not about to be appeased, Maggie paced restlessly, her gaze sliding with annoying regularity to where both men undressed. "You made me sit at the table naked. I can't believe I did that. Why the hell did I do that?"

"Because we made you."

"Because you wanted to."

Eb and Jeremiah both answered at the same time, looking at each other with a shrug, and resumed undressing, tossing their clothes into the corner.

Tossing his shirt aside, Eb watched thoughtfully as she paced. "You're going to tire yourself out before we even start. You stripped earlier because if you hadn't, we would have stripped you and you knew it. We also would have paddled your ass again for disobeying us. You knew that, too. Didn't you?"

Jeremiah stripped off his shirt, revealing a chest that never failed to make her hands itch to touch it.

"You also did it because you wanted to. You were soaking wet when we got here. Admit it, darlin'. You like it when we tease you."

Furious that he was right, Maggie stomped her foot, turning away to hide her expression at the way the leather moved against her clit, the ball attached to it shifting in her bottom.

She stilled as a commotion in the yard below caught her attention.

She watched as several of the hands surrounded Stockney, who looked as though he could barely stand, and even from this distance she could see that his face was swollen, his shirt blood-stained.

"What are they doing to him?"

Eb joined her at the window, pulling her back against his now naked body, his arms going around her as he looked at the scene below over her shoulder.

"They'll beat the hell out of him and send him on his way. It's one of our laws around here now, honey. Thanks to you. Any man who hurts a woman will have the shit beaten out of him and run out of town."

She tried not to react to his cock pressing against her back but couldn't stop the flow of heat from coating the leather between her thighs.

Jeremiah came up beside her and lifted her chin, his eyes twinkling in amusement. "And if he comes back, he'll be beaten and run out of town again." Running a finger down her cheek, over her jaw, and down to her neck, he smiled. "Our women are our most precious possessions and must be protected at all costs. All the men feel the same. That's how Desire will be run."

Maggie knocked his hand away, gasping as he stepped closer and his cock touched her belly. "He didn't hurt me, and I'm not a possession."

Eb pressed his cock into the small of her back. "He wanted to hurt you, but you knocked him out. Mad at us, were you?"

Maggie swallowed heavily as Eb's hand slid to her mound. "Still am. And I'm still not your possession."

Jeremiah's hand went back to her neck and down, teasing the curve of her breast, making her already pebbled nipples ache with the need to be touched.

"You're about to see how wrong you are about that, darlin'. You're about to be possessed in a way that'll leave you in no doubt that you're our most prized possession."

Maggie opened her mouth to say something but forgot it when he placed a hand over her breast and bent to take her mouth with his. She could practically feel herself melting as Jeremiah deepened his kiss, the heat from his naked body warming her from the front and Eb's warming her from behind.

Warm hands touched her everywhere, slow, long caresses that calmed her temper and excited her at the same time. Jeremiah's lips brushed over hers and nipped gently between long, drugging kisses that sent her senses soaring.

Eb's lips at the back of her neck set off a riot of tingles racing through her and moved on to her bare shoulders as her shirt somehow came loose. Over her shirt, his hands on her breasts cupped and caressed, his thumbs teasing her nipples.

She ached to feel the rough texture of his hands over her naked breasts and held her breath when his hands slid down her arms, taking her shirt with them. Naked from the waist up, she raised her hands to Jeremiah's shoulders, moaning into his mouth when Eb's hands covered her breasts from behind.

Jeremiah's hands went to her waist and within seconds, her skirt puddled at her feet, leaving her naked except for the leather strap between her legs. His lips left hers, trailing over her jaw.

"You're a hell of a woman all right, and you're all ours."

Hands continued to move over her, and she reveled in the fact that she could tell them apart. Eb and Jeremiah each had their own rhythm, their own way of touching her, and somehow the combination of both of them doing it at the same time sent her soaring like nothing else.

Being the center of attention of two men would be incredible enough, but to have two men such as Eb and Jeremiah using their hands and lips on her as though not being able to get enough of her made her inhibitions fall away with a speed that should have alarmed her.

When Eb's hands went to the fastening of the strap at her waist, she shuddered against Jeremiah, gripping his shoulders like a lifeline. The ball shifted inside her as Eb worked to undo the strap, sending chills chasing one after the other through her.

The fingers that moved lightly over her folds belonged to Jeremiah, his caress slightly different, more devious than Eb's and no less thrilling.

Eb's deliberate and firmer strokes to her nipples drove her insane as he finished loosening the strap. His hand dropped to her waist, holding her steady as he used the same deliberation to work the small metal ball from her bottom.

She shivered as he drew it out, her bottom hole forced to stretch as the ball widened before narrowing again. A whimper escaped as she came to her toes, her inner muscles still clenching as the feeling of possession lingered.

"Shh, that's my girl."

Jeremiah's soft whisper warmed her neck as he bent over her, gathering her against him. Lifting his head, he stared down at her, reaching up to take her face in his hands. "Trust us, darlin'."

Hearing the leather strap hitting the floor, Maggie trembled, a moan escaping when Eb ran his hands up and down her back and bottom.

"You're going to do it now, aren't you?"

She shook everywhere with anticipation and the overwhelming fear of the unknown. She'd loved everything they'd done to her. She'd even loved her spankings, although she'd never admit it. She didn't know, though, if she could handle what they planned to do to her now.

Eb's lips touched her back, moving lower. "Yes, we are. We'll be gentle with you, Maggie. I promise. If you don't like something, we'll stop. All you have to do is let us know. Talk to us, baby."

The feel of his lips trailing over her bottom made it even more sensitive and had her lifting into him, her head falling back in abandon when Jeremiah slipped a finger into her pussy.

Maggie struggled to get her mind to work, not sure if she'd understood. It proved to be difficult when Jeremiah began stroking, sliding a thumb over her clit. "Do you mean, ah, that, uh, oh God, that you'll stop if I say—oh!"

With a soft laugh, Jeremiah nuzzled her neck, wrapping his arms around her to absorb her shudders. "Yep, but you're not going to want to stop. Just let us take care of everything, and you're gonna come so hard, darlin', you'll scream the roof off."

He swung her off her feet, lifting her high against his chest and tossed her on the bed, immediately following her and lying on top of her. Pressing her into the soft bedding, Jeremiah gathered her close and rolled with her, pulling her knees to rest on either side of his hips.

Unused to being in such a position, Maggie met his eyes as he sat her up to straddle him. The feel of his abdomen against her naked folds sent a shock of awareness through her. It had become even more sensitive there now, so much so that even the lightest touch there now made her clit tingle with anticipation.

Meeting his eyes, she looked around to see Eb approaching the bed carrying the tin of salve. Licking her lips, she turned back to Jeremiah. "I don't know what to do."

Eb sat next to her, setting the tin down somewhere behind her back, his hand sliding over her belly as he bent to kiss her shoulder.

"You just have to trust us."

She moaned as his hand went to her hair as the other touched her bare folds, his finger moving in circles around her throbbing clit.

Eb leaned her back over his arm, his other hand sliding from her slit to her breasts.

"Do you know what you looked like coming across the yard like that? I couldn't take my eyes off of you. I didn't see Stockney until it was too late to stop him."

He bent close, rubbing his cheek against hers. "I couldn't stand it if anything happened to you. I know you're going to get mad at me for punishing you when you scare me that way, but it's better than what could have happened. I can't lose you, Maggie."

Stunned by his admission and by the shudder that went through him, Maggie threaded her fingers through his overlong hair, crying out when Jeremiah stroked her clit. Holding Eb close, she gasped when he applied more pressure to her nipple.

"I don't want to be punished. I'm not a child. Oh, God. I want to come." Her knees tightened on Jeremiah's hips, and she rocked against him, rocking harder when his finger left her clit to circle her pussy opening.

Eb scraped his teeth down her jaw, his hand firm at her back.

"Does this feel like we still consider you a child, baby? And your argument about not wanting to be punished might be more effective if you didn't get soaking wet every time we did it."

Jeremiah slid a finger deep, pressing at that sensitive place inside her.

"Wait until you earn your next spanking. I'm spanking your clit until you beg to come. I like the way this feels. I think she should be kept bare here."

The answering throb of her clit nearly sent her over, but Jeremiah pulled back slightly, no longer caressing her clit directly. Instead he played with her, touching her all around it but not giving her the friction she needed.

Eb lifted his head. "I think so, too. What do you think, Maggie? We're going to keep you this way."

He turned his head, blowing air over her wet folds, chuckling when she cried out. "Yes, I think I like you all open like this."

Holding on to him, Maggie moaned and rocked harder against the cock pressing into her back. More moisture coated Jeremiah's fingers as he continued to play with her pussy and clit while Eb lowered his mouth to her other breast and sucked a nipple, this time using his teeth.

Her body screamed for release, their combined play taking her quickly to the edge.

"Now."

Her eyes flew open at Jeremiah's curt tone, groaning in frustration when his hands left her slit to settle at her waist as Eb sat her up on his brother's stomach and released her. Flattening her hands on Jeremiah's muscular chest, Maggie rocked again, throwing her head back and rubbing her clit against his abdomen.

Jeremiah lifted her. "Another time, darlin', I would sit back and let you go, but I'm too fucking hungry for you right now."

"Damn it, Jeremiah. I was getting ready to come!"

She tried to twist out of his grasp so she could rub herself against him again but stilled when the head of his cock touched her pussy and began to press inside her. She gasped at the hard heat that slowly filled her, the width of it stretching her deliciously as it forged its way deep.

Fisting her hands, she struggled to take all of him, thankful that her juices made his possession easier. She stilled when the head of his cock touched her womb, her eyes shooting to his.

Jeremiah's eyes closed as a muscle worked in his jaw. "You took all of my cock, Maggie. Don't tighten up. I won't hurt you."

A string of curses followed, amusing her despite the circumstances. "Fuck. Maggie. Stay still, darlin'. Don't go ridin' me yet. Hell, you're tight."

The bed shifted behind her seconds before Eb's hands settled at her waist. "Slow down, baby. I don't want you coming until I'm in your ass."

She trembled with longing and fear as Eb wrapped an arm around her waist from behind, a fierce possessiveness in his hold that hadn't been there before. A prickling sensation at her neck was her only warning before his lips settled there.

"My cock's hard as iron just thinking about getting inside this ass."

Maggie cried out, clenching on the slick finger he slid deep and also on Jeremiah's cock, gasping when both moved inside her.

Every muscle became tight, trembling with apprehension and a desire so strong it made it nearly impossible to breathe, impossible to think.

"It's too tight like this. Oh, God. Too full."

Jeremiah groaned, holding her thighs against his side. "You're telling me. Hell, I can't even imagine what it's gonna feel like when Eb gets his cock inside you."

Holding on to Jeremiah's arms, she arched back as his hands closed over her breasts. Flattening her palms on his chest again, Maggie watched his face in fascination. Thrilled that the tortured look marring his features came from being inside her, she started to lean down toward him, hungry for his kiss but not willing to give up the expert way he manipulated her nipples.

She groaned when the finger in her bottom slid from her so fast it left her clenching, which drew another moan from Jeremiah.

Sliding his hands to her hips, Jeremiah held her steady. "Eb, I swear, when I take her ass, I'm going to tease her the way you are. See if you can hold out long enough."

Eb chuckled, a sound filled with tension more than amusement, the harsh tone of it sending a wave of erotic longing through her that made every inch of her skin tingle. "I don't want to hurt her. I want to make sure she has enough salve."

Maggie jolted as a salve-coated finger slid into her again with no warning. If not for Jeremiah's hold on her hips and Eb's on her back, she probably would have shot up to her knees.

The salve eased his way, and with her legs spread, her involuntary tightening did nothing to slow him down. He withdrew again, just as quickly, and pressed a hand down on her back.

"Hang on to her, Jeremiah. When I start to work the head of my cock into her, she's gonna try to buck me off."

Maggie shook, unable to believe this was really happening. As much as they'd talked about it, nothing could have prepared her for the feel of Jeremiah's cock filling her while Eb touched the head of his cock against her puckered opening and began to press into her.

Held against Jeremiah, she sank her fingers into his shoulders, turning her face into his chest. The chills racing through her now were nothing like those from before, stronger and more potent than ever as Eb's cock pressed insistently past the tight ring of muscle, stilling just inside her.

Struggling to get enough air in her lungs, Maggie whimpered. "It burns. Oh, God. I can't."

Eb wrapped his arms around her from behind and very gently lifted her from Jeremiah's chest, burying his face in her neck as he lightly stroked her breasts. In a voice as rough and jagged as broken glass, he spoke against her hair, his breathing as harsh as hers.

"I won't go any deeper until you're ready, baby. I promise."

Trusting him completely, she relaxed somewhat and opened her eyes. With a shuddering breath, she moaned, unable to stop clenching on both cocks inside her, unable to believe it was possible to be so full.

Their immediate and hoarse groans made her feel even better, giving her a confidence she desperately needed.

They could never have hidden their desire for her, but the caring that made them rein it in excited her more than anything else. It allowed her a freedom she'd been too frightened to experience before.

Jeremiah stared up at her, his eyes watchful, the love shining in them stealing her breath.

Smiling tremulously, she purposely clenched on both of them.

"You do love me, don't you? You're both soft on me, no matter how tough you try to be."

Jeremiah grinned, shifting beneath her, and started to thrust slowly in and out of her pussy.

Eb sank his teeth into her neck. "That's brave talk for a woman with a cock up her ass."

Turning her head, Maggie gasped, a shiver going through her as he nipped her shoulder. "I trust you, Eb. I've always trusted you and Jeremiah with my life."

She shuddered as both cocks inside her moved, all teasing forgotten. The tingles increased, the full feeling adding an element she'd never felt before. "I'm so full. I feel both of you everywhere."

Having the men she loved, the men she'd thought she'd lost forever, both inside her was like a dream. Their love surrounded her, every breath, every caress filled with desire and affection.

It was something she was grateful for right now as she tried to adjust to having two large cocks stretching her, filling her pussy and ass with a heat and uncompromising hardness that stroked her inner flesh more intimately than she ever thought possible.

Jeremiah groaned, sliding deep as Eb withdrew. "You are full, darlin'. Jesus, this is killing me."

Eb growled. "You should be in her ass. She's squeezing the hell out of my cock."

"You want to trade places?"

"No." With a hand on her back, Eb lowered Maggie a little more over Jeremiah and thrust as Jeremiah withdrew. "I like where I am just fine. Fuck, Maggie. Stop clenching."

Confident now, she did it again, a thrill going through her at their answering groans.

Jeremiah tightened his hands on her hips, his eyes flashing gold.

"I don't know about you, Eb, but I've just about had enough of our wife's teasing."

Rocking her hips, Maggie moaned at the friction on her clit.

"It's about time."

She cried out as both men started moving, stroking in and out of her with a rhythm that threatened her sanity. She kept crying out, beating on Jeremiah's chest as Eb went deeper with every thrust.

Chills accompanied the tingles that raced through her now, combining and making each of them stronger.

Impossibly full, Maggie shook everywhere, the fierce sizzles racing through her so fast now that she couldn't tell where one ended and the next began. They consumed her, blending into each other until they didn't stop at all, each one layering over the last.

Her clit felt swollen and heavy, the occasional brush along Jeremiah's abdomen like a hot jolt of lightning shooting through her.

Eb and Jeremiah spoke to her between groans and curses, their breathing labored as they continued to pump their cocks into her.

"Do it."

Eb's growled demand seemed to come up from the depths of his soul.

Not knowing what to expect, Maggie froze at the touch of Jeremiah's thumb to her clit. He didn't pause at all, circling the damp bundle of nerves with a feather-light touch that never faltered, throwing her fast and furiously over the edge.

Her scream didn't sound human as the enormous wave of blinding ecstasy washed over her. Losing complete control of her body, she screamed again as her inner muscles clamped down on both of them with a strength that she wouldn't have believed herself capable of.

Their cocks felt huge inside her, filling her like heated iron, unrelenting as they forged into her.

Both men roared their completion, the sound so animalistic and deep, it actually frightened her.

It was all too raw, too strong, too overwhelming, and she surrendered to it without a qualm.

Jeremiah's arms came around her, pulling her to his chest with a shudder.

Eb braced himself with a hand on either side of his brother and dropped his head onto her back, groaning and breathing heavily.

Snug between them, Maggie slumped against Jeremiah, wondering if she'd ever catch her breath. Trembling, she closed her eyes, so lethargic now that even the thought of opening them again was beyond her.

The hand running over her hair paused. "Are you all right, honey?"

Pleased with herself and with them, and happier than she'd ever thought she could be, Maggie smiled, not even attempting to open her eyes.

"I'm terrific."

Eb lifted his head, his lips warm on her back. "True."

The bed shifted as he straightened and, with a groan, withdrew from her bottom.

Maggie moaned as the head of his cock slid past the tight ring of muscle, knowing she'd never get used to such intimacy, jolting when a playful slap landed on her vulnerable ass. "Hey!"

Eb's lips moved over the place he'd just slapped. "You're terrific when you're not terrifying."

Jeremiah tightened his arms around her, pressing his cheek to her hair. "And when you scare us, you know what happens, so be warned."

Maggie lifted herself up to stare down at him, absently listening to Eb pour water into the wash bowl.

"You don't scare me anymore. You could have hurt me when you took me the way you just did, but both of you were scared to."

Jeremiah frowned. "We don't want to hurt you. What the hell made you think we'd want to hurt you? Hard-headed woman. We just want you to be safe. If beating your ass or using the harness on you makes you more aware of what you do, then that's what we'll do."

Maggie narrowed her eyes. "It's not a harness."

The bed shifted again and a few seconds later, a wet cloth swiped the place between her legs, making her jump.

"Move, Jeremiah, so I can take care of her."

"Stop that!" She tried to scramble to her knees, but Jeremiah held strong, withdrawing from her. With her face held against his chest, she shivered as the cloth swiped her pussy, the rough material sliding over her clit. "I can do it."

Eb finished there and parted the cheeks of her bottom, slapping it again when she squirmed. "So can I. It's part of taking care of you, baby. Don't try to tell me how to do my job."

As he finished, Jeremiah loosened his hold, his hands moving slowly up and down her back.

She heard more water being poured and turned to see Eb cleaning up before turning and coming back to the bed to sit beside her.

"Come here, baby."

Prepared to be transferred to his arms, Maggie reached out for him, stunned when Jeremiah pulled her back and buried his face in her neck.

"Did you mean it?"

Maggie shared a look with Eb, before turning her face toward Jeremiah, automatically softening her voice at the insecurity in his. "Did I mean what?"

Jeremiah held her slightly away from him, brushing her tangled hair back from her face. "Did you mean it when you said that you trust us with your life?"

Smiling, her heart nearly bursting with love for both of them, Maggie ran a finger over his lips. "Of course. You've always been my friends, my heroes." She drew a deep breath and let it out slowly, hardly able to believe that all her dreams had come true. "And now you're my husbands."

Jeremiah let out a breath she hadn't realized he'd been holding.

"That we are, and we'll be good husbands to you, honey. I don't ever want you to regret taking on two men as your husbands. It took

Eb and me some time to figure this out, and we're gonna make mistakes. I just don't want you to ever forget how much we both love you."

Maggie smiled through her tears. "And I love both of you. I've always loved you."

Eb gave her one of his rare grins and pulled her onto his lap. "I know you didn't think it would work, but it does, Maggie."

In a return of the arrogance she loved so much, he patted her shoulder. "Just let us take care of everything. You won't regret it."

Maggie watched Jeremiah rise from the bed, admiring his muscular physique as he moved gracefully to the wash bowl. Tugging one of Eb's chest hairs, she grinned when he growled at her and slapped her hand before grabbing it in his and kissing her fingers.

"Are you kidding? Every woman should have more than one husband. That way both sides of the bed are nice and warm. Maybe we should make it one of your laws."

Thinking about Savannah, Hayes, and Wyatt, she cuddled against Eb's chest, smiling again when his arms immediately came around her. She reached out a hand to Jeremiah as he came back to sit near her feet, his eyes twinkling with mischief.

"We've got enough laws regarding our women, laws we've already written down and that every man here has signed."

Maggie sat up, intrigued. "Really? Can I see them?"

Eb tumbled her to her back between them. "Nope. Man's work. Women just try to mess things up. As long as the men are in charge, Desire will flourish."

Maggie smiled to herself as they bundled her into bed, making sure the quilt covered her.

Straightening, Eb reached for his pants. "Go to sleep. We're going to check on a few things and bring supper back with us. After that, you can soak in the tub for a bit."

Jeremiah frowned worriedly and reached for his own clothes. "Do you think it was too soon? Hell, what if she's sore?"

Eb slid his arms into his sleeves, pausing to cover her shoulder when she turned to watch them. "I was easy with her. You saw how much salve I used, and we stretched her first."

Jeremiah followed Eb to the hallway, fastening his own shirt. "We should rub her down. She's probably going to be sore."

"I'll get some liniment from the storage shed."

"Did you get any of those fancy soaps? Maggie'll like them. She always smells so good and Esmeralda said she uses them."

"We bought everything in the damned store. If they were there, I got them."

"I'll find them. I'll ask Duke if he's seen them. He knows where everything is."

"If you don't find any, we'll order them in town the next time we go. She also needs new boots. Hers are getting worn."

Maggie listened until they went out the back door and their voices faded. Turning onto her side, she snuggled into the covers, smiling to herself as she traced a design on the quilt.

She closed her eyes, so worn out she could barely move, and wondered when they'd realize that their ingrained protectiveness meant she was in charge after all.

Picturing an entire town of women living the same way she did with the hard-edged cowboys she'd already met, she smiled as she slipped into sleep.

The laws of this town might just work out after all.

One thing was certain.

Desire would definitely be an unusual place to live.

Epilogue

"Are you sure that number's right?"

Sitting on a horse that Eb and Jeremiah had just recently given to her, Maggie watched in amusement as they finished putting up the sign at the edge of their land.

Eb shot her a look over his shoulder. "Of course it's right. We know how many men work at the Circle T."

Jeremiah grinned. "Plus one hot little woman."

Maggie smiled at the wooden squares with numbers painted on them scattered all over the ground. Reaching into her bag, she took out another biscuit to nibble on while she watched them.

"I have to admit, it was pretty smart to make the numbers that way so you can change them. Savannah, Hayes, and Wyatt should be coming soon, and you'll have to add them."

Finished with the sign, Jeremiah stepped away, wiping his brow with his sleeve. "Yeah, and so should all those mail-order brides we advertised for. Hell, we're going to have to come out here and change this number every week."

Eb tossed a hammer aside and picked up the remaining numbers and stuffed them into his saddlebag. "We'll make it Hayes' and Wyatt's responsibility. Hell, the sheriff should know how many people live in the town better than anybody else."

Finishing off her biscuit, Maggie slid from the saddle and approached the sign, smiling at each of them.

"Desire. I can't believe you really named your town Desire."

"Our town." Eb finished with his task and came to stand beside her, putting an arm around her, and she immediately cuddled into his warmth. He touched her like this all the time now, and she couldn't get enough of it. Every time they came near her, they reached out a hand for her as though they couldn't help themselves.

It was heady stuff.

She felt the same way, touching them at every opportunity, and it had become so obvious that even the ranch hands teased them about it.

Eb kissed her forehead, smiling indulgently. "Soon, it'll be everyone's town. The men are snapping up the adjoining land, ready to build homes. Some of this will be turned over to businesses so we'll have a place to get supplies and you women will have a place to shop."

Jeremiah came up on her other side and touched her hair, his fingers running over the strands as he stared down at her worriedly. "I won't believe it until I see it for myself. Some people aren't going to cotton to the way we live here, so I doubt if the town will get very big at all."

Eb nodded once, rubbing her back. "Good. It'll be easier to take care of the women if we weed out all the undesirables. I don't want just anybody living here."

Maggie grinned, unable to contain her secret any longer. It had only become obvious to her yesterday, and she'd wanted to wait for the perfect moment. When she found out they would be coming out here today with the sign, she knew that this would be it.

Her love for them had grown so much, and each day they became a little closer. Both men still had a lot of rough edges that she knew would always be a part of them, but it was a callousness born of necessity in this harsh land.

She still worried about the cattle rustlers they'd faced and knew they would face more. All of them faced danger every day, and she'd seen the trust between the men as they placed their lives in each other's hands.

Just yesterday, one of the men had almost been attacked by a bear, and the others had all rushed in to help without a thought to their own safety.

Knowing she'd never stop worrying about them, she also understood how they would worry about her and did her best to be careful. She didn't want them to be distracted by their concern for her and make a mistake that could get them killed.

She had to admit, though, she did like those spankings.

They were more playful now, but no less effective, usually earned when she teased them about watching her like a hawk. Nothing she ever did escaped their notice, and it amused her that this had.

Of course, they argued. A woman couldn't live with two such arrogant and demanding men and not expect to have to stand her ground, but the loving afterward was well worth it.

Leaning against Eb, she reached out to Jeremiah.

"You're too overprotective. I hope the other men aren't as bad as you two. I think you're going to be changing that sign quite a bit, especially if the men are like you."

Eb held her away from him, his fingers gentle as he lifted her chin. "What's that supposed to mean?"

Smiling through her tears, Maggie touched her abdomen. "The first child to be born here is already on his way."

Eb and Jeremiah froze, their eyes going wide as they looked at each other before turning back to her.

The slow smiles on their faces were the most beautiful things she'd ever seen, and the love in them stole her breath.

Jeremiah reached out to lay his hand over hers, his eyes sparkling with unshed tears. "Are you sure?"

Laughing through her tears, Maggie squealed when Eb gathered her in his arms, his face buried in her neck as he swung her around and carefully set her on her feet again.

"Hell, are you all right? I should have known. Oh, baby, I didn't even think. How could I have not known?"

Maggie gave him a teasing smile. "And you're supposed to be the breeders."

Jeremiah laughed and pulled her into his arms, hugging her close. "It appears we certainly are. Hell, how could we not have noticed?"

Maggie gestured toward the sign. "Thank you. Thank you for building this place so we can live together. Thank you for coming to get me. I love you both so much."

Eb picked her up, carrying her back to the horses. "Baby, we're the ones who should be thanking you. Every day, I thank God you came with us. If I loved you any more, I would burst."

Maggie giggled, happier than she'd ever been in her life. "If I remember correctly, I didn't have a choice."

Jeremiah bent over her, kissing her while Eb still held her, his lips warm and tender as they brushed over hers. "Smartest thing we ever did. Damn, woman, I love you. Come on. Let's get you home. You need your rest."

Riding away, Maggie looked over her shoulder, grinning at the sign Hayes, Wyatt, and Savannah would use to find them.

Desire, Oklahoma

Population 42

"Do you think she should be riding?" Eb's voice held a touch of panic.

"Hell, what do I know about this? No more riding until we check with the doctor in Tulsa. Hell and damnation—we need a doctor." Jeremiah didn't sound much better.

She had the strangest feeling that the protectiveness they'd shown up until now was nothing compared to what she'd experience over the next several months. Smiling, she shook her head. If their arguments ended like they usually did, she didn't mind a bit.

"We'll advertise for one."

"Does she look pale to you?"

Maggie turned back and grinned.

Yep, a town where the men were in charge.

She couldn't imagine a better place to live.

THE END

Siren Publishing, Inc.
www.SirenPublishing.com

LaVergne, TN USA
06 February 2011
215500LV00005B/274/P